PENGUIN CLASSICS

RUSSIAN SHORT STORIES FROM
PUSHKIN TO BUIDA

ROBERT CHANDLER has translated Sappho and Guillaume Apollinaire for Everyman's Poetry. His translations from Russian include Aleksandr Pushkin's *Dubrovsky*, Nikolay Leskov's *Lady Macbeth of Mtsensk* and Vasily Grossman's *Life and Fate*. With his wife Elizabeth and other colleagues he has co-translated numerous works by Andrey Platonov; *Soul* won the 2004 American Association of Teachers of Slavic and East European Languages award for best translation from a Slavonic language; *Soul* and *Happy Moscow* were both shortlisted for the Weidenfeld European Translation Prize; 'The Macedonian Officer' won second prize in the 2004 John Dryden Translation Prize.

Russian Short Stories from Pushkin to Buida

Edited and translated by
ROBERT CHANDLER

PENGUIN BOOKS

PENGUIN BOOKS

Published by the Penguin Group
Penguin Books Ltd, 80 Strand, London WC2R ORL, England
Penguin Group (USA) Inc., 375 Hudson Street, New York, New York 10014, USA
Penguin Group (Canada), 90 Eglinton Avenue East, Suite 700, Toronto, Ontario, Canada M4P 2Y3
(a division of Pearson Penguin Canada Inc.)
Penguin Ireland, 25 St Stephen's Green, Dublin 2, Ireland (a division of Penguin Books Ltd)
Penguin Group (Australia), 250 Camberwell Road, Camberwell, Victoria 3124, Australia
(a division of Pearson Australia Group Pty Ltd)
Penguin Books India Pvt Ltd, 11 Community Centre, Panchsheel Park, New Delhi – 110 017, India
Penguin Group (NZ), cnr Airborne and Rosedale Roads, Albany, Auckland 1310, New Zealand
(a division of Pearson New Zealand Ltd)
Penguin Books (South Africa) (Pty) Ltd, 24 Sturdee Avenue, Rosebank, Johannesburg 2196, South Africa

Penguin Books Ltd, Registered Offices: 80 Strand, London WC2R ORL, England

www.penguin.com

This collection first published in Penguin Classics 2005
8

The Acknowledgements (pp. 394–6) constitute an extension of this copyright page
Introductory material and notes copyright © Robert Chandler, 2005
Introductory material to Krzhizhanovsky and Dovlatov copyright © Joanne Turnbull, 2005
All rights reserved

The moral right of the translators and editor has been asserted

Set in 9.25/11 pt PostScript Adobe Sabon
Typeset by Rowland Phototypesetting Ltd, Bury St Edmunds, Suffolk
Printed in Great Britain by Clays Ltd, St Ives plc

ISBN-13: 978–0–140–44846–7
ISBN-10: 0–140–44846–2

www.greenpenguin.co.uk

Penguin Books is committed to a sustainable future
for our business, our readers and our planet.
The book in your hands is made from paper
certified by the Forest Stewardship Council.

Contents

Chronology

1703 Peter the Great founds St Petersburg.

1799 Birth of Aleksandr Sergeyevich Pushkin.

1812 Napoleon captures Moscow, but is forced to retreat.

1825 Decembrist Revolt: an unsuccessful coup by liberal members of the aristocracy. Tsar Nicholas I comes to the throne.

1833 Pushkin publishes *Yevgeny Onegin*.

1837 Death of Pushkin.

1840 Publication of Lermontov's *A Hero of Our Time*. He is killed in a duel the following year.

1842 Publication of Gogol's *Dead Souls* and 'The Greatcoat'.

1852 Publication of Turgenev's *A Hunter's Notebook*.

1853–6 The Crimean War, which ends in Russia's defeat.

1861 Emancipation of the serfs.

1865–9 Publication of Tolstoy's *War and Peace*.

1879–80 Publication of Dostoyevsky's *The Brothers Karamazov*.

1881 Aleksandr II assassinated by members of the terrorist *Narodnaya Volya* (People's Will) organization. Leskov publishes 'The Steel Flea'.

1891 Beginning of construction of Trans-Siberian railway.

1898 A revival of Chekhov's *The Seagull* is the main event in the opening season of the newly founded Moscow Arts Theatre.

1905 Russia is defeated in a war against Japan. The '1905 Revolution' is defused by liberal reforms. Russia becomes, in principle, a constitutional monarchy.

1910 Tolstoy's funeral is attended by several thousand people.

1914 Beginning of First World War. St Petersburg is given the more Russian-sounding name of Petrograd.

1916 Murder of Rasputin, a self-styled 'holy man' who exercised a malign influence on the Tsar and his family.

1917 Nicholas II abdicates after February Revolution. Workers' soviets (i.e., councils) are set up in Petrograd and Moscow. Lenin and his Bolshevik Party seize power in October.

1918–21 Russian Civil War. After 1919: Emigration of much of the upper and middle class, including Bunin, Nabokov and Teffi.

1924 Death of Lenin. Petrograd is renamed Leningrad. Stalin begins to take over power. First publication (in English translation) of Zamyatin's *We*.

1926 Babel's *Red Cavalry* first published in book form.

1927 Publication of Zoshchenko's *Nervous People*.

1929 Collectivization of agriculture begins.

1932 Foundation of Union of Soviet Writers.

1933 Nobel Prize is awarded to the émigré Ivan Bunin.

1934–9 The great purges. At least a million people are shot and several million sent to the Gulag.

1939 Stalin–Hitler pact. Beginning of Second World War. Kharms completes 'The Old Woman'.

1941 Hitler invades the Soviet Union. Leningrad is blockaded and Moscow under threat.

1945 End of Second World War.

1946 Control over the arts is tightened. Akhmatova and Zoshchenko are expelled from the Writers' Union. Platonov's 'The Return' is also fiercely criticized.

1953 Death of Stalin. Khrushchev begins to seize power.

1956 Khrushchev denounces Stalin at twentieth Party Congress. Shalamov returns to Moscow, one of several millions released from the camps. Start of more liberal period known as 'The Thaw'.

1958 Publication abroad of *Doctor Zhivago*. Under pressure from the Soviet authorities, Pasternak declines Nobel Prize.

1962 Publication of Solzhenitsyn's *One Day in the Life of Ivan Denisovich*.

1964 Fall of Khrushchev.

1966–7 First publication of Bulgakov's *The Master and Margarita* (written in the 1930s).

1974 Solzhenitsyn deported after publication in the West of *The Gulag Archipelago*. Shukshin dies of a heart attack; his film *Snowball Berry Red* enjoys huge success.

1985 Mikhail Gorbachev comes to power. Beginning of the period of liberal reforms known as perestroika; the next few years see the first publication in Russia of major works by Kharms, Grossman, Nabokov, Platonov, Shalamov, Solzhenitsyn and many others.

1989 Fall of Berlin Wall and reunification of Germany.

1991 Boris Yeltsin becomes President of the Russian Federation. Collapse of Soviet Union.

1994 Solzhenitsyn returns to Russia.

2000 Vladimir Putin elected President of the Russian Federation.

Introduction

The roots of literature lie in song, prayer and story. For all its sophistication, Russian literature is relatively young and therefore closer to these roots than the literature of Western Europe. Aleksandr Pushkin absorbed Russian folklore from a peasant housekeeper; the *anekdot*, usually a political story-cum-joke, was an important art form in the Soviet Union; and Russians still sing and recite poetry on social occasions. It is not surprising that both poems and short stories continue to have a central place in Russian literature; the English, in contrast, tend to pay only lip service to the importance of poetry and to look on the short story as a minor genre, something for an apprentice to cut his teeth on before the serious work of writing a novel.

Russian literature probably includes more great short stories than the literature of any other European country. There is no major Russian prose-writer who has not written short stories, and many of Russia's finest prose-writers wrote chiefly in this form. This may come as a surprise to English-speakers, who tend to assume that the supreme achievement of Russian literature is the epic novel. It is my hope, however, that the stories gathered here will convince readers there is as much vitality, linguistic creativity and emotional depth in the finest Russian short stories as in the novels of Tolstoy and Dostoyevsky or the poetry of Anna Akhmatova, Osip Mandelstam, Boris Pasternak and Marina Tsvetayeva.

Great literature often arises from marriages – or battles – between different cultures. Persian poetry arose from a collision between native Persian culture and imported Arabic beliefs and vocabulary. English literature began with Chaucer's fusion of English and French traditions and entered its greatest period during the sixteenth and seventeenth centuries, as writers struggled to absorb the impact of far-off cultures – the Americas in the distant present, and Greece and Rome in the distant past. The age of Pushkin, the so-called Golden Age of Russian poetry, is another such era of cultural collision. The Russian literary language was still a relatively new and fragile creation in the early nineteenth century, and there were furious debates between those who wanted to 'gallicize' Russian (to draw on French for both vocabulary and syntax) and those who preferred to borrow from Church Slavonic – a liturgical language closer to Bulgarian than to Russian. One of Pushkin's achievements was to assert his right to make use of every possibility available to him: colloquial Russian, Church Slavonic and borrowings from French, German and English.

Poetry always comes before prose in the creation of a national literature. Russian literature developed so fast, however, that there was no real interval between the great age of poetry (the 1820s and 1830s) and the first great age of prose (the 1830s and 1840s). The years 1831 to 1842 saw the publication of some of the finest works of Russian prose: Pushkin's 'The Queen of Spades' and *The Captain's Daughter*; Mikhail Lermontov's *A Hero of Our Time*, all of Nikolay Gogol's short stories and the great long novel of the period: Gogol's *Dead Souls*.[1] 'The Queen of Spades', Lermontov's 'The Fatalist' (from *A Hero of Our Time*) and Gogol's 'The Greatcoat' were obvious choices as the first three stories in this volume.

The second half of the nineteenth century – from the publication of Ivan Turgenev's *A Hunter's Notebook* (1852) – is the only period when the long novel really was more important in Russia than either poetry or short fiction. Count Leo Tolstoy and Fyodor Dostoyevsky wrote good and sometimes innovative short stories, but their supreme achievements are their novels. And apart from Nikolay Leskov – who wrote fine works in most prose genres – we find no great short story writer in this period until Anton Chekhov. Chekhov's achievement, however, is extraordinary – both in itself and as regards its importance to other writers. It is possible that not even Dostoyevsky had such an influence on the literature of Europe in the twentieth century.

The decade from 1910 was a period of intellectual and artistic innovation in Russia, the climax of a cultural Silver Age more brilliant than the Golden Age a century before. The years 1912–16 saw the publication of the first collections of poetry by Akhmatova, Mandelstam, Pasternak and Vladimir Mayakovsky, as well as the première of Igor Stravinsky's *The Rite of Spring* and the first showing of the painter Kasimir Malevich's notorious 'Black Square'. Once again, new developments in short fiction followed quickly after new developments in poetry: Isaak Babel, Mikhail Bulgakov, Andrey Platonov, Yevgeny Zamyatin, Mikhail Zoshchenko, and the émigrée Teffi all wrote many of their best works in the 1920s, registering and drawing creative energy from a linguistic ferment even wilder than that of Pushkin's time. People only semi-literate had suddenly assumed positions of power and there was a general sense that a New World required new words. The authorities called on writers to produce works of epic proportions, arguing that the heroic achievements of the Russian Revolution could only properly be celebrated in long poems or long novels; writers themselves, however, evidently felt that this confused and fragmented era could be better represented in shorter forms. The two great novels of the decade, Mikhail Sholokhov's *The Quiet Don* and Platonov's *Chevengur*, were completed only towards the end of the 1920s – and in any case, it would be another 60 years before *Chevengur* was first published in Russia.

The best Russian writers of the 1920s were often criticized by the authorities, but they were, in the main, able to publish their work. During the 1930s, however, it became increasingly difficult to publish good work in Russia. Ivan Bunin, Vladimir Nabokov, Teffi and Zamyatin were in France. Babel became a master – as he declared at the First Congress of Soviet Writers in 1934 – of the 'genre of silence'; Bulgakov, Sigizmund Krzhizhanovsky and Daniil Kharms wrote only 'for the drawer'; Leonid Dobychin managed to publish both a short novel and a collection of stories, but he committed suicide soon after being criticized at a Writers' Union meeting in 1936. Zoshchenko wrote interestingly and amusingly, but his work lost its edge. Only Platonov, with heroic tenacity, continued both to develop as a writer and, now and then, to publish. 'The River Potudan' appeared in 1937, at the height of Stalin's purges; 'The Return', published in 1946, was the last great work of the Stalin era. The post-war cultural clampdown (which began shortly before the publication of 'The Return') seemed for a while to have brought about the death of Russian literature.

The Gulag was a defining feature of the Soviet Union, and it is no accident that it was through writing about the Gulag that Russian literature was reborn in the mid-1950s, after Stalin's death. Varlam Shalamov wrote about little else; Aleksandr Solzhenitsyn wrote about little else during the first half of his literary career; and the Gulag is an important theme of the greatest Russian long novel of the second half of the twentieth century: Vasily Grossman's *Life and Fate*. During the 1960s and early 1970s Vasily Shukshin was one of the first writers after Platonov to look at another Soviet tragedy: the damage done by collectivization to the fabric of peasant life. Yury Trifonov – whose best works are too long for this anthology – examined the life of the Moscow intelligentsia under Stalin and in the decades that followed. Sergei Dovlatov wrote about labour camps with humour, from the position of a guard rather than that of a prisoner; this broadening of perspective marks another small step in Russia's recovery from

Stalinism. Georgy Vladimov went further still in his novel *Faithful Ruslan*, describing a labour camp from the perspective of a devoted guard-dog. And Asar Eppel asserted a writer's right simply to celebrate ordinary life and love.

I have chosen for this anthology only stories I have been able to reread many times, in both Russian and English, with increasing enjoyment. A few notable omissions are Maksim Gorky, Vasily Grossman, Boris Pasternak and Mikhail Sholokhov, all of whom are great writers but whose short stories are inferior to their work in other genres. Gorky is at his best in his memoirs and autobiographical writings; Pasternak is a finer poet than prose-writer; and the greatest works by Grossman and Sholokhov are their long novels. Nabokov is another writer whose novels are greater than his short stories; I would, however, have included him had I been able to reach an agreement with his publishers.

It was easier to decide where to begin this anthology than where to end it. The 1990s may prove to have been an important era for Russian prose, but no anthologist has unlimited space; of the writers who first became known in that decade, I have included only Yury Buida. Viktor Pelevin, Lyudmila Petrushevskaya, Aleksey Slapovsky and Lyudmila Ulitskaya are all good writers, but Buida is remarkable both for his philosophical reach and his ability to use postmodernist playfulness to express deep feeling. And, since almost all Russian writers – even writers as different from one another as Gogol, Dostoyevsky, Bunin, Pasternak, Tsvetayeva and Platonov – have turned to Pushkin for inspiration – I was glad of the chance to end this volume with a homage to one of his most famous poems; I was all the more glad because it happens to be the first Russian poem I learned by heart myself.

NOTES

1. Gogol referred to *Dead Souls* as a *poema*, i.e., a long poem, rather than a novel.

Further Reading

I list only translations which, in my view, do justice to their originals. As well as short stories, I include a few novels and narrative poems. I do not include writers such as Tolstoy who are readily available in a number of good editions.

Babel, Isaak, *Collected Stories*, tr. David McDuff (London: Penguin, 1994).

Brown, Clarence (ed.), *Twentieth-Century Russian Reader* (London: Penguin, 1993).

Buida, Yury, *The Zero Train* (London: Dedalus, 2001); *The Prussian Bride* (London: Dedalus, 2002); both tr. Oliver Ready.

Bulgakov, Mikhail, *A Country Doctor's Notebook,* tr. Michael Glenny (London: Harvill, 1975); *The Fatal Eggs*, tr. Hugh Aplin (London: Hesperus, 2003); *The Master and Margarita*, tr. Michael Glenny (London: Harvill, 1996).

Chekhov, Anton, *About Love and Other Stories*, tr. Rosamund Bartlett (Oxford: Oxford University Press, 2004); *Early Stories*, tr. Patrick Miles and Harvey Pitcher (Oxford: Oxford University Press, 1999); *The Steppe*, tr. Robert and Elizabeth Chandler and Rosamund Bartlett (London: Hesperus, 2006).

Dostoyevsky, Fyodor, *The Brothers Karamazov*, tr. Richard Pevear and Larissa Volokhonskaya (London: Vintage, 1992).

Eppel, Asar, *The Grassy Street*, tr. Joanne Turnbull (Moscow/Birmingham: Glas, 1994).

Gogol, Nikolai, *Diary of a Madman*, tr. Ronald Wilks (London: Penguin, 1972); *Dead Souls*, tr. Robert A. Maguire (London: Penguin, 2004).

Grossman, Vasily, *Life and Fate*, tr. Robert Chandler (London: Harvill, 1995).

Kharms, Daniil, *Incidences*, tr. Neil Cornwell (London: Serpent's Tail, 1993).

Leskov, Nikolay, *Satirical Stories of Nikolay Leskov*, tr. William B.

Edgerton (New York: Pegasus, 1969); *Lady Macbeth of Mtsensk*, tr. Robert Chandler (London: Hesperus, 2003); *The Priest who was Never Baptized*, tr. James Muckle (Ilkeston: Bramcote Press, 2004).

Nabokov, Vladimir, *Collected Stories*, tr. Dmitri Nabokov (London: Penguin, 1997).

Pelevin, Viktor, *The Life of Insects*, tr. Andrew Bromfield (London: Faber, 1999); *A Werewolf Problem in Central Russia*, tr. Andrew Bromfield (London: Harbord, 1999).

Petrushevskaya, Ludmila, *The Time is Night*, tr. Sally Laird (London: Virago, 1994); *Immortal Love*, tr. Sally Laird (New York: Pantheon, 1995).

Platonov, Andrey, *The Foundation Pit*, tr. Robert Chandler and Geoffrey Smith (London: Harvill, 1996); *The Return and Other Stories*, tr. Robert and Elizabeth Chandler and Angela Livingstone (London: Harvill, 1999); *The Portable Platonov*, tr. Robert and Elizabeth Chandler et al. (Moscow: Glas, 1999); *Happy Moscow*, tr. Robert and Elizabeth Chandler et al. (London: Harvill, 2002); *Soul*, tr. Robert and Elizabeth Chandler and Olga Meerson et al. (London: Harvill, 2004).

Pushkin, Aleksandr, *The Bridegroom*, tr. Antony Wood (London: Angel, 2002); *Dubrovsky*, tr. Robert Chandler (London: Hesperus, 2003); *Yevgeny Onegin* – Pushkin's greatest work has been well translated by James Falen (Oxford: Oxford University Press, 1995). For extracts from Stanley Mitchell's still finer translation-in-progress see *Modern Poetry in Translation*, nos. 11, 15 and 18 (Queen's College, Oxford).

Shalamov, Varlam, *Kolyma Tales*, tr. John Glad (London: Penguin, 1994). Though omitting important details, this still conveys much of Shalamov's greatness.

Shukshin, Vasily, *Stories from a Siberian Village*, tr. John Givens and Laura Michael (DeKalb: Northern Illinois University Press, 1997).

Solzhenitsyn, Aleksandr, *One Day in the Life of Ivan Denisovich*, tr. Harry Willetts (London: Harvill, 1996); *Invisible Allies*, tr. Alexis Klimoff and Michael Nicholson (London: Harvill, 1997).

Struve, Gleb (ed.), *Russian Stories* (New York: Dover, 1990). Twelve stories by writers from Pushkin to Zoshchenko. Bilingual edition.

Zamyatin, Yevgeny, *We*, tr. Clarence Brown (London: Penguin, 1993).

Zinik, Zinovy, *Mind the Doors*, tr. Andrew Bromfield and Bernard Meares (New York: Context Books, 2001).

Zinovyeva-Annibal, Lidiya, *The Tragic Menagerie*, tr. Jane Costlow (Evanston: Northwestern University Press, 1999).

Zoshchenko, Mikhail, *A Man is not a Flea*, tr. Serge Shishkoff (Ann

Arbor: Ardis, 1989); *The Galosh and Other Stories*, tr. Jeremy Hicks (London: Angel, 2000).

Reference

The following works of criticism and reference, and annotated editions of texts, have been especially useful:

Bartlett, Rosamund, *Chekhov: Scenes from a Life* (London: Simon and Schuster, 2004).

Classe, Olive (ed.), *Encyclopedia of Literary Translation into English* (London/Chicago: Fitzroy Dearborn, 2000).

Cornwell, Neil (ed.), *Reference Guide to Russian Literature* (London: Fitzroy Dearborn, 1998).

—, *Pushkin's The Queen of Spades* (London: Bristol Classical Press, 1993).

Graffy, Julian, *Gogol's The Overcoat* (London: Bristol Classical Press, 2000).

Kharms, Daniil, *The Old Woman* (London: Bristol Classical Press, 1995).

Lermontov, Mikhail, *A Hero of our Time* (London: Bristol Classical Press, 1992).

Mirsky, Prince D. S., *A History of Russian Literature* (Evanston: Northwestern University Press, 1999).

Popkin, Cathy, *The Pragmatics of Insignificance* (Stanford: Stanford University Press, 1993).

Skatov, N. N., *Russkie Pisateli*: XX Vek (Moscow: Prosveshchenie, 1998).

Woodward, James, *Ivan Bunin: A Study of His Fiction* (North Carolina: University of North Carolina Press, 1980).

Sovlit.com (www.sovlit.com) has also been a useful source of biographical information.

Note on the Translations

It has been a privilege both to be able to retranslate such masterpieces as 'The Queen of Spades' and to have the chance to introduce great writers like Platonov who are still undervalued in the West; or, like Dobychin and Krzhizhanovsky, little known even in Russia. And I am proud both to be including unpublished translations by other translators I admire and to be republishing two old but shamefully neglected translations: William Edgerton's translation of Leskov's 'The Steel Flea', and the translation of Bunin's 'The Gentleman from San Francisco' by S. S. Koteliansky together with D. H. Lawrence and Leonard Woolf. Both these works have, I believe, gained more in translation than they have lost.

All the translations credited to myself are the product of greater or lesser degrees of collaboration with my wife Elizabeth, with the many people who have checked through drafts, and – in the case of the earlier and better known stories – with previous translators. Many translators avoid looking at the work of their predecessors; others evidently do look but are ashamed to admit it. This is surprising: in most fields of human endeavour ignorance of previous work in a given field is considered unacceptable. I have many times been saved from a misunderstanding, or helped towards a more satisfactory rendering, by looking at earlier translations – especially those of the often under-rated Constance Garnett.

One last point: for all our lip service to cultural pluralism, both British and American readers are often surprisingly intolerant of 'Americanisms' or 'Britishisms'. This volume contains work by both British and American translators; I enjoy their different styles and have not attempted to reduce them to a pallid norm. It may even be the case that some stories translate more readily into particular varieties of English. It is hard, for example, to imagine Vasily Shukshin's 'In the Autumn' sounding as effective in British English as in the American version by John Givens and Laura Michael.

The order of stories in this volume is first by author's birthdate and then by date of publication, except in the case of stories from Babel's *Red Cavalry* and Shalamov's *The Kolyma Tales*, where I have followed the order in which they were arranged by the authors.

Russian Short Stories from Pushkin to Buida

ALEKSANDR SERGEYEVICH PUSHKIN (1799–1837)

Pushkin was born in Moscow and brought up mainly by tutors and governesses. One of his great-grandfathers, Abram Gannibal, was an African slave who became a favourite and godson of Peter the Great. Like many aristocrats, Pushkin learned Russian mainly from household serfs.

As an adolescent, he attended the new élite lycée at Tsarskoye Selo, outside St Petersburg. In his early twenties he was exiled for several years because of his political poems. Although several of his friends took part in the Decembrist Revolt, Pushkin did not. It is unclear why; it may simply be that his friends were not confident he could keep a secret. In 1826 Pushkin returned to St Petersburg, with the Tsar as his personal censor. He suffered a variety of humiliations in his last years, including serious debts and worries about the fidelity of his young wife, Natalya Goncharova. He was fatally wounded in a duel with D'Anthès, the Dutch Ambassador's adopted son, who was said to be having an affair with Natalya.

Pushkin's position in Russian literature can best be compared with that of Goethe in Germany. Not only is he Russia's greatest poet; he is also the author of the first major works in a variety of genres. As well as his masterpieces – the verse novel Yevgeny Onegin and the narrative poem The Bronze Horseman – Pushkin wrote one of the first important Russian dramas, Boris Godunov, the first great Russian historical novel, The Captain's Daughter, and the greatest of all Russian short stories, 'The Queen of Spades'.

Pushkin did not start writing prose until 1827. His prose style is clear and succinct. He himself said that 'Precision and brevity are the most important qualities of prose. Prose demands thoughts and more thoughts – without thoughts, dazzling expressions serve no purpose.' In 'The Queen of Spades', as in several of his later works, Pushkin shows a remarkable ability to treat dark, difficult material (obsessive madness, insoluble personal and socio-political conflict) with clarity and grace. Unlike the writers of the French Enlightenment, he writes clearly without being in any way simplistic. And unlike many later writers, he can evoke the most terrifying aspects of human nature without, even momentarily, losing his own balance.

'The Queen of Spades' is laconic and enigmatic. It can be read as a social comedy, a tale of the supernatural, a parody of the then popular E. T. A. Hoffmann or as a meditation on the symbiosis between rationalism and superstition. Above all, it is a gripping story, one whose structure – in the words of the literary historian D. S. Mirsky – 'is as tense as a compressed spring'.

Mirsky also said that 'The Queen of Spades' is 'so economic and terse in its noble baldness that even Prosper Mérimée, that most fastidious of French writers, had not the courage to translate it as it was, and introduced various embellishments and amplifications into his French version'. A Russian friend, hearing we were translating the story, said: 'That must be very difficult. You can't afford to change a single comma.' We have tried to follow her advice.

Readers will enjoy the story more if they have some understanding of the card game faro (also known as stoss), a game of pure chance that was popular with the European aristocracy during the eighteenth and early nineteenth centuries. Each punter – and there can be any number of them – has his own pack of cards; as does the banker. A punter looks at his pack, selects a card and puts it face down on the table, placing his stake on top of the card or chalking the amount on the card itself. The banker then deals out the cards from his own pack in pairs, placing one card, face up, on each side of each of the punters' cards. If a punter's card matches the card to his right, the banker wins; if it matches the card to his left, the punter wins; if it matches neither of the banker's cards, a more complex reckoning (the details are irrelevant to this story) is carried out at the end of the round. A punter can double the stake by bending back a corner of his card, or quadruple it by bending back two corners. The game continues, unless the bank is broken, until the banker has dealt out his whole pack.

THE QUEEN OF SPADES

The Queen of Spades signifies secret malice.
The latest guide to fortune-telling.

I

> In rainy weather
> They gathered together
> To play.
> To double – redouble –
> A stake was no trouble,
> They say.
> They did not find it hard
> To entrust to a card
> Their pay,
> So no day of rain
> Ever slipped by in vain,
> They say.

That night their host was Narumov, an officer in the Horse Guards. The long winter night slipped by unnoticed; only after four in the morning did they sit down to supper. The winners ate heartily; the others sat there abstractedly, refusing all offers of food. But then champagne appeared, the conversation livened up and everyone joined in.

'How did you do, Surin?' asked Narumov.

'Same as always – I lost. You have to admit I'm unlucky. I play cautiously, I never get carried away, nothing distracts me, but I just keep on losing.'

'And you've never been tempted? Never been fooled by a card that seems fortunate? I'm astonished at your self-control.'

'How about Hermann, though?' said one of the guests, pointing at a young engineer. 'Never touched a card in his life, never once doubled a stake, but he sits with us until five in the morning and watches us play.'

'Cards hold a fascination for me,' said Hermann. 'But I cannot afford to sacrifice the essential in the hope of acquiring the superfluous.'

'Hermann's a German. He counts the pennies, that's all,' said Tomsky. 'But if there's one person I can't understand, it's my grandmother, the countess Anna Fedotovna.'

'Why? How's that?' people called out.

'I can't understand,' Tomsky went on, 'why my grandmother never gambles.'

'But what's so astonishing,' asked Narumov, 'about a lady in her eighties who doesn't gamble?'

'You mean you really haven't heard about her?'

'No, not a word!'

'Well then, listen! About sixty years ago, my grandmother went to Paris and became the toast of the town. People chased after her to catch a glimpse of *La Vénus Moscovite*. Richelieu paid court to her, and my grandmother assures me that he almost shot himself because she was so cruel to him.

'In those days ladies used to play faro. At Court one evening, grandmother lost a large sum of money to the Duke of Orléans. When she got home, as she was peeling off her beauty spots and undoing her hooped petticoat, she informed grandfather of her gambling losses and told him to settle up. My late grandfather, as far as I recall, was a kind of butler to my grandmother. He feared her like fire; hearing of these terrible losses, however, he flew into a rage, fetched his accounts book, pointed out that they had got through half a million in six months and that neither their Moscow estate nor their Saratov estate happened to be in reach of Paris – and flatly refused to pay. Grandmother gave him a slap on the face, and retired to bed on her own to indicate her displeasure.

'The following day she sent for her husband, hoping that this domestic punishment would have had its effect, but she found him unshakeable. For the first time in her life she went so far as to argue and reason with him; she pointed out condescendingly, thinking this would shame him, that there are debts and debts and that a prince is not the same as a coach-builder. All in vain: grandfather was in revolt. No meant no! Grandmother didn't know what to do.

'Among her close acquaintances was a most remarkable man. I am sure you have heard of Count Saint-Germain,[1] the subject of so many wonderful tales. You know he claimed to be the Wandering Jew, to have discovered the elixir of life and the philosopher's stone, and so on. People laughed at him and called him a charlatan, while Casanova[2] says in his memoirs that he was a spy; in spite of his mysteriousness, however, Saint-Germain was a man of dignified appearance and the most agreeable of company. Grandmother still adores him and gets angry if anyone says a word against him. Grandmother knew that Saint-Germain had large sums of money at his disposal. She decided to appeal to him. She wrote him a note, asking him to come and see her at once.

'The old eccentric came immediately and found her in terrible distress. Grandmother described her husband's barbarous conduct in the blackest of colours and ended by saying that her only hope lay in Saint-Germain's friendship and courtesy.

'Saint-Germain thought for a while.

'"I can do you this service," he said, "but I know you won't feel at ease until you've repaid the sum and I'd rather not involve you in yet more worries. There's another solution: you can win back the money." "But my dear Count," answered grandmother, "I've told you, we have no money at all." "There's no need for money," said Saint-Germain. "Be so kind as to hear me out." And he revealed a secret to her for which every one of us here would be willing to pay dearly.'

The young gamblers doubled their attention. Tomsky lit his pipe, drew on it and went on: 'That same evening grandmother appeared at Versailles, *au jeu de la Reine*.[3] The Duke of Orléans was keeping the bank; grandmother casually apologized for not bringing the money she owed, making up some little story by way of excuse, and began playing against him. She chose three cards and played them one after the other; all three won, and grandmother quite recovered her losses.'

'Luck!' said one of the company.

'A fairy tale!' said Hermann.

'Perhaps the cards were marked,' said someone else.

'I think not,' Tomsky replied gravely.

'What!' said Narumov. 'You have a grandmother who can predict three cards in sequence and you still haven't got her to tell you her cabalistic secret?'

'Not a hope in hell!' replied Tomsky. 'She had four sons, one of them my father; all four were incorrigible gamblers, but she didn't let any of them know her secret – although it would certainly have been quite a help to them, and to me too. But this is what I was once told by my uncle, Count Ivan Ilyich, and he swore it was all true. The late Chaplitsky – you know, the one who died penniless after squandering millions – once, when he was young, lost around three hundred thousand. To Zorich, if I remember rightly. He was in despair. Grandmother always took a stern view of youthful foolishness, but for some reason she took pity on Chaplitsky. She gave him three cards to play in sequence, making him give his word of honour never to gamble again. Chaplitsky went back to the man who had defeated him; they sat down to play. Chaplitsky put fifty thousand on the first card and won straight off; he doubled the stake, doubled again – and recovered his losses and more.

'But it's time we went to bed. It's already quarter to six.'

Indeed, day was dawning. The young men drained their glasses and left in their carriages.

2

'Il paraît que monsieur est décidément pour les suivantes.'
'Que voulez-vous, madame? Elles sont plus fraîches.'[4]
   from a society conversation

The old Countess —— was in her dressing room, sitting in front of the mirror. Three maids were standing round her. One was holding a pot of rouge, the second a box of pins, the third a tall bonnet with flame-coloured ribbons. The Countess had no pretensions to beauty, her own having faded long ago, but she maintained all the habits of her youth, still kept strictly to the fashions of the seventies and took as much time and trouble over her toilette as she had done sixty years before. By the window, sitting at an embroidery frame, was a young lady, her ward.

'Good morning, *Grand'maman*,' said a young officer as he entered the room. '*Bonjour, Mademoiselle Lise. Grand'maman*, I have a favour to ask you.'

'What is it, Paul?'

'Will you allow me to introduce one of my friends to you, and to bring him to your ball on Friday?'

'Bring him straight to the ball. You can introduce him to me there. Were you at N.'s last night, may I ask?'

'Of course I was! It was very gay; we danced until five in the morning. Yeletskaya looked ever so pretty.'

'My dear fellow! What's pretty about her? You should have seen her grandmother, Princess Darya Petrovna . . . But I suppose she must have aged a great deal by now, Princess Darya Petrovna?'

'What do you mean "aged"?' Tomsky replied carelessly. 'She's been dead seven years.'

The young lady looked up and made a sign to the young man. He remembered that the deaths of her contemporaries were kept secret from the old Countess and bit his lip. The Countess, however, greeted this news with considerable indifference.

'Dead!' she said. 'And I didn't know. We were appointed maids of honour together, and when we were presented at Court, the Empress . . .'

And for the hundredth time, the Countess repeated this story to her grandson.

'Well, Paul,' she said afterwards, 'now you can help me to my feet. Lizanka, where's my snuffbox?'

And the Countess went behind the screen with her maids to finish her toilette. Tomsky was left alone with the young lady.

'Who is it you want to introduce?' Lizaveta Ivanovna asked quietly.

'Narumov. Do you know him?'

'No. Is he a soldier or a civilian?'

'A soldier.'

'An engineer?'

'No, he's in the Cavalry. What made you think he's an engineer?' The young lady laughed but did not answer.

'Paul!' the Countess shouted from behind the screen. 'Send me some new novel or other – only, please, not the kind they write nowadays.'

'What do you mean, *Grand'maman*?'

'I want the kind of novel where the hero doesn't strangle either his father or his mother, and where there are no drowned bodies. I have a terrible fear of drowned bodies!'

'Your kind of novel doesn't exist any longer. Unless you'd like a Russian one?'

'A Russian novel? I didn't know there were any. Send me some, old boy, please do!'

'Goodbye, *Grand'maman*: I must hurry. Goodbye, Lizaveta Ivanovna! What made you think Narumov was an engineer?'

And Tomsky left the dressing room.

Lizaveta Ivanovna was now on her own. She stopped her work and began gazing out of the window. After a short while, a young officer appeared from behind the house on the opposite corner of the street. A blush spread over her cheeks: she returned to her work, bending low over the canvas. Just then the Countess came in, fully dressed.

'Order the carriage, Lizanka,' she said. 'We'll go for a drive.'

Lizanka got up from behind her frame and began putting away her work.

'What's the matter with you, old girl? Have you gone deaf?' shouted the Countess. 'Order the horses to be harnessed at once!'

'Yes!' the young lady said quietly and hurried out into the ante-room.

A servant came in and handed the Countess some books from Prince Pavel Aleksandrovich.

'Good! Thank him,' said the Countess. 'Lizanka, Lizanka! Where are you off to in such a hurry?'

'To dress.'

'There's time enough for that, my dear. Stay here. Open the first volume. Read to me.'

The young lady took the book and read a few lines.

'Louder!' said the Countess. 'What's the matter with you, old girl? Lost your voice or something? Wait. Bring me my footstool. Closer . . . There!'

Lizaveta Ivanovna read two pages. The Countess yawned.

'Enough of that,' she said. 'What nonsense! Send it back to Prince Pavel, with our thanks . . . Well, where's the carriage?'

'The carriage is ready,' said Lizaveta Ivanovna, looking out on to the street.

'Then why aren't you dressed?' said the Countess. 'I'm always having to wait for you. It's intolerable.'

Liza ran off to her room. Within three minutes the Countess was ringing her bell with all her might. The three maids rushed in through one door, a manservant through the other.

'Why don't you come when you're called?' said the Countess. 'Tell Lizaveta Ivanovna I'm waiting for her.'

In came Lizaveta Ivanovna, wearing a cape and bonnet.

'About time too, old girl,' said the Countess. 'And what finery! Whatever for? Whose eye are you hoping to catch? And what's it like outside? Windy, I suppose?'

'Not at all, your ladyship,' said the manservant, 'it's very still.'

'Think before you speak. Open the top pane. Just as I said: wind, and an extremely cold wind at that! I shan't be wanting the carriage. Lizanka, we're not going anywhere – you needn't have got all dressed up.'

'And such is my life,' thought Lizaveta Ivanovna.

Lizaveta Ivanovna was indeed a most unfortunate creature. Bitter is a stranger's bread, says Dante, and steep the steps to a stranger's door – and who can better understand all the bitterness of dependency than the poor ward of a highborn old woman? The Countess did not, of course, have an evil soul, but she had the self-will of a woman who has been spoilt by society; she was miserly and had sunk into a cold egotism, in the way of old people who are done with loving and who have become strangers to the present day. She took part in all the vanities of high society, dragging herself along to balls, where she sat in a corner, heavily rouged and dressed in the fashion of an age gone by, like some hideous but indispensable ballroom ornament; newly arrived guests went up to her with low bows and curtsies, as if according to some established ritual, and after that no one took any more notice of her. She still received the entire city, observing strict etiquette and not recognizing anyone's face. Her numerous servants, grown stout and grey in the maids' room and the ante-room, did as they pleased, competing with one another in robbing the dying old woman.

Lizaveta Ivanovna was a domestic martyr. She poured out tea and was scolded for using too much sugar; she read novels out loud and was blamed for all the author's mistakes; she accompanied the Countess on her outings and was responsible for the weather and the state of the roads. She was supposed to receive an allowance, which was never paid in full; and she was required to dress like everyone – that is to say, like extremely few. In society she played the most pitiable of roles. Everyone knew her and no one noticed her; at balls she would dance only when someone was without a partner, and ladies would take her arm each time they had to go out and set something right in their dress. She was proud, she felt her position keenly and she was constantly looking around, waiting impatiently for a saviour; but the young men, calculating in their flighty vanity, judged her unworthy of their attention, even though Lizaveta Ivanovna was a hundred times sweeter than the cold yet immodest maidens whose favours they courted. How many, many times, slipping out of the tedious and splendid salon, she had gone off to weep in her own poor room, with its papered screen, its chest of drawers, its little mirror and painted bedstead, and its tallow candle burning darkly in a brass candlestick.

One morning – this was two days after the evening recorded at the beginning of this tale, and one week before the scene from which we have digressed – Lizaveta Ivanovna was sitting by the window at her embroidery frame when, chancing to look out on to the street, she saw a young engineer: he was standing there stock-still, his eyes fixed on her window. She bowed her head and went on with her work; five minutes later she looked out again – the young officer was still standing on the same spot. Not being in the habit of flirting with passing officers, she stopped looking out and went on sewing for another two hours without once raising her head. Lunch was announced. She got up, began putting away her embroidery frame and, chancing to look out on to the street, she once again saw the officer. This seemed rather strange. After lunch she went up to the window with a certain unease, but the officer was no longer there – and she forgot about him.

A couple of days later, as she was leaving the house to go for a drive with the Countess, she saw him again. He was standing right by the front porch, his face hidden by a beaver collar: black eyes glittered from beneath his cap. Lizaveta Ivanovna felt frightened, not knowing why, and sat down in the carriage with a quiver of ineffable agitation.

On her return home she ran to the window – the officer was standing in the same place as before, eyes fixed upon her; she turned away, tormented by curiosity and troubled by a feeling entirely new to her.

Since then not a day had passed without the young man appearing, always at the same hour, beneath the windows of their house. An unspoken understanding was established between them. Sitting and working in her usual place, she would sense his approach, raise her head and look at him – for a little longer each day. The young man, it seemed, was grateful to her for this: with the keen sight of youth she noticed a quick flush pass over his pale cheeks each time their eyes met. After a week she smiled at him.

When Tomsky asked the Countess for permission to introduce a friend, the poor girl's heart had begun to beat faster. Discovering, however, that Narumov was not an engineer but a Horse Guard, she regretted that her indiscreet question had let the flighty Tomsky know of her secret.

Hermann was the son of a Russified German who had left him a small inheritance. Firmly convinced of the need to buttress his independence, Hermann did not even touch the interest on this sum; he lived on his salary alone and did not allow himself the smallest extravagance. He was secretive and proud, however, and his comrades seldom had occasion to joke about his excessive thrift. He had strong passions and a fiery imagination, but his self-discipline saved him from the usual errors of youth. Thus, for example, having the soul of a gambler, he never touched cards, believing that he could not afford (as he used to say) 'to sacrifice the essential in the hope of acquiring the superfluous'; nevertheless, he would sit whole nights by the card tables, following the ups and downs of the game with quivering agitation.

The story of the three cards had affected his imagination powerfully and had stayed in his mind all through the night. 'What if,' he thought as he wandered about Petersburg the following evening, 'what if the old Countess were to reveal her secret to me? Or tell me those three sure cards? Why shouldn't I try my luck? I could be introduced to her, win her favour, maybe become her lover – but that all takes time, and she's eighty-seven, she might be dead in a week, even in a couple of days! And what of the story itself? Is it to be believed? No! Calculation, moderation, and hard work – those are my three sure cards, they are what will treble my capital, increase it sevenfold and win me peace and independence!'

Taken up by such thoughts, he found himself on one of the main streets of Petersburg in front of a house built a long time ago. The street was packed with carriages; one after another, they drew up by the lit porch. From out of these carriages would appear the shapely leg of a young beauty, a boot with clinking spurs, the shoe and striped stocking of a diplomat ... Fur coats and capes flitted past a majestic hall porter. Hermann stopped.

'Whose house is this?' he asked a policeman in his box at the corner of the street.

'The Countess N.'s,' answered the policeman.

Hermann gave a start. The surprising story presented itself once again to his imagination. He began to pace about in front of the house, thinking of its mistress and her miraculous ability. It was late when he returned to his own humble quarters; he was unable to get to sleep for a long time and, when sleep did overtake him, he dreamed of cards, a green table, heaps of bank notes and piles of gold coins. He played card after card, resolutely kept doubling his stakes, and went on and on winning, raking the gold coins across the table and pocketing the bank notes. He woke up late, sighed over the loss of his fantastic wealth, again began wandering about the city and again found himself in front of the Countess N.'s house. A mysterious force seemed to be drawing him towards it. He stopped and looked at the windows. In one he saw a dark-haired head: bent down, probably over a book or some work. The head looked up. Hermann saw a fresh young face and black eyes. This moment decided his fate.

3

Vous m'écrivez, mon ange, des lettres de quatre pages plus vite que je ne puis les lire.[5]
  from a personal correspondence

No sooner had Lizaveta Ivanovna taken off her cape and bonnet than the Countess sent for her and was ordering the carriage again. They went out on to the street. Just as two footmen lifted the old woman up and pushed her through the carriage door, Lizaveta Ivanovna saw her engineer standing by one of the wheels; he seized her hand; she was overcome by fright – the young man vanished: in her hand lay a letter. She slipped it inside her glove and, throughout the drive, heard nothing and saw nothing. The Countess was in the habit, when they were in a carriage, of constantly asking questions: Who was that, going the other way? What's the name of this bridge? What's written there on that sign? On this occasion, Lizaveta Ivanovna's answers were random and nonsensical, and the Countess grew angry:

'What's up with you, old girl? Are you in a daze? Can't you hear? Or is it that you don't understand? I don't mumble, thank God, and I haven't lost my mind yet!'

Lizaveta Ivanovna was not listening. Back at home, she ran straight to her room and took the letter out of her glove: it had not been sealed.

Lizaveta Ivanovna read it. The letter contained a confession of love: it was tender, respectful and taken word for word from a German novel. But Lizaveta Ivanovna knew no German and was very content with the confession.

Nevertheless, she was extremely troubled by what she had done. She was entering for the first time into close, secret relations with a young man. His audacity appalled her. She reproached herself for her imprudent conduct and didn't know what to do. Should she stop sitting by the window and, through a show of indifference, chill the young officer's desire to make further advances? Should she return his letter? Answer coldly and resolutely? There was no one she could turn to for advice; she had neither close friend nor mentor. Lizaveta Ivanovna made up her mind to reply.

She sat down at her little writing-table, took up pen and paper – and thought. Several times she began her letter – then tore it up: her words seemed either too forbearing or too cruel. In the end she managed to write a few lines she was content with. *I am certain*, she wrote, *that you have honourable intentions and that you did not wish to insult me by a thoughtless act; but our acquaintance ought not to begin in this manner. I am returning your letter to you, and I hope I shall not again have reason to complain of an undeserved lack of respect.*

The following day, seeing Hermann approach, Lizaveta Ivanovna got up from her embroidery frame, went into the hall, opened the little window and threw the letter out on to the street, trusting in the young officer's alertness. Hermann ran forward, picked up the letter and went into a confectioner's shop. Breaking the seal, he found his own letter and Lizaveta Ivanovna's reply. This was as he had expected and he returned home, much taken up with his scheming.

Three days after this, a quick-eyed young mamselle brought Lizaveta Ivanovna a note from a milliner's. Lizaveta Ivanovna opened it apprehensively, anticipating a demand for payment, and suddenly recognized the hand of Hermann.

'You've made a mistake, my dear,' she said. 'This note isn't for me.'

'It most certainly is!' replied the bold girl, not attempting to hide a knowing smile. 'Do please read it!'

Lizaveta Ivanovna quickly read the note through. Hermann was asking for a tryst.

'It's not possible!' said Lizaveta Ivanovna, frightened by both the precipitateness of the request and the means used to convey it. 'No, it really can't be addressed to me.' And she tore the letter into little pieces.

'If the letter wasn't addressed to you, then why have you torn it up?' said the young mamselle. 'I could have returned it to the person who sent it.'

'Be so kind, my dear,' said Lizaveta Ivanovna, incensed by this remark, 'as not to bring me any more letters. And tell whoever sent you here that he should be ashamed . . .'

But Hermann persisted. Every day, by one means or another, letters arrived from him. They were no longer translations from German. Hermann wrote in the inspiration of passion and he was speaking a language that came naturally to him: one that expressed both the intransigence of his desires and the disorder of an unbridled imagination. Lizaveta Ivanovna no longer thought of sending the letters back; she revelled in them and began to reply to them, and her messages grew longer and more tender by the hour. In the end, she threw out of the window to him a letter which read:

There is a ball tonight at the —— Ambassador's. The Countess is attending. We shall stay till about two o'clock. This gives us an opportunity for you to see me alone. As soon as the Countess goes out, her servants will probably leave their stations; the hall-porter will remain by the entrance, but even he usually retires to his closet. Come at half past eleven. Walk straight up the stairs. If you meet anyone in the ante-room, ask whether the Countess is at home. They will say 'No' – and that will be that. You will have to leave. But probably you won't meet anyone. The maids will be in their room, all together. Go left out of the ante-room and keep straight on till you come to the Countess's bedroom. In the bedroom, behind the screen, you will see two small doors. The one on the right is to a study, which the Countess never enters; the one on the left opens on to a passage – and then there's a narrow little spiral staircase, which leads to my bedroom.

Hermann quivered like a tiger as he waited for the appointed time. By ten o'clock in the evening he was standing outside the Countess's house. The weather was terrible: the wind howled, wet flakes of snow were falling; the lanterns burned dim; the streets were deserted. From time to time, on the lookout for a late fare, a cabby would drive by with a scrawny horse. Wearing only a frock coat, Hermann felt neither the wind nor the snow. At last the Countess's carriage was brought round. Hermann watched as the footmen brought out a hunched-up old woman wrapped in a sable coat; behind her, in a chilly cloak, her head adorned with fresh flowers, he glimpsed her ward. Doors slammed. The carriage moved heavily off through the soft snow. The hall porter closed the front door. The windows went dark. Hermann paced up and down in front of the deserted house: he went up to a lantern and looked at his watch – it was twenty past eleven. He stayed under the lantern, eyes fixed on the hands of his watch, as he waited out the remaining minutes. At exactly half past eleven, Hermann walked up the steps to the Countess's porch and entered the brightly lit lobby. There was no hall porter. Hermann ran up the stairs, opened the door into the ante-room and found a servant asleep under a lamp in an ancient, stained armchair. With a light, resolute step Hermann walked past him. The hall and drawing room were dark, lit only dimly from the ante-room. Hermann entered the bedroom. Before a case filled with ancient icons burned a gold lamp. Standing in sad symmetry along walls hung with Chinese silk were down-cushioned sofas, their gilt flaking off, and chairs upholstered in faded damask. On one of the walls hung two portraits painted in Paris by Mme Lebrun.[6] The first was of a stout, florid man, about forty years old, in a light-green uniform with a star; the other was of a young beauty with an aquiline nose and a rose in her powdered hair, which was combed back off the temples. Every nook and corner was filled with porcelain shepherd-esses, clocks made by the celebrated Leroys,[7] little boxes, bandalores, fans, and other ladies' playthings that had been invented, along with the Montgolfier balloon and Mesmer's magnetism,[8] at the end of the previous century. Hermann went behind the screen. There he found a small iron bedstead. To the right was the door to the study; to the left – the other door, into the passage. Hermann opened this door and saw the narrow spiral staircase that led to the bedroom of the poor young ward. But he turned back and entered the dark study.

Time passed slowly. Everything was quiet. In the drawing room a clock struck twelve; in one room after another clocks struck twelve – and everything fell silent again. Hermann stood there, leaning against the cold stove. He was calm; his heart was beating evenly, as does the heart of a man who has resolved upon something dangerous but unavoidable. The clocks struck one, then two – and he heard the distant rumble of a carriage. He was seized by an involuntary excitement. The carriage drew up and stopped. He heard a knock as the steps were let down. The household began to stir. People ran about, voices were raised and lights were lit. Three aged maids hurried into the bedroom and the Countess, half dead, lowered herself into a Voltaire armchair.[9] Hermann watched through a crack: Lizaveta Ivanovna walked past him. Hermann heard her hurrying steps on the treads of her stairs. In response something like a pang of conscience answered in his heart, then fell silent. He became like stone.

The Countess began to undress in front of the mirror. Her rose-decked bonnet was unpinned; her powdered wig was removed from her grey and close-cropped head. Pins showered down around her. A yellow dress, embroidered with silver, dropped to her swollen feet. Hermann was a witness to the revolting mysteries of her toilette. At last the Countess was in her bedjacket and nightcap; in this garb, more appropriate to her age, she seemed less terrible and hideous.

Like a great many old people, the Countess suffered from insomnia. After undressing, she sat down by the window in her Voltaire armchair and dismissed her maids. The candles were taken away; once more the room was lit only by the icon-lamp. The Countess sat there, all yellow, twitching her pendulous lips and rocking from side to side. Her cloudy eyes showed a total absence of thought; looking at the frightening old woman, one might have imagined that this rocking was effected not by her will but by the action of some hidden galvanism.[10]

An extraordinary change came over the dead face. Her lips stopped twitching, her eyes came to life: before the Countess stood a man she had never seen.

'Don't be frightened, for the love of God, don't be frightened!' he said in a clear, quiet voice. 'I have no intention of harming you; I've come to beg a favour of you.'

The old woman looked silently at him and seemed not to hear him. Hermann thought she was deaf, bent down over her ear and said the same thing again. The old woman remained silent.

'You have the power,' Hermann went on, 'at no cost to yourself, to make me a happy man. I know you can guess three cards in sequence . . .'

He stopped. The Countess, it seemed, had understood what was being asked of her; it seemed she was trying to find words for an answer.

'That was a joke,' she said at last. 'I swear to you! It was a joke!'

'This is no joking matter,' Hermann replied crossly. 'Remember Chaplitsky, how you helped him win back his losses.'

The Countess was visibly perturbed. Her features registered a strong movement of the soul, but she quickly fell back into her former apathy.

'Can you,' Hermann went on, 'tell me those three true cards?'

The Countess remained silent; Hermann went on: 'For whom are you keeping your secret? For your grandchildren? They're rich anyway; they don't know the value of money. Your three cards can't help a spendthrift. He who doesn't look after his patrimony will die in poverty; the devil himself can't change that. I'm not a spendthrift; I know the value of money. Your three cards will not be wasted on me. Well?'

He waited, quivering, for her answer. The Countess said nothing; Hermann fell to his knees.

'If ever,' he said, 'your heart has known the feeling of love, if you can remember its ecstasies; if you have ever smiled at the cry of a new-born son; if anything human has at any time stirred in your breast, then I implore you by your feelings as a wife, as a mistress, as a mother, by all that is sacred in life – do not refuse me what I ask! Tell me your secret! What use is it to you? Maybe it is linked to some terrible sin, to the loss of eternal bliss, to a diabolical pact. Think: you are old; you don't have long to live, and I am willing to take your sin upon my own soul. Only tell me your secret. Think: a man's happiness lies in your hands. Not only I, but my children, my grandchildren and great-grandchildren will bless your memory and hold it sacred.'

The old woman answered not a word.

Hermann stood.

'Old witch!' he said, through clenched teeth. 'Then I shall force you to answer.'

With these words he drew a pistol from his pocket.

Seeing the pistol, the Countess for the second time showed strong feeling. She nodded her head and raised one hand, as if shielding herself from a shot. Then she fell back . . . and remained motionless.

'Don't be childish,' said Hermann, taking her by the hand. 'I'm asking for the last time: will you tell me your three cards? Yes, or no?'

The Countess did not answer. Hermann realized she was dead.

4

7 May 18—
Homme sans mœurs et sans religion![11]
from a correspondence

Lizaveta Ivanovna was sitting in her room, still in her ball gown, plunged deep in thought. On returning home, she had been quick to dismiss the sleepy maid who reluctantly offered her services; she said she would undress on her own and went quivering to her room, hoping to find Hermann and wanting not to find him. One glance was enough to assure her of his absence, and she thanked Fate for the obstacle that had prevented their tryst. She sat down without undressing and began to recall all the circumstances that had enticed her such a great distance in so short a time. It was not yet three weeks since she had first, through the window, seen this young man – and she was already corresponding with him, and she had yielded to his demand for a nocturnal tryst! She knew his name only because some of his letters were signed; she had never spoken to him, never heard his voice, never heard anything about him – until this evening. It was strange. This very evening, at the ball, Tomsky, in a huff with the young Princess Polina ——, who had been flirting for once with someone other than him, had wanted to avenge himself through a show of indifference; he had taken Lizaveta Ivanovna and danced an endless mazurka[12] with her. All through it, he teased her about her liking for engineers; he assured her that he knew a great deal more than she might imagine, and some of his jokes were so near the mark that Lizaveta Ivanovna more than once thought he knew her secret.

'Who have you learned all this from?' she asked, laughing.

'From a most remarkable fellow,' Tomsky replied. 'A friend of someone you know.'

'And who is this remarkable fellow?'

'His name is Hermann.'

Lizaveta Ivanovna said nothing; but her hands and feet turned to ice.

'This Hermann,' Tomsky went on, 'is a truly romantic figure. He has the profile of Napoleon – and the soul of Mephistopheles. Weighing on his conscience, I believe, are at least three evil deeds. How pale you've gone!'

'I've got a headache. So what did you learn from this Hermann – or whatever his name is?'

'Hermann is most annoyed with his friend. Were he in his friend's place, he says, he would act quite differently. I even think Hermann has designs on you himself. At the very least, he seems far from indifferent when he listens to the enamoured outpourings of his friend.'

'But where has he seen me?'

'In church, perhaps, or when you were out and about. God knows! Perhaps while you were asleep in your room. I wouldn't put it past him.'

Three ladies came up to them with the question *oubli ou regret?*,[13] cutting short a conversation that Lizaveta Ivanovna was finding unbearably fascinating.

Tomsky's new partner was the Princess Polina. Dancing one more time round the room and spinning round one more time in front of her chair, she managed to make her peace with him. By the time he returned to his place, Tomsky was no longer thinking either of Hermann or of Lizaveta Ivanovna. Lizaveta Ivanovna had desperately wanted to renew the interrupted conversation, but the mazurka had come to an end and soon afterwards the old Countess had taken her leave.

Tomsky's words were mere ballroom chatter, but they had sunk deep into the soul of the young dreamer. The portrait sketched by Tomsky was similar to the image she had formed herself and, thanks to the latest novels, this already hackneyed figure frightened and captivated her imagination. She sat in her room, her bare arms crossed and her head, still adorned with flowers, bent down over her breast. Suddenly the door opened and Hermann came in. She quivered.

'Where have you been?' she asked in a frightened whisper.

'In the old Countess's bedroom,' said Hermann. 'I've just left her. The Countess is dead.'

'My God! What are you saying?'

'And I seem,' Hermann went on, 'to have been the cause of her death.'

Lizaveta Ivanovna looked at him; in her soul echoed Tomsky's words: *on his conscience are at least three evil deeds*! Hermann sat down beside her, on the window seat, and told her everything.

Lizaveta Ivanovna listened to him in horror. So the passionate letters, the ardent demands, the audacious, persistent pursuit – all this had not been love! What his soul craved was money! She herself had no power to assuage his desires and make him happy. The poor ward had been nothing but a blind accomplice to a brigand, to the murderer of her aged benefactress! She wept bitterly in her belated, anguished remorse. Hermann watched her in silence; he too was in torment, but what troubled his stern soul was neither the poor girl's tears nor the surprising charm of her grief. Nor did he feel any pang of conscience at the thought of the old woman's death. Only one thing appalled him: the irrevocable loss of a secret that was to have brought him wealth.

'You monster!' said Lizaveta Ivanovna at last.

'I didn't want her to die,' said Hermann. 'My pistol is not loaded.'

They fell silent.

Day was breaking. Lizaveta Ivanovna extinguished the candle, now burning down; pale light illumined her room. She wiped the tears from her eyes and glanced up at Hermann: he was sitting on the window-seat, arms folded, frowning grimly. In this pose he looked astonishingly like a portrait of Napoleon. This likeness amazed even Lizaveta Ivanovna.

'How are you going to leave the house?' said Lizaveta Ivanovna at last. 'I'd meant to take you down the secret staircase, but that means going through the Countess's bedroom, and I'm frightened.'

'Tell me how to find this secret staircase; I must leave.'

Lizaveta Ivanovna got up, took a key from her chest, handed it to

Hermann and gave him detailed instructions. Hermann pressed her cold, unresponsive hand, kissed her bowed head and left.

He went down the spiral staircase and once again entered the Countess's bedroom. The dead old woman sat there, turned to stone; her face expressed a deep calm. Hermann stopped in front of her; he looked at her for a long time, as if wanting to be sure of the terrible truth; at last he entered the study, felt behind the wall hangings till he found the door, and began to descend a dark staircase, troubled by strange feelings. Up this same staircase, Hermann was thinking, perhaps sixty years before, at this same hour, his hair coiffured *à l'oiseau royal*,[14] wearing an embroidered coat and pressing his three-cornered hat to his heart, a fortunate young man – now long rotted away in his grave – had crept to the same bedroom; and today the heart of his aged mistress had ceased to beat.

At the foot of the staircase Hermann came to a door, which he unlocked with the key – and he found himself in a passage that led him out on to the street.

5

That night the late Baroness von V——— appeared to me. She was all in white and she said to me: 'Good evening, Mister Councillor!'
    Swedenborg[15]

Three days after the fateful night, at nine o'clock in the morning, Hermann set out for the convent where the funeral rites for the body of the deceased Countess were to be sung. Though unrepentant, he could not altogether silence the voice of his conscience, which kept repeating, 'You are the old woman's murderer!' Having little true faith, he had a great number of superstitions. He believed that the dead Countess might have an evil influence on his life, and he had resolved to attend her funeral and so win her forgiveness.

The church was full. Hermann could barely make his way through the crowd of people. The coffin stood on an opulent catafalque under a velvet canopy. The deceased lay with her arms folded across her breast, in a lace cap and a white satin dress. Around the coffin stood her household: the servants holding candles and wearing black kaftans with the family crest sewn onto the shoulder; the relatives – children, grandchildren and great-grandchildren – all in deep mourning. No one wept: tears would have been *une affectation*. The Countess was so very old that her death could not have been a surprise to anyone, and her family had long seen her as someone from another era. A young bishop gave the funeral address. In simple and moving words he described the peaceful dormition of a righteous woman whose long years had been a quiet, touching preparation for a Christian end. 'The angel of death discovered her,' he said, 'vigilant in pious thought and waiting for the Midnight Bridegroom.' The service was conducted with sad decorum. The relatives were first to go up and take leave of the body. They were followed by the Countess's numerous guests, who had come to pay their respects to one who for so long had been a part of their vain merriments. Next came the household servants. Last of all, an old retainer, a woman the same age as the deceased, went up to the coffin; two young girls supported her, each taking an arm. She did not have the strength to bow down to the ground, and she alone shed tears as she kissed the cold hand of her mistress. After her, Hermann summoned his resolve to go up to the coffin. He bent down to the ground and prostrated himself for several minutes on the cold floor, which was strewn with sprigs of fir. Finally, pale as the deceased, he got to his feet, climbed the steps to the catafalque and bent down towards her. At that moment it seemed to him that the dead woman screwed up one eye and gave him a mocking wink. Hermann stepped quickly backwards, lost his footing and crashed to the ground, flat on his back. He was helped to his feet. At the same time, Lizaveta Ivanovna was carried out of the church in a faint. The solemnity of the sombre rite was disturbed by this episode for several minutes. The visitors all began murmuring and a gaunt chamberlain, a close relative of the deceased, whispered into the ear of an Englishman standing beside him that the young officer was her illegitimate son, to which the Englishman responded with a cold 'Oh?'

All that day Hermann felt extremely upset. Dining at an out-of-the-way tavern, he uncharacteristically drank a great deal in the hope of stifling his inner turmoil. But the wine only further inflamed his imagination. Returning home, he threw himself fully clothed on his bed and fell into a deep sleep.

It was night when he woke; his room was lit by the moon. He glanced at his watch: it was a quarter to three. He was no longer sleepy; he sat up, thinking about the funeral of the old Countess.

Just then someone out on the street looked in through the window and immediately stepped back. Hermann paid no attention. A minute later he heard the sound of the ante-room door being opened. Hermann thought his orderly was returning, drunk as usual, from a night-time spree. But he heard unfamiliar footsteps: someone was softly shuffling along in slippers. The door opened; in came a woman dressed in white. Hermann took her for his old nurse and wondered what could have brought her to him at such an hour. But the white woman, gliding forward, was suddenly in front of him – and Hermann recognized the Countess.

'I have come to you against my will,' she said in a firm voice, 'but I have been ordered to grant your request. The three, the seven and the ace will win for you in sequence – on condition you play only one card in twenty-four hours and that you never, as long as you live, gamble again. I forgive you my death on condition you marry my ward, Lizaveta Ivanovna.'

With these words she quietly turned round, shuffled to the door and disappeared. Hermann heard her slam the door to the entrance room and saw someone looking in at him again through the window.

It took Hermann a long time to come back to himself. He went into the other room. His orderly was asleep on the floor; Hermann could barely wake him up. As usual, the man was drunk; it was impossible to get any sense out of him. The door into the entrance room was locked. Hermann returned to his room, lit a candle and wrote down his vision.

6

'*Attendez!*'
'How dare you speak to me like that?'
'Your Excellency, I said: "*Attendez*, sir!" '[16]

Two *idées fixes* cannot coexist in the moral sphere, just as two bodies cannot occupy the same space in the physical world. The image of the dead old woman was soon eclipsed in Hermann's imagination by the three, the seven and the ace. The three, seven and ace were always in his thoughts and on his lips. Seeing a young woman, he would come out with, 'She's so slender! A real three of hearts.' When asked the time, he might reply, 'Five minutes to the seven.' A pot-bellied man always made him think of an ace. The three, the seven and the ace pursued him through his dreams, assuming every conceivable guise: the three blossomed before him like a large and splendid flower, the seven became a gothic portal, the ace a huge spider. All his thoughts merged into one unchanging thought: how could he make use of a secret for which he had paid dearly? He began thinking about resigning his commission and travelling. In the public casinos of Paris he would wrest treasure from an enchanted Fortuna. Chance spared him the trouble.

In Moscow there was a circle of wealthy gamblers presided over by the famous Chekalinsky, who had spent his entire life at the card table and had at one time made millions, accepting promissory notes when he won and paying his losses in cash. Long experience had won him the trust of his fellow gamblers; his open house and famous chef, along with his courteous and cheerful manner, gained him the respect of society in general. He came to Petersburg. Young men flocked to him, forsaking ballrooms for cards and preferring the temptations of faro to the allures of philandering. Narumov brought Hermann to his house.

They passed through a series of magnificent rooms, filled with attentive servants. Generals and privy councillors were playing whist; young men were lounging on damask sofas, eating ice creams or smoking pipes. In the drawing room, twenty or so gamblers were crowded around a long table behind which sat the host, who was keeping the bank. He was a most respectable-looking man of about sixty; he had a fine head of silvery-grey hair; his full, fresh face was the picture of benevolence; his eyes shone, animated by a constant smile. Narumov introduced Hermann to him. Chekalinsky shook his hand warmly, asked him not to stand on ceremony and went on dealing.

The round went on for a long time. More than thirty cards were on the table. After dealing to a player, Chekalinsky would pause, allowing everyone time to decide what they wanted; he noted down losses, listened politely to requests and still more politely straightened out a card whose corner was being bent back by an absent-minded hand.[17] At last the round was over. Chekalinsky shuffled the cards and got ready to deal another.

'Allow me to play a card,' said Hermann, reaching forward from behind a stout gentleman, one of the gamblers. Chekalinsky smiled silently and nodded his head, indicating his obedient consent. Narumov laughingly congratulated Hermann on breaking his long fast and wished him a lucky beginning.

'There!' said Hermann, chalking a number of figures on the back of his card.

'How much, sir?' asked the banker, screwing up his eyes. 'Forgive me, I can't quite see.'

'Forty-seven thousand,' Hermann replied.

At these words every head turned instantly, and all eyes were fixed on Hermann. 'He's gone mad,' thought Narumov.

'Allow me to observe,' Chekalinsky said with his same unchanging smile, 'that your stake is very high. Until now no one has placed an initial stake of more than two hundred and seventy-five.'

'What of it?' replied Hermann. 'Will you play against my card or not?'

Chekalinsky bowed with the same air of humble compliance.

'I merely wished to point out,' he said, 'that, being honoured with the trust of my fellows, I can play only against ready cash. For my own part, of course, I am confident that your word is enough, but, for the sake of clarity in our reckonings and the conduct of the game, I must ask you to place your money on your card.'

Hermann took a bank note out of his pocket and handed it to Chekalinsky, who, after a quick glance at it, placed it on Hermann's card.

He began to deal. A nine to the right, a three to the left.

'My three wins,' said Hermann, turning over his card.

The players all began whispering. Chekalinsky frowned, but a smile instantly returned to his face.

'Would you like your winnings now?' he asked.

'If you please,' answered Hermann.

Chekalinsky took several bank notes from his pocket and settled up with him then and there. Hermann took his money and left the table. Narumov felt bewildered. Hermann drank a glass of lemonade and set off back home.

The next evening he appeared at Chekalinsky's again. The host was dealing. Hermann went up to the table; the other gamblers at once made room for him. Chekalinsky bowed courteously.

Hermann waited till the next round and placed a card on the table; on top of it he placed both his original forty-seven thousand and the previous day's winnings.

Chekalinsky dealt to Hermann. To the right – a knave; to the left – a seven.

Hermann turned over his seven.

Everyone gasped. Chekalinsky was visibly perturbed. He counted out ninety-four thousand and handed it to Hermann. Hermann accepted the money with sang-froid and left straight away.

The following evening, Hermann appeared again at the card table. Everyone was expecting him. The generals and privy councillors abandoned their whist to watch such extraordinary play. The young officers leaped up from their sofas; the servants all congregated in the drawing room. Everyone clustered around Hermann. The other gamblers let their turns pass, impatient to see how Hermann would end. Hermann stood by the table, about to play alone against a pale but still smiling Chekalinsky. Each unsealed a new pack. Chekalinsky shuffled. Hermann chose his card and placed it on the table, covering it with a heap of bank notes. It was like a duel. Deep silence reigned all around.

Chekalinsky dealt; his hands were trembling. To the right – a queen; to the left – an ace.

'My ace wins,' said Hermann, turning over his card.

'Your Queen's lost,' Chekalinsky said courteously.

Hermann shuddered. Before him, instead of an ace, stood the Queen of Spades. He couldn't believe his eyes, unable to understand how he could have played the wrong card.

At that moment the Queen of Spades seemed to him to wink and smirk. Hermann was struck by an extraordinary likeness.

'The old woman!' he cried out in horror.

Chekalinsky gathered in Hermann's bank notes. Hermann stood there stock-still. When at last he walked away, there was a sudden hubbub. 'Splendid play,' said the other gamblers. Chekalinsky shuffled again; the game continued its course.

Conclusion

Hermann went mad. He is in room 17 of the Obukhov Hospital; he doesn't answer any questions and he keeps muttering with extraordinary rapidity, 'Three, seven, ace! Three, seven, queen!'

Lizaveta Ivanovna has married a very pleasant young man; he works in some government office and has a respectable fortune of his own: he is the son of the old Countess's former steward. Lizaveta Ivanovna is bringing up a young ward, a poor relation.

Tomsky has been promoted to captain and is marrying Princess Polina.

First published in 1834
Translated by Robert and Elizabeth Chandler and Olga Meerson

MIKHAIL YURYEVICH
LERMONTOV (1814–41)

Born in Moscow, Lermontov was raised mainly by his grand-mother on her Central Russian estate. He returned to Moscow in 1827 and attended the School for the Nobility and Moscow University, where he studied ethics, politics and literature. After two years at a military academy in St Petersburg, he became a junior officer in the Life Guard Hussars. He made his name with a poem on Pushkin's death, accusing court circles of complicity; the resulting controversy led to his exile to the Caucasus. After his return to St Petersburg, Lermontov was exiled a second time – for duelling with the son of the French Ambassador.

Lermontov was hailed as Pushkin's successor and his career fol-lowed a similar pattern. Like Pushkin, he mastered a variety of poetic genres: lyric, narrative and satirical. Like Pushkin, he turned to prose in his last years, publishing the novel A Hero of Our Time only a year before his death. And, like Pushkin, he died in a duel, in the spa town of Pyatigorsk in the northern Caucasus. Nearly all of Lermontov's best work dates from his last two years; this makes his premature death still more tragic.

Lermontov's prose, like Pushkin's, seems surprisingly modern. A Hero of Our Time consists of five separate stories linked by a common hero. Each story is in a distinct genre. The first two, told by two different narrators, introduce the figure of Pechorin, a young officer serving in the Caucasus; the last three are extracts from his journal. Both attractive and repulsive, Pechorin is thus seen from several perspectives; it is for the reader to bring these perspectives together.

'The Fatalist', the last story in the novel, can be read both as a meditation on chance, causality and fate and as an exploration of Pechorin's inner contradictions. Pechorin claims to believe in free will, yet he accepts that Vulich's death is 'written in the heavens'. Lermontov may have intended Pechorin to represent Russia, poised between the individualistic West and the fatalistic East.

Russia had secured most of Transcaucasia by 1830. Two parts

of the northern Caucasus, however, remained largely independent: Circassia in the west and Chechnya in the east. In Lermontov's day, Russia's attempt to assert her power in these areas was largely a matter of sending brief punitive expeditions into enemy territory. Chechnya and Circassia were not subdued until 1864. Even after that, however, there were periodic rebellions and the collapse of the Soviet Union has led to two more wars between Russia and Chechnya.

THE FATALIST

I happened once to spend a couple of weeks in a Cossack village on the left flank.[1] An infantry battalion was stationed there and in the evenings the officers gathered in one another's quarters to play cards, taking it in turn to be host.

One evening at Major S——'s we grew tired of boston, threw the cards under the table and sat up until very late; the conversation, for once, was interesting. We were talking about the way many Christians accept the Muslim belief that a man's fate is written in the heavens; each of us had unusual stories to tell – for or against.

'None of this, gentlemen, proves anything at all,' said the old major. 'Not one of you, I take it, has witnessed the strange happenings with which you back up your views.'

'That's true,' several of us admitted, 'but we heard about them from people we can trust.'

'It's all nonsense!' said somebody else. 'Where are these trustworthy people who have seen the records on which the hour of our death is inscribed? And if there really is such a thing as predestination, why have we been given free will and reason? Why must we account for our actions?'

At that moment, an officer sitting in the corner got to his feet. He walked slowly up to the table and looked at us all with a calm and solemn look. He was a Serb by birth, as was clear from his name.

Lieutenant Vulich's looks perfectly matched his character. His height, his swarthy face, his black hair and penetrating black eyes, the large but straight nose so characteristic of his nation, the sad cold smile constantly wandering on his lips – all this seemed to give him the air of someone apart, unable to share his thoughts and passions with the men Fate had given him as companions.

He was brave; he spoke little, but to the point; there was no one to whom he confided the secrets of his soul or his family; he hardly ever drank wine and he never chased after the young Cossack girls –

whose charms, unless you have seen them, cannot be imagined. It was said, admittedly, that the Colonel's wife was not indifferent to his expressive eyes, but any insinuations about this made him extremely angry.

There was just one passion he did not hide – his passion for gambling. Once he was at the green table, he would forget everything, and he usually lost; but repeated bad luck only exacerbated his obstinacy. It was said that one night, while out on an expedition, he and his fellows had been playing faro, using a pillow as a table; he had been keeping the bank himself and was enjoying terrific luck. Suddenly there were shots, the alarm sounded, and everyone jumped up and rushed for their weapons.

'Place your card – I'm staking the bank!' Vulich shouted, without moving from his seat, to one of the most ardent punters. 'I'm playing a seven,'[2] said the punter as he ran off. In spite of the general commotion, Vulich finished the round; the card he chanced to deal to the punter was a seven.

When Vulich caught up with the others, he found himself amid a heavy exchange of fire. Not bothering in the least about either the bullets or the swords of the Chechens, he began to search for the fortunate punter.

'I dealt you a seven!' he shouted, finally catching sight of his man in the line of marksmen who were beginning to force the enemy out of the wood. He went up closer, took out his purse and wallet and handed them to the lucky man, ignoring his protests that this was no time or place for payment. After discharging this unpleasant duty, Vulich rushed forward, taking our soldiers along with him, and went on coolly exchanging shots with the Chechens until the end of the engagement.

When Lieutenant Vulich went up to the table, everyone fell silent, expecting something out of the ordinary.

'Gentlemen!' he said (his voice was calm, though a tone below its usual pitch). 'Gentlemen, what use are empty arguments? What you need is evidence. I suggest we test here and now whether a man is able to dispose of his life at will, or whether the fateful minute has been assigned to each of us in advance. Who'll be the one?'

From every side came cries of 'Not me! Not me!' and 'He's crazy! What on earth's got into him?'

'I'll place a bet,' I said jokingly.

'Which way?'

'I assert that there is no predestination,' I said, dropping twenty gold coins – all I had in my pocket – on to the table.

'I accept your bet,' Vulich answered in a low voice. 'Major, you will be umpire. Here are fifteen gold pieces. You owe me the other five yourself – do me a favour: add them to these.'

'Very well,' said the Major, 'but I really don't understand what this is all about or how you're going to settle the argument.'

Without a word Vulich stepped into the Major's bedroom; we followed behind. He went up to the wall where the Major had hung his weapons and, quite at random, took down from its nail one of the various-calibred pistols. We still didn't understand, but when he cocked the pistol and poured some gunpowder into the pan, several of us yelled out involuntarily and grabbed him by the arms.

'What do you want to do? You're mad!'

'Gentlemen,' he said slowly, freeing his arms, 'are any of you willing to pay twenty gold coins on my behalf?'

We all fell silent and walked away.

Vulich went back into the other room and sat down at the table; we followed him. He motioned to us to sit down around him. We obeyed in silence: he had acquired some mysterious power over us. I looked him hard in the eye, but he met my scrutiny with a calm, steady gaze and his pale lips smiled; yet for all his sang-froid I felt I could see the mark of death on his pale face. I have observed – and many seasoned fighters have confirmed this observation of mine – that the face of a man who is going to die within a few hours often bears some strange sign of a fate that cannot be avoided; an experienced eye is rarely mistaken.

'You're going to die soon,' I said to him.

He turned round quickly but answered slowly and calmly, 'Maybe, maybe not.'

Then he asked the Major if the pistol was loaded. The Major was too confused to remember clearly.

'All right, Vulich!' someone shouted. 'That'll do. If it was hanging by the head of the bed, it's sure to be loaded. Stop playing the fool!'

'Yes, stop fooling around,' said someone else.

'Fifty roubles to five the pistol's not loaded!' shouted a third person.

Fresh bets were laid.

This ritual was dragging on too long for me.

'Listen,' I said. 'Either shoot yourself or put the pistol back where it came from so we can all go to bed.'

'That's right,' several of us shouted. 'Let's get some sleep.'

'Gentlemen, please don't move,' said Vulich, putting the muzzle to his forehead. Everyone froze.

'Mr Pechorin,' he continued, 'take a card and throw it in the air.'

I took a card from the table – it was the ace of hearts, I can see it now – and threw it into the air. Everyone held his breath; everyone's eyes, full of fear and a certain undefined curiosity, were darting between the pistol and the fateful ace, which hung trembling in the air; when it reached the table, Vulich pulled the trigger. The pistol misfired.

'Thank God!' people shouted. 'It wasn't loaded.'

'Let's just see,' said Vulich. He cocked the pistol again and took aim at a cap hanging over the window. A shot rang out; the room filled with smoke. Once the smoke had cleared, someone took down the cap: there was a hole right through the middle, and a bullet was lodged deep in the wall.

For several minutes no one could say a word. With absolute composure, Vulich poured my gold pieces into his purse.

A discussion began as to why the pistol had misfired the first time. Some said the pan must have been clogged; others whispered that the powder had been damp and that Vulich had then added fresh. But I said this last suggestion was unfair, because I had not once taken my eyes off the pistol.

'You've been lucky!' I said to Vulich.

'For the first time in my life,' he replied, smiling complacently. 'This is better than faro or stoss.'

'But a little more dangerous.'

'So, do you believe in predestination now?'

'Yes, I do,' I replied. 'Only I can't understand why I was so sure you were going to die today.'

The man who, only a moment ago, had been so calmly pointing a pistol at his own forehead suddenly looked flushed and confused.

'That'll do,' he said, getting to his feet. 'Our bet has been settled and your remark, it seems to me, is out of place.' He took his cap and left. I thought this strange – and not without reason.

Soon afterwards the other officers went off to their lodgings, each with his own interpretation of Vulich's eccentricities and all, no doubt, in agreement about how heartless I'd been to bet against a man who wanted to shoot himself – as though he couldn't have found an opportunity without me!

I walked home through the empty side streets. A full moon, red as the glow of a distant blaze, was just rising over a jagged horizon of rooftops. Stars were shining calmly in the deep blue heavens and it made me laugh to think there had once been people of great wisdom who believed that the stars took part in our petty quarrels over a patch of land or some imaginary rights or other. And what had happened?

Those lamps, which they imagined had been lit only to shine on their battles and triumphs, still burned on as bright as ever, while all their passions and hopes, and they themselves, had long been extinguished, like a little fire lit on the edge of a forest by some carefree traveller. And yet what strength of will they had derived from the certainty that the whole sky, with its countless inhabitants, was watching them with a sympathy that was mute but never failing. And we, their pitiful descendants, roaming the earth without convictions or pride, with no pleasure or fear except the involuntary fear that grips the heart at the thought of our inevitable end – we are no longer capable of great sacrifices, whether for the good of mankind or even for our own personal happiness, whose impossibility we well know; and, just as our ancestors once rushed from one delusion to another, we ourselves move indifferently from doubt to doubt, without our ancestors' hope, without even that undefined but real delight the soul derives from any struggle with men or with Fate.

And many other similar thoughts passed through my mind. I didn't try to hold on to them, since I prefer not to dwell on abstract ideas: where do they lead you? As a boy I was a dreamer: I loved to caress the images, now gloomy, now iridescent, traced by my restless and avid imagination. But what did that leave me with? Weariness – as if I had been struggling all night with a phantom – only weariness and some dim memory, filled with regrets. In this hopeless battle I exhausted all the ardour of soul and constancy of will required for life; I entered real life only after living through it all in my mind and I felt bored and disgusted, as if I were reading a poor imitation of a book I had known for a long time.

The events of the evening had made a rather deep impression on me and had irritated my nerves. I no longer know for sure whether or not I believe in predestination, but that evening I was certain of it: the evidence for it had been startling and, although I laughed at our ancestors and their obliging astrology, I found myself slipping into their way of thinking. This, however, is a dangerous path and I managed to pull myself up in time; since it is a rule of mine never to believe anything blindly or reject anything absolutely, I put metaphysics to one side and began to look at the ground under my feet. This precaution proved most timely: I almost fell, stumbling against something fat and soft but apparently not alive. I bent down – the moon was now shining straight on to the road – and what did I see? Before me lay a pig, sliced in two by a sword . . . I'd barely had time for a proper look when I heard steps. Two Cossacks rushed out of a side street. One of them came up to me: had I seen a drunken Cossack chasing a pig? I told them I hadn't, then pointed to the unfortunate victim of the man's frenzied daring.

'Damn him,' said the second Cossack. 'Gets some *chikhir*[3] inside him – and off he goes, hacking up everything he sees. Come on, Yeremeich, we must catch him – or else . . .'

They went off and I continued on my way with more caution; in the end I got safely home.

I was billeted with an old Cossack sergeant, a man I loved for his good nature and – even more – for his pretty young daughter, Nastya.[4]

As usual, she was waiting for me by the gate, wrapped in a fur coat; I could see in the moonlight that her sweet lips were blue from the night cold. She smiled when she saw me, but I had other things on my mind. 'Good night, Nastya!' I said, and walked past her. She almost said something back, but instead she just sighed.

I closed the door of my room, lit a candle and threw myself down on the bed; sleep, however, kept me waiting longer than usual. The east was beginning to turn pale by the time I dropped off – but it was clearly written in the heavens that I was not to get my fill of sleep. At four in the morning, two fists started pounding at my window. I jumped up: what was going on? There were shouts of 'Get up! Get dressed!' I dressed quickly and went out. 'Do you know what's happened?' asked the three officers who had come for me, all trying to speak at once; they were as pale as death.

'What?'

'Vulich has been killed.'

I stood stock-still.

'Yes, killed,' they repeated. 'Quick!'

'Where to?'

'We'll tell you on the way.'

We set off. They told me all that had happened, interjecting a variety of comments about the strangeness of predestination – which had saved Vulich from certain death only half an hour before he died. Vulich had been walking alone down a dark street. Up ran the drunken Cossack who had sliced through the pig. Probably the man would have gone on his way, paying no attention to Vulich, except that Vulich suddenly stopped and said, 'Who are you looking for, brother?' 'You!' answered the Cossack, striking him a blow with his sword that split him in two, from the shoulder almost to the heart. Then the two Cossacks I'd seen had come up; they picked up the wounded officer, but he was already at his last gasp, and he said only three words: 'He was right!' I alone understood the dark meaning of this: he was referring to me. Involuntarily I had foretold the poor man's fate. My instinct had not deceived me: in the changed look on Vulich's face I really had seen a sign of his imminent death.

The murderer had locked himself up in an empty hut at the end of the village: that was where we were going. Crowds of sobbing women were hurrying the same way; now and again a Cossack would dash belatedly on to the street, hurriedly fastening on his dagger, and come running past us. The commotion was terrible.

At last we were there. Around the hut, whose doors and shutters were locked from inside, we could see a crowd of people. Officers and men were arguing excitedly; women were howling, lamenting, keening. I was immediately struck by the look of crazed despair on the face of one old woman. She was sitting on a thick log, her elbows propped on her knees and her hands supporting her head; she was the murderer's mother. From time to time her lips moved: were they whispering a prayer or a curse?

Meanwhile we had to decide on some way of seizing the criminal. No one, however, was daring enough to be first through the door.

I went up to the window and looked through a crack in the shutter. There he was, white-faced, lying on the floor and holding a pistol in his right hand; a bloodstained sword lay beside him. His eyes were rolling about wildly; sometimes he shuddered and put his hands to his head, as if dimly recalling the events of the night. I could see little resolution in those restless eyes and I asked the Major why he didn't order the Cossacks to break down the door and rush in, since it would be better to act now rather than wait until the man had recovered his senses.

Just then an old Cossack captain walked up to the door and called out the man's name. The murderer answered.

'You've done wrong, brother Yefimych,' said the Captain. 'There's nothin' for it – you must give yourself up!'

'I won't!'

'Have you no fear of the Lord? You're an honest Christian, aren't you, not some accursed Chechen? If sin has led you astray, there's nothin' for it. There's no escapin' your fate.'

'I won't give in!' the Cossack shouted fiercely, and there was the click of a pistol being cocked.

'Hey, you there!' the Captain then said to the old woman. 'Have a word with your son – perhaps he'll listen to you. Or he'll bring down the wrath of the Lord. And these gentlemen here have been waitin' two hours now.'

The old woman looked at the Captain intently and shook her head.

He went up to the Major.

'Vasily Petrovich,' he said, 'I know him – he won't give in. And if we smash down the door, he'll slaughter a good few of our lads. Wouldn't it be better to give orders to shoot him? There's a wide crack in the shutter.'

Just then a strange thought flashed through my mind: I took it into my head, like Vulich, to test Fate.

'Wait,' I said to the Major. 'I'll take him alive.' I told the Captain to engage the murderer in conversation, and I posted three Cossacks by the door, ready to break in and rush to my aid the moment I gave the signal. Then I went round the hut and approached the fateful window; my heart was pounding.

'Ay, you cursed wretch!' the Captain was shouting. 'Laughin' at us, are you? Think we can't get you, do you?' He began banging on the door as hard as he could. My eye to the crack, I watched the Cossack, who was not expecting to be attacked from this side. Suddenly I wrenched off the shutter and flung myself head first through the window. There was an explosion just above my ear, and the bullet ripped off one of my epaulettes. But the smoke filling the room prevented my adversary from finding his sword. I seized him by the arms, the Cossacks broke in, and within three minutes the criminal had been bound and taken away under guard. The crowd melted away and the officers began congratulating me – and not without reason.

How, after all that, could a man not become a fatalist? But who can ever be sure whether he's convinced of something or not? And how often what seems like conviction is simply the deceit of the senses or an error of reasoning! I like to doubt everything. Such a disposition of mind is no impediment to resoluteness of character. With me, at least, it's the opposite: I always go forward more boldly when I don't know what awaits me. After all, the worst that can happen to you is death – and death is inescapable!

Back in the fortress, I told Maksim Maksimych all I had seen and been through and I asked him what he thought about predestination. At first he didn't understand the word, but I explained it as best I could. He then replied, shaking his head ponderously, 'Well yes, of course . . . Quite a tricky matter. But then these Asiatic triggers often do misfire if they're badly oiled or you don't press hard enough with your finger. I must admit, I don't like Circassian rifles either; somehow they don't seem right for the likes of us. And with that short butt of theirs you've got to watch out – you can easily get your nose burnt. But the swords they make – no, you can't do better than Circassian swords!'

After thinking for a moment, he added, 'Pity about that poor fellow, though . . . What the devil made him start chatting to a drunk at night? But I suppose that must have been the fate he was dealt at birth!'

That was all I could get out of Maksim Maksimych; he's not someone who likes metaphysical discussions.

First published in 1839
Translated by Robert Chandler

NIKOLAY VASILYEVICH GOGOL
(1809–52)

Born near Poltava in the Ukraine into a family of minor gentry, Gogol
first travelled to St Petersburg at the age of nineteen. There he worked
as a civil servant, progressing from the lowest of the fourteen ranks to
the eighth. He then taught at a girls' school and attempted, with little
success, to teach history at St Petersburg University. From 1837 to
1839 he lived in Rome, and he spent much of the rest of his life
travelling in Russia and Western Europe.

Gogol made his name with colourful, often fantastic, stories about
the Ukrainian peasantry, collected in the volumes Evenings on a Farm
near Dikanka and Mirgorod. These were followed by his Petersburg
stories, which fuse fantasy and realism. Pushkin had been quick to
recognize Gogol's talent, and Gogol claimed that Pushkin gave him
the plots for his satirical play The Government Inspector and his one
long work, Dead Souls.

Dead Souls (published, like 'The Greatcoat', in 1842) was intended
as the first part of a Russian Divine Comedy. Gogol's inability to
conceive of a Purgatorio, let alone a Paradiso, seems to have triggered
a lasting depression. In 1847 he published Selected Passages from
Correspondence with Friends, a collection of tedious moral exhort-
ations that alienated liberals and even many conservatives and was
famously denounced by the influential radical critic Vissarion Belin-
sky. In despair, Gogol went on a pilgrimage to the Holy Land, but
this only deepened his depression. Feeling it lacked true moral content,
he burned much of the second part of Dead Souls. He died ten days
afterwards, in March 1852, probably of starvation; he had refused to
eat any food at all since the beginning of Lent.

The hero of 'The Greatcoat', the last and most famous of Gogol's
St Petersburg stories, bears the unusual name of Akaky Akakiyevich;
this is probably derived both from kaka, a child's word for 'faeces',
and from the Greek akakos, meaning 'innocent'. Several saints bore
the name of Acacius, and one, a monk (and tailor), died after being
tormented for years by a cruel elder, who later repented. Like 'The

Queen of Spades', this story has given rise to a variety of interpretations. Some critics read it as a defence of the 'little man' against an oppressive bureaucracy. Others see it as an allegory about sexual and material temptation, the greatcoat being a devilish lure. Still others have seen the greatcoat as a paradigm of humanity's search for meaning; in the words of the critic Cathy Popkin, 'our own quest for significance – for something substantial and important – is closely re-enacted in Akaky Akakiyevich's ill-fated quest for a coat. In his seeking and losing the "thread", the meaning and the reason to go on, we recognize our own vain pursuit of sense, significance, and substance.'[1]

Gogol's influence on Russian literature has been huge. The statement 'We have all come out of Gogol's Greatcoat' has been quoted countless times, sometimes attributed to Dostoyevsky, sometimes to Turgenev. Leskov, Bulgakov, Zoshchenko and Platonov are only a few of the many writers who followed Gogol's example in exploiting the comic and philosophical effects of mixing different registers of speech: colloquial, literary, religious and bureaucratic.

THE GREATCOAT

In the department of . . . but it's better not to name the department. There is nothing more touchy and bad-tempered than all these departments, regiments, government offices – in a word, all these official bodies. Nowadays, if you say a word against any private individual he carries on as if the whole of society has been insulted. Not so very long ago, I've heard, a petition was received from some police captain, I don't remember of what town, in which he makes it quite plain that governmental decrees are going to rack and ruin and that his own sacred name is being taken most decidedly in vain. In substantiation of this, he appended to his petition a most exceedingly enormous tome of some romantic work in which, every ten pages, a police captain appears, sometimes even in a totally drunken state. And so, in order to avoid any unpleasantness, it's best if we call the department in question *a certain department*. And so, in *a certain department* there served *a certain clerk* – a clerk who cannot be described as especially remarkable: of shortish height, somewhat pockmarked, somewhat red-haired, even apparently somewhat short-sighted, going a little bald in front, and with wrinkles on both cheeks and the kind of complexion we call haemorrhoidal . . . This just cannot be helped: the Petersburg climate is to blame. As for his rank (for here in Russia a man's rank is the very first thing that must be announced), he was what people call an eternal titular councillor; a rank which, as is well known, has been the butt of many a sneer and jeer from various writers possessed of the commendable habit of attacking those who cannot bite back. The clerk's surname was Bashmachkin. It is immediately clear that this surname came at some time or other from the word *bashmak* or 'shoe'; but when, at what time, and in what manner, it came from *bashmak* – none of this is known. His father, his grandfather and even his brother-in-law – absolutely every Bashmachkin – walked about in boots, which they had resoled two or three times a year. His first name and patronymic were Akaky Akakiyevich. This may seem somewhat strange and far-fetched, but the reader can be assured that it was not fetched from anywhere and that circumstances simply occurred of themselves which made it quite impossible for him to be given any other name – and here now is the precise way that it all came about. Akaky Akakiyevich was born, if my memory serves me right, on the night of 23 March. His late mother, the wife of a clerk and a very good woman, intended, as was fitting, to have the child christened. She was still lying in bed, opposite the door, while to her right stood the godfather, a most excellent man, Ivan Ivanovich Yeroshkin, who served as a head clerk in the Senate,[1] together with the godmother, Arina Semyonovna Belobryushkova,[2] the wife of a police officer and a woman of rare virtue. The new mother was offered a choice of any of three names, whichever she wanted to choose: Mokkiya, Sossiya, or she could call the baby after the martyr Khozdazat.[3] 'No,' thought his late mother, 'none of these names are right.' To please her, they opened the calendar at another page; out came another three names: Trifily, Dula and Varakhasy. 'What have we done to deserve this?' said the good woman. 'What names they all are. Really, I've never heard the like. Varadat or Varukh would be one thing, but not Trifily or Varakhasy.' They turned over another page; out came Pavsikakhy and Vakhtisy. 'Well,' said the good woman, 'it's plainly to be seen that this is his fate. If that's the way it is, then let him be called after his father. The father was Akaky, so let the son be Akaky.' So it was that Akaky Akakiyevich came about. The boy was christened. During the ceremony he cried and made such a face it was as if he understood that he was to be a titular councillor. Yes, this is how it all came about. We have related this in order that the reader should be able to see for himself that it happened entirely out of necessity and that it was quite impossible to give him any other name. When and at what time he entered the department, and who appointed him, is something that no one could recall. However many directors and other higher officials might come and go, he was always to be seen in one and the same place, in the same position, at the same task, the very same copying clerk; eventually people came to believe that he must have come into the world all ready and prepared, in uniform and going bald in front. No respect whatsoever was shown to him in the department. Not only did the caretakers remain seated when he went by, they did not even look at him; it was as if a mere fly had flown through the waiting room. The directors treated him with a kind of cold despotism. Some assistant head clerk would simply thrust papers under his nose without so much as a 'Copy these' or a 'Here's an interesting little job for you' or some other pleasant remark of the kind that is customary in well-bred offices. And he would take these papers, not looking at anything else, not noticing who had put them there or whether they had the right to do this. He would take the papers and immediately set about copying them. The young clerks joked and made witticisms at his expense, as far as their office wit would stretch. There, in his presence, they told all kinds of stories they had made up about him and his landlady, an old woman of seventy; they said she beat him, asked when the wedding would be, and showered little scraps of paper on to his head, saying it was snowing. But not a word of response came from Akaky Akakiyevich, who carried on as if there were no one else there; it did not even affect his work: amid all these aggravations he made not one error in his copying. Only when the joke became too unbearable, when they jogged his elbow and stopped him carrying on with his work, would he say, 'Let me be. Why do you torment me?' And there was something strange in the words, and in the voice that uttered them. In that voice was something so evocative of pity that one young man, who had recently been appointed, and who, following the example of others, was on the point of allowing himself to make fun of Akaky Akakiyevich, suddenly stopped, as if transfixed, and from that moment everything was changed before him and appeared in a different light. Some strange power pushed him away from his colleagues, whom he had taken, on first meeting them, to be decent, cultivated men. And for a long time afterwards, at moments of the greatest merriment, there would appear before him the figure of the little clerk with the balding forehead, uttering his piercing words, 'Let me be. Why do you torment me?' In these piercing words was an echo of other words: 'I am your brother.' And the poor young man would bury his face in his hands, and many a time in his life he would shudder to see how much inhumanity there is in man, how much savage coarseness can lie concealed in refined, cultivated manners and – dear God! – even in a man society regards as noble and honourable.

It would be difficult to find anyone who lived so much in his work as Akaky Akakiyevich. It is not enough to say he served zealously; no, he served with love. There, in his copying, he found a delightful and varied world of his own. His pleasure could be seen on his face; some letters of the alphabet were his especial favourites, and when he came to one of them he was transported: he chuckled and winked and helped it on with his lips, so that it seemed as if one could read on his face each letter being traced by his pen. Had he been rewarded in accord with his zeal, he might perhaps, to his own astonishment, even have been promoted to state councillor,[4] but all he got for his pains, in the words of his witty comrades, was a badge for his buttonhole and a haemorrhoid for his butt. Still, it would be wrong to say that no notice at all was taken of him. One director, being a kind man and wanting to reward him for his long service, ordered him to be given something rather more important than his usual copying – he was asked, in fact, to rewrite an already existing file, addressing it to another government office; it was simply a matter of writing out the new heading and changing a verb here and there from the first to the third person. This was such a struggle for him that he came out all in a sweat, kept rubbing his brow and finally said, 'No, it would be better if you could find me something to copy.' After that he was left to go on copying forever. Beyond this copying, nothing seemed to exist for him. He gave no thought at all to his clothes: his uniform was not green but some reddish-browny-mealy colour. The collar was so narrow and short that his neck, in reality also quite short, appeared unusually long, like the necks of those head-nodding plaster-of-Paris kittens that foreigners peddle, carrying them about in whole trayfuls on their heads. And then there was always something clinging to his uniform, a wisp of straw or a bit of thread; he possessed, moreover, a particular knack, as he walked down a street, of passing under a window just at the moment that rubbish of all kinds was being thrown out, which is why he was eternally carrying bits of melon rind or watermelon rind or other such nonsense on the top of his hat. Not once in his life had he paid any attention to the daily goings-on out on the street, to the many happenings which, as we know, never escape the attention of his brother-clerks, young men who have so sharpened their sharp eyes that they even notice a loose ankle-strap on the trousers of a man on the other side of the street – a sight which never fails to bring a sly grin to their faces.

But if Akaky Akakiyevich ever did look at anything, all he saw everywhere was his own neat, evenly written lines, and only if a horse's muzzle, suddenly appearing from goodness knows where, placed itself

on his shoulder and its nostrils directed a whole gale at his cheek –
only then did he realize that he was not in the middle of a line, but
rather in the middle of a street. When he got home, he would immediately sit at the table, quickly spoon up his cabbage soup and eat a piece
of beef with onions, not noticing how anything tasted; he swallowed all
this down along with the flies and whatever else God had sent at that
time. Noticing that his stomach was beginning to bulge, he would rise
from the table, take out a bottle of ink, and start copying papers he
had brought home with him. If there happened to be no more papers to
copy, he would copy something just for himself, for his own pleasure,
especially if the document was remarkable not for its beauty of style
but for being addressed to some new or important figure.

Even at those hours when the grey Petersburg sky has completely
faded and all clerical folk have eaten their fill, each dining as best he
can, according to the salary he receives and his personal fancy; when
everything and everyone has come to a rest after the departmental
scraping of pens, after all the rush and bustle, after the conclusion
both of all the business necessary to oneself and others and of all the
business that indefatigable man takes upon himself by choice, above
and beyond what is necessary; when civil servants are hastening to
devote to pleasure what remains of their time (one hurrying briskly
off to the theatre, another going out to gaze at silly hats of one kind
or another, another intending to spend the evening paying compli-
ments to some pretty young woman, the star of a small clerical circle,
another – and this is what happens most often – going to visit a
colleague who lives on some second or third floor in two small rooms
with an ante-room or a kitchen and fashionable pretensions of one
kind or another, perhaps a lamp or some other little article, obtained
at the cost of many a sacrificed dinner or evening's entertainment); in
a word, even at that time when all clerks are scattered about their
friends' little apartments, playing knockout whist, sipping tea from
glasses and nibbling one-kopek rusks, drawing on their long chibouks[5]
and, as the cards are dealt, retelling some scandal that has filtered
down from high society – for no Russian, regardless of his condition,
can ever renounce high society – or even, should there be nothing to
talk about, retelling the age-old joke about the commandant who
received word that the tail had been cut off the horse of Falconet's
Peter the Great;[6] in a word, even then, when everything and everyone
is eagerly seeking to be entertained, Akaky Akakiyevich did not give
himself up to any entertainment at all. No one could claim ever to
have seen him at an evening gathering. After copying to his heart's
content, he would lie down to sleep, smiling in anticipation of the day

to come and wondering what God would send him to copy. Thus flowed the peaceful life of a man who, with a salary of four hundred roubles a year, knew how to be content with his lot, and so, perhaps, his life might have flowed on, deep into old age, were it not for the various calamities that lie scattered across the path not only of titular, but also of privy, state, court and all other councillors, even those who never give counsel to anyone or receive it themselves.

There is in Petersburg a mighty enemy of all who receive a salary of four hundred roubles a year or thereabouts. This enemy is none other than our northern frost, although there are some who say it is very beneficial to the health. Between eight and nine o'clock in the morning, just when the streets are crowded with people walking to their departments, it starts to deliver such mighty and stinging nips to every nose, quite indiscriminately, that the poor clerks well and truly don't know what to do with their noses. At a time when even those who occupy senior positions have aching brows and tears welling up in their eyes, poor titular councillors are often without defence. The whole of salvation lies in running as fast as you can, in your wretched little greatcoat, the length of five or six streets, and then having a good stamp in the porter's lodge until all your talents and capacities for official duties, which have become frozen stiff on the way, have thawed out again. For some time now Akaky Akakiyevich had been beginning to feel that his back and shoulders were being burnt especially fiercely, even though he tried to scurry across the decreed space as quickly as he possibly could. It occurred to him in the end to wonder whether it might not be his greatcoat that was to blame. After giving it a thorough examination at home, he discovered that in two or three places – namely, on the back and shoulders – it had become just like cheese-cloth: it was so worn as to be threadbare, and the lining had fallen to pieces. It has to be said that Akaky Akakiyevich's greatcoat was also an object of mockery to the other civil servants; it had even been deprived of the noble title of greatcoat and become known as his dressing gown. And its structure was indeed rather peculiar: the collar had been growing smaller year by year, since bits of it now served as patches for other parts of the coat. The patching was no advertisement of the tailor's art and the general effect was, in fact, baggy and far from beautiful. Seeing how things were, Akaky Akakiyevich decided the greatcoat would have to be taken to Petrovich, a tailor who lived somewhere up a back staircase on a third floor and who, despite having only one eye and pockmarks all over his face, was doing rather well for himself mending the trousers and frock coats of clerks and all manner of people – when he was sober, that is, and not entertaining any other project in his head. I should not, of course, be saying much about this tailor, but, since it is now the rule that the character of every person in a tale be fully delineated, well, there's nothing for it: let's have a look at Petrovich too. At first he had simply been called Grigory and he had been a serf belonging to some landowner or other; he took to using the name Petrovich[7] when he got his freedom and began drinking pretty heavily on all holidays, at first only on the most important holidays, but then on all church holidays indiscriminately, as long as there was a little cross in the calendar.[8] In this respect, he was true to the customs of his forefathers and, when he quarrelled with his wife, he would call her a depraved woman and a German. Since we have now mentioned the wife, it will be necessary to say a few words about her too; but unfortunately not much was known about her, only that Petrovich had a wife, and that she even wore a bonnet rather than a headscarf;[9] but beauty, so it seems, was not something of which she could boast – at any rate, it was only guards-men who tried to peep under her bonnet when they met her, winking their moustaches and mouthing a rather peculiar sound.

Climbing the stairs leading to Petrovich – which, to do them justice, had all been anointed with water and slops and were saturated through and through with that odour of spirits which makes the eyes smart and, as is well known, is a permanent presence on all the back stairs of Petersburg buildings – climbing the stairs, Akaky Akakiyevich was already wondering how much Petrovich would ask for the job, and he had made up his mind not to give him more than two roubles. The door stood open because Petrovich's wife, while cooking some kind of fish, had filled the kitchen with so much smoke that it was impossible to make out even the very cockroaches. Akaky Akakiyevich made his way through the kitchen, unnoticed even by the housewife herself, and finally entered a room where he saw Petrovich on a wide, unpainted wooden table, sitting cross-legged like a Turkish pasha. His feet, as is the custom with tailors sitting at their work, were bare. And the first thing to strike the eye was his big toe, which Akaky Akakiyevich already knew very well, with its somehow deformed nail that was as thick and strong as the shell of a tortoise. From Petrovich's neck hung a skein of silk and some cotton, and on his knees lay an old piece of cloth. He had been trying for several minutes to thread his needle but had had no success and was very angry with the darkness and even with the thread itself, muttering under his breath, 'So you barbarian, you won't go in? Well, I've had it with you, you bitch!' Akaky Akaki-yevich regretted that he had come just at the moment when Petrovich was getting angry: he liked to order something from Petrovich when the latter was a little under the influence or, as his wife put it, 'had been hitting the bottle, the one-eyed devil'. In that state, Petrovich was usually very ready to give way and be reasonable, and he would even keep bowing and saying he was grateful. Later, it's true, his wife would come round, wailing that her husband had been drunk and had asked too little, but all you had to do was throw in another ten kopeks and you had it all sewn up. But now it seemed that Petrovich was sober – and therefore tough and intractable and the devil knows what price he'd be asking. Akaky Akakiyevich grasped this and was, as they say, about to beat a retreat, but it was too late. Petrovich looked at him very intently, screwing up his one and only eye, and Akaky Akakiyevich involuntarily came out with the words, 'Good day, Petrovich!'

'I wish you a good day, sir!' said Petrovich, and fixed his eye on Akaky Akakiyevich's hands, wanting to make out what kind of booty the man was bringing.

'So, Petrovich, here, er, I've . . .'

It needs to be said that Akaky Akakiyevich expressed himself for the main part through prepositions, adverbs and, finally, such little particles as have decidedly no meaning at all. And if the matter was very awkward indeed, he even had a habit of not finishing sentences at all, and so it often happened that he would begin a speech with the words, 'That, really, er, is altogether . . .' and that was the end of it, and he himself would be oblivious, thinking everything had already been said.

'What is it?' asked Petrovich, at the same time examining with his one eye the whole of Akaky Akakiyevich's uniform, beginning with the collar and going on to the sleeves, the back, the skirts and the buttonholes; everything was familiar to him, since it was his own work. Such is the custom among tailors: it is the first thing they do on meeting someone.

'I've come, er, Petrovich . . . this greatcoat, the cloth . . . you see, it's quite strong everywhere in other places, it's just got a little dusty so it seems old, but it's new, though there's just one place where, er, it's a little . . . on the back, and here on one shoulder it's a little worn, I know, and a little on this shoulder – that's all, you see. Not a lot of work.'

Petrovich took the dressing gown, laid it out on the table, examined it for a long time, shook his head, then reached out to the window sill for his round snuffbox with a portrait of some general on it – exactly which general is unknown, because a finger had been poked through the place where the face was and a rectangular scrap of paper pasted over it. After taking a pinch, Petrovich held the dressing gown up in his hands and examined it against the light and once more shook his head. Then he held it up with the lining towards him and again shook his head, again removed the lid with the papered-over general, filled his nose with snuff, closed the box, put it away and finally said, 'No, it's a wretched garment. It's beyond repair!'

At these words, Akaky Akakiyevich's heart missed a beat.

'Why, Petrovich?' he asked in a childlike, almost pleading voice. 'Why, it's only a bit worn on the shoulders – and you have those little pieces . . .'

'Yes, I can find pieces of cloth, there are pieces of cloth all right,' said Petrovich, 'but how can I sew them on? The whole thing's rotten. Put a needle to it and it'll fall to pieces.'

'That's all right – just patch it again straightaway.'

'But there's nowhere to put a patch, there's nothing to anchor it to, the cloth's too far gone. It's stretching a point even to call it cloth. One puff of wind and it'll fly apart.'

'You must reinforce it then. I mean, really, you know, er!'

'No,' said Petrovich decisively, 'there's nothing I can do. It's no good. You'd do better, come the winter cold, to make it into foot-cloths,[10] because there's no warmth in stockings. It was Germans thought them up, so as to make more money for themselves.' (Petrovich never missed a chance to have a go at the Germans.) 'But as for a greatcoat, you'll clearly be needing a new one.'

At the word 'new' Akaky Akakiyevich's eyes clouded and everything in the room began to swim before him. All he could see clearly – there on the lid of Petrovich's snuffbox – was the general with the pasted-over face.

'What do you mean – "new"?' he asked, still as if he were in a dream. 'I don't have the money for that.'

'Yes, new,' said Petrovich, with barbaric calm.

'But if, say, a new one had to be, what would it . . . ?'

'You mean, what will it cost?'

'Yes.'

'Well, it'll be a hundred and fifty roubles and then some,' said Petrovich – and pursed his lips with significance. He had a great fondness for dramatic effects; he liked somehow to confound a man suddenly and completely, then look out of the corner of his eye at the look on the face of whomever he had confounded.

'One hundred and fifty roubles for a greatcoat!' poor Akaky Akakiyevich cried out – cried out, perhaps, for the first time since his birth, for he had always been distinguished by the softness of his voice.

'Yes sir, and that would just be a very ordinary coat. If we were to put marten on the collar and add a hood with a silk lining, then it could set you back as much as two hundred.'

'Please, Petrovich,' Akaky Akakiyevich said in a pleading voice, neither hearing nor even trying to hear Petrovich's words and all his dramatic effects, 'mend it somehow or other, so it'll serve at least a little longer.'

'No, it's no good. That'd be a waste of effort, and money down the drain,' said Petrovich; and after these words Akaky Akakiyevich left, completely destroyed. Petrovich, however, stood there for a long time, pursing his lips with significance and not resuming his work, satisfied that he had neither demeaned himself nor betrayed the art of tailoring.

When he got back outside, Akaky Akakiyevich was as if in a dream. 'So ... so that's how things are,' he said to himself. 'I really never thought, you know, it was like ...' and then, after a silence, he added, 'So there we are! That's how it finally stands and I'd never have guessed, really I could never have guessed things were ...' This was followed by another long silence, after which he pronounced, 'So that's the way! What an, indeed, altogether, er, unexpected ... who could have ... what a turn of events!' Having said this, instead of going home, he went in quite the opposite direction without realizing what he was doing. On the way, a chimney sweep brushed the whole of his unclean side against him and blackened his shoulder; a hatful of lime poured down on him from the top of a building that was under construction. He noticed none of this, and it was only when he had knocked into a sentry who, his halberd propped beside him, was shaking snuff from his snuff-horn on to his calloused fist, that Akaky Akakiyevich began to come to his senses, and even then only because the policeman said, 'What are you doing barging straight into me like that? Isn't there enough pavement for you?' This made him look round and turn homeward. Only at this point did he begin to gather his thoughts; clearly seeing his position for what it was, he began talking to himself not in broken snatches, but reasonably and frankly, as if to a sensible acquaintance with whom he could discuss the most intimate matters of the heart. 'No,' said Akaky Akakiyevich, 'it's no use talking to Petrovich now. Now he's, er ... seems his wife must have been knocking him about a bit. I'd do better to go and see him on Sunday morning. After his Saturday night he'll be hung over and still half asleep and he'll be needing a touch of the hair of the dog, but his wife's not going to be giving him any money, so just at that time, er, I'll slip ten kopeks into his hand and he'll be more reasonable and the greatcoat will, er ...' Thus Akaky Akakiyevich reasoned with himself and cheered himself up; he waited until the next Sunday, watched from a distance until he saw Petrovich's wife go off somewhere, and went straight in. Petrovich was indeed nursing a mighty hangover from his Saturday night; still half asleep, he was barely able to hold his head up; nevertheless, as soon as he realized why Akaky Akakiyevich had come, it was as if the devil were there at his elbow. 'No, I can't,' he said. 'Be so good as to order a new greatcoat.' At this point Akaky Akakiyevich slipped him ten kopeks. 'I thank you, sir, and I shall drink a little fortifying drop to your health,' said Petrovich. 'But please, sir, don't keep troubling yourself about that greatcoat of yours: it ain't no use for nothing. I'll sew you a splendid new coat, yes sir, you have our word on it!'

Akaky Akakiyevich tried again to say something about mending, but Petrovich refused to listen and said, 'I shall most certainly sew you a new one. Depend upon it, sir, I shall make every effort. And seeing as it's now the fashion, we could even have little silver appliqué clasps to fasten the collar.'

At this point Akaky Akakiyevich realized there was no getting away from this new greatcoat, and his heart sank completely. Really, indeed, how could he, where would the money come from? He could, of course, to some extent count on a bonus for the coming holiday, but that money had long been earmarked and accounted for. He needed to buy new trousers and to settle a long-standing debt with the cobbler who had put new vamps on his boots; he also had to order three shirts from the seamstress, as well as a couple of pairs of an item of underwear that cannot properly be named in print; in a word, absolutely all of the money was already spent and even if the director were so gracious as to appoint him a bonus, not of forty roubles, but of forty-five or fifty, there would still be only the merest trifle left over – just a drop in the ocean when it came to the capital required for a greatcoat. Although he knew, of course, that Petrovich had a way of suddenly naming the devil knows what exorbitant price, so that sometimes even his own wife couldn't help shouting, 'Have you taken leave of your senses, you fool? One day he takes on work for nothing, the next day the Devil gets into him and he asks for more than he's worth himself!' Although he knew, of course, that Petrovich would undertake to make the coat for eighty roubles – but where was he to find those eighty roubles? He might be able to come up with half that sum; yes, half of it could be found – maybe even a little more than half; but where was he to find the other half? But first of all the reader needs to know how he would find the first half. Akaky Akakiyevich was in the habit, every time he spent a rouble, of putting aside half a kopek into a small locked box with a little slit in the lid for coins. At the end of every six months he inspected the coppers that had piled up and exchanged them for small pieces of silver. He had been doing this for a long time, and the sum thus accumulated over a number of years turned out to be more than forty roubles. And so half of the sum was at hand; but where was he to find the other half? Where was he to find the other forty roubles? Akaky Akakiyevich thought and thought and decided, at least for a year, to cut down on his living expenses: to put an end to the use of tea in the evening; to give up burning candles in the evening and, if there was something that had to be done, to go into his landlady's room and work by the light of *her* candle; to step as lightly and carefully as possible, almost on tiptoe, over cobbles and flagstones, so as not to wear out his soles too quickly; to send his clothes to the laundress as seldom as possible and, to prevent them getting dirty, to remove them as soon as he got back home and, for the rest of the day, wear only his cotton housecoat – a garment of great age that had been spared even by Time itself. If the truth be told, he did at first find it rather hard to get used to these restrictions, but then everything became a habit and began to go smoothly; he even entirely succeeded in training himself to go without food in the evenings; but then he was, on the other hand, receiving spiritual nourishment, carrying in his thoughts the eternal idea of his future greatcoat. From then on it was as if his very existence somehow became fuller, as if he had married, as if someone else were there at his side, as if his days of loneliness were now over and some charming soulmate had agreed to walk down life's path beside him – and this companion were none other than this selfsame greatcoat with its thick quilting and its strong lining that would never wear out. He became somehow livelier, even stronger-willed, like a man who has defined a goal for himself and set it before him. Doubt and indecision – in a word, all the shilly-shallying and indefiniteness in his character – vanished as if of their own accord from his face and actions. A fire sometimes gleamed in his eyes and through his head flashed even the very boldest and most audacious of thoughts: perhaps, after all, he really should have a marten collar? These reflections almost led him into moments of absent-mindedness. Once, copying some papers, he very nearly even made a mistake, with the result that he cried 'Oh!' almost out loud and then crossed himself. In the course of each month he called in at least once on Petrovich, to talk about the greatcoat and discuss where it would be best to buy the cloth, what colour it should be, and what price – and, though somewhat preoccupied, he would always return home contented, thinking that, in the end, the time would come when everything had been purchased and the greatcoat would be finished.

Things even progressed faster than he had anticipated. Contrary to all expectation, the director appointed Akaky Akakiyevich a bonus not of forty or forty-five, but of no less than sixty roubles: he might have had a presentiment that Akaky Akakiyevich needed a greatcoat or it might have happened simply by chance, but as a result of this, in any case, Akaky Akakiyevich ended up with an additional twenty roubles. This circumstance accelerated the course of events. Another two or three months of moderate fasting and Akaky Akakiyevich truly did find himself with around eighty roubles. His heart, which was usually extremely calm, began to pound. The very next day he set off with Petrovich to the shops. They bought some particularly fine cloth – and no wonder, since they had been thinking about this for the previous six months and hardly a month had gone by without their going round the shops to compare prices; now Petrovich himself said there was no better cloth to be had. For the lining they chose calico, but such sturdy and high-quality calico that, in the words of Petrovich, it was better than silk, glossier even and more handsome to look at. They did not buy marten, because it was indeed expensive; instead they chose cat, the very best to be had in the shop, cat that from a distance could always be taken for marten. Petrovich took two whole weeks over the greatcoat, because there was a lot of quilting to be done; otherwise it would have been ready sooner. For his work Petrovich charged twelve roubles – anything less was out of the question: everything had quite decidedly been sewn with silk, in fine double seams, and Petrovich had then gone over every seam with his teeth, imprinting various patterns on it. It was . . . it is hard to say on exactly what day, but it was probably on the most sublimest day of Akaky Akakiyevich's life that Petrovich at last brought him the greatcoat. He brought it in the morning, just as Akaky Akakiyevich was due to leave for the department. The greatcoat could not have come at a better time because sharpish frosts were already setting in and threatening, it seemed, to turn sharper still. Petrovich appeared with the greatcoat, as a good tailor does. On his face was such a meaningful expression of significance as Akaky Akakiyevich had never seen. He seemed to know very well that his was no mean achievement and that he had suddenly revealed, in his own person, the gulf that divides tailors who merely put in linings and do repairs from those who cut new garments. He took the greatcoat out of the handkerchief in which he had brought it; the handkerchief had just come back from the laundry and he folded it and put it in his pocket for use on his nose. Having taken the greatcoat out, he looked at it with great pride and, holding it in both hands, threw it with great deftness across Akaky Akakiyevich's shoulders; then he gave it a pull and settled it on his back with a downward stroke, draping it over Akaky Akakiyevich rather jauntily, like a cape. Akaky Akakiyevich, being no longer a young man, wanted to try it on properly; Petrovich helped him put his arms through the sleeves – it fitted there too. In a word, the greatcoat turned out to be an exact and perfect fit. Petrovich did not forbear to mention that it was only because he lived on a small street and had no signboard, and also because he had known Akaky Akakiyevich for a long time, that he had charged so little; on Nevsky Prospekt, Akaky Akakiyevich would have had to pay seventy-five roubles for the work alone. This was not something Akaky Akakiyevich wanted to discuss with Petrovich, for he was frightened by the mighty sums that came rolling off Petrovich's tongue when he was trying to impress. He settled up with him, thanked him, and set off at once to the department, wearing the new greatcoat. Petrovich followed him out, stood for some time in the street to look at the greatcoat from a distance, then made a detour down a twisting lane so that he could overtake Akaky Akakiyevich, run out into the street ahead of him and look again at his greatcoat, this time from the other side, that is, straight in the face. Meanwhile Akaky Akakiyevich walked along with all his feelings in their most festive mood. Every moment of the minute he could feel the new greatcoat on his shoulders, and several times he even grinned out of inner satisfaction. The coat was, in fact, doubly advantageous: in the first place, it was warm; in the second, it was good. He barely noticed his journey – and, all of a sudden, there he was in the department; he took off the greatcoat in the porter's lodge, looked it over, and entrusted it to the porter's special safekeeping. Just how this happened is unknown, but suddenly everyone in the department knew that Akaky Akakiyevich had a new greatcoat and that the dressing gown was no more. They all immediately dashed out into the porter's lodge to look at Akaky Akakiyevich's new greatcoat. They began greeting him and congratulating him and he could do nothing but smile, and then he even began to feel ashamed. And when everyone surrounded him and began saying that the new greatcoat should be baptized and that the very least he could do was to throw a party for them all, Akaky Akakiyevich felt completely at a loss and had no idea what to do with himself, what to reply or how to make his excuses. After several minutes, blushing all over, he began simple-mindedly assuring them that it really wasn't a new greatcoat, that it was just, just the old greatcoat. In the end, one of the civil servants – probably even an assistant to the Head of the desk – wanting most likely to show that he was not in the least a snob and that he even hobnobbed

with his inferiors, said, 'So be it, I shall give a party on behalf of Akaky
Akakiyevich and I invite you all to have supper with me. By good
chance, today happens to be my nameday.' The clerks, of course, at
once congratulated the assistant to the Head of the desk and eagerly
accepted his invitation. Akaky Akakiyevich began making excuses,
but everyone said this would be most discourteous and there were
repeated cries of 'For shame! For shame!' and so it became quite
impossible for him to refuse. Afterwards, however, he felt pleased,
realizing that now he could go out for a walk in his new greatcoat
even in the evening. That whole day was for Akaky Akakiyevich like
the grandest and most sublimest of holidays. He returned home in the
happiest of moods, took off his greatcoat and carefully hung it up on
the wall, once again admiring the cloth and the lining, and then, for
purposes of comparison, took out the old dressing gown, which had
now fallen to pieces completely. He took one look and even began to
laugh: what a difference there was between them! And for a long time
afterwards, over dinner, he kept on grinning whenever he remembered
the present state of his dressing gown. He dined cheerfully and after
dinner he wrote nothing, not a single document, but just lay sybariti-
cally on his bed for a while, until it grew dark. Then, without further
ado, he dressed, put on his greatcoat and went out on to the street.
Where exactly the civil servant who had invited him lived, we cannot
unfortunately say; our memory has begun to let us down mightily and
everything to be found in Petersburg, every street and every house,
has so blended and blurred in our head that we can hardly summon
up anything at all from there in an orderly state. However that may
be, it is certain that the civil servant lived in the better part of town
and consequently not very close to Akaky Akakiyevich. At first Akaky
Akakiyevich had to pass down some deserted streets with very scant
illumination, but as he drew nearer to the civil servant's apartment,
the streets grew more lively, more crowded and better lit. Passers-by
became more frequent, smartly dressed ladies could be seen here and
there, beaver collars began to appear on the men, and there were fewer
peasant cabbies with their slatted wooden sleighs studded with gilded
nails; instead there were coachmen in raspberry-coloured velvet hats,
with lacquered sleighs and bearskin rugs, and fine hammerclothed
carriages bowling down the street, wheels squealing over the snow.
Akaky Akakiyevich looked at all this as if he had never seen anything
like it. It was several years since he had gone outside in the evening.
He stopped with curiosity before a lighted shop window to look at a
painting of some beautiful woman taking her shoe off, baring her
whole leg, a very shapely one at that, while behind her back a gentle-

man with sideburns and a dapper imperial on his chin poked his head round the door. Akaky Akakiyevich shook his head and grinned, then went on his way. Why he grinned, whether because he had encountered something quite unfamiliar but for which every one of us, nevertheless, retains some kind of instinctive feeling, or whether because, like many other clerks, he thought: 'Well, really, these Frenchmen! What's there to say? They take it into their heads they want something, and er, it's just as if, really, er . . .' Or maybe he didn't even think that – after all, it's not as if you can clamber into a man's soul and learn all his thoughts. Finally he reached the building where the assistant to the Head of the desk had his rooms. The assistant to the Head of the desk lived in grand style: the stairway was lit and his rooms were on the first floor. On entering the ante-room, Akaky Akakiyevich saw whole rows of galoshes. Between these rows, in the middle of the room, stood a samovar, hissing and letting out clouds of steam. The walls were dense with greatcoats and cloaks, some of which even had beaver collars or velvet lapels. From behind the wall he could hear a general clamour and voices that suddenly became clear and ringing when the door opened and a footman came out bearing a tray laden with empty glasses, a cream jug and a basket of biscuits. It seemed the clerks had all been there for some time and had already drunk their first glass of tea. Akaky Akakiyevich, after hanging up his greatcoat himself, entered the room – and before him, all at once, flashed candles, clerks, pipes and card tables, while his ears were assailed by a hubbub of conversation, coming from every side, and the sound of chairs being moved about. He stood most awkwardly in the middle of the room, looking around and trying to think what to do. But he had been noticed – and they all greeted him loudly and at once went out into the ante-room and again examined his greatcoat. Akaky Akakiyevich was partly embarrassed, yet, being simple at heart, he couldn't help but be pleased at the way they all praised his greatcoat. Then, of course, everyone abandoned both him and his greatcoat and turned their attention, in the usual way, to the tables set for whist. All this – the noise, the talk, the great crowd of people – seemed somehow strange to Akaky Akakiyevich. He simply did not know what to do, where to put his hands, his feet, his whole self; in the end he sat down beside some of the card-players, looked at the cards, peered into one face after another – and after some time began to yawn and feel bored, all the more so since it was long past the time when he usually went to bed. He wanted to take his leave but they wouldn't let him go, saying that he absolutely must drink a glass of champagne to the new greatcoat. An hour later dinner was served; it consisted of Russian salad, cold veal, paté, sweet pastries and champagne. Akaky Akakiyevich was made to drink two glasses, after which the room began to feel merrier, but he still couldn't forget that it was twelve o'clock and long past the time for him to be going home. Lest his host take it into his head to detain him, he slipped out of the room and searched in the ante-room for his greatcoat, which, not without regret, he discovered to be lying on the floor; he gave it a shake, removed every last bit of fluff, draped it over his shoulders and went downstairs and on to the street. It was still light outside. A few little grocers' shops – those round-the-clock clubs for servants and all manner of people – were still open, while those that were closed showed a long sliver of light all the way down the door jamb, indicating that they were not yet deserted and that maids or menservants were probably still spinning out their tales and discussions, leaving their masters quite bewildered as to their whereabouts. Akaky Akakiyevich walked on in his merry frame of mind; he even almost began to run, for some unknown reason, after a certain lady who passed by like lightning, every part of her body filled with extraordinary movement. Nevertheless he slowed down at once and resumed his previous quiet pace, as astonished as anyone at the animation that had come over him as if from nowhere. Soon he came to those long, deserted streets that are far from cheerful even during the daytime, let alone in the evening. Now they had become still more silent and lonely; the street lamps were fewer and farther between – oil was obviously in short supply; houses and fences were now made of wood; not a soul could be seen anywhere; there was no light except from the snow on the streets, while the low sleeping hovels with their closed shutters looked sad and black. He was near the place where the street was interrupted by an endless square which, with houses on the far side that were almost invisible, looked like a terrible desert.

Far away, God knows where, there was a glimmer of light from a policeman's booth that seemed to be standing at the very edge of the world. Here, somehow, Akaky Akakiyevich's merry good cheer diminished significantly. He stepped out into the square, not without a certain involuntary fear, as if his heart had a foreboding of something bad. He looked to either side: it was as if there were a sea all round him. 'No, better not look,' he thought, and walked on with his eyes shut – and when he opened them to see if it was far to the end of the square, what he saw, right there before him, almost in front of his nose, was some men with moustaches, but what kind of men they were was something he could not even discern. His eyes clouded and there was a pounding in his chest. 'Hey, that greatcoat's *mine*!' said one of them in a voice like thunder, seizing him by the collar. Akaky Akakiyevich was on the point of screaming 'Help!' when another man put a fist the size of a clerk's head right up against his mouth and said, 'Just you try shouting!' Akaky Akakiyevich felt only that someone removed his greatcoat and jabbed him with their knee, whereupon he fell on his back in the snow and no longer felt anything at all. A few minutes later he came to his senses and got back onto his feet, but there was nobody to be seen. It felt cold out in the open with no greatcoat and he tried to shout, but his voice, it seemed, had not the least intention of carrying to the end of the square. In despair, shouting continuously, he started running across the square straight towards the booth, beside which stood a policeman, leaning on his halberd and watching with apparent curiosity, as if wondering why the devil a far-away man was running towards him and shouting. Akaky Akakiyevich ran up to him and, gasping for breath, went on shouting. Why had the policeman been sleeping when he should have been on watch? Why hadn't he seen that a man was being robbed? The policeman replied that he had seen nothing, that he had seen two men go up to Akaky Akakiyevich in the middle of the square but had thought they were people he knew, and he told Akaky Akakiyevich that, instead of abusing him for nothing, he should go the next day to see the sergeant, and the sergeant would find out who it was had taken his greatcoat. Akaky Akakiyevich ran home in a terrible state: his hair, of which he still had a small amount on his temples and the back of his head, was completely dishevelled; his side, his chest and his trousers were covered in snow. Hearing a dreadful knocking at the door, his elderly landlady leaped out of bed and, wearing only one slipper, ran down to open it, modestly clasping her shift to her bosom with one hand; but on opening the door and seeing what a state Akaky Akakiyevich was in, she stepped back. When he told her what had happened, she threw up her hands and said he must go straight to the district superintendent; the local sergeant would deceive him, tell lies and generally lead him around by the nose, and so it really would be best to go straight to the district superintendent; she even knew him herself, because Anna, the Finnish woman who had once worked for her as a cook, had been taken on by him as a nursemaid and she often saw him driving past their house and he also went to church every Sunday, where he prayed and at the same time looked round merrily at everyone, and this all went to show, therefore, that he must be a good man. After hearing this judgement, Akaky Akakiyevich sadly dragged himself to his room, and how he spent the night there must be left to the imagination of those who can enter to some degree into the feelings of others. Early next morning he set off to see the superintendent but was told he was asleep; he went round at ten – and was again told he was asleep; he went round at eleven – and was told the superintendent was out; he went round at lunchtime – but the clerks in the waiting-room would not let him in on any account and insisted on knowing what he had come about and what business had brought him there and what it was that had happened. And so at last, for once in his life, Akaky Akakiyevich took it into his head to show just what he was made of: he said quite bluntly that he needed to see the superintendent himself, in person, that they dare not refuse him admission, that he had come from his department on official business and that if he lodged a complaint against them, they would find themselves in trouble. The clerks dared say nothing to this, and one of them went to call the superintendent. The superintendent somehow responded very strangely to the account of the theft of the greatcoat. Instead of paying attention to what was important, he began to question Akaky Akakiyevich – why had he been going back home so late? Had he not, perhaps, called in at some house of ill repute? – with the result that Akaky Akakiyevich felt completely confused and left with no idea whether the case of his greatcoat would progress in an appropriate manner or not. All that day he was absent from the office (for the only time in his life). He appeared the following day, all pale and wearing his old dressing gown, which now looked more pitiful than ever. Though there were some clerks who did not let slip even this chance to jeer at Akaky Akakiyevich, many of his colleagues were moved by the story of the theft of the greatcoat. They resolved then and there to make a collection for him, but they collected only the merest trifle, because the clerks had already exhausted their funds contributing not only towards a portrait of the director, but also, at the suggestion of the Head of the section, who was acquainted with the author, towards some book or other – and so the sum collected was trifling in the extreme. One of them, moved by compassion, resolved at least to assist Akaky Akakiyevich with good advice, telling him not to go to the local sergeant because, although it was possible that the latter, eager to win the approval of his superiors, might somehow find the greatcoat, the greatcoat would nevertheless remain in the police station unless Akaky Akakiyevich were able to present legal proofs of its ownership; the best thing would be to appeal to a certain *significant person*, since this *significant person*, by communicating and consulting with the necessary people, could push the case through more successfully. There was nothing for it; Akaky Akakiyevich resolved to go to the *significant person*. Exactly what was the office held by this *significant person* and what it entailed remains unknown to this day. It should be noted that this *certain significant person* had only recently become a significant person, having previously been an insignificant person. Even after this advancement, however, his position was not considered significant in comparison with others of yet greater significance. Still, one can always find a circle of people for whom what is insignificant in the eyes of others is significant. Moreover, he tried to increase his significance through adopting a variety of measures: his subordinates were required to meet him on the stairs when he came in to work; none of them should venture to appear directly before him, everything instead being carried out in accord with the strictest of protocols: a collegiate registrar should report to a provincial secretary, a provincial secretary to a titular councillor or whoever else might be appropriate, and in no other way should anything be brought to his attention. Thus the whole of Holy Russia is polluted by imitation – everyone copies and apes his superior. It is even said that a certain titular councillor, on being put in charge of a small, separate chancellery, immediately partitioned off a special room for himself, which he called the 'Audience Chamber', and stationed gold-braided and red-collared ushers outside this room, with instructions to hold the handle of the door and open it for every visitor – even though there was barely enough space in the 'Audience Chamber' for an ordinary writing desk. The manners and habits of the *significant person* were dignified and majestic, but of no especial complexity. The cornerstone of his system was strictness. 'Strictness, strictness, and – strictness,' he often used to say, and at the last word he would look very significantly into the face of the man he was addressing. Not, however, that there was any reason for him to do this; the ten officials who made up the entire administrative mechanism of his office were in an appropriate state of fear and trembling anyway. Seeing him in the distance, they would immediately stop what they were doing and stand to attention until their superior had passed through the room. His usual conversation with his subordinates was strict as strict could be and consisted almost entirely of three phrases: 'How dare you? Do you realize to whom you are talking? Are you aware who is standing before you?' He was, however, a good man at heart, loyal to his friends and ready to oblige, but the rank of general had completely turned his head. His promotion had somehow bewildered him and thrown him off balance, and he really had no idea how he should behave. When he was with his equals, he was quite a decent man, very gentlemanly in fact, and in many respects even intelligent; but as soon as he chanced to be in the company of men even only one rank beneath him, he was simply a lost soul: he could not say a word, and people felt pity for him, all the more so since even he sensed that he could have been spending his time incomparably better. Sometimes his eyes betrayed a strong wish to join some interesting group or conversation, but he was always stopped by the thought that this might be going too far, that such over-friendliness on his part might detract from his significance. And so, as a result of these considerations, he remained forever in the same condition of silence, pronouncing only the occasional monosyllable and so acquiring the reputation of being exceptionally boring. This was the *significant person* to whom our Akaky Akakiyevich appealed, and he appealed at a very unfortunate moment, a moment that was most inopportune for him, although, on the other hand, opportune for the significant person. The significant person was in his office, having the jolliest of conversations with an old acquaintance, a childhood friend who had only recently arrived in the capital and whom he had not seen for several years. Just then he was informed that a certain Bashmachkin was asking to see him. 'Who's he?' he asked curtly. 'Some clerk or other,' came the reply. 'Oh, he can wait. This isn't the right moment,' said the significant person. Here I must observe that the significant person was telling a barefaced lie: it was precisely the right moment. He and his friend had long since said everything they had to say to one another and had begun to punctuate their conversation with extremely long silences, during which they merely slapped one another gently on the thigh and repeated, 'Well, well, Ivan Abramovich!' and 'So there we are, Stepan Varlamovich!' Nevertheless, he kept the clerk waiting, so he could make it clear to his friend, who had some time ago left the civil service to settle down on his country estate, how long clerks had to wait in his ante-room. In the end, after talking – and, still more, remaining silent – to his heart's content, and after smoking a cigar in an extremely comfortable armchair with a sloping back, he seemed suddenly to remember, and he said to a secretary who was standing by the door with some papers, waiting to report: 'Ah, yes, I think there's a clerk wanting to see me. Tell him he may come in.' Seeing Akaky Akakiyevich's humble appearance and elderly uniform, he suddenly turned to him and said, 'What can I do for you?' in a voice that sounded abrupt and firm and which he had specially practised alone in his room, in front of a mirror, for an entire week before being promoted to the rank of general and taking up his present position. Akaky Akakiyevich, who had been feeling suitably timid for some time, became somewhat flustered and began as best he could, as much as his tongue-tied state allowed and, with even more frequent than usual employment of the particle 'er', to explain that his greatcoat had been entirely new and that he had been robbed in the most inhuman fashion, and that he was now appealing to him to, er, intercede on his behalf and write to his honour the police superintendent, or else to somebody else, and so discover the whereabouts of the greatcoat.

The General, for some unknown reason, thought he was being addressed in too familiar a manner. 'What is this, my dear sir?' he said abruptly. 'Do you not know the proper procedure? Why have you come here to me? Do you not know the right way to go about things? You should first have submitted a petition to the office; the petition would have gone to the chief clerk, then to the section chief, then it would have been conveyed to a secretary, and the secretary would have presented it to me.'

'But Your Excellency,' said Akaky Akakiyevich, trying to summon all of the modest portion of presence of mind he possessed and sensing at the same time that he had broken out in a terrible sweat, 'I ventured to trouble your Highest Excellency because, er, secretaries are an unreliable lot . . .'

'What, what, what?' said the significant person. 'Who's taught you such insolence? Where have you got such ideas from? What is this spirit of sedition infecting young people against their chiefs and seniors?' The significant person appeared not to have noticed that Akaky Akakiyevich was already over fifty. Were it possible, therefore, to refer to him as a young man, this would be only relatively speaking, that is, in relation to someone who was already at least seventy. 'Do you know who you are speaking to? Do you understand who is standing before you? Do you realize this, I ask you, do you realize this?' At this point he stamped his foot, raising his voice so powerfully that even better men than Akaky Akakiyevich would have been terrified. Akaky Akakiyevich was petrified; he staggered, his whole body began to shake, and he was unable to stay upright; if the doormen had not run up to support him, he would have flopped down on the floor; he was carried out almost motionless. And the significant person, pleased that he had produced an effect still greater than he had anticipated, and quite entranced by the thought that words of his could deprive a man even of his senses, gave his friend a sidelong glance to see what he was making of all this; he noticed not without satisfaction that his acquaintance was in a most uncertain state and was even beginning to feel frightened himself.

How he got down the stairs, how he got out on to the street, Akaky Akakiyevich was quite unable to remember. He had no feeling in either his arms or his legs. Never in his life had he been given such a dressing down by a general, let alone one from another department. Repeatedly stumbling off the edge of the pavement, his mouth agape, he walked through the blizzard that was whistling up and down the streets; the wind, as is its wont in Petersburg, was blowing at him from all four points of the compass, out of every side street. In only a moment this wind had blown a quinsy into his throat and, by the time he got home, he was unable to say a single word; all swollen up, he took to his bed. So powerful, at times, is the effect of a good and proper dressing down! The following day he was found to have a high fever. Thanks to the gracious assistance of the Petersburg climate, his illness progressed more rapidly than could have been expected and, when the doctor came and took his pulse, all he felt able to do was to prescribe a poultice, just so that the sick man would not be left entirely without the benefit of medical help; at the same time, however, he declared that it would definitely be all up with Akaky Akakiyevich within a day and a half. After which he turned to the landlady and said, 'And you, dear lady, had better not waste time. You should order him a pine coffin straightaway, since an oak one will be too expensive for him.' Whether or not Akaky Akakiyevich heard this fateful pronouncement, whether or not, if he did hear it, it had a shattering effect on him, whether or not he regretted his wretched life – none of this is known, since he was in a state of delirium and fever. Apparitions, each stranger than the one before, were continuously presenting themselves to him: one moment he could see Petrovich and was ordering him to make a greatcoat with some kind of traps to snare the thieves whom he kept imagining were under the bed, and he was endlessly begging his landlady to drag away a thief who had even got under the quilt; next he was asking why the old dressing gown was still hanging there now that he had a new greatcoat; next he fancied he was standing before the General, being dressed down good and proper and repeating, 'I'm sorry, Your Excellency!' and then, in the end, even blasphematizing and uttering the most terrible of words, so that his old landlady, never having heard anything of the kind from him in all her life, even had to keep crossing herself – all the more so because these most terrible words always came immediately after the words 'Your Excellency!'. After that, he spoke utter gibberish and it was impossible to understand anything at all; it was clear only that his incoherent words and thoughts all centred upon one and the same greatcoat. Finally, poor Akaky Akakiyevich gave up the ghost. Neither his room nor his belongings were put under seal because, in the first place, he had no heirs and, in the second place, he had left very little behind: namely, a bundle of goose quills, a quire of official white paper, three pairs of socks, two or three buttons that had come off his trousers, and the dressing gown with which the reader is already familiar. To whom all this went, God knows; I have to confess that not even the teller of this tale troubled to inquire. Akaky Akakiyevich was taken away and buried. And Petersburg was left without Akaky Akakiyevich, just as if he had never been there at all. Dead and gone was a being whom no one had defended, whom no one had held dear, and in whom no one, not even a naturalist always ready to mount even an ordinary fly on a pin and examine it under a microscope, had ever shown any interest; a being who had patiently endured the mockery of his office colleagues and who had gone to his grave without excessive fuss, but before whom, nevertheless, if only at the end of his life, momentarily enlivening his poor life, had appeared a bright guest in the form of a greatcoat – and on whom calamity had then crashed down, as harshly as it has crashed down on the sovereigns and tsars of the world. A few days after his death, a porter came to his lodgings with orders that Akaky Akakiyevich should go at once to the department: his boss was asking for him. But the porter was obliged to return alone and report that the clerk was unable to come to work any more. To the question 'Why?' he responded: 'Well, you see, he's dead. He's been buried three days now.' Thus the news of his death reached the department; and the following day his place was taken by a new clerk, who was much taller and whose handwriting was not so upright but considerably more slanting and oblique.

But who could have imagined that this was not the end for Akaky Akakiyevich, that he was destined to make a noise in the world for some time after his death, as if to compensate for a life no one had noticed? But so it happened, and our poor story unexpectedly acquires a fantastic ending. Rumours suddenly spread through St Petersburg that around the Kalinkin Bridge, and far beyond it, a stiff had taken to appearing at night in the form of a civil servant searching for a stolen greatcoat and that, under the pretext of trying to recover the greatcoat, this stiff was stripping from everyone's shoulders, regardless of rank or calling, greatcoats of every kind: coats lined with cat fur and beaver fur, coats quilted with cotton, coats lined with racoon, fox and bear – coats, in short, made from every kind of fur and pelt that people have devised to cover their own. One clerk from the department saw the stiff with his own eyes and immediately recognized it as Akaky Akakiyevich; this, however, instilled such terror in him that he rushed off as fast as his legs would carry him and so failed to examine the stiff properly, just seeing it wag a threatening finger far off in the distance. Complaints came in from all sides that the backs and shoulders not only of titular councillors but even of the priviest of councillors were being exposed to the most severe chills as a result of this nocturnal stripping of greatcoats. Orders were issued to the police to capture the stiff dead or alive, regardless of cost, and to subject it, as an example to others, to the harshest of punishments – and in this they very nearly even succeeded. That is, a policeman somewhere on Kiryushkin Lane actually seized the stiff by the collar at the very scene of the crime, as it attempted to snatch a frieze greatcoat off the back of a certain retired musician who in his day had whistled on the flute. After seizing hold of its collar, the policeman called out to two of his colleagues, whom he then instructed to hold the stiff for a moment while he quickly reached down into his boot for his snuffbox, since his nose had already suffered frostbite six times and he needed to revive it a little; but his snuff was evidently so strong that not even a stiff could bear it. No sooner had the policeman closed his right nostril with one finger and drawn a half-handful of snuff up into his left nostril than the stiff sneezed so violently as completely to bespatter the eyes of all three of them. While they raised their fists to wipe their eyes clean, the stiff vanished into thin air, so that they were no longer even quite certain if it had ever really been in their hands at all. After that the policemen developed such a fear of stiffs that they felt wary even of arresting the living, and instead they just shouted out from a distance, 'Hey you there, move along now!' And the clerk who was a stiff began to appear even on the wrong side of the Kalinkin Bridge, striking no little fear into the hearts of all timid people. But we have, however, completely forgotten the *certain significant person* who was himself, as a matter of fact, all but responsible for the fantastic direction that this, incidentally, entirely truthful story has now taken. First, justice requires me to record that, soon after the departure of poor, well and truly dressed-down Akaky Akakiyevich, the *certain significant person* began to feel something in the way of remorse. Compassion was not alien to him; his heart was open to many kind impulses, in spite of the fact that his rank all too often prevented them from being expressed. As soon as his acquaintance from the country had left his office, he even began to give some thought to Akaky Akakiyevich. And from then on he saw images almost every day of the pale clerk who had been unable to withstand an official dressing down. The thought of Akaky Akakiyevich so troubled him that after a week he went so far as to send a clerk round to find out how he was doing and whether there was, in fact, any way he could help him. And when it was reported to him that Akaky Akakiyevich had died of a sudden fever, he even felt shocked; he could hear his conscience murmuring at him and he felt out of sorts all day. Wanting to amuse himself a little and to put this unpleasantness out of his mind, he went round that evening to one of his acquaintances, where the company was respectable and – best of all – he felt quite free of constraint, since everyone else was of more or less the same rank as he was. This had an astonishing effect on his state of mind. He loosened up, became affable and made pleasant conversation – in short, he greatly enjoyed the evening. He had a glass or two of champagne with his supper – something we all know to be an effective means of inducing merriment. The champagne put him in the mood for particular measures: that is, he decided not to go home yet, but to call on a certain lady he knew, Karolina Ivanovna, who was apparently of German extraction and with whom he was on the friendliest of terms. It has to be mentioned that the significant person, no longer young, was a good husband and a respectable family man. Two sons, one of whom was already in the civil service, and a good-looking sixteen-year-old daughter, whose nose was rather snub though quite pretty all the same, used to come and kiss his hand every day, saying, 'Bonjour, Papa.' His spouse, who was still blooming and even far from unattractive, would first give him her own hand to kiss and then kiss his, turning it the other way up. But the significant person, although he was, by the way, entirely satisfied with the domestic tendernesses of his family, considered it proper to conduct a special friendship with a lady in another part of the city. This lady companion was not in any way either prettier or younger than his wife; but there are many such riddles in the world and it is not our business to resolve them. And so the significant person went downstairs, got into his sleigh, said to the driver 'To Karolina Ivanovna's!' and, wrapped up most luxuriously in a warm greatcoat, lapsed into that pleasant state, better than which nothing is imaginable to a Russian, where you yourself do not think of anything at all and yet thoughts – each more pleasant than the one before – slip into your head of their own accord, without putting you to the trouble of chasing after them and searching for them. Full of contentment, he effortlessly recalled all the merriest moments of the evening, all the words that had raised peals of laughter in his small circle. He even repeated many of them under his breath and found them as amusing as before; not surprisingly, this led him to chuckle to himself in delight. Now and again, however, he was disturbed by sudden gusts of a wind that sprang up from God knows where and for no apparent reason, cutting him in the face, flinging bits of snow in his eyes, making his coat collar billow out like a sail or suddenly throwing it over his head with supernatural force, causing him no end of bother in his attempts to extricate himself. Suddenly the significant person felt someone seize him extremely firmly by the collar. Turning round, he saw a short man in a shabby old uniform and, not without horror, recognized him as Akaky Akakiyevich. The clerk's face was as pale as snow and looked just like that of a stiff. But the horror of the significant person exceeded all measure when he saw the dead man's mouth start to twist and, letting out a terrible stench of the grave, utter the following words: 'Ah! So there you are at last. Now at last, er, I've collared you. It's your greatcoat I'm after. You couldn't be bothered to help me find mine, and you even gave me quite a dressing down into the bargain – so now give me yours!' The poor *significant person* almost died. For all the strength of character he displayed in the office and before those of inferior rank more generally, and even though one look at his manly figure and bearing was enough to make people say 'Goodness, what character!' – nevertheless, at this moment, like many a man with the air of a heroic warrior, he felt such terror that he even began to fear, and not without reason, that he was about to suffer some kind of nervous fit. He even threw off his greatcoat himself as quick as he could, and shouted out to the driver in a voice that didn't belong to him 'Home! As fast as you can!' The driver, hearing a tone of voice associated with moments of crisis and which was usually, even, accompanied by something decidedly more forceful, drew his head down between his shoulders to be on the safe side, cracked his whip and sped off like an arrow. In a little over six minutes the significant person was outside the entrance to his house. Pale, badly frightened and with no greatcoat, instead of calling on Karolina Ivanovna, he had returned home; he staggered somehow or other to his room and spent the night there in a state of great agitation, with the result that over breakfast his daughter said to him straight out, 'You look very pale today, Papa.' But Papa held his tongue; not a word did he say to anyone about what had happened, where he had gone or where he had intended to go. The incident made a powerful impression on him. Far less often, indeed, did he say to his subordinates 'How dare you? Do you realize who is standing before you?' – and if he did come out with these words, it was only after first hearing what the subordinate had to say. But still more remarkable is the fact that, from then on, the apparitions of the clerk who was a stiff entirely ceased. The General's greatcoat was evidently a perfect fit; nothing more, in any case, was heard of snatchings of greatcoats. Nevertheless, many active and concerned people simply refused to be reassured and went on saying that the clerk who was a stiff was still appearing in outlying parts of the city. And one Kolomna[11] policeman truly, with his own eyes, saw a ghost appear from behind a building; but being somewhat lacking in strength – to such a degree that an ordinary fully grown young pig, hurtling out of some private house, had once knocked him to the ground, to the great amusement of the cabbies standing around, whom he had then fined half a kopek each so he could buy some snuff – being, as I said, somewhat lacking in strength, he did not dare to stop it, but merely followed it in the dark until, at last, the ghost suddenly looked round, stopped, asked 'What are *you* after?' and displayed a fist such as you won't find even among the living. The policeman said 'Nothing' and turned back at once. This ghost, however, was a great deal taller, it had a simply enormous moustache and, apparently making for the Obukhov Bridge, it disappeared completely into the darkness of night.

First published in 1842
Translated by Robert Chandler

IVAN SERGEYEVICH TURGENEV
(1818–83)

Turgenev was born in Oryol and raised by a tyrannical mother on her family estate. After attending both Moscow and St Petersburg Universities, Turgenev studied in Berlin from 1838 to 1841. He inherited his mother's estate in 1850, but never stayed there for long. He spent much of his life abroad, mainly in France and Germany. More cosmopolitan than any other Russian writer of his time, he was a friend of Gustave Flaubert, Henry James, George Sand and other European literary figures. The most important relationship of his adult life was with the singer Pauline Viardot; he was close both to her and to her husband.

Turgenev's first important work was the story-cycle A Hunter's Notebook *(1852). It has been said that these evocations of a nobleman's experiences during hunting trips helped to bring about the emancipation of the serfs in 1861. Turgenev seldom, however, attacks the evils of serfdom directly. What shocked or delighted his contemporaries was that he portrays the peasants as human beings with their own thoughts and feelings. This implicitly undermined the legitimacy of a social order in which peasants were seen as their master's possessions.*

During the decade after the publication of A Hunter's Notebook, *Turgenev wrote many of his finest works: the short story 'Mumu', a more direct attack on serfdom; the short novels* Asya *and* First Love; *and four of his six novels – including the most famous,* Fathers and Sons. *Like his other long novels, this is a novel of ideas that covers a broad social canvas. Its central theme is the conflict between Turgenev's own generation of liberals and the younger generation whose iconoclastic attitudes led him to refer to them as nihilists.*

'The Knocking' is one of several stories added to A Hunter's Notebook *more than twenty years after its first publication; it is at once comic, lyrical and realistic – and free of the sentimentality that mars much of Turgenev's work.*

THE KNOCKING

'What I've got to tell you,' said Yermolay, coming into the hut to see me – and I'd just finished my lunch and lain down on the camp bed to have a bit of a rest after a reasonably successful, if exhausting, shoot of black grouse (it was around the middle of July and frightfully hot) – 'what I've got to tell you, is that there's no more shot left.'

I jumped up from the bed.

'What d'you mean, there's no shot left? You know very well we had around thirty pounds when we left the village! There was a whole bagful!'

'You're right, sir, and it was a big bag; it should've been enough for a whole fortnight. I dunno. Maybe it got torn somehow. Anyway, makes no difference how it happened, there's no shot . . . well, maybe enough for another ten rounds or so.'

'What are we going to do now, then? We haven't even got to the best places yet, and they promised there'd be six new broods . . .'

'Send me off to Tula – it's not all that far, only about thirty miles. I can get some shot for you – three stone of it, if you like. I'll be there and back in no time.'

'But when can you set off?'

'Right away this minute. No point putting it off. The only thing is, we'll have to borrow some horses.'

'Borrow some horses? But we've got our own!'

'Ours are no good. The shaft-horse has gone lame, it's terrible.'

'When did that happen?'

'Just the other day, sir. The coachman took it to be shod – but the blacksmith clearly didn't know what he was doing. Now it can't even put its hoof down. It's the front leg. It's lifting it up, like a dog.'

'Well, at least they've unshod it, I suppose?'

'No they haven't, but they certainly ought to. Could be they hammered a nail right into its flesh.'

I called out the coachman, and it turned out that Yermolay was right: the shaft-horse simply couldn't rest its leg on the ground. Straight away I ordered it to be unshod and stood on some wet clay.

'So, do you want me to hire some horses and go to Tula?' Yermolay persisted.

'Are there really any horses to hire in a dump like this?' I was unable to control my irritation.

The village where we found ourselves was indeed in the back of beyond, well out of everyone's way. All the inhabitants seemed to be desperately poor, and it had been hard to find a single decent-sized hut, albeit without a chimney.

'Yes,' replied Yermolay, with his usual imperturbability. 'You're right about this village, but there used to be a really clever peasant living here. Well-off too – he had nine horses. He's dead now, but his eldest son is in charge of everything. He's as thick as they come, but he won't have had time yet to get through everything his dad left behind. We'll be able to get some horses out of him. You just tell me, and I'll bring him to you. I've heard his brothers are pretty smart, but it's him that's the boss.'

'Why's that?'

'Because he's the eldest! That means the younger ones have to know their place!' At this point Yermolay uttered some caustic and unprintable words about younger brothers in general. 'I'll get him over here. He's a simple sort of bloke. You should be able to do a deal with him.'

While Yermolay went off to find this 'simple' sort of person it occurred to me that it might be better if I went to Tula myself. Firstly, wise from experience, I knew I couldn't rely on Yermolay. Once I'd sent him to town on a shopping expedition; he promised to do everything all in one day – and he disappeared for a week, spent the money on drink and came back on foot (he'd left in a droshky). Secondly, I knew a horse-dealer in Tula from whom I could get a replacement for the lame shaft-horse.

'No doubt about it,' I thought. 'I'll go myself. I should be able to have a nap on the way, as it's a comfortable wagon.'

'Here he is!' Yermolay shouted quarter of an hour later, as he lurched into the hut. Behind him entered a well-built peasant in a white shirt, dark-blue trousers and bast shoes, tow-haired, weak-sighted, with a little pointed sandy beard, a long pudgy nose and a wide-open mouth. He did indeed look a bit of a 'simple Simon'.

'And here you are,' said Yermolay. 'He's got some horses and he agrees.'

'That is, sort of, I . . .' the peasant croaked. Then he started to stutter, shaking his sparse hair and fingering the band round his cap, which he was holding in his hands. 'I, sort of . . .'

'What's your name?' I asked.

The peasant looked down at the floor and seemed to be lost in thought.

'What's my name then?'

'Yes. What's your first name?'

'Well, my first name is Filofey.'

'Right then, my good friend Filofey. I've heard that you have some horses. Bring three of them over here, we'll harness them to my wagon – it's not a heavy one – and you can take me in to Tula. There's a good moon at the moment, you'll be able to see the way, and it'll be nice and cool. What's the road like in these parts?'

'The road? The road isn't bad. It'll only be about twelve miles to the main road. There's one bad bit, but otherwise it's all right.'

'What's the bad bit?'

'You 'ave to ford the river.'

'So you're going to Tula yourself?' enquired Yermolay.

'Yes, I'll go myself.'

'Well!' said my faithful servant and shook his head. 'Well, well!' he repeated. Then he spat and left the room.

Evidently the trip to Tula no longer struck him as in any way attractive. For him it had become just a waste of time.

'Do you know how to get there?' I asked Filofey.

' 'Course I do. The only thing is that I, sort of, if you don't mind, I can't – 'ow can I suddenly . . .'

It turned out that when he was hiring Filofey, Yermolay merely told him not to ask foolish questions and that of course he would be duly recompensed. But Filofey, even if he was, as Yermolay put it, a simpleton, wouldn't take this assurance as sufficient on its own. He asked me for fifty roubles in paper money – a huge sum. I offered him ten roubles, a low price, and we started to haggle. At first Filofey held his ground, but then he began to yield, albeit reluctantly and taking his time. Yermolay came in for a moment and started to assure me that 'this simpleton' (' 'E really does like that word!' muttered Filofey under his breath), 'this simpleton hasn't the least idea what the going rate is', and reminded me in this context that about twenty years ago a coaching inn opened by my mother on a prime site for business at the junction of two main roads went into decline and failed, because the old house-serf installed to run the place genuinely had no idea of the value of money and thought that the more coins he had, whatever their denomination, the better he was doing. So, for instance, he would gladly exchange one silver quarter for six copper groats – though he still didn't leave off cussing and swearing while he was about it.

'Oh Filofey, Filofey, you're such a simpleton!' Yermolay finally exclaimed, and he went out, angrily banging the door.

Filofey didn't answer back, as though he realized that he did indeed have a rather silly name and even that it was quite acceptable to make fun of a man for being called something like that, although the guilty

party here was the village priest, who really ought to have come up
with something more appropriate at the christening.[1]

Anyway, we finally clinched the deal at twenty roubles. He set off
to get the horses and an hour later produced no fewer than five of
them, so that I could choose. The horses proved to be quite serviceable,
although their manes and tails were matted and their bellies were
large and swollen like drums. Filofey was accompanied by two of his
brothers, who were completely unlike him in appearance. Short, with
dark eyes and sharp noses, they did indeed give the impression of
being pretty smart, speaking quickly and volubly (or, as Yermolay put
it, babbling away) but deferring to their eldest brother.

They wheeled the wagon out from the shed and spent about an hour
and a half fussing around with it and the horses. First they would
loosen the traces, then they would fasten them up as tightly as they
possibly could. The two younger brothers insisted that the roan be the
shaft-horse because 'it knows best how to go downhill', but Filofey
decided it should be the one they called 'Shaggy'. And so Shaggy was
put in the shafts.

The wagon was stuffed full of hay, and under the seat they shoved
the harness from the lame shaft-horse in case I happened to buy a new
horse in Tula. Filofey, who had managed to dash home and return in
his late father's long white loose cloak, high formless hat and blacked
boots, solemnly climbed up into the driver's seat. I got in and looked
at my watch. It was a quarter past ten. Yermolay didn't even say
goodbye; he began beating Jack, his dog. Filofey tugged at the reins
and shouted 'Come on, me dearies!' in his squeaky, high-pitched voice,
while his brothers jumped on at each side, whipping the trace-horses
under their bellies – and the wagon moved off and went out through
the gates and onto the road. Shaggy was on the point of rushing off
into his own familiar yard, but Filofey brought him back to his senses
with a few blows of the whip, and soon the village was behind us and
we were coasting along a fairly smooth road between thick, unbroken
clumps of hazel.

It was a gloriously quiet night, ideal for a journey. One moment the
wind would rustle through the bushes and rock the branches, the next
moment it would completely die down. Small, silvery, motionless
clouds could be seen here and there in the sky. The moon stood high
in the heavens and clearly illuminated the area around us. I stretched
out on the hay and was on the point of dropping off to sleep when I
remembered about the 'bad place' and shook myself awake.

'Hi there, Filofey, how far is it to the ford?'

'To the ford? It'll be about five miles.'

'Five miles,' I thought. 'We won't be there for at least an hour. Time for a nap.'

'Filofey, you do know the road well, do you?' I asked again.

''Ow could I not know it well, this 'ere road? It's not the first time I've been 'ere . . .'

He added something else, but I was no longer listening. I was asleep.

I was aroused not by my own intention of waking up exactly one hour later, the way one often does, but by a strange, if faint, squelching and gurgling right next to my ears. I raised my head.

What was going on? I was lying in the wagon as before, but all around the wagon – and not more than half an arm's length below its floor – there was a smooth, moonlit, watery expanse, trembling and breaking up into small, distinct ripples. I looked in front: on the driver's seat, hanging his head and slouching forward, Filofey was sitting as motionless as a stuffed dummy, and a little further away, above the murmuring water, lay the curved shaft-bow and the backs and heads of the horses. And everything was as still, as silent, as if we were in a magic realm, as if it were all a dream, a fabulous dream. What on earth was going on? I looked behind, from under the hood at the rear of the wagon. Why, we were in the very middle of the river, a good thirty paces from either bank!

'Filofey!' I yelled.

'What?' he replied.

'What do you mean "What?" For goodness sake! Where on earth are we?'

'In the river.'

'I can see we're in the river. And any minute now we might drown. Is this how you ford a river? Come on! Filofey, are you asleep? Answer me!'

'I just made a little mistake,' my driver replied. 'Sorry to say I went a bit to one side – now we just have to sit an' wait.'

'What do you mean, "sit an' wait"? What on earth is there to wait for?'

'Just give Shaggy time to look about 'im. Whichever way 'e chooses, that'll be the way to go.'

I sat up in the hay. The head of the shaft-horse was motionless above the surface of the water. In the clear light of the moon I could just see one ear twitching – first backwards, then forwards.

'But he's asleep as well, that Shaggy of yours!'

'No 'e ain't,' responded Filofey. ''E's sniffing the water.'

And everything fell silent again; only the water, as before, was quietly gurgling. I was numb with cold.

Moonlight, night, the river and ourselves in the river . . .

'What's that hissing?' I asked Filofey.

' 'Issing? It's ducks in the bulrushes . . . or maybe snakes.'

Suddenly the head of the shaft-horse began to shake, its ears pricked up, it snorted and began to feel its way forward.

'Gee-up, gee-up!' Filofey bellowed at the top of his voice, getting to his feet and brandishing his whip. The wagon immediately gave a start, lurched forward, cutting across the current, and moved off, jerking and swaying from side to side. At first I thought we were sinking, going deeper into the river, but after some jolts and two or three plunges, the smooth watery expanses suddenly seemed to have got lower. Yes, the water level was getting lower and lower, the wagon was emerging from the river, now I could see the wagon wheels and the horses' tails, and then, churning up powerful and abundant plumes of spray that shot up like diamond – or rather sapphire – shafts of light through the dull haze of the moon, the horses quickly and glee-fully dragged us up on to the sandy bank and set off up the road, out of step and awkwardly pounding their wet, glistening legs.

'What,' I wondered, 'is Filofey going to say now? "See, I was right all along!" or something of that sort?' But Filofey said nothing. Conse-quently I felt there was no need to tell him off for being so careless and, settling down in the hay, I tried again to get off to sleep.

But I simply couldn't drop off, not because I wasn't tired after the shoot, and not because anxiety had dispelled my sleepiness, but be-cause of the great beauty of the countryside we were going through. There were vast, open, grassy water-meadows with a multitude of small swards, ponds, rivulets and creeks, overgrown at their ends by osiers and willows, truly Russian places, places loved by the Russian people, just like those places where the heroes of old Russian folklore used to go to shoot white swans and grey ducks. The well-worn road unwound before us like a yellowish ribbon, the horses cantered along easily, and I couldn't *not* look – it was a feast for the eyes! And it all floated past so gently and harmoniously under the kindly moon . . . Even Filofey was captivated by it.

'These 'ere meadows of ours are called after St George,' he said, turning towards me. 'And further on are the ones they call the Grand Dukes's. You won't find no meadows like them anywhere else in Russia. Lor', they're beautiful!' Shaggy snorted and shook himself. 'Bless yer 'eart!' said Filofey gravely under his breath. 'There's beauty for you!' he said. He sighed, then gave a protracted grunt. 'And soon it'll be 'aymaking time, and there'll be a veritable mountain of all that 'ay! And these creeks are fair teeming with fish. You've never seen such bream!' he added in a sing-song voice. 'Yes, far too soon to give up the ghost, you know.'

He raised an arm.

'Eh, look! In the lake . . . Is that an 'eron standing there? Don't tell me they fish at night! Aah! It isn't an 'eron, it's a branch. Well I never! It's that moon 'aving me on.'

And so we continued, further and further, until the meadows came to an end and gave way to groves of trees and ploughed fields. Two or three lights in a little village to one side winked at us, and it was now only about three miles to the main road. I fell asleep. And once again I didn't wake up of my own accord. This time I was aroused by the sound of Filofey's voice.

'Mister! Eh, Mister!'

I sat up. The wagon was standing on a smooth patch in the middle of the road. Looking at me from the driver's seat with wide open eyes (I was surprised – I'd never have imagined his eyes were so big), Filofey whispered meaningfully and mysteriously, 'Knocking! Something's knocking!'

'What's that you're saying?'

'I'm saying there's a knocking. Bend down and listen. Can't you 'ear?'

I leant out of the wagon, held my breath, and I really did hear a weak, intermittent knocking sound somewhere far, far away behind us, something like the sound of wheels.

'Can't you 'ear?' said Filofey again.

'Well, yes,' I answered. 'There's some sort of a vehicle coming along.'

'If you can't 'ear it proper, then listen! There! Bells – and whistling too. Can you 'ear it now? Take your cap off, you'll 'ear better.'

I didn't take my cap off, but I listened for all I was worth.

'Well yes, could be . . . But what of it?'

Filofey turned towards the horses.

'It's a cart with iron-rimmed wheels . . . careering along without a load,' he said, and picked up the reins. 'It'll be people who are up to no good, Mister. There's a lot of mischief goes on round 'ere, yer know, near Tula.'

'You're talking rubbish! What makes you think they're up to no good?'

'I'm telling yer the truth. Bells, and an empty cart. They're up to no good all right.'

'Well, is it still a long way to Tula?'

'About ten miles, and there's nobody at all lives round these 'ere parts.'

'Well, get a move on then, stop wasting time.'

Filofey brandished his whip, and the wagon moved off once again.

Although I didn't believe Filofey, I just couldn't drop off to sleep again. Suppose, after all, he was right? An unpleasant feeling began to stir within me. I sat up in the wagon – until then I had been lying down – and began to look to either side. While I was asleep a thin mist had been forming, not on the ground but up in the sky, so that it was high above us, with the moon hanging inside it and looking like a whitish blotch surrounded by smoke. Everything was dim and blurred, although at ground level you could see more clearly. Round about us it was flat and depressing, just field after field with a few bushes and gullies and then more fields, mostly lying fallow and sometimes covered with weeds. Empty . . . and dead! Not even the occasional cry of a quail.

This went on for about half an hour. Now and again Filofey would swing his whip and click his tongue, but neither he nor I said a single word. Then we reached the top of a small incline. Filofey stopped the troika and said, 'Knocking. I can still 'ear this knocking, Mister!'

I thrust my head out of the wagon again, but I might just as well not have bothered, so clear now, if far away, was the rumble of cart wheels, the sound of people whistling, bells jingling and even hooves thudding. I fancied I could hear singing and laughter. True, the wind was coming from that direction, but there could be no doubt that these unknown travellers had now drawn at least half a mile closer, maybe even a mile.

Filofey and I looked at one another in silence. He merely shifted his hat forward from the back of his head to his brow and immediately, bending over the reins, began to whip the horses. They set off at a gallop, but they couldn't keep up the pace for long and fell back to a trot. Filofey continued to whip them. We simply had to get away! I couldn't explain to myself why, having not shared Filofey's anxieties earlier, I was now suddenly convinced that the people following hot on our tracks were indeed up to no good. The sounds were the same as before – the jangling of little bells, the rattling of an empty cart, a whistling, an indistinct hubbub. But now I was in no doubt. Filofey was right!

Another twenty minutes or so went by. As well as the knocking and rumbling of our own wagon, during the last few of these twenty minutes we could hear another sort of knocking and rumbling.

'Rein the horses in, Filofey,' I said. 'It's no good, we won't be able to get away.'

Filofey, clearly scared, whoahed the horses, who came to a stop immediately, as if glad of a chance for a rest.

Good Lord! Those little bells were right behind us now, really screeching away. The cart was clanking and clattering, people were whistling, shouting and singing, while their horses were snorting and pounding the earth with their hooves.

They'd caught us up!

'We're up the cree-e-eek now!' whispered Filofey, dragging the words out. Clicking his tongue, he hesitantly urged his horses to get moving again. But at that very moment something suddenly seemed to break loose and then there was a roar and a crash, and an enormous, very broad and low-hung cart, harnessed to three muscular horses, suddenly swept past us like a whirlwind, careered on a little way ahead and then slowed to a walking pace, blocking our way.

'That's what robbers always do,' whispered Filofey.

I have to admit that I broke out into a cold sweat. I began to stare into the murky, vapour-ridden moonlight. In the cart just ahead of us were half a dozen men, sitting or lying with heavy peasants' coats over their shoulders. Two of them were bareheaded; jackboots covering powerful legs were dangling over the side of the cart, arms were flailing up and down for no apparent reason, and their bodies were all swaying about. No doubt about it: they were drunk. Some of them were bawling out whatever came into their heads; one was letting out some very clear and deafening whistles; another was blaspheming. Ensconced in the coachman's seat was a giant of a man in a sheepskin jacket. They were going at a walking pace and appearing to take no notice of us at all.

What were we to do? There was nothing for it but to trundle along after them, also at a walking pace.

In this manner we covered about two hundred yards. The wait was excruciating. There could be no question of trying to escape or of putting up any resistance. There were six of them, and I didn't even have a stick. If we turned round and went back they would catch us up right away. I remembered a line from a poem by Zhukovsky,[2] about the murder of Field Marshal Kamensky:

The filthy axe of a highway robber . . .

And if they haven't got an axe they'll strangle us with a dirty rope and throw us into the ditch where we'll be wheezing and writhing like hares in a trap.

Yes, things were looking bad . . .

And there they were, still plodding on at a walking pace and not paying us the slightest attention.

'Filofey,' I whispered. 'See if you can get past them, there's enough room on the right.'

Filofey had a go. He veered over to the right, but the men ahead of us immediately did exactly the same. It was impossible to overtake them. Filofey made another attempt. He swung over to the left. Again, they didn't let him move ahead of the cart. They even burst out laughing. They clearly weren't going to let us pass.

'Real 'ighway robbers,' Filofey whispered to me over his shoulder.

'But what are they waiting for?' I asked, also in a whisper.

'A bit further on, where the road dips, there's a stream . . . and a bridge. That's where they'll get us. They like bridges. We're done for, Mister,' he went on with a sigh. 'They're not going to let us off alive now. They've got to cover up their tracks. There's just one thing makes me sad, Mister. It's me 'orses. Me brothers'll never see them again.'

I would have been surprised that Filofey should be worrying about his horses at a moment like this, except that, I have to admit, it wasn't really him I was thinking about. 'Are they really going to kill me?' I kept on thinking to myself. 'Why? After all, I'll give them everything they want anyway.'

But the bridge was getting closer and closer. You could see it more and more clearly.

Suddenly there was a shrill whooping, the troika ahead of us rushed forward, almost leaving the ground, and when it got to the bridge it stopped dead in its tracks, a bit to one side of the road. My heart sank into my boots.

'Well, Filofey, my friend,' I said, 'you and I are going to meet our maker. Forgive me for cutting short your life.'

'It's not your fault, Mister! What will be, will be! Well, Shaggy, me dearie,' said Filofey, turning to the shaft-horse, 'forward march, brother! 'Elp us out for the last time! Nothing for it . . . Oh Lord, have mercy on us!'

And he ordered the horses to trot.

Now, as we approached the bridge and the motionless, threatening cart, everything, as though by design, went completely quiet. Not a single sound! Just like a pike or a hawk or any predator when its prey is close. Now we were almost level with the cart, and the giant in the sheepskin jacket suddenly jumped down and was coming straight towards us.

Not a word did he say to Filofey, who nonetheless immediately pulled on the reins, and we came to a halt.

The giant placed his hands on the side of the wagon, inserted his hairy head, smirked and said, in a quiet, smooth voice, with a factory worker's drawl: 'Good Sir, we're on our way home from a festive gathering, a wedding feast. We've sort of married off our hero and laid him out to rest. All the lads here are young daredevils, they drank the place dry and now they've nothing to help them sober up come the morning after. Might you not find it within yourself, sir, to be so compassionate and generous as to spare a mere trifle so that they can each purchase a little hair of the dog that bit them? We would offer a toast to the health of your worship, sir. But should you find it impossible to offer us any of your charity, well, then you'll have only yourself to blame!'

'What's all this?' I wondered. 'Is he just taunting and mocking us?'

The giant stayed put, his head lowered. Just then the moon came out of the mist and lit up his face. It was grimacing, this face – both eyes and lips. But there was no sign of menace, he just looked very much on his guard. And the teeth were so large and white.

'Glad to oblige. Here you are,' I said hastily, getting my purse out of my pocket and extracting a couple of silver roubles (at that time silver coins still hadn't gone out of circulation in Russia). 'Here you are, if that will suffice.'

'Deeply grateful!' bawled out the giant, like a soldier on parade, and in a flash his thick fingers pounced – not on the purse, just on the two roubles. 'Deeply grateful!' He shook back his hair and ran back to the cart.

'Listen, lads!' he shouted. 'This worthy gentleman who happened to be passing by has spared two whole roubles for us!' They all suddenly started to roar with laughter, and the giant ensconced himself again on the driving seat.

'And the very best of good luck to you!'

And without further ado, they were off. The horses raced ahead and the cart thundered on up the hill, reappeared for a moment against the dark line dividing earth and sky, then dropped out of sight and was gone.

And even the knocking and the shouting and the little bells could no longer be heard.

The silence of the grave.

It took some time for me and Filofey to regain our wits.

'Phew, there's a joker for you!' said Filofey at last, taking off his hat and starting to cross himself. 'A real joker,' he added, and turned round to face me, glowing with joy. 'And 'e must be a good man too, I really think so. Gee-up, me dearies! Step lively! You'll be all right! We'll all be all right! 'E's the one 'oo wouldn't let us pass, yer know. 'E's the one 'oo was driving the horses. What a joker that feller is! Gee-up, gee-up! God be with us – with all of us!'

I said nothing, but my soul too was exulting. 'We'll be all right!' I repeated to myself and stretched out on the hay. 'We got off cheaply!' I even felt a bit ashamed that I had recalled that line by Zhukovsky. Suddenly a thought hit me.

'Filofey!'

'What?'

'Are you a married man?'

'Yep.'

'Any children?'

'Yep.'

'How come you didn't say a word about them? You felt sorry for the horses, but what about your wife and children?'

'Why'd I be sorry for my wife and children? They wouldn't 'ave fallen into the 'ands of thieves. But I was thinking of 'em all the time. And I'm thinking about 'em right now. And that's a fact.' Filofey fell silent. 'Maybe it's all because of them that the Lord God just had mercy on you and me.'

'But maybe they weren't highway robbers at all?'

''Ow can you tell? It's a mystery. You can't see into another man's soul. You know what they say: another man's soul is a riddle. It's always safer to go along with God. And my family . . . I'll always . . . Gee-up, me dearies, God be with you!'

It was almost dawn by the time we got to the outskirts of Tula. I was half-asleep and half-awake.

'Eh, Mister,' Filofey said suddenly. 'Take a look at that! There they are – at the tavern. And there's the cart.'

I looked up. Yes, there they were, along with their cart and their horses. And on the threshold of the public house suddenly appeared the unmistakable figure of the giant in his sheepskin jacket.

'Good sir!' he exclaimed, waving his cap. 'We're drinking our way through your kindly donation! And as for you, driver,' he added, shaking his head at Filofey, 'I dare say you just had the fright of your life, eh!'

'A real card, isn't he?' remarked Filofey, when the tavern was about forty paces behind us.

We finally made it to the centre of Tula. I got plenty of shot, took the chance to stock up on tea and liquor, and even bought a horse from the dealer. We set off on our journey back at noon. As we went past the place where we'd first heard the knocking, Filofey, who turned out, after having had something to drink in Tula, to be a very talkative sort of person – he was even telling me all kinds of cock and bull stories – well, as we went past that place, Filofey suddenly began to laugh.

'Do you remember, Mister, 'ow I kept on saying, "something's knocking . . . Knock, knock, knock!"?'

He struck the air several times with the back of his hand. He seemed to find this 'knock' word tremendously funny.

That same evening we got back to his village.

I told Yermolay about our adventure. As he was sober he didn't utter a word of sympathy and only hummed and hawed – whether approvingly or reproachfully I dare say he himself didn't know. But a couple of days later he told me with glee that on the very night when Filofey and I were going to Tula, and on that very same road, some merchant or other had been robbed and murdered. At first I couldn't believe this, but later I had no choice. The district police superintendent, who was hurrying to be in on the investigation, confirmed to me that it was true. Was this not the 'festive gathering' from which those fine lads were returning, and was this merchant not the 'hero' who, in the words of the giant joker, had been 'laid out to rest'? I stayed in Filofey's village for another five days or so. I got into the habit of saying, every time I met him, 'Well, anything knocking today?'

'Quite a card!' he replies each time, and starts to laugh himself.

First published in 1874
Translated by Martin Dewhirst

FYODOR MIKHAILOVICH
DOSTOYEVSKY (1821–81)

Dostoyevsky was born in Moscow. His pious mother died when he was sixteen and his father – a dedicated doctor, but a tyrant in his home and on his estate – was murdered by his own serfs when Dostoyevsky was eighteen. His first published work, Poor Folk *(1846), was an immediate success. In 1849, along with other members of the radical 'Petrashevsky Circle', Dostoyevsky was sentenced to death; this was commuted to penal servitude only after a mock execution intended, grotesquely, to teach the conspirators a lesson. Four years in a Siberian penal settlement and five years as a soldier in Semipalatinsk changed Dostoyevsky's view of human nature. Mankind's capacity for evil is so deep, he came to believe, that no merely political change can alter our lives; true change arises only from the transformation of the soul – which can be achieved only through Christ.*

Dostoyevsky married Mariya Isayeva in 1857, but she died in 1864, as did his brother Mikhail. In the following years he conducted an unhappy liaison with Apollinariya Suslova; burdened by debts, he turned to gambling. In 1867 he married Anna Snitkina, the stenographer to whom he had dictated The Gambler *in 1866. Their marriage was an unusually happy one, and Anna's importance to his work was enormous. According to the critic Donald Rayfield, 'Not only is so much of [Anna] reflected in the novels, every sentence was filtered through her. Anna Dostoyevskaya may appear to have collaborated simply as her husband's typist, but it was impossible for Dostoyevsky to write a word without wondering about her reaction to it.'[1]*

Dostoyevsky's journalism was anti-Semitic, anti-Western and reactionary. His greatness as a novelist, however, stems at least in part from his ability to give vivid and sympathetic expression to points of view opposed to his own; his socialists and atheists are as attractive, and come out with arguments as powerful, as the characters who express Dostoyevsky's views. Rayfield, in fact, has gone so far as to remark on the 'inexplicable phenomenon ... that Dostoyevsky's characters seem to think more deeply and coherently than he did himself.'[2] It was clearly in his novels that Dostoyevsky did his truest thinking.

Four of Dostoyevsky's greatest works – Notes from Underground, Crime and Punishment, The Gambler and The Idiot – were published between 1864 and 1869. 'Bobok' was published in 1873, after The Demons and before Dostoyevsky's last and greatest novel, The Brothers Karamazov. 'Bobok' encapsulates much that is central to Dostoyevsky: his bold humour, his capacity for self-parody, the way he delighted – in the words of the translator Richard Pevear – 'in the richness of spoken language, its playfulness, its happy mistakes, its revealing quirks and peculiarities'.[3] 'Bobok' was first published as one of Dostoyevsky's regular contributions to The Citizen, a weekly newspaper for which he was a joint editor from 1873 to 1876. The word bobok ('little bean') appears to be used simply as a nonsense word. It is possible, however, that Dostoyevsky may, in his characteristic way, be parodying an image of great importance to him and which he used as an epigraph to The Brothers Karamazov: 'Except a corn of wheat fall into the ground and die, it abideth alone: but if it die, it bringeth forth much fruit' (John 12:24 (Authorized Version)).

BOBOK

This time I am including 'Notes of a Certain Person'. It's not me; it's someone quite different. There is no need, I think, for any preface.

Notes of a Certain Person

Just the day before yesterday, Semyon Ardalyonovich said to me, 'Are you ever, Ivan Ivanych, going to be sober?'

A strange thing to ask. I don't take offence, I'm a quiet man; but, you see, they've made me out to be quite mad. An artist happened to paint a portrait of me: 'After all,' he says, 'you are a man of letters.' So I let him, and he exhibited it. Then I read, 'Go and look at this morbid, almost insane face.'

All right, maybe it's true, but still, why must they go and say it in print? Everything in print should be noble; here, on the other hand . . .

They might at least put it obliquely – isn't that what style's for? But no, no one wants to be oblique any more. Nowadays humour and good style are disappearing, and abuse is taken for wit. I don't take offence; I'm not such a man of letters as to lose my mind over all this. I wrote a story – it wasn't published. I wrote an article – it was rejected.

I took a lot of these articles to different editorial offices – they were all rejected. 'No salt in them,' I was told.

'What kind of salt are you after?' I ask. 'Attic salt?'[1]

He doesn't even understand me. Mostly I translate from French for booksellers. And I write advertisements for merchants: *A rarity! Finest quality tea from our own plantations.* For a panegyric to His Excellency the late Pyotr Matveyevich I got quite a sum. A bookseller commissioned me to put together *The Art of Pleasing Ladies.* I've done six little books like that in my life. I'd like to do a collection of Voltaire's bons mots, but I'm afraid they might seem insipid today. Who wants Voltaire now? These days we'd rather pick up a cudgel! We've knocked one another's last teeth out! Well, that's the entirety of my literary activity. Except I also send letters to editors free of charge, and with my full signature. I'm always giving admonitions and advice, criticizing and pointing out the correct course of action. Last week I sent one editor my fortieth letter in two years; I've paid four roubles in stamps alone. I've got a vile temper, that's what.

I think the artist painted me not for the sake of literature, but for the sake of the two symmetrical warts on my forehead: quite a phenomenon, he said. They've got no ideas, so they trade on phenomena. And my warts certainly came out well in that portrait – they're alive! This they call realism.

As for insanity, a lot of us were written off as madmen last year. And how stylishly: 'With such an original talent . . . and in the end it turns out . . . but then this should have been foreseen long ago.' It's all rather clever; yes, from a purely artistic point of view it even deserves praise. Now, however, those very *madmen* have turned out wiser than ever. And that's the way it goes – people here know how to pronounce a man mad all right, but they've yet to pronounce anyone wise.

The wisest person of all, the way I see it, is the one who calls himself a fool at least once a month – an unheard-of ability in this day and age. In the old days a fool understood at least once a year that he was a fool, but nowadays – not a hope! And nowadays everything's got so tangled you can't tell a fool and a wise man apart. This has been done on purpose.

I remember a Spanish witticism from two hundred and fifty years ago, when the French built their first madhouse: 'They've locked all their fools into a special building to prove how wise they are themselves.' Very to the point: you don't prove your own wisdom by locking someone else up in a madhouse. 'K.'s gone mad, so we've grown wise.' No, that doesn't follow.

But then, what the hell? And why all this fuss about my own mind? Grumbling and grumbling. Even my maidservant's sick of it. Yesterday a friend dropped by. 'Your style's changing,' he said, 'it's getting very choppy. You chop and you chop, then a parenthesis, then a parenthesis inside the parenthesis, then you stick in some other phrase in brackets, then it's back to your chopping . . .'

My friend's right. Something strange is happening to me. My character's changing, and my head aches. I'm starting to see and hear some very strange things. Not quite voices, but as if someone nearby were going, '*Bobok, bobok, bobok*!'

What is this *bobok*? I need to take my mind off things.

Going out to take my mind off things, I happened across a funeral. A distant relative. All the same, a collegiate councillor.[2] A widow, five daughters, all young girls. Think what it must cost just to keep them in shoes! The deceased used to provide for them, but now – just a wretched little pension. They'll be tightening their belts all right. Not that I ever used to get much of a welcome from them myself. And I wouldn't have gone along at all if it hadn't been a sort of special occasion. I followed him to the graveyard along with the rest of them; they kept their distance and looked at me haughtily. My uniform is in truth a bit shabby. It must have been twenty-five years since I was last in a graveyard; a lovely little place – I don't think!

First, the smell. About fifteen corpses had shown up. Palls of various prices. Even two catafalques: one for a general and one for some fine lady. A lot of mournful faces, a lot of pretend mourning, and a lot of outright gaiety. The clergy can't complain; it's a living. But there was one hell of an odour – not much of a place, really, to be in holy orders.

Afraid of my own impressionability, I glanced cautiously at the corpses' faces. There were some gentle expressions, some unpleasant ones. In general the smiles weren't so very nice, even quite the reverse. Horrible: like in dreams.

During the Mass I left the church for some air: it was rather a grey day, but dry. Cold too; but it was, after all, October. I had a little walk among the graves. There are various classes. Third class costs thirty roubles: respectable enough, and not too expensive. First and second are inside the church and under the porch; for them, you have to pay through the nose. This time there were around half a dozen people being buried third class, among them the General and the fine lady.

I peeked into the open graves – horrible! Water – and not just any

old water! It was completely green and ... well, never mind! The
gravedigger was continually bailing it out with a scoop. While the
service continued, I went for a walk outside the gate. By the gate
there's an almshouse, and a little further on – a restaurant. Quite a
decent little restaurant, not bad at all; you can have a bite to eat, and
something with it. There was quite a crowd there, mourners too. I saw
a lot of merriment and sincere animation. I had something to eat, and
a drink.

Then, with my own hands, I helped carry the coffin from the church
to the grave. What makes these corpses so damned heavy in their
coffins? I've heard say it's because of some kind of inertia, that the
body somehow loses control over itself. Or some such nonsense that
flies in the face of both common sense and the laws of mechanics.
I don't like it when people with only a general education start holding
forth on specialist questions; in this country it happens all the time.
Civilians love to pronounce on military matters, even ones that could
only be decided by a field marshal, while trained engineers prefer to
discuss philosophy and political economy.

I didn't go to the wake. I have my pride; and if I'm received only on
the most special occasions, then why should I drag myself along to
one of their dinners? So what if it's just after a funeral? The only thing
I don't understand is why I stayed behind at the graveyard; I sat on a
tombstone and, in an appropriate manner, became lost in thought.

I began with the Moscow Exhibition and ended up thinking, in the
most general of ways, about the theme of astonishment. Here's the
conclusion I reached: 'Being astonished at everything is, of course,
stupid, while not being astonished at anything is a great deal more
becoming and is for some reason seen as good form. But I doubt if
this is so in reality. To my mind, being astonished at nothing is a great
deal more stupid than being astonished at everything. And moreover,
to be astonished at nothing is almost the same as to feel respect for
nothing. And a stupid man is incapable of respect.'

'What I wish, more than anything, is to feel respect. I *yearn* to feel
respect,' a friend of mine said to me the other day.

He yearns to feel respect! 'Good God!' I thought. 'What would
happen to you today if you dared publish that?'

At this point I sank into oblivion. I don't like reading inscriptions
on tombstones: they're eternally one and the same. Beside me, on the
stone, lay a half-eaten sandwich; it looked stupid and out of place.
I threw it on to the ground, since it wasn't bread but merely a sandwich.
Anyway, what's sinful, I think, isn't throwing crumbs on to the ground,
but throwing them on to the floor. Look it up in Suvorin's Almanac.[3]

I suppose I must have sat there a long time, maybe even too long; that is, I even lay down on a long stone shaped like a marble coffin. And how did it happen that I suddenly began to hear one thing after another? At first I paid no attention and adopted an attitude of contempt. But nevertheless, the conversation continued. I listened: the sounds were muffled, as if coming from mouths covered with pillows; all the same, they were distinct, and they seemed to be from close by. I came to, sat up, and began to listen intently.

'It just isn't possible, Your Excellency. You called hearts, I'm your partner, and all of a sudden you have seven diamonds. We should have agreed on diamonds beforehand.'

'What do you mean – play from memory? Where's the fun in that?'

'It's impossible, Your Excellency, without a guarantee it's quite impossible. There absolutely must be a dummy and a blind open.'

'Well, you won't find any dummies here.'

What devil-may-care words! Strange, unexpected. One voice that was weighty and dignified; the other as if slightly sweetened. I wouldn't have believed it if I hadn't heard it with my own ears. I didn't appear to be at a wake. Yet how could they be playing card games here – and was this really a general? That the voices were coming from under the gravestones there was no possible doubt. I bent down and read the inscription on the memorial:

Here rests the body of Major-General Pervoyedov[4] ... Knight of the Orders of This and of That. Hm ... Died in August of the year ... age of fifty-seven ... Rest, beloved dust, until the joyful morning!

So, damn it, a real general! The neighbouring grave, where the ingratiating voice came from, was still without a headstone; there was just a slab on the ground: a newcomer, no doubt. A court councillor[5] by his voice.

'Oh-oh-oh-oh!' came an entirely new voice, from an absolutely fresh little grave about a dozen yards away from the General's place – the voice of a man, a common voice, but softened by a touch of sanctimoniousness. 'Oh-oh-oh-oh!'

'There he is, hiccuping again!' came the fastidious, haughty voice of an irritable lady apparently from high society. 'What torment to be next to this shopkeeper!'

'I didn't hiccup in the least, nor have I even partaken of food. It's just my nature, that's all. Anyway, dear lady, if you can't get any peace here, it's because of your own whims and caprices.'

'But why did you have to come and lie here?'

'I was laid here, I was laid here by my spouse and my little children. I didn't come and recline here myself. The mystery of death! And I wouldn't have chosen to lie down beside you for anything, no, no matter what they paid me. But I've paid the price, yes, it was my own capital I laid by so I could lie here. Yes, that's something we can always do – pay up for a little third-class grave.'

'Did you make a pile by short-changing people?'

'We could hardly have short-changed you. We haven't had a kopek from you, by my reckoning, since January. You've run up quite a nice little bill at the shop.'

'Well, that really is stupid. Trying to collect debts where we are now, in my view, is very stupid indeed! Go upstairs and ask my niece. She's my heir.'

'There's no one I can ask now, and nowhere I can go now. We have both reached the end now, and before the judgement seat of the Lord we stand equal in our trespasses.'

'In our trespasses!' the deceased lady scornfully repeated his words. 'Don't you dare speak another word to me!'

'Oh-oh-oh-oh!'

'A shopkeeper does, you see, obey a lady, Your Excellency.'

'And why wouldn't he obey her?'

'Well, Your Excellency, there is, as is generally recognized, a new order here.'

'What sort of new order?'

'Well, Your Excellency, we are, so to speak, all dead.'

'Ah, yes! All the same, order . . .'

Very obliged to you, yes indeed! A real comfort you've all been to me! If things are this bad down below, why should we expect anything better up above? Quite a to-do, yes indeed! I went on listening, however, even if it was with unbounded indignation.

'No. I could live a little! No . . . I, you know . . . I could live a little!' All of a sudden there was a new voice, from somewhere between the General and the irritable lady.

'Listen, Your Excellency, there's our friend – harping away again on his usual theme. Not a word for three days on end, and then, all of a sudden: "I could live a little! No. I could live a little!" And with such, you know, gusto, tee-hee!'

'And such frivolity.'

'He's upset, Your Excellency, and then, you know, he's falling asleep, he really is falling asleep now. He's been lying here ever since April – and all of a sudden: "I could live a little!"'

'It is rather boring, though,' observed His Excellency.

'It is indeed, Your Excellency. What do you think – shall we have a bit of fun with Avdotya Ignatyevna again, tee-hee?'

'No, I beg you, anything but that. I can't stand that quarrelsome bitch.'

'And I, for my part, cannot stand either of you,' the woman retorted with disgust. 'Both of you are utterly boring and quite unable to talk about anything true and ideal. And as for you, Your Excellency, please don't go putting on airs – I can tell a little story about you, how one morning a footman swept you out with his broom from under a certain married lady's bed.'

'Foul creature!' the General muttered through his teeth.

'Avdotya Ignatyevna, dearie,' the shopkeeper suddenly piped up again. 'Dear lady, let bygones be bygones and tell me what's happening: are these the torments we meet after death, or is this something different?'

'Oh, there he goes again. I expected as much. I can smell the odour he gives off – he must be tossing and turning.'

'I'm not tossing and turning, dearie, and I have no particular odour since I have preserved myself in all the fullness of my body, while you, dear lady, really have begun to turn. The odour truly is unbearable, even by the standards of this place. I have remained silent only out of politeness.'

'Filthy slanderer! Stinking away himself – and he blames it on me!'

'Oh-oh-oh-oh! If only my fortieth day[6] would come soon! I should hear their tearful voices above me, the wailing of my spouse and my children's quiet weeping.'

'A fine thing he's found to weep about: they'll just stuff their faces and then they'll be off back home. Oh, if only someone new would wake up!'

'Avdotya Ignatyevna,' said the obsequious court councillor. 'Just be a little bit patient – it won't be long till the new lot start talking.'

'Are there any young men?'

'Yes, Avdotya Ignatyevna. Even some very young men.'

'Just the thing!'

'Oh, haven't the new lot started yet?' enquired His Excellency.

'Even the day-before-yesterday's lot have still to wake up. You know very well, Your Excellency, sometimes they stay silent for a whole week. It's a good thing a whole new batch has been brought in at once – yesterday, the day before yesterday, and now today! Otherwise almost everyone within twenty-five yards has been here nearly a year.'

'Yes, it will be interesting.'

'Today, Your Excellency, they buried Full Privy Councillor[7] Tarasevich. I could tell by the voices. His nephew's an acquaintance of
mine, he was helping to lower the coffin.'

'Hm, where is he?'

'About five yards away from you, Your Excellency, to the left.
Almost at your feet, sir. You should really make his acquaintance,
Your Excellency.'

'Hm, no . . . I mean, I can hardly make the first – '

'But he'll make the first move himself, Your Excellency. He'll even
be flattered. Leave it to me, Your Excellency, and I'll – '

'Ah, ah . . . ah, what on earth's happening to me?' groaned some
frightened, brand new little voice.

'Someone new, Your Excellency, someone brand new, and so soon!
Sometimes they stay silent for a whole week.'

'Ah, I think it's a young man,' squealed Avdotya Ignatyevna.

'I . . . I . . . I . . . from complications, and so sudden!' the youth
started to babble again. 'Schultz says to me, only the day before, "You
have complications" – and then all of a sudden, towards morning, I'm
finished. Ah! Ah!'

'Well, there's nothing for it, young man,' the General observed
graciously, evidently glad of the new arrival, 'you must take comfort!
Welcome to our, so to speak, Valley of Jehoshaphat.[8] We're good
people, you'll get to know us and like us. Major General Vasily
Vasilyevich Pervoyedov, at your service.'

'Ah, no! No, no, I just can't! I was under Schultz. I developed
complications, you see. First it was my chest, and coughing, then
I caught a cold: my chest, and influenza . . . then all of a sudden and
quite unexpectedly . . . above all, quite unexpectedly – '

'You say it was your chest first of all?' the court councillor gently
interrupted, as if wishing to encourage the newcomer.

'Yes, my chest and phlegm, then all of a sudden there was no more
phlegm, and my chest – and I can't breathe . . . and you know . . .'

'I know, I know. But if it was your chest, you should really have
gone to Eck, not to Schultz.'

'Well, you know, I kept meaning to go to Botkin . . . and then, all
of a sudden . . .'

'But Botkin really stings you,' remarked the General.

'No-o, he's not like that at all. I've heard that he's ever so attentive
and that he gives you a complete prognosis.'

'His Excellency was referring to his fees,' the court councillor corrected him.

'Oh, come now, only three roubles, and his examinations are so . . .

and his prescriptions . . . and I really wanted to see him, because I'd
been told . . . Well, gentlemen, what do you think: should I go to Eck
or to Botkin?'

'What? Where?' the General's corpse heaved with good-natured
laughter. The court councillor accompanied him, in a falsetto.

'My dear boy, my dear delightful boy, how I love you!' Avdotya
Ignatyevna squealed ecstatically. 'Oh, if only they'd laid someone like
him next to me!'

No, this is more than I can tolerate! So this is the contemporary
corpse! Still, I must listen a bit more and not jump to conclusions. As
for this snivelling new arrival, I remember him in his coffin only a
moment ago: the expression of a terrified chicken, the most repulsive
expression in the world! What next, though?

But next such a hullabaloo broke out that I have been unable to retain
it all in my memory. This was because a great number of them woke
up all at once. A civil servant, with the rank of state councillor,[9] began
there and then, without further ado, to talk to the General about a
project for a new subcommittee in the Ministry of —— Affairs and a
probable transfer of personnel in connection with this subcommittee
– all of which the General found most entertaining. I too, I admit,
learned a great deal that was new, and I marvelled at the paths through
which, in this capital of ours, administrative news can sometimes be
learned. Then some engineer half woke up, but for a long time he
went on muttering such complete nonsense that our lot didn't bother
with him at all and simply left him to it. Finally the distinguished lady
who had been brought in that morning under a catafalque showed
signs of sepulchral animation. Lebezyatnikov[10] (for that turned out to
be the name of the fawning court councillor, the one I disliked so
much and who was lying beside General Pervoyedov) really got quite
agitated, astonished that everyone was waking up so quickly this time.
I must admit I was astonished too; but then some of them had already
been lying there for all of two days – one very young girl, for example,
about sixteen years old, who kept on giggling . . . vilely and lasciviously
giggling.

'Your Excellency, Privy Councillor Tarasevich is awakening,'
announced Lebezyatnikov with great haste.

'Eh? What?' mumbled the Privy Councillor who had so suddenly
woken up. He had a fastidious, lisping voice that sounded both
capricious and imperious. I listened with curiosity, for I had recently
heard something about this Tarasevich, something suggestive and
alarming to the highest degree.

'It's me, Your Excellency. So far, it's just me, sir.'

'What is your request and how can I oblige you?'

'I was merely inquiring after Your Excellency's health. Not being used to it here, sir, everyone feels a little cramped when they first . . . General Pervoyedov would like to have the honour of making Your Excellency's acquaintance, and he hopes . . .'

'Never heard of him.'

'But surely, Your Excellency – General Pervoyedov, Vasily Vasilyevich . . .'

'Are you General Pervoyedov?'

'No, Your Excellency, I am only merely Court Councillor Lebezyatnikov, at your service, whereas General Pervoyedov . . .'

'Stuff and nonsense! I beg you to leave me in peace.'

'Leave him alone,' said General Pervoyedov with dignity, finally putting a stop to the disgusting haste of this graveyard flunkey.

'He still hasn't woken up, Your Excellency. You must bear that in mind, sir. It's because he's not used to it, sir. Once he's awake, he'll behave quite differently, sir.'

'Leave him alone,' the General repeated.

'Vasily Vasilyevich! Hey, Your Excellency!' a new voice called out loudly and unabashedly from just beside Avdotya Ignatyevna; it was an insolent, aristocratic voice, with fashionably languid articulation and a cheeky drawl. 'I've been observing you all for the last two hours. Yes, I've been lying here three days now. Remember me, Vasily Vasilyevich? Klinevich. We used to meet at the Volokonskys, where, goodness knows why, you too were received.'

'What! Count Pyotr Petrovich . . . but surely you can't . . . and so young . . . How sorry I am!'

'I'm sorry myself, only it's all the same to me now, and I want to make the most of wherever I am. And I'm not Count but Baron, just a mere baron. We're just mangy little barons – and how we came to be barons, I don't know, and I don't give a damn. I'm just a scoundrel, from the pseudo-beau monde, with a reputation for being a "charming scapegrace". My father was some kind of minor general and my mother was once received *en haut lieu*.[11] Last year Siffel the Jew and I forged fifty thousand worth of counterfeit bank notes, but then I informed on him and Yulka Charpentier de Lusignan[12] took all the money with her to Bordeaux. And just imagine, I was already well and truly betrothed – to the Shchevalevsky girl, three months short of sixteen, still at her boarding school, and with a dowry of around ninety thousand. Avdotya Ignatyevna, do you remember how you seduced me about fifteen years ago, when I was just a fourteen-year-old page?'

'So it's you, you scoundrel! Well, at least God's sent *you* to us now. Without you it's been –'

'You were wrong to blame the bad smell on your tradesman neighbour. I just kept quiet and laughed to myself. It's me – I had to be buried in a nailed-down coffin.'

'How loathsome you are! But I'm glad all the same. You can't imagine, Klinevich, you simply can't imagine the absence of life and wit down here.'

'Quite so, quite so, and it's my intention to introduce something rather novel. Your Excellency – no, not you, Pervoyedov – Your Excellency, the other one, Mister Tarasevich, the privy councillor! Answer me! It's Klinevich. It's me who used to take you to Mademoiselle Furie during Lent. Can you hear me?'

'I can hear you, Klinevich, and I'm very glad, and believe me –'

'No, I don't believe a single word – and I don't give a damn. I'd simply love to kiss you, my dear old man, but thank God I can't. Do you know, gentlemen, what this *grand-père* got up to? He died three or four days ago and – can you imagine it? – he left the fund he administered short of no less than four hundred thousand. It was a fund for widows and orphans and for some reason he ran it all on his own, and the books ended up not being audited for nearly eight years. I can well imagine all the long faces now, and the names he's been called. A voluptuous thought, isn't it? All last year I kept wondering how a nasty old seventy year old with gout and arthritis could still have so much strength left for debauchery – and now I know! Those widows and orphans – the mere thought of them must have been enough to inflame his ardour! I knew about it for some time, I was the only one, Charpentier told me, and as soon as I found out, it was in Holy Week, I went and said to him, in the friendliest of tones, "Give me twenty-five thousand – or you'll be audited tomorrow." Well, just imagine, he only had around thirteen thousand just then, so it seems he chose the right time to die. *Grand-père, grand-père*, can you hear me?'

'*Cher* Klinevich, I agree with you entirely, and really there was no need for you to . . . go into such detail. There is so much suffering and torment in life, and so little recompense. I wished finally to find peace and, as far as I can see, here too I can hope to make the most of –'

'I'll bet he's already sniffed out Katiche[13] Berestova.'

'Katiche? What Katiche?' the old man's voice quavered lasciviously.

'What Katiche, eh? Well, she's over to the left, five yards from me, and ten from you. This is her fifth day here, and if you knew, *grand-père*, what a little bitch she is. From a good family, well educated and

– a fiend, a fiend to the *n*th degree! I never showed her to anyone up above, I was the only one who knew. Katiche, say something for yourself!'

'Hee, hee, hee!' came the cracked sound of the voice of a little girl, but in it was something as sharp as the prick of a needle. 'Hee-hee-hee.'

'Is . . . she . . . blonde?' came the three-note staccato of *grand-père*'s babyish voice.

'Hee-hee-hee!'

'I have . . . I have for a long time,' the old man began breathlessly, in his babyish voice, 'cherished the dream of a little blonde, around fifteen years old, and in exactly such surroundings as these.'

'You monster!' exclaimed Avdotya Ignatyevna.

'That'll do!' said Klinevich. 'I can see we have first-rate material here. Soon we'll have our lives arranged in the best possible way. The main thing is to have a good time – but how much time is there left? Hey, you from some Ministry or other, Lebezyatnikov – isn't that what I heard someone call you?'

'Lebezyatnikov, Court Councillor, Semyon Yevseyich, at your service, and with the very, very greatest of pleasure!'

'I don't give a damn about your pleasure, but you seem to have some idea of what's what round here. First of all, tell me (I've been wondering about this since yesterday) how is it we can talk here? After all, we're dead, yet we're talking; we seem to move, yet we're not moving any more than we're talking. What's going on?'

'If you so wish, Baron, Platon Nikolayevich could explain this to you better than I can.'

'Who's Platon Nikolayevich? Don't mumble – get to the point.'

'Platon Nikolayevich, our local home-grown philosopher and Master of Sciences. He's published several little books of philosophy, but he's been fast asleep for three months now and it's impossible to shake him awake. Once a week he mutters a few words that have nothing to do with anything.'

'Get to the point!'

'He explains it all in the very simplest way: namely, that we were wrong, while we were still alive, to take our death up above for death. Here the body seems to come to life once again, the remnants of life concentrate together, but only in our consciousness. It's as if – I don't know how best to put it – life keeps going out of inertia. Everything is concentrated – in his view – somewhere in our consciousness, and it all keeps going for another two or three months, sometimes even six months. There's one fellow here, for example, who's almost completely decomposed, but every six weeks or so he still mutters some little word,

something quite meaningless of course, about some kind of bean –
bobok, *bobok* – which means that in him too an imperceptible spark
of life still flickers.'

'How ridiculous. How is it then that I have no sense of smell, yet
can smell the stench?'

'That . . . heh, heh . . . Well, here our philosopher is all in a fog. On
the subject of the sense of smell he observed that the stench we smell
here is, so to say, a moral stench . . . heh, heh . . . a stench, as it were
of the soul, so that we should have time, during these two or three
months to reconsider . . . and that this, so to speak, is the final mercy
. . . Only I think, Baron, that this is just mystical raving, entirely
excusable in his position.'

'That'll do. I'm sure the rest is all nonsense too. The main thing is:
two or three months of life, and then – *bobok*. I propose we spend
these two months as enjoyably as possible, and that to this end we
should base our lives on different principles. Ladies and gentlemen!
I propose we should feel ashamed of nothing!'

'Oh yes, yes, let's be ashamed of nothing!' cried a number of voices,
and, surprisingly, there were even some quite new voices that must
have belonged to people who had newly awoken. An engineer, who
had by then fully come to, thundered his consent in a bass voice and
with especial eagerness. Little Katiche giggled gleefully.

'Oh, how I long to feel ashamed of nothing!' Avdotya Ignatyevna
exclaimed in rapture.

'Listen, if even Avdotya Ignatyevna wants to feel ashamed of
nothing . . .'

'No, no, no, Klinevich. Up there, whatever you may think, I still felt
ashamed, but here, I terribly, terribly want to feel ashamed of nothing.'

'As I understand it, Klinevich,' said the engineer in his bass voice,
'what you are proposing is that we arrange our, so to speak, life here
according to new and rational principles.'

'I don't give a damn about all that. We can wait for Kudeyarov –
he was brought in yesterday. When he wakes up, he'll explain everything to you. He's a real personality, a giant of a personality!
Tomorrow I think they'll be dragging in another scientist, probably a
certain officer, and – in three or four days if I'm not mistaken – some
newspaper columnist, probably along with his editor. To hell with
them, though! We shall have a little group of our own and everything
will be arranged perfectly. Meanwhile, though, I want there to be no
lying. That's what I want, because that's what matters most of all. It's
impossible to live on earth and not lie, because living and lying are
synonymous, but here, just for the fun of it, we'll have no lying. Devil

take it, the grave does – like it or not – have some meaning! We can all tell our stories out loud and no longer feel ashamed of anything. Let me tell you about myself first of all. I was a lover of flesh, you know. Up above, all that was bound with rotten cords. Away with all cords and let us live these two months in the most shameless truth! Let's strip naked and bare ourselves!'

'Let's bare ourselves, let's bare ourselves!' they all shouted at the tops of their voices.

'I terribly, terribly want to bare myself!' squealed Avdotya Igna-tyevna.

'Oh . . . oh . . . oh, I can see it's going to be fun here. I don't want to go to Eck!'

'No. I could live a little. No, you know, I could live a little!'

'Hee, hee, hee,' giggled Katiche.

'The main thing is that no one can forbid us, and though I can see that Pervoyedov is angry, he still can't lay a hand on me. *Grand-père*, do you agree?'

'I completely, completely agree, and with the greatest of pleasure, provided Katiche will be the first to give us her au-to-bio-graphy.'

'I protest, I protest with all my might,' General Pervoyedov declared resolutely.

'Your Excellency!' said the vile Lebezyatnikov. Lowering his voice and babbling in excited haste, he went on, 'Your Excellency, it really is in our own interest to agree. There's that girl, you know . . . and, in short, well, you know . . .'

'The girl, I grant you that, but . . .'

'It's in our own interest, Your Excellency, I swear by God it is! Well, let's just see what happens, let's at least give it a try.'

'They won't let me rest even in the grave!'

'In the first place, General, you weren't resting but playing cards, and, in the second place, we don't give a damn about you anyway!' drawled Klinevich.

'My dear sir, I ask you not to forget yourself.'

'What? You can't lay a finger on me, but I can carry on teasing you as if you were Yulka's lapdog. And first of all, ladies and gentlemen, what kind of general can he be down here? He was a general up there, but here – pooh!'

'No, not pooh . . . Here too I –'

'Here you will rot away in your coffin, and all that will be left of you is six brass buttons.'

'Bravo, Klinevich! Ha-ha-ha!' bellowed more loud voices.

'I served my sovereign . . . I have a sword –'

'Your sword is only good for sticking mice, and anyway, you never even drew it.'

'That makes no difference, sir. I constituted a part of the whole.'

'There are all kinds of parts in a whole.'

'Bravo, Klinevich, bravo! Ha-ha-ha!'

'I don't understand what a sword is,' declared the engineer.

'We'll run from the Prussians like mice. They'll make mincemeat of us!'[14] shouted a distant voice I had not heard before, positively choking with glee.

'A sword, sir, means honour!' – and that shout was the last I heard from the General. This was followed by hubbub and uproar, by long and furious howls, and I could make out nothing but Avdotya Igna-tyevna's hysterically impatient squeals: 'Come on, come on now! Oh, when are we going to start feeling ashamed of nothing?'

'Oh-oh-oh! Verily my soul is passing through torments!' came the voice of the simple tradesman, and –

And here I sneezed. This happened suddenly and unintentionally, but its effect was remarkable: everything dissolved like a dream, there was just deathly silence. Yes, the silence was truly sepulchral. I don't think it was a matter of them feeling shame in my presence: they had resolved, after all, to feel ashamed of nothing! I waited another five minutes or so – and not a word, not a sound. Nor is it to be supposed that they were afraid of being reported to the police, for what could the police have done? I am forced to conclude that those under the ground must, after all, have some secret unknown to mortals and which they are careful to conceal from mortals.

'Well, my dears,' I thought, 'I shall visit you again.' And with that I left the graveyard.

No, this I cannot tolerate; truly I cannot! What disturbs me is not *bobok* (so this is what *bobok* amounts to!).

No – but debauchery in such a place, the debauching of last hopes, depravity of worn-out and rotting corpses, and not even sparing the last moments of consciousness. These moments are given to them, bestowed on them, and . . . And worst of all, worst of all – in such a place! No, this I cannot tolerate . . .

I'll visit other classes of grave, I'll listen everywhere. That's it, I must listen everywhere, and not just from the edge, so as to develop an understanding.

But I'll go back to this lot without fail. They promised their autobio-graphies and all kinds of funny stories. Pah! But I'll go back, I'll go without fail; it's a matter of conscience!

I'll take this to *The Citizen*. The portrait of one of their editors was also in the exhibition. Maybe he'll print it.

First published in 1873
Translated by Robert Chandler

LEV NIKOLAYEVICH TOLSTOY
(1828–1910)

Born near Tula into an aristocratic family, Tolstoy was orphaned in 1837. His next guardians, a grandmother and an aunt, also died. He and his four siblings were sent to another aunt in Kazan. Tolstoy studied at Kazan University, first in the Faculty of Oriental Languages, then in that of Law, but he failed to graduate. From 1852 to 1856 he served in the Army, seeing action in the Caucasus and the Crimea; he commanded an artillery battery during the siege of Sebastopol, and it was his Sebastopol Sketches (1855–6) that first made his name. He married Sofya Behrs in 1862, and from then lived mainly on his family estate in Yasnaya Polyana.

Tolstoy was as fiercely moralistic as he was sensual. His social conscience led him to establish a school for his peasants; the primer he wrote for it ran to twenty-eight editions in his lifetime. Between 1879 and 1881 he wrote A Confession, an account of a spiritual crisis that led him to renounce all of his previous writing as immoral. His wife's sceptical attitude towards his new piety exacerbated the already severe difficulties between them, and Tolstoy tried unsuccessfully to leave home in 1884. In 1885 he founded a publishing house, Posrednik ('The Intermediary'), which provided educational and morally improving literature at a price the poor could afford; three million books were sold in 1889 alone. After several attempts, Tolstoy gave up meat, alcohol and tobacco in 1888. Between 1891 and 1893 he organized famine relief in the province of Ryazan. The International Tolstoy Society was founded in 1900 to promote his ascetic and pacifist ideals. In 1901 the Orthodox Church (denounced by Tolstoy as having nothing to do with Christianity) excommunicated him. He died at Astapovo railway station, soon after leaving home on an undefined quest – or perhaps just to escape his increasingly unhappy marriage.

No one in Europe around the beginning of the twentieth century enjoyed greater moral and spiritual authority than Tolstoy. Maksim Gorky once joked that there could be no room for God and Tolstoy in one universe, since they would be like two bears in one den. Tolstoy's teachings influenced, among others, Mahatma Gandhi and the founders of the kibbutz movement.

Tolstoy's most famous novels, War and Peace (1865–9) and Anna Karenina (1875–7), are by no means his only important works. His early autobiographical trilogy Childhood, Boyhood, Youth has a unique charm. His novella The Death of Ivan Ilyich examines the wish to deny the reality of death. The Kreutzer Sonata, another short novel, constitutes a plea for absolute chastity. The long novel Resurrection proclaims the need for the rebirth both of the individual and of society. And Tolstoy's last major work of fiction, Hadji Murat, is a sympathetic portrait of a famous Chechen leader.

Tolstoy believed, at least after his spiritual crisis, that the function of art was to provide moral instruction. In What is Art? (1897) he picked out 'God Sees the Truth, but Waits' – an expanded version of a fable told by Platon Karatayev in the last pages of War and Peace – as one of only two examples of his own work that he still considered 'good art'. The tension between Tolstoy the artist and Tolstoy the moralist is embodied in this story's textual history. In what has long been considered the standard text, Aksyonov tells a white lie when questioned by the Governor, saying, 'I've seen nothing and I know nothing.' In 1885, however, Tolstoy's disciple Chertkov wrote to him to say that he was troubled by this: 'he is resorting to a deliberate lie in order to save his comrade. Moreover, this very act gives the impression of being the greatest deed of his life. But this act could remain such even if he were freed from deceit. Aksyonov could say that he did not dig the tunnel and remain silent about whether or not he knew who did.'[1] Tolstoy was evidently convinced by Chertkov's argument, and he rewrote Aksyonov's speech; it is this later version that I have translated.

GOD SEES THE TRUTH, BUT WAITS

In the city of Vladimir there lived a young merchant by the name of Aksyonov. He had two shops and a house of his own.

Aksyonov was a handsome fellow with light-brown curly hair; he was the life and soul of a party and he was fond of singing. As a young man he had drunk a lot, then got into brawls, but when he married he stopped drinking, except very occasionally.

One summer he was about to go to Nizhny Novgorod, to the fair.

As he began saying goodbye to his family, his wife said to him, 'Don't go today, Ivan Dmitrych, I've had a bad dream about you.'

Aksyonov laughed and said, 'Still afraid I'll go on a binge at the fair?'

'I don't know myself what I'm afraid of,' said his wife. 'All I know is that I've had a bad dream. I dreamt you'd just got back from the fair. You took off your hat – and your hair had turned grey.'

Aksyonov laughed. 'That means good luck. Just you wait – I'll sell all my goods and I'll come back with expensive gifts for you.'

He said goodbye to his family and set off.

When he was halfway there, he met a merchant he knew and the two of them put up at the same inn for the night. They had some tea together and then went to bed in adjoining rooms. Aksyonov didn't like sleeping late; he woke while it was still dark and, wanting to set off before it got hot, he woke his driver and told him to harness the horses. Then he settled up with the landlord, who lived in a small hut at the back, and set off.

After about twenty-five miles, he stopped at an inn to feed the horses. He rested for a while in the entrance room, then went out on to the porch to have something to eat and drink himself. He told them to heat up the samovar, got out his guitar and began to play.

Suddenly a troika with a bell drove into the yard. Out got an official, together with two soldiers. He went up to Aksyonov and asked him who he was and where he had come from. Aksyonov answered these questions and asked the official if he wouldn't like to drink some tea with him. But the official kept on with his questions: 'Where did you spend the night? Alone, or with a merchant? Did you see the merchant this morning? Why did you leave so early?'

Aksyonov wondered why he was being questioned like this. He recounted everything that had happened, then said, 'Why are you interrogating me as if I were a thief or a robber? I'm travelling on business, and you've no reason to question me like this.'

Then the official called the soldiers over and said to Aksyonov, 'I'm the district police captain and I am questioning you because the merchant you spent last night with has had his throat cut. We have to search you and your belongings.'

They went inside, took his trunk and his bag and began going through them. Suddenly the police captain took a knife out of the bag and shouted, 'Whose knife is this?'

The knife was covered in blood: Aksyonov felt frightened.

'Why is there blood on this knife?'

Aksyonov wanted to answer, but he couldn't get the words out. 'I . . . I don't know . . . I . . . the knife . . . I . . . it's not mine . . .'

Then the police captain said, 'The merchant was found in bed this morning with his throat cut. No one but you can have done this. The hut was locked from the inside, and there was no one else there. Now we've found a bloodstained knife in your bag, and anyway I can tell from the look on your face. Tell me how you killed him and how much money you stole.'

Aksyonov swore he had done nothing; he had not seen the merchant after having supper with him, he had eight thousand roubles of his own and the knife was not his. But his voice quavered, his face was pale and he was trembling all over from fear, as if he were guilty.

The police captain told his soldiers to arrest Aksyonov and put him on the cart. When he was flung on to the cart with his legs tied together, Aksyonov crossed himself and began to cry. His goods and money were confiscated and he was taken to the nearest town and put in prison. Enquiries were made about him in Vladimir, and all the merchants and other inhabitants of Vladimir attested that Aksyonov might have drunk and caroused when he was young, but that he was a good man. Soon the trial began; Aksyonov was charged with the murder of a merchant from Ryazan and the theft of twenty thousand roubles.

His wife was in despair; she didn't know what to believe. Her children were all little; she was still nursing the youngest. She took them with her and went to the town where her husband was in prison. At first she was not admitted but, after begging the officers in charge, she was taken in to his cell. When she saw him in prison clothes, in chains, locked up with criminals, she passed out, fell to the ground and only came back to her senses after a long time. Then she gathered her children around her, sat down beside him, said how things were at home and asked him to tell her what had happened. He told her everything. 'What can we do?' she said.

'We must appeal to the Tsar,' said Aksyonov. 'He can't let an innocent man perish!'

His wife said that she had already submitted a petition to the Tsar, but it had not been accepted. Aksyonov didn't say anything; he just bowed his head. Then his wife said, 'It was not for nothing I dreamt your hair had turned grey. Remember? Now you really have gone grey with grief. You shouldn't have left home that day.' Running her fingers through his hair, she went on, 'Vanya, dearest, tell the truth to your wife. Wasn't it you who did it?'

'So you suspect me too,' said Aksyonov. He hid his face in his hands and began to weep. Then a soldier came in and said it was time for his wife and children to leave. And Aksyonov said goodbye to his family for the last time.

After his wife had left, Aksyonov thought everything over. When he thought about how his wife had suspected him and asked him if he had killed the merchant, he said to himself, 'It seems no one but God can know the truth. It is to Him alone I must appeal, and from Him alone that I must expect mercy.' And Aksyonov gave up writing petitions and abandoned all hope; all he did was pray to God.

Aksyonov was sentenced to a flogging, followed by penal servitude. And so he was flogged with a knout and, when his wounds had healed, he was marched with a group of other convicts to Siberia.

For twenty-six years Aksyonov lived the life of a convict. The hair on his head became white as snow, and his beard grew long, thin and grey. His merriment vanished. He grew hunched and began to move more slowly; he spoke little, never laughed, but often prayed to God.

In prison Aksyonov learned to make boots. With the money he earned he bought *The Lives of the Saints* and, when it was light enough inside the prison, he read. On Sundays and feast days he went to the prison church, read the Epistle and sang in the choir – he still had a good voice. The authorities liked Aksyonov for his meekness and his fellow convicts respected him, calling him 'Grandfather' and 'a godly man'. When they wanted to petition the authorities, they always chose Aksyonov as their spokesman; and when they quarrelled with one another, they always called on him to adjudicate.

Aksyonov received no letters from home; he did not even know if his wife and children were still alive.

One day some new convicts were brought to the prison. In the evening the old convicts gathered round the new arrivals, asking each of them which town or village he was from and what he had been sentenced for. Looking down at the ground, Aksyonov sat on the bed-boards beside the newcomers and listened. A tall, strong-looking old man of about sixty, with a short grey beard, was explaining why he had been arrested.

'Well, brothers,' he said, 'I've ended up here for no reason at all. I took a horse that was tied to a sledge. I was arrested and accused of theft. I said I'd been in a hurry to get home and that I'd let the horse go. And that the coachman was a friend of mine – so everything was above board. "No," they said, "you're a thief." What I really did steal, and where, they never discovered. By rights I should have been sent here long ago, but I was never found out. And now I've been sent here for nothing. But I'm lying: I've been in Siberia before, though I didn't hang about long.'

'Where are you from?' someone asked.

'My family are small merchants from the city of Vladimir. My name's Makar, my father's name was Semyon.'

Aksyonov looked up and asked, 'Tell me, Semyonych, have you heard anything of the Aksyonov family? They're Vladimir merchants. Are they still living?'

'How could I not have heard of them? They're rich merchants – even though the father's in Siberia. Seems he's a sinner like us. And what about you, Granddad, what brought you here?'

Aksyonov did not like to speak of his misfortune. He sighed and said, 'Because of my sins I've been here for twenty-six years, doing forced labour.'

'What sins?' asked Makar Semyonov.

'Great sins,' Aksyonov replied, 'or I wouldn't still be here.' He did not want to say any more, but the other convicts recounted how it was that Aksyonov had ended up in Siberia. On the road, they said, someone had killed a merchant and hidden the knife in Aksyonov's bag. He had been unjustly sentenced.

When Makar Semyonov heard this, he looked at Aksyonov, slapped his hands on his knees and said, 'Who'd have believed it? Who'd ever have believed it? But you've grown old, Grandfather!'

The others asked what he was so surprised about and where he had seen Aksyonov before, but he just answered, 'Who'd have believed we'd end up meeting here?'

At this Aksyonov began to wonder if this man might not know who had killed the merchant. He asked, 'Have you heard about all this before, Semyonych? Or have you seen me somewhere before?'

'How could I not have heard about it? The world's full of stories. But it was all a long time ago. Whatever I heard, I've forgotten.'

'Maybe you heard who killed the merchant?' asked Aksyonov.

Makar Semyonov laughed and said, 'Must have been the man with the bag they found the knife in. If someone else really did put a knife in your bag – well, *no one's a thief till he's caught*. Anyway, how could a man put a knife in your bag when it was under your head? You'd have woken up!'

When Aksyonov heard this, he felt sure that this was the man who had killed the merchant. He got up and walked away. All that night Aksyonov lay awake. He fell into melancholy and began to see things in his mind's eye. He saw his wife saying goodbye to him before he set off on his last journey to the fair. He saw her as if she were there before him; he saw her face and her eyes, he heard her talking and laughing. Then he saw his children as they were then – very small, one in a little fur coat, the youngest at his mother's breast. And he remembered the man he had once been – young and merry. He remembered sitting on the porch of the inn where he had been arrested; he had been playing the guitar, without a care in the world. And he remembered the town square where he had been flogged, and the man with the knout, and the people watching, and his chains, and the other convicts, and his twenty-six years of prison life, and how he had grown old. And Aksyonov felt so sad he wanted to kill himself.

'And all because of *that* villain!' he said to himself. And he felt furious with Makar Semyonov: even if it was his own undoing, he had to revenge himself. He said prayers all night, but this did nothing to calm him. During the day he did not go near Makar Semyonov or even look at him.

Two weeks went by like this. Aksyonov couldn't sleep at night, and in the daytime he felt so wretched he didn't know what to do with himself.

One evening, as he was walking about the prison, he saw earth spilling out from somewhere beneath the bed-boards. He stopped to look. All of a sudden Makar Semyonov crept out and gave Aksyonov a frightened look. Aksyonov tried to walk on by, so he wouldn't see who it was, but Makar grabbed him by the hand and told him that he was digging a tunnel under the wall; he was taking the earth away in his boots, emptying the earth onto the ground when they were escorted to work in the morning. 'You just be quiet, old man,' he said, 'and I'll take you with me. But if you breathe a word, I'll be flogged – and I won't let you off lightly. I'll kill you.'

When Aksyonov realized it was his enemy, he trembled all over with rage, pulled his hand away and said, 'I've no need to escape, and you've no need to kill me. You killed me long ago. And as to whether or not I say what I've seen, that's as God wills.'

The next morning, when they'd escorted the convicts to work, the soldiers saw the earth that had been emptied onto the ground by Makar Semyonov. They searched the prison and found the hole. The Governor himself came and began questioning the prisoners: who had dug the hole? Everyone kept their mouths shut. Those who knew did not betray Makar Semyonov; they knew he'd be flogged almost to death. Then the Governor turned to Aksyonov, whom he knew to be a righteous man. 'You're an honest man,' he said. 'Tell me, before God: who did it?'

Makar Semyonov stood there as if this were a matter of no concern to him, looking at the Governor and not glancing at Aksyonov for even a moment. Aksyonov's lips and hands, however, were trembling, and for a long time he was unable to utter a word. 'Why should I protect him?' he was thinking. 'Why should I forgive the man who ruined my life? Let him pay for what I have suffered. But if I do tell, they'll flog the life out of him. And what if I'm wrong? Anyway, am I going to feel any better for it myself?'

'Well, old man?' the Governor said once again. 'Tell me the truth: who's been digging under the wall?'

Aksyonov glanced at Makar Semyonov and said, 'I cannot say, Your Excellency. God does not permit me to tell. And I will not. Do what you like with me; I am in your power.'

No matter how hard the Commandant struggled with him, Aksyonov said nothing more. And so they never found out who had dug the tunnel.

The following evening, as Aksyonov was dozing off, he heard someone draw near and then sit down by his feet. He looked into the darkness and recognized Makar. 'What do you want from me now?' he asked. 'What are you doing here?'

Makar Semyonov said nothing. Aksyonov raised himself up on one elbow and said, 'What do you want? Go away or I'll call the guard!'

Makar Semyonov bent over towards Aksyonov and whispered, 'Ivan Dmitrych, forgive me!'

'What for?' asked Aksyonov.

'I killed the merchant, and I hid the knife in your bag. I'd have killed you too, but there was a noise outside. I left the knife in your bag and climbed out of the window.'

Aksyonov was silent. He did not know what to say. Makar Semyonov got down off the bed-boards, knelt on the ground and said, 'Ivan Dmitrych, forgive me, forgive me for the love of God! I'll confess that I killed the merchant and you will be pardoned. You'll go back home.'

'Fine words,' said Aksyonov, 'but do you know what I've suffered? My wife is dead, my children have forgotten me. Where can I go now?'

Still on his knees, Makar Semyonov beat his head against the floor. 'Ivan Dmitrych,' he said, 'forgive me! The knout on my back was easier for me to bear than the sight of you now. And yet you had pity on me, you didn't tell. Forgive me, for the love of Christ! Forgive me, cursed wretch that I am!' And he began to sob.

When Aksyonov heard Makar Semyonov weeping, he began to weep too. 'God will forgive you,' he said. 'Maybe I myself am a hundred times worse than you are.' At this, he felt a weight off his heart. He stopped feeling homesick, he no longer wanted to leave the prison, and his only wish was to die.

Aksyonov told him not to say anything, but Makar Semyonov confessed to the murder. And by the time the order for his release came, Aksyonov had died.

First published in 1872
Translated by Robert Chandler

NIKOLAY SEMYONOVICH LESKOV
(1831–95)

Born in the province of Oryol, Leskov's ancestry was unusually hybrid. His mother was born to an impoverished gentleman who married a merchant's daughter. His father, though technically ennobled as a result of promotion in government service, came from a line of village priests; dismissed from his administrative post after a conflict with the provincial governor, he unsuccessfully farmed a small estate. There Nikolay Leskov grew up in close contact with the peasantry and much of his education was informal, although he attended a secondary school in Oryol for several years. All this combined to endow him with a broader knowledge of Russian society than any other writer of his time; he wrote that, since he had grown up among the common people, it was not for him 'either to place the peasants on a pedestal or to trample them beneath [his] feet'.[1] Aged sixteen, Leskov started work for the civil service in Oryol, moving to Kiev two years later. This was followed by three years in estate management for the firm of Scott (his uncle by marriage) & Wilkins; this entailed a vast amount of travel over the whole of European Russia.

In 1860 Leskov began his career as a professional writer, living briefly in Moscow and then in St Petersburg. Among the most important of his many works are Life of a Peasant Woman (1863); Lady Macbeth of Mtsensk (1865), later used by Shostakovich for the plot of his opera; the long novel Cathedral Folk (1872); and two more explorations of Russian spirituality, The Sealed Angel and The Enchanted Wanderer (both 1873). The Sealed Angel is one of the few adequate portrayals in Russian literature of the life of the Old Believers, the outlawed schismatics who rejected the seventeenth-century liturgical reforms and who, by the end of the nineteenth century, made up a fifth of the country's population.

No great Russian writer of the nineteenth century is so little known to the English-speaking reader today as Leskov. This is in part due to the variety of his novels, stories and journalism; literary historians tend to prefer writers who are easier to pigeon-hole. It is also because of the complexity of his language. For Leskov, according to Hugh McLean, 'language was not simply a medium of communication, but a potential art object in its own right, something to be played with, sculpted into interesting shapes'.[2] The language of many of his works moves between the colloquial, the folk-poetic and the pseudo-educated, and these shifts of register are difficult to reproduce in translation.

Even in Russia Leskov has been undervalued, under both the Tsarist and the Soviet regimes. During his lifetime he was more popular with the public than with the critics. His undoctrinaire liberalism offended both religious conservatives and radical socialists, while the latter also disapproved of his religious concerns. And he has suffered from the misfortune of being identified with his characters, many of whom are bigoted and xenophobic. This is especially absurd: Leskov was in fact unusually open to Western ideas. He was strongly influenced, for example, by British Low Church morality.

'The Steel Flea' is Leskov's most brilliant work. In his preface to his outstanding translation, William Edgerton writes:

> Underneath the deceptive gaiety of Leskov's prose there runs a caustic commentary on Russian social and political life. Its effect is all the more powerful because it is ironically placed in the mouth of a narrator who is a staunch supporter of things as they are. This so-called skaz manner, the device of telling a story through one of its characters and in his own peculiar language, is the most prominent feature of Leskov's storytelling technique. He almost always uses it ironically; and his malapropisms and other deformations of language reinforce his satire.
>
> Much of the delight that generations of Russian readers have found in 'The Steel Flea' arises from the fact that Leskov puts only a part of his verbal effects out in plain view. He hides many others in the bushes of innocent-looking prose or camouflages them to make them look so familiar that the unsuspecting reader may pass them by completely before he realizes that crafty old Leskov has put one over on him again.
>
> For the translator who ventures to turn 'The Steel Flea' into English it is not enough merely to find trite English equivalents for Leskov's malapropisms. He must also cultivate Leskov's subtlety. If his translation of the Russian verbal effects is so obvious that the reader becomes aware of them all on his first trip through the story, then the translator has failed to convey the full effect of Leskov's wily genius.[3]

THE STEEL FLEA

(The Tale of the Cross-Eyed, Left-Handed Gunsmith from Tula and the Steel Flea)

I

When Emperor Aleksandr the First had finished the Council of Vienna[1] he decided he would like to take a trip around Europe and look at the marvels in the different countries. He travelled through all the nations, and everywhere his friendliness always helped him get into the most intimidating conversations with all kinds of people, and everybody would amaze him with one thing or another and try to win him over to their side. But along with him was the Don Cossack Platov,[2] who didn't like all this persuasion; he hankered to get back to his farm, and he kept trying to talk the Emperor into going home. And if Platov noticed the Emperor getting really interested in something foreign, then just as soon as all the guides stopped talking for a minute, Platov would pop up and say this, that and the other, telling them ours at home was just as good, and one way or another he would get their minds onto something else.

The Englishmen knew this, and they thought up all kinds of shifty tricks for the Emperor's visit, so as to get him in their power with their outlandishness and get his mind off the Russians, and in a lot of cases they managed it, especially at their big meetings, where Platov couldn't say everything completely in French. But then he was not very much interested in that, since he was a married man and looked on all French conversations as trifles not worthy of serious imagination. And when the Englishmen started inviting the Emperor into all their store houses, gun works and soapy-rope factories, so as to show how much better they were than us in everything and then brag about it, Platov said to himself, 'Well, this has gone far enough. I've put up with it so far, but I can't take any more. Maybe I'll succeed and maybe I'll fail, but at least I won't go back on my own people.'

And he had no sooner said this to himself than the Emperor told him, 'Tomorrow you and I are going to look at their military museum. There they've got such natures of perfection that just as soon as you've seen them you'll agree that we Russians with our significance don't mean a thing.'

Platov said nothing in reply to the Emperor, but just stuck his humpbacked nose down into his shaggy felt overcoat and went to his room. He told his orderly to get a bottle of Caucasian grape vodka out of their travelling supplies. He gulped down a big glassful, said his prayers before the folding travelling icon, covered himself with his overcoat and started snoring such a time that none of the Englishmen in the whole house could get any sleep.

He thought, 'Wait until the morning light; it's always wiser than the night.'

2

The next day the Emperor and Platov went to the museums. The Emperor took none of his other Russians with him, because the carriage they gave him was only a two-sitter.

They came to a great big building, with an entrance beyond description, corridors beyond measure, and one room after another, until at last they came into the biggest hall of all, with tremendulous estuaries, and right in the middle, under a canoply, stood the Apollo Velvet Ear.[3]

The Emperor glanced around sideways at Platov to see what he was looking at and whether he was very much amazed; but Platov was walking along with his eyes looking down at the ground as if he didn't see anything, and he was only winding his moustaches into rings.

The Englishmen started at once to show off all sorts of marvels and explain how everything in them was fitted together with everything else for military circumstances. There were nautical whether-meters, gamblehair coats for the infantry and waterproof rein coats for the cavalry. The Emperor was glad to see all this, and he thought everything looked very good; but Platov held his impatience and said it all didn't mean a thing for him.

The Emperor said, 'How is that possible? How can you be so unfeeling? Doesn't anything at all impress you here?'

And Platov replied, 'Just one thing impresses me here: my Don River boys fought without all this and drove out old Bony Part.'

The Emperor said, 'That's just prejudunce.'

Platov answered, 'I don't know what to call it, but I ain't allowed to argue so I'll keep quiet.'

The Englishmen, seeing this exchange between the Emperor, at once took him up to the statue of Apollo Velvet Ear itself and took a Mortimer rifle out of one hand and a pistol out of the other.

'Here's the kind of production we've got,' they said, and they handed him the rifle.

The Emperor looked calmly at the Mortimer rifle, because he had some like it at home in his Summer Palace, and then they handed

him the pistol and said, 'This is a pistol of unknown and inimit-
able workmanship. Our admiral snatched it off the belt of a robber
chieftain at Candelabria.'

The Emperor fastened his eyes on the pistol and couldn't get enough
of looking at it.

He oh-ed and ah-ed something awful.

'Oh! Oh! Oh!' he says. 'What do you know about that! How is it
possible to do such fine work!' And he turned to Platov and said to
him in Russian: 'Now if only I had just one craftsman like that in
Russia I would be a very happy man; I'd be so proud I would make a
nobleman of him on the spot.'

At these words Platov stuck his right hand into his big wide trousers
and pulled out a gunsmith's screwdriver. The Englishmen said, 'This
won't come open,' but Platov, paying no attention to them, started
tinkering with the gunlock. He turned it once, he turned it twice – and
the gun opened up. Platov showed the Emperor the trigger, and right
there in the crook was a Russian inscription: *Ivan Moskvin in Tula
Town.*[4]

The Englishmen were amazed and nudged each other: 'Uh-oh!' they
said. 'We slipped up that time.'

But the Emperor said sadly to Platov, 'Why did you have to embarrass them so much? Let's go.'

They got into their two-sitter again and started off, and the Emperor
went to a ball that evening, but Platov downed a still bigger glass of
grape vodka and slept the sound sleep of the Cossacks.

He had been glad to put the Englishmen to rout and attract conten-
tion to the Tula gunsmith, but he had been put out as well: why did
the Emperor have to feel sorry for the Englishmen in a case like this?

'Why did the Emperor feel bad about it?' thought Platov. 'I can't
figure it out at all.' And in this consideration he got up twice, crossed
himself, and drank vodka until at last he forced himself into a sound
sleep.

At that same time the Englishmen were not asleep either, because
their heads were spinning, too. While the Emperor was having a good
time at the ball, they cooked up such a new marvel for him that they
completely knocked the imagination out of Platov.

3

The next day, when Platov reported to the Emperor to say good
morning, he told Platov, 'Have the two-sitter carriage hitched up, and
let's go to look at some more museums.'

Platov even made bold to ask the Emperor whether they hadn't looked at enough outlandish products, and wouldn't it be better to get ready to go back to Russia, but the Emperor said, 'No, I wish to see still other novelties here; they have boasted to me about how they make sugar of the very highest quality.'

They started off.

The Englishmen showed everything to the Emperor – just how many different highest qualities they had – and Platov looked and looked, and then suddenly he said, 'But won't you show us your factories where you make Molvo sugar?'

The Englishmen didn't know what 'Molvo'[5] was. They whispered back and forth to each other, winked back and forth to each other, and repeated to each other, 'Molvo, Molvo,' but they couldn't understand what kind of sugar that was that we made in our country, and they had to admit that they had all kinds of sugar – but no 'Molvo'.

Platov said, 'Well, then, you haven't got anything to brag about. Come to our country and we'll fill you full of tea with genuwine Molvo sugar from Bobrinsky's factory.'[6]

But the Emperor tugged him by the sleeve and said quietly: 'Now, please don't go and spoil my politics.'

Then the Englishmen invited the Emperor to their very latest museum, where they had brought together mineral stones and nymphusorias from all over the world, beginning with the most enormous Egyptian hobble lists and coming down to the hide-bound flea, which you can't see with your eyes but can only feel when he bites you between your hide and your body.

The Emperor set out.

They looked at the hobble lists and all kinds of stuffed animals, and then came out and Platov thought to himself, 'There now, thank the Lord, everything is turning out all right: the Emperor hasn't marvelled at anything.'

But as soon as they got to the very last room, there were workmen standing around in everyday jackets and aprons holding a tray that had nothing on it.

Then the Emperor really did marvel because they offered him an empty tray.

'What does this mean?' he asked, and the English craftsmen replied, 'This is our humble offering to your Highness.'

'But what *is* it?'

'Well,' they said, 'does your Highness kindly see this little speck?'

The Emperor took a look and saw that there really was the tiniest little speck lying on the tray.

The workmen said, 'Be so kind as to spit on your finger and pick it up and put it on your hand.'

'What good is that speck to me?'

'That,' they answered, 'is not a speck but a nymphusoria.'

'Is it alive?'

'No, sir,' they answered, 'it's not alive. We made it in the shape of a flea out of pure English steel, and inside it is a motor and a spring. Be so kind as to wind it up with the key: then it will do a little *dansez*.'

The Emperor got curious and asked, 'But where is the key?'

The Englishmen replied, 'Here is the key, right in front of your eyes.'

'Then why can't I see it?' asked the Emperor.

'Because,' they said, 'you have to blow it up in a nitroscope.'

A nitroscope was brought in, and the Emperor saw that a little key really was lying on the tray beside the flea.

'Be so kind as to take it in your hand,' they said. 'There's a hole in its belly for the key, and the key will take seven turns. Then it will start its *dansez*.'

The Emperor could barely pick up the key and barely hold it in his fingers. He took hold of the flea with his other hand and hadn't hardly stuck the key in before he felt the whiskers move, and then the legs started working, and at last it suddenly jumped up and in one bound did a straight *dansez* and two fairiations to one side and then to the other, and danced like that through a whole cod drill in three fairiations.

The Emperor gave orders on the spot to give a million to the Englishmen in any kind of money they wanted – either in silver five-kopek coins, if they wished, or else in small bills.

The Englishmen asked for it in silver, because they couldn't make heads or tails out of paper money, and then right off they pulled another one of their shifty tricks: they handed over the flea as a gift, but they hadn't brought any case for it. Without a case you couldn't keep either the flea or the key, because they would get lost and thrown out with the trash. But they had made a case out of a diamond in the shape of a nut, with a hole dug out of the middle for the flea. They didn't make a gift of this, because they said the case was government property, and they are very strict over there about government property, even for the Emperor – you can't give it away.

Platov was about to get hot under the collar, and he said, 'What's the idea of all this swindle! They gave us a gift and they got a million for it, and still that isn't enough! The case,' he says, 'always goes with such things as these.'

But the Emperor said, 'Leave off, please, this isn't your affair – don't go and spoil my politics. They have their own customs.' And he asked, 'How much does that nut cost that the flea fits into?'

The Englishmen reckoned that would be five thousand more.

Emperor Aleksandr said, 'Pay them,' and put the flea in that nut himself, and the key along with it, and so as not to lose the nut he put it into his gold snuffbox, and he ordered the snuffbox put into his little travelling casket, which was all covered with the mother of pearl and fishbones. The Emperor dismissed the English workmen with honour and said to them, 'You are the finest workmen in the whole world, and my men can't do anything compared to you.'

They were very pleased with this, and Platov could say nothing against the words of his Emperor. Only he took the nitroscope and slipped it in his pocket without saying anything, because 'it goes with it,' he says, 'and you've taken a lot of money from us already.'

The Emperor knew nothing about that till he got to Russia. They left right away, because military affairs had filled the Emperor with melancholy and he wanted to go to spiritual confession before Father Fedot in Taganrog.[7] On the way he and Platov had a mighty unpleasant conversation, because they had entirely different ideas in their heads: the Emperor thought nobody could come up to the Englishmen in art, and Platov begged to report that our people could make anything once they got a good look at it, only they didn't have any useful training. And he pointed out to the Emperor that the English workmen have completely different rules of life, science and production for everything, and every man among them has all the absolute circumstances before him, and for that reason he has a completely different meaning.

The Emperor would not listen very long to that, and when Platov saw this he didn't insist. So they rode along in silence, only Platov would get out at every station and in his aggravation he would drink up a big glass of vodka, eat a little salt mutton, light up his enormous pipe, which was big enough to hold a whole pound of Zhukov tobacco,[8] and then take his seat and sit without saying a word beside the Tsar in the carriage. The Emperor would look off in one direction, and Platov would stick his chibouk[9] out the other window and smoke into the wind. This was how they rode all the way to Petersburg, and when the Emperor went on to see Father Fedot he didn't take Platov at all.

'You,' he said, 'are intemperate in spiritual conversation, and you smoke so much that my head is full of soot from your pipe.'

Platov felt insulted and he lay down at home on his bed of ire, and just kept on lying there, smoking his Zhukov tobacco without intercession.

4

The marvellous flea of blue English steel remained in Aleksandr the First's little fishbone casket until he died in Taganrog, after turning it over to Father Fedot to pass on to the Empress when she calmed down. Empress Elizabeth Alexeyevna looked at the flea's fairiations and smiled, but she didn't take an interest in it.

'My affairs now,' she said, 'are widow's affairs, and no amusements can win my attention,' and when she got back to Petersburg she handed over this wonder with all her other valuables as an inheritance for the new emperor.

In the beginning Tsar Nicholas the First also paid no attention to the flea, because there was trouble at the time he got up on the throne, but after that one day he started looking through the little casket that had come down to him from his brother, and he took out the snuffbox, and out of the snuffbox he took the diamond nut, and in it he found the steel flea, which had not been wound up in a long time and for that reason was not moving, but lay there quietly like it was numb.

The Emperor looked at it in amazement.

'What can this trifle be, and to what purpose did my brother preserve it in this way?'

The courtiers wanted to throw it out, but the Emperor said, 'No, this must mean something.'

They called a druggist from the pharmacy effacing the Anichkin Bridge, who weighed poisons in the very finest scales. They showed it to him, and he took the flea and put it on his tongue and said, 'I feel something cold, like strong metal.' And then he mashed it a little with his teeth and announced, 'Say what you please, but this is not a genuine flea but a nymphusoria, and it is made of metal, and the work is not ours – not Russian.'

The Emperor ordered that inquiries should be made at once about where it had come from and what it signified.

They plunged into an examination of the records and the lists, but nothing was written in the records. They began asking this one and that, but nobody knew anything. By good luck, though, Platov the Don Cossack was still alive and even still lying on his bed of ire and smoking his pipe. As soon as he heard about all that disturbance at the Court, he rose up from his bed, threw down his pipe and reported to the Emperor with all his decorations. The Emperor said, 'What need have you of me, courageous old man?'

And Platov answered, 'I need nothing for myself, Your Majesty, since I eat and drink all I want and I'm satisfied with everything. But,' he says, 'I have come to report about that nymphusoria they found. This is the way it was,' he says, 'this is how it happened right before my eyes in England, and right here beside it is the key, and I've got their own nitroscope, that you can use to blow it up and look at it, and with this key you can wind up the nymphusoria through its belly, and it will hop around in any space you want and do fairiations to each side.'

They wound it up, it began to jump, and Platov said, 'You're right, Your Majesty,' he says, 'that the work is mighty fine and interesting, only it's not right for us to marvel at it with nothing but the rapture of our feelings. It ought to be submitted for Russian inspection at Tula or Sesterbek (at that time Sestroretsk was still called Sesterbek), to see whether our craftsmen can't outdo it, so that the Englishmen won't keep lording it over us Russians.'

Emperor Nicholas had great confidence in his Russian men and didn't like to yield to any foreigner, and so he answered Platov, 'You speak well, courageous old man, and I charge you with the task of proving this matter. With all my cares I do not need this little box. You take it with you, and lie no more on your bed of ire, but go to the silent Don, and strike up intimidating conversations there with my Don people about their life and devotion and what is pleasing to them. And when you go through Tula, show this nymphusoria to my Tula craftsmen, that they may ponder over it. Tell them from me that my brother marvelled at this thing, and he praised above all others the foreigners who made this nymphusoria, but I place my hope in my own people, that they are surpassed by no one. They will heed my word and will do something.'

5

Platov took the steel flea, and when he went through Tula toward the Don, he showed it to the Tula gunsmiths and passed the Emperor's words on to them and then asked, 'Now what can we do about it, Orthodox brethren?'

The gunsmiths replied, 'Worthy old man we feel the gracious word of the Emperor, and we never can forget it, because he puts his hope in his own people, but what we can do about it in this here case we can't say in just one minute, because the English nation ain't stupid either; they're even sort of cunning, and their art is full of horse sense. We mustn't go out after them till we've pondered about it and got God's blessing. Now, if you have confidence in us like the Emperor, then journey hence to your home upon the silent Don, and leave us this here little flea just like it is, in its case and in the golden snuffbox of the Tsar. Make yourself merry along the Don and heal the wounds you have suffered for our fatherland, and when you return through Tula, tarry and send for us: by that time, God willing, it may be that we'll have something thunk up.'

Platov was not completely satisfied because the Tula workmen demanded so much time and didn't talk very clearly about just what they hoped to make. He asked them this way and that, and using his Don Cossack cunning he talked with them in every sort of way, but the Tula men were no less cunning than he was, because they already had thought up such a plan that they couldn't really hope even Platov would believe them, and they wanted to carry out their bold idea right away and then hand it over.

They said, 'Even we ourselves don't know yet what we'll do, but we'll only rest our faith in God and trust that the Tsar's word won't be put to shame through our doings.'

Platov kept twisting and turning this way and that, and so did the men from Tula.

Platov wriggled and wriggled till he saw that he couldn't outwriggle a Tula man, and then he handed over the snuffbox with the nymphusoria and said, 'Well, there's nothing to do. Let it be your way,' he says. 'I know you – what kind you are. Still, there's nothing to do – I believe you. Only take care and don't try to swap diamonds on me, and don't spoil the fine English workmanship, and don't fool around very long, because I travel fast. Two weeks won't go by before I return again from the silent Don to Petersburg. At that time see to it that I have something to show the Emperor.'

The gunsmiths reassured him completely, 'We ain't going to harm the fine workmanship,' they said, 'and we won't change diamonds on you, and two weeks are enough time for us, and by the time you come back you will have *something* worthy to be shown to his Imperial Splendour.'

But exactly *what* it was they just wouldn't say.

6

Platov departed from Tula; and three of the gunsmiths, the most skilful of them all – one of them a cross-eyed left-handed man with a birthmark on his cheek and bald spots on his temples where the hair had been pulled out when he was an apprentice – these three bade farewell to their fellow workmen and their families, and without saying anything to anybody they took their bags, put what food they needed into them, and disappeared from town.

The only thing anybody noticed was that they didn't go out through the Moscow gate, but through the one on the other side, in the direction of Kiev, and people thought they had gone to Kiev to bow down before the saints resting there in peace or to take counsel with some of the holy men still alive there, who were always available in abundance in Kiev.

But this was only close to the truth and not the truth itself. Neither time nor distance allowed the Tula craftsmen in three weeks to walk to Kiev and then on top of that to make something that would put the English nation to shame. They might have done better to go and pray in Moscow, which was only 'twice fifty miles away', and a good many holy saints rest in peace there too. In the other direction too it was 'twice fifty miles' to Oryol and then another good three hundred from Oryol to Kiev. You won't get over that much ground in a hurry, and even when you've done it you won't get rested in a hurry: for a long time your feet will feel as numb as glass and your hands will tremble.

Some people even thought the craftsmen had bragged a little too much to Platov and then after they thought it over had got scared and run away for good, taking along the Tsar's gold snuffbox, and the diamond, and the English steel flea in its case that had brought them all the trouble.

However, this supposition too was completely unfounded, and was unworthy of the clever men on whom the hope of the nation now rested.

7

The inhabitants of Tula, who are intelligent people and knowledgeable about metal work, are also well known as the finest experts in religion. Their fame in this connection has spread all over their native land and has even reached Mount Athos: they are not only masters at singing their fancy trills; they also know how to paint the picture *Evening Bells*, and if any of them dedicate themselves to greater service and enter monastic life, they become famous as the best managers of monastery household affairs, and they make the most capable collectors of alms. On holy Mount Athos everybody knows that the Tula inhabitants are a most remunerative people, and if it wasn't for them, most likely the dark corners of Russia would not see very many holy relics from the distant East, and Mount Athos would be deprived of many useful contributions from Russian generosity and piety. Today the 'Tula men of Mount Athos' carry holy relics all over our native land and skilfully collect contributions even where there is nothing to collect. The Tula man is full of churchly piety and is highly practical in this matter, and so the three master craftsmen who took it on themselves to uphold Platov, and with him all Russia, made no mistake when they headed south instead of towards Moscow. They didn't go to Kiev at all but to Mtsensk, to the district town of Oryol Province in which there stands the ancient 'stone-graven' icon of Saint Nicholas, which was brought here in the most ancient times along the river Zusha on a large cross, likewise made of stone. This icon is 'awesome and most terrible' in appearance. The sainted archbishop of Myra in Lycia is represented on it full-length, clothed all over in silver-gilt clothing, swarthy of face and holding a temple in one hand and the sword of 'Military Conquest' in the other. It was just this 'Conquest' that held the meaning of the whole thing: Saint Nicholas in general and 'Nicholas of Mtsensk' in particular was the patron saint of commerce and warfare, and so the Tula gunsmiths went to make their bows to him. They held their prayer service right in front of the icon, and then in front of the stone cross, and finally, returning home by night and saying nothing to anybody, they set about their work in awful secrecy. All three of them got together in Lefty's house; they locked the doors, boarded up the windows, lighted a lamp before the icon of Saint Nicholas and started to work.

One day, two days, three days they sat without going out anywhere, all of them tapping away with their hammers. They were making something, but what it was they were making nobody knew.

Everyone was curious, but nobody could find out a thing, because the workmen said nothing and never stuck their noses outside. All sorts of people would go up to the little house and knock on the door with all sorts of excuses, to ask for fire or borrow some salt, but the three experts would not open up for any kind of request. Even how they got food nobody knew. People tried to scare them, and pretended that the house next door was on fire to see whether they wouldn't run out in fright and give away the secret of what they were making, but nothing could take in those shrewd workmen. Lefty stuck his head out only once and shouted, 'Go ahead and burn up; we ain't got time,' and then he drew in his plucked head, banged the shutters tight and got to work again. Through the tiny cracks people could only see the glitter of a light and hear the ringing blows of tiny hammers tapping on anvils.

In a word, the whole thing was handled in such awful secrecy that there was no way to find out anything about it, and it lasted right up to the return of the Cossack Platov from the silent Don on his way to the Emperor, and during all that time the craftsmen saw nobody and said nothing.

8

Platov travelled in great haste and ceremony: he himself sat in the carriage, and on the coach-boxes two Cossack scurriers holding whips sat on each side of the driver and poured it on him unmercifully so as to make him hurry. If either one of the Cossacks dozed off, Platov would give him a kick from inside the carriage, and they would tear along even more wildly. These measures worked so well that there was no holding back the horses at a single station anywhere; they would always gallop on a hundred paces past the halting-place. Then the Cossack would work on the driver once more in the opposite direction, and they would go back to the entrance.

That was the way they rolled into Tula: there too at first they flew a hundred paces beyond the Moscow gate, and then the Cossack worked on the driver with his whip in the opposite direction, and at the entrance they started hitching up fresh horses. Platov didn't get out of the carriage, but only told his scurrier to go as fast as possible and get the craftsmen he had left the flea with.

One scurrier dashed off to get them to come as fast as possible and bring him the work that was to put the Englishmen to shame, and that scurrier had run only a short distance when Platov sent first one and then another after him so as to speed things up.

He sent off all his scurriers and then began dispatching ordinary people from the curious crowd, and in impatience he even stuck his own legs out of the carriage and was about to start running impatiently himself, and he gritted his teeth because they were all so slow in coming into sight.

In those days everything had to be done just right and very fast, so as not to lose a minute that might be useful to Russia.

9

At that very moment the Tula craftsmen who were making the marvellous thing had finished their work. The scurriers ran up to them puffing and blowing, and the ordinary people from the curious crowd – well, they didn't even get there at all, because their legs, being out of practice, scattered and fell all along the way, and then in terror, for fear they might catch sight of Platov, they lit out for home and hid wherever they could.

As soon as the scurriers ran up, they gave a shout, and when they saw that nobody opened up, they jerked at the bolts on the shutters, but the bolts were so strong they wouldn't give at all; they pulled at the doors, but the doors were fastened from the inside with heavy oak bars. Then the scurriers picked up a beam from the street and stuck it under the eave of the roof the way firemen do, and in one blow they prized the whole roof off the hut. But as soon as they got the roof off, they themselves keeled over, because the workmen with their unceaseless labour in their crowded little shanty had expired so much that a man who wasn't used to it, coming right in when the wind was dead, instinkly choked.

The messengers cried out, 'What are you doing, you so-and-so's, you swine? What do you mean by knocking us over with that expiration? Or ain't you got any fear of God left in you?'

And they answered, 'Just a minute, we're driving in the last nail, and as soon as we hammer it down we'll bring out our work.'

The messengers said, 'He'll eat us alive before then and won't even leave our souls for the funeral.'

But the craftsmen answered, 'He won't have time to gobble you up, because we drove the last nail in while you were standing there talking. Run and tell him we're bringing it right now.'

The scurriers dashed off, but their hearts weren't in it, because they thought the craftsmen might fool them, and for that reason they ran and ran, but kept looking back. But the craftsmen were coming along behind them, and they had hurried so fast they hadn't even got dressed quite the way they ought for a meeting with an important person, and while they ran they were still fastening the hooks of their kaftans. Two of them had nothing in their hands, but the third one, Lefty, had the Tsar's jewel casket wrapped in a green cloth cover with the English steel flea inside.

10

The scurriers ran up to Platov and said, 'Here they are in person!'

Platov barked at the craftsmen, 'Is it ready?'

'It's all ready,' they answered.

'Give it here.'

They handed it over.

The carriage was already hitched up, and the driver and postillion were in their places. The Cossacks at once took their seats beside the driver and raised their whips over his head and held them brandished there.

Platov snatched off the green cover, opened the little casket, took the gold snuffbox out of its padding and the diamond nut out of the snuffbox. He saw the English flea lying there just the way it had before, and apart from it nothing else was there.

Platov said, 'What's the meaning of this? Where is your work that you wanted to console the Emperor with?'

The gunsmiths answered, 'Our work is right there.'

Platov asked, 'What kind of work?'

The gunsmiths answered, 'What's the use of explaining? Everything is right there in front of your eyes. Just take a look at it.'

Platov squared his shoulders and shouted, 'Where's the key to the flea?'

'Why, it's right here,' they answered. 'Where the flea is, there the key is – in the same nut.'

Platov tried to take hold of the key, but his fingers were too stubby. He grabbed and grabbed but couldn't catch either the flea or the key to its bellyworks, and suddenly he burst out and started swearing with colourful Cossack words.

He shouted, 'You scoundrels, you've done nothing at all, and on top of it you've probably ruined the whole thing! I'll take off your heads!'

But the Tula men answered him, 'There ain't no use insulting us. From you, as the Emperor's messenger, we've got to put up with all insults, but just because you wouldn't trust us and thought we were the kind that would even cheat the Emperor hisself, we ain't going to tell you the secret of our work now; just be so kind as to take it to the Emperor, and he'll see what sort of men he's got in us, and whether we've done anything to make him ashamed of us.'

Platov shouted, 'You're lying, you scoundrels, and I won't let you get away from me like that. One of you will go with me to Petersburg, and there I'll get out of him what kind of scullduggery you've been up to.'

And with this he reached out, grabbed the cross-eyed Lefty by the collar with his stubby fingers, so that all the hooks flew off his kazakin shirt, and pitched him into the carriage at his feet.

'Lie there like a puddle,' he said, 'till we get to Petersburg. You'll answer to me for all of them. And you,' he said to the scurriers, 'get a move on! Look sharp now, and see to it that I'm in Petersburg at the Emperor's the day after tomorrow!'

The craftsmen stuck their necks out for their comrade and asked how he could be taken away from them like that without his grasp port. Then he would have no way to get back! But instead of answering them Platov just showed them his fist – a frightful one, all knotty and hacked apart and somehow grown back together again – and waving it in front of them he said, 'There's a grasp port for you!'

And he said to his Cossacks, 'Let's go, boys!'

His Cossacks, drivers and steeds all started working at once and they whisked Lefty away without his grasp port, and two days later, just as Platov had ordered, they rolled up to the Emperor's palace, arriving at such a properly furious gallop that they drove right past the columns.

Platov stood up, hooked on his decorations and went in to the Emperor, telling his Cossack scurriers to keep watch at the entrance over cross-eyed Lefty.

11

Platov was afraid to report to the Emperor in person, because it was awful how noticeable and memorable Tsar Nicholas was – he never forgot anything. Platov knew he was bound to ask him about the flea. And even though he was afraid of no enemy on earth, right here he got cold feet: he carried the little casket into the palace and very quietly laid it down in the hall behind the stove. With the box hidden he presented himself to the Emperor in his office and quickly began reporting on the intimidating conversations he'd had with the Cossacks on the silent Don. He figured he would try to keep the Emperor busy with this. Then if the Emperor remembered and started talking about the flea, he would have to hand it over and answer, but if the Emperor didn't say anything about it, he could just keep quiet. He would tell the Emperor's servant to hide the little casket and lock up Lefty in a fortress cell so as to keep him handy in case he might be needed.

But Emperor Nicholas forgot about nothing, and Platov had barely finished about the intimidating conversations when he asked at once,

'And how about it – how did my Tula craftsmen justify themselves against the English nymphusoria?'

Platov answered the way the matter looked to him.

'Your Majesty,' he says, 'the nymphusoria is still lying in that same space, and I have brought it back, but the Tula craftsmen couldn't make anything more marvellous.'

The Emperor replied, 'You are a courageous old man, but what you report to me cannot be so.'

Platov tried to convince him and told him how the whole thing had happened, and when he got to the part where the Tula workmen asked him to show the flea to the Emperor, Tsar Nicholas slapped him on the back and said, 'Give it here. I know my men won't let me down. Something has been done here that is past all understanding.'

12

They brought the little casket out from behind the stove, they took the cloth cover off, they opened the gold snuffbox and the diamond nut – and there the flea was, lying just the way it had before.

The Emperor took a look and said, 'What a misfortune!' But his faith in his Russian craftsmen didn't slacken, and he sent for his favourite daughter Aleksandra and commanded her, 'You have slender fingers: hasten, take that little key and wind up the bellyworks of that nymphusoria.'

The princess began to wind it up, and the flea at once started wiggling its whiskers, but it didn't move its feet. Aleksandra pulled on the whole works, but still the nymphusoria wouldn't do a single *dansez* or fairiation, the way it used to.

Platov turned green all over and shouted, 'Oh those rascally dogs! Now I understand why they wouldn't tell me anything. It's lucky I brought one of their blockheads along with me.'

With these words he ran out to the entrance, grabbed Lefty by the hair, and began to swing him back and forth so hard that tufts of it started flying. When Platov had stopped beating him, Lefty straightened himself out and said, 'That's the way all my hair got pulled out while I was an apprentice. I don't know what need there is now to go through all that again.'

'That's because I'd counted on you and vouched for you,' said Platov, 'and then you went and spoiled that rarity.'

Lefty answered, 'We're mighty glad you vouched for us, and as for spoiling – we didn't spoil nothing. Just blow it up in your strongest nitroscope and take a look.'

Platov ran back to tell them about the nitroscope, but to Lefty he only warned, 'I'll give you this-that-and-the-other even yet.'

He ordered the scurriers to twist Lefty's arms even harder behind his back, and he himself went up the steps, puffing and blowing and repeating the prayer, 'Blessed Tsar's Most Blessed Mother, immaculate and pure,' and so on, as needed. And the courtiers who were standing on the steps all turned their backs on him. They thought, 'Platov is done for now, and he'll soon be chased out of the palace,' because they couldn't stand him on account of his bravery.

13

As soon as Platov reported Lefty's words to the Emperor, he said full of joy, 'I know my Russian men will not let me down.' And he ordered the nitroscope to be brought forward on a pillow.

The nitroscope was brought forward that very minute, and the Emperor took the flea and laid it under the glass, first on its belly, then on its side and then on its back. In a word, it was turned in every direction, but nothing could be seen. Still the Emperor didn't lose faith. He only said, 'Bring hither at once that gunsmith who is waiting below.'

Platov reported, 'They'd have to dress him up. He's still got the clothes on he was caught in, and now he's in bad shape.'

But the Emperor replied, 'Never mind; bring him in just as he is.'

Platov said, 'Come in here, now, you so-and-so, and answer to the Emperor before his eyes.'

Lefty replied, 'Why, sure, I'll go like this and I'll answer.'

He went like he was: in ragged boots, with one trouser-leg tucked in and the other dangling, with an old jacket that wouldn't fasten because the hooks were lost, and with the collar that was torn; but it didn't matter – he wasn't embarrassed.

'What of it?' he thought. 'If the Emperor wants to see me, I've got to go, and if I ain't got a grasp port, it ain't my fault, and I'll tell him how it happened.'

As soon as Lefty came in and bowed, the Emperor said to him, 'What does this mean, my good man? We have looked this way and that and have blown it up in the nitroscope and we still can't find anything remarkable.'

Lefty answered, 'Did Your Majesty be so kind as to look at it the right way?'

The nobles motioned to him to tell him that was not the way to talk, but he didn't understand how to talk courtier language – with flattery or cunning – and he kept on talking simply.

The Emperor said to them, 'Stop making things complicated for him; let him answer as he knows how.'

And then he explained to Lefty, 'This is the way we laid it,' he says. And he put the flea under the nitroscope. 'Look at it yourself,' he says. 'You can't see a thing.'

Lefty answered, 'You can't see nothing that way, Your Majesty, because our work is a lot too secret for that size.'

The Emperor asked, 'Then how *do* we manage it?'

'You have to put just one of its feet in detail under the whole nitroscope, and look one at a time at each foot it walks on.'

'Goodness Gracious,' said the Emperor. 'That's powerfully small.'

'But what else can you do,' answered Lefty, 'if that's the only way you can get a look at our work? Then you can see the whole amazement.'

They laid it down the way Lefty said and as soon as the Emperor looked in the upper glass, he beamed all over. He grabbed Lefty just the way he was – dirty, dusty, unwashed – and put his arms around him and kissed him on the cheek, and then he turned to all the courtiers and said, 'You see, I knew better than everybody that my Russians would not let me down. Just look: why, the rascals have taken the English flea and nailed flea-shoes on its feet!'

14

They all came up to look: all the flea's feet really were shod with genuine flea-shoes, and Lefty reported that this was not the only marvel.

'If you had a better nitroscope,' he said, 'one that would blow it up five million times, then you could be so kind as to see that a craftsman's name was put on each shoe, so as to show which Russian gunsmith made that shoe.'

'Is your name there too'?' asked the Emperor.

'No, sir,' answered Lefty. 'Mine is the only one that ain't.'

'Why isn't it?'

'Because I did smaller work than these flea-shoes,' he said. 'I made the nails the shoes were fastened on with, and they are too small for any nitroscope to blow them up.'

The Emperor asked, 'But where is your nitroscope, which you used to produce this marvel?'

Lefty answered, 'We are poor people – too poor to own a nitroscope, so we just sharpened our eyes.'

Seeing that Lefty's business had turned out well, the other courtiers began to kiss him and Platov gave him a hundred roubles and said, 'Forgive me, brother, for dragging you around by the hair.'

Lefty answered, 'God will forgive you – it ain't the first time that kind of snow has fallen on my head.'

He would say no more – and he didn't even have time to say more, because the Emperor ordered the iron-shod nymphusoria to be packed up and sent back at once to England, as a sort of gift, to make them understand that it wasn't any marvel to us. And the Emperor ordered the flea to be carried by a special courier who was learned in all languages, and ordered the left-handed smith to go with him so that he himself could show their work to the Englishmen and show them what kind of craftsmen we have in Tula.

Platov made the sign of the Cross over him.

'Blessings be upon you,' he said. 'I'll send you some of my own grape vodka for the journey. Don't drink too little and don't drink too much – drink middlesome.'

And so he did – he sent it.

Count Nestlebroad[10] gave orders to wash Lefty in the Tula Public Baths, cut his hair in a barber shop, and deck him out in the full-dress coat of a singer in the royal choir, so that he would look like he had some kind of paid government rank.

As soon as they had worked him over this way, they filled him with tea and Platov's grape vodka, drew up his belt as tight as possible so that his guts wouldn't shake, and sent him off to London. That is when foreign sights started happening to Lefty.

15

The courier travelled powerfully fast with Lefty, so that they didn't stop to rest anywhere between Petersburg and London, but only drew their belts another notch tighter at every station, so that their guts wouldn't get mixed up with their lungs; but since Lefty on Platov's orders was allotted as much government vodka as he wanted after he had been presented to the Emperor, he kept up his strength on this alone, without eating anything, and he sang Russian songs all the way through Europe – only adding a refrain of foreign words,

> *Aye loolee*
> *Say tray Joe Lee.*

As soon as the courier got him to London, he reported to the proper authorities and handed over the box, and then put Lefty down in a hotel room; but there he soon began to get restless, and besides, he was hungry. He knocked on the door and pointed to his mouth when the servant came, and the servant took him right off to the feeding room.

Here Lefty sat down at a table and waited. He didn't know how to ask for anything in English. But then he figured it out, again he just tapped on the table with his finger and pointed to his mouth; the Englishmen guessed what he meant and served him, only they didn't always bring what he wanted. But he wouldn't take anything that didn't suit him. They brought him their kind of hot glum pudding in flames. He said, 'I don't see how anybody can eat that,' and he wouldn't take a bite. They exchanged it for him and brought him something else to eat. He wouldn't drink their vodka, either, because it was green – like they had flavoured it with sulphuric acid. He picked out the plainest stuff they had, and waited in the cool with his canteen for the courier.

And the people the courier had handed the nymphusoria over to looked at it that very minute through their strongest nitroscope and sent a description right off to a calumnist on the *Daily Telegraft*, so that he could tell everybody about it the very next day.

'And as for that craftsman,' they said, 'we want to see him at once.' The courier took them to the hotel room and from there to the feeding room, where our Lefty had begun to glow very decently, and said, 'There he is.'

The Englishmen slapped Lefty on the back right away and took him by the hands just like their own equal. 'Comrade,' they said, 'comrade, you're a good craftsman. We'll talk to you afterwards when there is time, but now we want to drink to your prosperity.'

They ordered a lot of wine and gave Lefty the first glass, but out of politeness he wouldn't be the first to drink. He thought, 'Maybe you're so aggravated you want to poison me.'

'No,' he said, 'that's not the way to do it. Even with a Polish thirst, you have to let the host drink first. You yourselves drink on ahead.'

The Englishmen tasted all their wines in front of him and then started filling his glass. He stood up, crossed himself with his left hand, and drank to the health of them all.

They noticed that he had crossed himself with his left hand, and they asked the courier, 'What is he – a Lutheranian or a Protesterian?'

The courier answered, 'He's not either a Lutheranian or a Protesterian; he belongs to the Russian faith.'

'But why does he cross himself with his left hand?'

The courier replied, 'He's a left-handed man, and he does everything with his left hand.'

The Englishmen marvelled even more and started pumping both Lefty and the courier full of wine, and kept on this way for three whole days, and then they said, 'Now that's enough.' They symphonied some water out of a bottle with impressed air, and when they were refreshed all over they started asking Lefty all about where had he studied, and what had he studied, and how far had he gone in arithmetic.

Lefty answered, 'Our learning is simple – according to the Psalter and the *Dream-Book*. We don't know no arithmetic at all.'

The Englishmen looked at each other and said, 'That's amazing.'

And Lefty answered, 'It's that way all over in our country.'

'But what sort of book is that in Russia,' they asked, 'that dream-book?'

'That book,' he said, 'refers to if King David didn't reveal some fortune-telling clearly in the Psalter, then you can get some extra fortunes out of the *Dream-Book*.'

They said, 'That's too bad. It would be better if you at least knew the four rules of addition; that would be a lot more utilifying to you than your whole *Dream-Book*. Then you would be able to understand that every machine has its balance of forces. As it is, even though you are mighty skilful with your hands, you didn't realize that such a little machine as the one in the nymphusoria was calculated for the most accurate exactness, and it can't carry the flea-shoes. That's why the nymphusoria won't jump or dance any *dansez*.'

Lefty agreed, 'About that there ain't no argument,' he said. 'We didn't get very far in book-learning, but only faithfully serve our fatherland.'

And the Englishmen said to him, 'Stay here with us; we'll give you a big education and you'll turn out to be a superbluous craftsman.'

But Lefty wouldn't agree. 'I've got my parents at home,' he said.

The Englishmen offered to send his parents money, but Lefty wouldn't take it.

'We are devoted to our country,' he said, 'and my daddy's an old man and my mother's an old woman, and they're used to going to church in their own parish, and it would be mighty lonely here for me all by myself, because I'm still a bachelor by calling.'

'You'll get used to it,' they said. 'You'll accept our laws, and we'll get you married.'

'That can never be,' answered Lefty.

'Why not?'

'Because,' he answered, 'our Russian faith is the rightest one, and the way our forefathers believed is just the way their dissentants have to believe.'

'You don't know our faith,' said the Englishmen. 'We've got the same Christian law and hold to the same Gospel.'

'It's true,' said Lefty, 'that everybody's got the same Gospel, but our books are thicker than yours, and our faith is fuller.'

'How can you judge that way?'

'We've got all the evident proofs of it,' he answered.

'What kind?'

'Why, we've got God-wondering icons and prism-working relics, and you ain't got nothing – except for Sunday you ain't even got any special holidays. And the second reason is that even if I was married in the law to an English girl it would be confusing to live with her.'

'How's that?' they asked. 'Don't turn up your nose at our girls – they too dress neatly and they're good housekeepers.'

But Lefty said, 'I don't know them.'

The Englishmen replied, 'That's no problem – you'll get to know them. We'll fix up a roundy-view for you.'

Lefty started blushing. 'What's the use of stringing the girls along for no reason?' he said, and he wouldn't budge. 'That's something for fine gentlemen. It wouldn't suit us. And if they found out about it at home, in Tula, they'd make fun of me something awful.'

The Englishmen got curious, 'Then suppose we did it without a roundy-view,' they said. 'How do you manage in your country so as to make a favourable choice?'

Lefty explained our way to them. 'In our country,' he said, 'when a man wants to reveal a circumstantial intention in regard to a girl, he sends over a conversational woman, and when she has made a preposition, they politely go to the house together and look the girl over without concealment, and in front of all the relationships.'

They understood, but they answered that they had no conversational women and followed no such custom, and Lefty said, 'That's all the better, because if you go in for that kind of thing you have to do it with a circumstantial intention, and since I don't feel none towards a foreign nation, what's the use of stringing the girls along?'

The Englishmen were pleased with him for these opinions too, and so they started off again in their friendly way, slapping him on the back and the knees, and they asked: 'Just out of curiosity,' they said, 'we'd like to know what signs of defects you've noticed in our girls, and why you keep away from them?'

At this Lefty answered them frankly, 'I don't mean to run them down; I just don't like the way their dresses sort of swish back and forth, so that you can't make out just what they've got on and what it's for. There'll be one thing here, and below something else will be pinned on, and on their arms they'll have some kind of socks. In them velveteen coats of theirs they look just like capuchin monkeys.'

The Englishmen laughed and said, 'Why does that get in your way?'

'It don't get in my way,' answered Lefty, 'only I'm scared I'd be ashamed to look and wait until she got untangled from all that stuff.'

'But do you really think your fashions are better?' they asked.

'Our fashions in Tula,' he replied, 'are simple: every girl is dressed in her own lace. Our lace is worn even by fine ladies.'

Then they showed him off to their own ladies, and there they served him tea and asked him, 'What are you frowning for?'

He answered that 'We ain't used to drinking it so sweet.'

Then they served it to him in the Russian way, with a lump of sugar to suck.

This didn't seem to be as good to them, but Lefty said, 'To our taste this way it's tastier.'

The Englishmen couldn't find any bait at all that could make him take to their life. They could only talk him into staying with them for a short while as their guest, and said they would take him to all sorts of factories and show him all their arts.

And after that, they said, they would put him on their own ship and 'deliver him safe and sound in Petersburg.'

He agreed to that.

16

The Englishmen took charge of Lefty and sent the Russian courier back to Russia. Even though the courier had government rank and was learned in various languages, they weren't interested in him, but they *were* interested in Lefty, and they set out to take Lefty around and show him everything. He looked at all their production: he really liked their metallic mills and their soapy-rope factories, and the way they managed things – especially the way they took care of their workers. Every one of their workmen was always well fed, none was dressed in rags, each one had on a capable everyday jacket and wore thick hard-nail boots with iron caps, so that he wouldn't stump his toes anywhere on anything. Along with his work he got teaching instead of beatings, and he worked with comprehension. In front of each one, hung up right in full view, was a stultification table, and within arm's reach was a racing slate. Whatever any craftsman did, he would look up at the tables, and then check it with comprehension, and then write one thing down on the slate, race another thing, and put it together accurately: whatever was written down in the figures really came out that way. And when a holiday came, they would all get together in couples, each one would take a walking stick in his hand, and they would go for a walk in a proper way, all proud and polite.

Lefty got a good look at all their life and all their work, but above all else he paid attention to something that surprised the Englishmen a lot. He wasn't interested so much in how they made new rifles as in how they took care of the old ones. He would walk around everything and praise it and say, 'We can do that too.'

But whenever he came to an old rifle, he would stick his finger in the barrel, rub it around inside, and sigh, 'That is way yonder better than ours.'

The Englishmen couldn't figure out what Lefty noticed. He asked them, 'Might I know whether or not our generals have ever looked at this?'

They answered, 'Those who have been here must have taken a look.'

'But when they were here,' he asked, 'did they have gloves on or not?'

'Yours are full-dress generals,' they said. 'Gloves come with them, so they must have had them on here.'

Lefty said nothing. But suddenly he began to feel an uneasy homesickness. He pined away and pined away and said to the Englishmen, 'I thank you kindly for your entertainment, and I like everything in your country, and I've seen everything I needed to see – and now I'd like to go home in a hurry.'

They couldn't hold him back any longer. There was no way to let him go by land because he didn't know all languages, and it was a bad time to go by sea because it was the fall of the year and stormy, but he insisted, 'Let me go.'

'We've looked at the whether-meter,' they said. 'A storm is coming; you could drown; after all, this is not like your Gulf of Finland – this is the real Militerranean Sea.'

'It's all the same where a man dies,' he answered. 'It's all God's will alone, and I want to get back home in a hurry; because if I don't, I might get a kind of craziness in the head.'

They couldn't hold him back by force. They fed him till he creaked, they rewarded him with money, they gave him an alarmed gold watch as a souvenir, and for the cold weather at sea on the late fall voyage they gave him a woollen overcoat with a windy hurricane hat for his head. They dressed him warmly and took him down to the ship that was sailing for Russia. There they gave Lefty the very best cabin, like a real nobleman, but he felt ashamed and didn't like to sit shut up with the other gentlemen, and he would go up on deck and sit down under the tar poling and ask, 'Where is our Russia?'

The Englishman he asked would point or nod off in that direction, and then Lefty would turn his head that way and impatiently look for his native land.

When they sailed out of the bay into the Militerranean Sea, his longing for Russia became so strong that there was no way to calm him down. The rolling and pitching was awful, but Lefty still wouldn't go down to his cabin; he sat under the tar poling, pulled his hurricane hat down over his eyes and kept looking towards his homeland.

Often the Englishmen would come up and invite him to a warm spot down below, and he even began to lie his way out so that they would stop bothering him. 'No,' he would answer. 'I feel better out here; if I went inside with all this rolling and pitching the sea wretch would get me.'

And so the whole time he would never go below until he had to for special reasons, and because of this the thirst mate took a liking to him. This thirst mate, to the misfortune of our Lefty, knew how to talk Russian, and he couldn't get over marvelling that a Russian landlubber could hold out like that through all the rough weather.

'Good lad, Russ!' he said. 'Let's take a drink!'

Lefty took a drink.

And the thirst mate said, 'Another one!'

So Lefty took another one, and they drank themselves tight. The thirst mate asked him, 'What kind of secret is it you're taking to Russia from our country?'

Lefty answered, 'That's my business.'

'Well, if that's the way it is,' answered the thirst mate, 'then let me make an English bet with you.'

Lefty asked, 'What kind?'

'That we'll never drink alone and will always drink the same – one just as much as the other – and whoever drinks the other one down will win.'

Lefty thought, 'Dark skies, bellies rise; the boredom's strong and the way is long. We still can't see the homeland beyond the waves – it will be merrier after all to make the bet.'

'All right,' he said. 'It's a bet.'

'Only let it be honest.'

'As far as that goes,' he said, 'you ain't got no worry.'

They agreed and shook hands on it.

17

Their bet began in the Militerranean Sea, and they drank all the way to the Riga Dunamunde,[11] but they ran neck and neck, and neither one fell behind the other, and they kept so strictly even with each other that when one of them looked down into the sea and saw a devil climbing up out of the water, the very same thing immediately appeared to the other one. Only, the thirst mate saw a red-headed devil, and Lefty claimed it was dark, like a blackamoor.

Lefty said, 'Cross yourself and turn away; that's a devil from the deep.'

But the Englishman argued that it was only a 'deep-sea driver'. 'If you want me to,' he said, 'I'll pitch you overboard. Don't be afraid – he'll bring you right back to me.'

And Lefty answered, 'If that's true, then pitch me over.'

The thirst mate picked him up by the shoulders and carried him to the rail.

The sailors saw this and stopped them and reported it to the captain. He ordered them both to be locked up below and kept on rations of rum and wine and cold food, so that they could both eat and drink and stick to their bet, but he gave orders that they were not to get any hot glum pudding in flames, for fear the spirits in their innards might catch fire.

So they travelled locked up all the way to Petersburg, and neither one of them won the bet. There they were spread out in separate sleighs, and the Englishman was sent to the embassy on the English quay and Lefty to the police station.

From this point their destinies became very different.

18

When the Englishman was brought to the Ambassador's house, they at once called in a doctor and a druggist for him. The doctor ordered him put into a warm bath on the spot, and the druggist right away rolled up a gutta-percha pill and personally stuck it in his mouth, and then both of them together took and laid him on a feather bed and covered him over with a fur coat and left him to sweat; and to keep anyone from disturbing him the order was sent out through the whole embassy to let nobody sneeze. The doctor and the druggist waited till the thirst mate went to sleep, and then they made another gutta-percha pill for him, laid it on a little table at the head of his bed and went off.

But at the police station they threw Lefty on the floor and started questioning him, 'Who was he, and where was he from, and did he have a grasp port or any other kind of document?'

But he was so weak from his illness and the drinking and the rolling and pitching that he didn't answer a word, but only groaned.

Then they searched him right away, relieved him of his colourful clothes and his alarmed watch and fleeced him of his money; and the police officer gave orders that the first passing sleigh-driver should take him free to the hospital.

The policeman took Lefty out to put him into a sleigh, but for a long time he couldn't catch a single one, because sleigh-drivers avoid policemen. Lefty was lying all this time on the cold depravement. Then the policeman caught a sleigh-driver, only one without a warm fur lap-robe, because in cases like that they hide the fur lap-robe by sitting on it, in order to make policemen's feet freeze faster. So they carried Lefty in an open sleigh, and whenever they transferred him from one sleigh to another they would keep dropping him, and when they picked him up they would pull his ears to make him come to. They got him to one hospital, but there they wouldn't accept him without a grasp port; they took him to another, and they wouldn't accept him there either; and then to a third, and a fourth. All night long they kept dragging him through all the little winding alleys and transferring him over and over, until he was half dead. Then one doctor's assistant told the policeman to take him to the Obukhvin Public Hospital, where everybody of unknown social class was taken in to die.

There they gave orders to write out a receipt and deposit Lefty on the floor in the corridor till they could inspect him.

And at that very same time the next day the English thirst mate got up, swallowed the second gutta-percha pill down to his innards, ate a light breakfast of chicken and rice, took a drink of impressed air, and said, 'Where is my Russian buddy? I'm going to look for him.'

19

He got dressed and off he ran.

In some amazing way the thirst mate found Lefty very quickly; only, they hadn't yet put him on a bed. He was still lying in the hall on the floor, and he complained to the Englishman. 'I've just got to have two words with the Emperor,' he said.

The Englishman ran off to Count Kleinmichel[12] and ripped and roared, 'Really, now, this is the limit!' he said. 'Though only a sheepskin coat it be, in its wearer a human soul we see.'

For this statement the Englishman was turned out at once, so that he shouldn't dare mention the human soul again. After that somebody said to him, 'You'd do better to go around to Platov the Cossack; he's got simple feelings.'

The Englishman got hold of Platov, who by this time was lying again on his bed. Platov listened to his story and remembered Lefty.

'Why, of course, brother,' he said. 'I know him very well. I've even dragged him around by the hair. Only, I don't know how I can help him in this kind of trouble, because I've served out my time and got a full apple plexy – now they don't pay attention to me any more. But you just run over to the Commandant Skobelev;[13] he's in full force, and he's also had experience in this line – he'll do something.'

The thirst mate went to Skobelev and told all about what sort of illness Lefty had and how it had happened. Skobelev said, 'I understand that illness; only, the Germans don't know how to treat it; here you have to have some kind of doctor from the spiritual profession, because they have grown up with these cases and they can help; I'll send over the Russian doctor Martyn-Solsky right away.'[14]

But when Martyn-Solsky got there, Lefty was already dying, because he had cracked open the back of his head when they dropped him on the cold depravement; and he was able to say only one thing clearly, 'Tell the Emperor that the English don't clean their rifles with brick dust, and we must stop it too, or else God save us from a war, because they won't be any good for shooting.'

And with this loyalty, Lefty crossed himself and kicked the bucket.

Martyn-Solsky went out at once and reported this to Count Chernyshov,[15] so that he could tell the Emperor, but Count Chernyshov shouted at him, 'Look here now,' he said, 'your job is laxatives and purgatives. Don't stick your nose into other people's business: in Russia we've got generals for that.'

So nothing was said to the Emperor, and the cleaning went on in the same old way right up to the Crimean War. At that time when they started loading their rifles, the bullets just rattled around in them, because the barrels had been cleaned out with brick dust.

Then Martyn-Solsky reminded Count Chernyshov about Lefty, and Count Chernyshov said, 'Go to the devil, you public enema, and don't stick your nose into other people's business or I'll deny I ever heard about that from you, and then you yourself will catch it.'

Martyn-Solsky thought, 'And he really will deny it.' So he kept quiet.

But if only they had reported Lefty's words in time to the Emperor, the war against the enemy in Crimea would have taken an entirely different turn.

Now all this is 'affairs of long-gone days' and 'traditions of yore'[16] even though this yore is not very old. But there is no need to be hasty about forgetting these traditions, despite the incredible nature of the legend and the epic character of its principal hero. Lefty's real name, like the names of many of the greatest geniuses, has been lost to posterity forever; but he is interesting as the embodiment of a myth in the popular imagination, and his adventures can serve to remind us of an epoch whose general spirit has been portrayed here clearly and accurately.

It goes without saying that Tula no longer has such master craftsmen as the legendary Lefty: machines have evened up the inequalities in gifts and talents, and genius no longer strains itself in a struggle against diligence and exactness. Even though they encourage the raising of salaries, machines do not encourage artistic daring, which sometimes went so far beyond ordinary bounds as to inspire the folk imagination to create unbelievable legends like this one.

The workmen, of course, can appreciate the advantages they have gained through practical applications of mechanical science, but they still recall those olden times with pride and affection. These memories are their epic – an epic that has a genuinely 'human soul'.

First published in 1881
Translated by William Edgerton

ANTON PAVLOVICH CHEKHOV
(1860–1904)

Chekhov was born in Taganrog, a port on the Sea of Azov. His father was a grocer. While studying medicine at Moscow University Chekhov published hundreds of comic sketches in order to pay his way and support his parents and siblings. After becoming famous in the late 1880s, he practised as a doctor only intermittently; most of his medical work was on behalf of the peasants, and unpaid. In 1890 he travelled across the whole of Siberia to Sakhalin Island, where he investigated the living conditions of the settlers, of the native Ainu and Gilyak, and – most importantly – of the thousands of exiled convicts. During the 1890s Chekhov's tuberculosis worsened and from 1897 he had to spend most of his time in the Crimean resort of Yalta. There he composed his plays The Three Sisters *and* The Cherry Orchard, *as well as some of his finest stories. In 1901 he married the actress Olga Knipper, for whom he wrote the part of Ranevskaya in* The Cherry Orchard.*

Unlike Tolstoy, whom he admired, Chekhov refused to moralize in his art; he wanted his readers to think for themselves. There is a fine tribute to Chekhov in Vasily Grossman's novel Life and Fate:

> *Chekhov brought Russia into our consciousness in all its vastness – with people of every estate, every class, every age. More than that! It was as a democrat that he presented all these people – as a Russian democrat . . . Chekhov said, let's put God – and all these grand progressive ideas – to one side. Let's begin with man; let's be kind and attentive to the individual man – whether he's a bishop, a peasant, an industrial magnate, a convict in the Sakhalin Islands or a waiter in a restaurant. Let's begin with respect, compassion and love for the individual – or we'll never get anywhere.[1]*

Chekhov's father was unusually devout and his children received a strict religious upbringing. No Russian writer – except possibly Leskov – had a more precise knowledge of the rites and tenets of Orthodoxy than the atheistic Chekhov. It is only recently, however, that critics have noticed the hints of religious symbolism in Chekhov's work; at the end of 'In the Cart', for example, a 'baptism' in the river and a glimpse of a church with 'its crosses blazing as they reflected the evening sun' herald a moment of epiphany.

Chekhov's writing can seem deceptively ordinary on first reading, but even his early stories touch unexpected depths. And 'In the Cart', both in its evocation of a life of tedium and in its moment of illumination, exemplifies the critic Janet Malcolm's words about the 'bark of the prosaic in which Chekhov consistently encases a story's vital poetic core, as if such protection were necessary for its survival'.[2]

No great Russian writer – except perhaps Andrey Platonov – was as unostentatiously practical as Chekhov, and the huge number of trees he planted testifies to the inseparability of his love of beauty and his concern for the useful. Rosamund Bartlett tells us that 'Chekhov once made a note about the Muslim custom of digging wells to save one's soul, adding: "It would be good if each of us left a school or a well or something similar, so that our lives did not go by . . . without trace." '[3] Chekhov himself built no less than three schools, but I am still more struck by the reference to digging a well. Chekhov did not, like Tolstoy and Dostoyevsky, leave us vast cathedrals of words; his plays and stories are, however, at least a little like wells – modest, mysterious, and as necessary as they are inexhaustible.

IN THE CART

They left town at half past eight in the morning.

The road was dry and the beautiful April sun was very warm, but there was still snow lying in the ditches and in the forest. The long, dark, mean winter was not long past and spring had arrived suddenly, but neither the sunshine, nor the thin listless forests warmed by the breath of spring, nor the black flocks flying over enormous puddles which were like lakes in the fields, nor the glorious sky into whose boundless expanses one could have joyously disappeared seemed new or interesting to Marya Vasilyevna sitting there in the cart. She had been a teacher for thirteen years and had lost count of the number of times she had travelled to town for her wages; whether it was spring, like now, or a rainy autumn evening, or winter – it was all the same to her, and each time she only ever wanted one thing: to get the trip over as quickly as possible.

She felt as if she had been living in these parts for ages and ages, a hundred years at least, and it seemed as if she knew every single stone and every single tree on the road from the town to her school. Here was her past and her present and she could imagine no other future than school, the journey to town and back, more school, the journey again . . .

She had already got out of the habit of remembering her life before she became a schoolteacher, and had forgotten almost everything about it. At one point she had a father and mother; they lived in Moscow near the Red Gates, in a large apartment, but all that was left of that life was a dim blurred memory, like a dream. Her father had died when she was ten years old, and her mother had died soon after . . . Her brother was an officer and they had corresponded at first, but then he got out of the habit of writing and stopped answering her letters. All she had left from her former possessions was a photograph of her mother, but it had faded because the school was so damp, and now all you could see was her hair and her eyebrows.

When they had travelled a few miles, old Semyon, who was holding the reins, turned round and said, 'They've arrested an official in town. Sent him off to jail. People are saying apparently he and some Germans killed Mayor Alekseyev in Moscow.'

'Who told you that?'

'People were reading about it in the newspaper at Ivan Ionov's inn.'

Then they were silent again for a long time. Marya Vasilyevna was thinking about her school and about the exam coming up at which she would be presenting four boys and one girl. And just as she was thinking about exams, Khanov the landowner overtook her in his four-horse carriage – the same man who had examined at her school the year before. As he drew level he recognized her and nodded his head in greeting.

'Hello there!' he said. 'You homeward bound?'

This man Khanov, who was about forty and had a haggard face and a sluggish expression, had already begun to age noticeably, but he was still handsome and attractive to women. He lived by himself on his large estate and did not have a job; people said that he did nothing at home except play chess with his old servant and walk around whistling. People also said that he drank a lot. In fact, at the exams last year, even the papers he brought with him stank of wine and cologne. Everything he had worn then was brand new and Marya Vasilyevna had been very attracted to him; she had felt completely tongue-tied while she was sitting next to him. She had grown used to cold and formal examiners at her school, but this one could not remember a single prayer and did not know what questions to ask; he was exceptionally polite and considerate and gave everyone top marks.

'I'm on my way to see Bakvist,' he continued, turning to Marya Vasilyevna, 'but I've heard he is not at home!'

They turned off the highway on to the road leading to the village, Khanov in front and Semyon following behind. Khanov's four horses plodded along the road, straining to drag the heavy carriage through the mud. Semyon, meanwhile, was weaving about, going over hillocks and through the meadows in order to avoid the road, and he kept having to get off the cart to help the horses. Marya Vasilyevna was still thinking about school and whether the exam would be difficult or easy. And she was feeling annoyed with the local *zemstvo*[1] because there had been no one in the office when she stopped by the day before. What disorder! She had been asking them for two years now to dismiss the caretaker, who did not do his job, was rude to her and beat the schoolchildren, but no one ever listened to her. It was difficult to get hold of the head of the *zemstvo* when he was at work, and even when you did, he would just tell you with tears in his eyes that he was too busy; the school inspector came only once every three years and did not understand anything because he had worked in excise before and had got the job through the back door; the board of trustees met very infrequently and no one knew where they met; the school's trustee was an uneducated peasant who ran a tanning business and was rude, slow-witted and in cahoots with the caretaker, so goodness knows to whom she was supposed to address complaints and enquiries . . .

'He really is good-looking,' she thought, glancing at Khanov.

The road was getting worse and worse. They had entered a forest. There was nowhere to turn off here, the ruts were very deep and there was gurgling water streaming along them. Prickly branches were hitting her face.

'How do you like the road?' asked Khanov with a laugh.

The teacher looked at him and could not understand why this odd person lived here. What possible use was there for his money, his interesting appearance and his fine manners in this boring, muddy place in the middle of nowhere? He was not getting anything out of life, and here he was just like Semyon, having to plod along this frightful road and putting up with the same discomforts. Why did he live here when he could live in Petersburg or abroad? And you would have thought a rich man like him might have considered it worth improving this dreadful road so as not to have to put up with this nightmare, and not have to see the despair etched on the faces of his driver and Semyon; but he just laughed; he clearly could not care less and had no interest in living better. He was a gentle, naïve and kind man who did not understand this crude life, and his knowledge of it was as poor as his knowledge of the prayers they said at exams. All he gave the school were globes of the world, and he genuinely thought he was being useful and doing a lot to improve national education. But what use were his globes here!

'Hold tight, Vasilyevna!' said Semyon.

The cart tilted heavily and almost keeled over; something heavy fell on to Marya Vasilyevna's feet – it was her shopping. Now there was a steep climb up the hill through mud as thick as clay; noisy streams were running down the winding ditches, and it was as if the water had been eating away at the road – travelling round here was dreadful! The horses were snorting. Khanov climbed out of his carriage and started walking along the edge of the road. He was hot.

'How do you like the road?' Khanov asked again with a laugh. 'My carriage is going to be wrecked at this rate.'

'No one is making you travel in weather like this, are they?' said Semyon severely. 'You should have stayed at home.'

'It's boring at home, old man. I don't like staying at home.'

He seemed slim and sprightly next to old Semyon, but there was something in his bearing, barely noticeable, which gave him away as a person who was already done for, weak and close to ruin. And just then the forest suddenly started smelling of wine. Marya Vasilyevna started to feel afraid and sorry for this person who was going into decline for no apparent reason, and it occurred to her that if she was his wife or his sister she would probably devote her whole life to saving him from ruin. If she was his wife? Life had ordained that he should live on his own on his large estate and she should live on her own in a remote village, but even just the thought that she and he could be equals and intimate with each other seemed impossible and ridiculous for some reason. Life was generally arranged in such an incomprehensible way and relationships with people were so complicated that you ended up feeling terrified, with your heart sinking, however you looked at it.

'And it's impossible to understand,' she thought, 'why God gives beauty and charm, and such sweet, sad eyes to such useless, weak and unhappy people, and why they are so attractive.'

'We're turning to the right here,' said Khanov as he got into his carriage. 'Goodbye then! All the best!'

And again she started thinking about her pupils, about the exam, about the caretaker and the board of trustees; and when the wind brought the sound of the receding carriage over from the right, these thoughts started mingling with the previous ones. She wanted to think about beautiful eyes, about love, about the happiness she would never have . . .

Be a wife? It was cold in the morning, there was no one to light the stove, the caretaker was never there; the schoolchildren would start arriving at first light, bringing snow and mud and noise; everything was so uninviting and cheerless. Her home was just one room with a kitchen in it. Her head ached every day after classes, and after dinner she felt a burning sensation in her chest. She had to collect money from her pupils for firewood and for the caretaker, take it to the school trustee, and then beg that self-satisfied, brazen peasant to be so kind as to deliver the firewood. Then at night she would dream of exams, peasants and snowdrifts. And this life had aged her and made her coarse and unattractive, she had become awkward and clumsy, as if she were filled with lead; she was afraid of everything, and in the presence of a councillor or the school trustee she would stand up, not daring to sit down again, and when she referred to them in conversation she would be needlessly deferential. No one liked her, and her life was passing by miserably, without affection, without the sympathy of friends and without any interesting acquaintances. What a terrible thing it would be if she fell in love in her position!

'Hold on tight, Vasilyevna!'

Another steep climb up a hill . . .

She had trained as a teacher out of necessity rather than any sense of vocation; she had never actually thought about a vocation, or the benefits of learning; it had always seemed to her that the most important thing in her job was not pupils or education but exams. And anyway, when did she have the time to think about a vocation or the benefits of learning? With all the work they have to do, teachers, hard-up doctors and medical assistants never even have the consolation of thinking that they are devoting themselves to an ideal or helping the people, because their heads are always full of thoughts about firewood, getting enough to eat, bad roads and illnesses. Life is difficult and uninteresting, and only docile cart-horses like Marya Vasilyevna put up with it long term; lively, sensitive, impressionable people who talk about their vocation and dedication to ideals soon become worn out and give up.

Semyon was doing his best to drive on ground that was dryer, taking short cuts through the fields and backways; but either the peasants did not always let them through or there was the priest's land and that was no thoroughfare or there was the land that Ivan Ionov had bought from the landowner and dug a trench around. Sometimes they had to turn back.

They arrived at the little town of Lower Gorodishche. Near the inn, on ground strewn with manure, underneath which there was still snow, stood carts which had been transporting large drums of oil of vitriol. There were a lot of people in the inn, all drivers, and it smelt of vodka, tobacco and sheepskin. The conversation was loud and the weighted door kept slamming. Behind the partition in the shop someone was playing an accordion continually. Marya Vasilyevna sat drinking tea, while at the next table some peasants were drinking vodka and beer, red-faced from all the tea they had drunk and the stuffiness in the inn.

'Hey, Kuzma!' some unruly voices shouted out. 'What's going on? God save us! Ivan Dementyich, I can sort things! You watch out!'

A small peasant with a short black beard and a pitted face, long drunk, was suddenly taken off guard by something; he let out a string of curses.

'What's all that swearing for? Hey, you!' Semyon called out angrily from the far corner where he was sitting. 'Surely you can see there's a lady here!'

'A lady . . .' mimicked someone in the opposite corner.

'You swine!'

'Look, we didn't mean any harm,' said the small peasant in embarrassment. 'Sorry. We'll keep to our patch, and let the lady do the same. Good morning to you!'

'Hello,' said the teacher.

'Thank you most kindly.'

Marya Vasilyevna enjoyed her tea and went red in the face like the peasants, and she started thinking again about the firewood and the caretaker . . .

'Hang on!' came a voice from the next table. 'She's the teacher from Vyazovye . . . we know her! She's a good lady.'

'Honourable!'

The weighted door kept banging as people came in and out. Marya Vasilyevna sat and thought about the same old things while the accordion played on behind the partition. There were patches of sunshine on the floor; then they transferred to the counter and onto the wall, and then they completely disappeared, which meant the sun had crept past midday. The peasants at the next table started getting ready to move. Tottering slightly, the small peasant went up to Marya Vasilyevna and shook her hand; seeing this, the others also shook her hand to say goodbye as they left one by one, and the door squeaked and banged ten times.

'Come on, Vasilyevna, time to get going,' called Semyon.

They set off. And again they had to walk.

'They built a school here not long ago, in Lower Gorodishche,' said Semyon, turning round. 'That was a bad business!'

'Why?'

'Apparently the *zemstvo* chief pocketed a thousand, and the trustee took a thousand too, and the teacher got five hundred.'

'But building a whole school only costs a thousand. It's not good to speak ill of people. That's all nonsense.'

'I don't know . . . That's what people said.'

But it was clear that Semyon did not believe the teacher. The peasants never believed her; they thought she was paid far too much – twenty-one roubles a month (when five would have been enough), and they thought that she kept most of the money she collected to pay for firewood and the caretaker. The trustee thought the same as all the peasants; he earned a bit on the side himself from the firewood, and he received a salary from the peasants for being trustee, which was something the authorities did not know about.

The forest had come to an end, thank goodness, and now it was flat all the way to Vyazovye. And there was not much further to go; they had to cross the river, then the railway line, and Vyazovye was immediately after that.

'Where are you going?' Marya Vasilyevna asked Semyon. 'You ought to take the road to the right, over the bridge.'

'What? We'll be all right this way. It's not too deep.'

'Watch out, we don't want to drown the horse.'

'What?'

'There's Khanov going across the bridge,' said Marya Vasilyevna, seeing a horse and four a long way over to the right. 'That is him, isn't it?'

'Yes, that's him. Bakvist can't have been at home. What a fool he is, heaven help us, going that way for no good reason, when it's two miles shorter this way.'

They arrived at the river. In summer it was not much more than a stream, which was easy enough to ford and had usually dried up by August, but now after the floods it was a river about forty feet across, fast-flowing, turbulent and cold, and there were fresh tracks on the bank by the water's edge – people had obviously been crossing here.

'Giddy up!' shouted Semyon angrily and with anxiety, pulling hard on the reins and waving his elbows up and down like a bird flapping its wings; 'Giddy up!'

The horse walked into the water up to its belly and stopped, then started again at once, straining every muscle, and Marya Vasilyevna felt a sharp coldness in her feet.

'Giddy up!' she also shouted out, as she stood up. 'Come on, giddy up!'

They reached the other bank.

'And anyway, what's the point of all this, for heaven's sake?' mumbled Semyon, adjusting the harness. 'It's downright murder having to deal with that *zemstvo*.'

Her shoes and galoshes were full of water, the bottom of her dress and her coat and one of her sleeves were dripping wet, and the sugar and flour were sodden – that was more upsetting than everything else and Marya Vasilyevna just threw up her hands in despair and said, 'Ah, Semyon, Semyon! . . . Really!'

The barrier was lowered at the railway crossing: the express train was coming from the station. Marya Vasilyevna stood by the crossing and waited for the train to pass, her whole body trembling with cold. You could already see Vyazovye – the school with its green roof, and the church with its crosses blazing as they reflected the evening sun; the windows in the station were also blazing, and there was pink smoke coming from the train engine . . . And it seemed to her that everything was shivering with cold.

Here was the train: its windows were flooded with bright light like the crosses on the church, and it hurt to look at them. On the platform at the end of one of the first-class carriages stood a lady and Marya Vasilyevna glanced at her fleetingly: it was her mother! What a resemblance! Her mother had the same luxuriant hair, the same forehead, and her head was inclined in the same way. And with amazing clarity, for the first time in all these thirteen years, she was able vividly to remember her mother and father, her brother, the apartment in Moscow, the aquarium with the little fish and everything else down to the smallest detail; suddenly she heard the sound of the piano and her father's voice; she felt as if she was young, pretty and well-dressed in a bright, warm room, surrounded by her family, as she had been then; a feeling of joy and happiness suddenly enveloped her and she pressed her palms to her temples in rapture and called out softly in supplication:

'Mama!'

And for no apparent reason she burst into tears. Just at that moment Khanov drove up in his coach-and-four, and when she saw him she imagined the happiness she had never had and smiled at him, nodding her head as if she was a close acquaintance and his equal, and it felt to her as if her happiness, her exultation, was reflected in the sky, in all the windows and in the trees. No, her father and mother had never died, and she had never been a teacher; that was just a long, terrible, bizarre dream, and she had just woken up . . .

'Vasilyevna, get in!'

And suddenly everything disappeared. The barrier was slowly rising. Shivering and numb with cold, Marya Vasilyevna got into the cart. The coach-and-four crossed the tracks, and Semyon followed. The guard at the crossing took off his hat.

'Here's Vyazovye. We're home.'

First published in 1897
Translated by Rosamund Bartlett

LIDIYA ZINOVYEVA-ANNIBAL
(1866–1907)

Zinovyeva-Annibal was born in Kogore on the Gulf of Finland, into an aristocratic family (her mother was descended from the African Gannibal, Pushkin's great-grandfather). Lidiya was educated at home and in private boarding schools, from which she was expelled for her rebellious behaviour. Somewhat against her parents' wishes, she married her history tutor Konstantin Shvarsalon in 1884; she left him in 1890. In 1893, in Rome, after three years travelling in Western Europe, she met the classical scholar and Symbolist poet Vyacheslav Ivanov (1866–1949), who saw her as an embodiment of the Dionysian principle he had spent so long studying. They lived together in Western Europe until 1899, when Zinovyeva-Annibal was finally able to divorce her husband and marry Ivanov. Soon after this they returned to Russia.

Ivanov and Zinovyeva-Annibal presided together over an influential weekly salon, known as 'The Tower', where they received the leading figures of St Petersburg's 'Silver Age'; Zinovyeva-Annibal, in her flowing robes, was a vivid and emotional presence there. Her plays and poetry, however, now seem of only historical interest.

She died in 1907, during an outbreak of scarlet fever (she had been ministering to peasants suffering from the disease). Her two most important works, the short novel Thirty-three Abominations *and the story-cycle* The Tragic Menagerie *were published shortly before her death. The former is one of the first Russian works of literature devoted to a lesbian relationship; it is the latter, however, that is her masterpiece. In the words of a contemporary, the poet Maksimilian Voloshin, 'Zinovyeva-Annibal, who has until now been recherchée, artificial, obscure . . . has found herself at last, has found her own language, simple and expressive, her own style, her own wings.'[1] The book was no less admired by the poets Aleksandr Blok and Marina Tsvetayeva. Nevertheless, it was forgotten both in the Soviet Union and by the émigré world, and the Russian text was not republished as a whole until 1997.*

The connected stories, told in the first person by the tomboy heroine,

Vera, seem to be re-creations of the author's own childhood. Much of the book is set on her family's estate near the Baltic. Several chapters – including the one I have chosen, 'The Monster' – are centred on various wild creatures she encounters; another evokes her awakening both to her own sexuality and to social injustice. Like D. H. Lawrence, Zinovyeva-Annibal writes equally perceptively about the wildness within us and the wildness outside us. Vera's behaviour is appalling: she kills pet animals through neglect, steals from her favourite brother and torments everyone around her. Her acts of cruelty are presented without self-justification or self-recrimination.

The longest chapter, 'The Devil', is set in St Petersburg, which Vera sees as a prison, and in a German boarding school. Sent there after yet another governess has proved unable to govern her, she conducts simultaneous 'affairs' with two of her fellow-pupils; by arranging trysts with Gertrude and Lucia in adjacent hiding places, she forces Gertrude to witness her intimacies with Lucia. Gertrude suffers an emotional breakdown and Vera is expelled; no one, least of all she herself, can cope with the 'devil' that has got into her. Only in the final story, in the words of her translator Jane Costlow, does she intuit 'a mode of being that involves neither violence nor the will to power'.[2]

THE MONSTER

Dedicated to
Konstantin Aleksandrovich Siunnerberg[1]

In the spring I caught a monster with a net in the bog.

It didn't come by itself. I brought it home in a small bucket, poured everything I'd caught into a jam jar and put the jar on the small round table by the window in my room.

If you looked through the murky water towards the light, a whole bog world appeared there.

Some kind of whirligig minnows, thin, almost transparent, with heads and whiskers, turned jaunty somersaults. Scratchy little sticks, like bits of narrow twig, went swinging forward, and suddenly a shaggy head emerged from one of their ends. A small snake cut the murk with an angular clearing motion, first gathering its tiny body in a rose-coloured clump, then spreading it out in a slender thread.

Then there were lots of shadowy, incredible grubs, just awakening to life, which I barely remembered having caught; they shifted among the grasses at the bottom of my jar.

Jellylike frogs' eggs lay in dense clusters. Inside each murky green egg was a black seedlet-embryo.

Soon the black seedlets started growing, and the egg jelly melted off somewhere. And suddenly I saw that each seedlet had grown a small tail.

Often I would come stand by my bog jar, watching the bog life, waiting: now I would see it, now it would begin. But nothing noticeable was wrong. I kept waiting for the monster to reappear.

I had seen him then for only one moment, that morning when a ray of sunlight suddenly illuminated the boggy murk, held in the net above the water, but not yet lifted completely out; it had swum towards the top and then slipped once more into darkness.

Had I in fact dreamed him, but clearly, as things can only be when waking, not in sleep? Yellowish-brown, a small tough body of flat, linked pieces, a strong rudder tail and two claws coming out of the head; huge, strong and round, with sharp linked tips. I observed it all in a sunny moment, despite the fact that the monster was no longer in size than one quarter of my pinky, and me only ten years old.

It lay in hiding three days or more, and I finally almost stopped believing I'd caught it. The net probably had a tear somewhere, or it had died in the jar. And I grew bored . . .

I longed to see the monster. And I did see him, of course.

It swam up once from the mass of frogs' eggs, quite unexpectedly, so that I cried out abruptly, 'There it is!'

My startled teacher asked severely, 'Who? . . . You frightened me.'

I was silent. For some reason I never wanted to talk about the monster.

'What are you so happy about?'

Was I, in fact, happy? I hadn't known I was happy, and I looked once more at the disgusting flat body of links and claws, swimming slowly, with sinister confidence, steering true with its strong, sharp tail.

'I'm not happy,' I finally answered decisively.

'Then why did you shout that way?'

'I found a monster.'

Now my teacher laughed, with her mirthless, condescending laugh, and came towards me.

We stood in front of the jar and scrutinized it.

I found it revolting, but at the same time that fear and revulsion drew me to it.

'It's a disgusting grub!' my teacher said, after a long pause. 'Throw it out. It will make all sorts of trouble here.'

But I didn't throw it out, and it disappeared once more.

The frog jelly melted not by the day but by the hour and, instead of the indistinct seedlets, fat black heads appeared, indisputably ugly and awkward, near the broad, transparent grey tails that I found so dapper.

They were tadpoles being born and swimming to freedom; lethargic, kind, soft all through and amusingly slow, despite the ardour of their broad, dapper, waving tails. They knocked awkward heads with a kind of trust and muddle-headedness; their muslin tails got entangled one with another.

I loved them tenderly.

In innocence they grew, in innocence they fed – on what and how I had no idea.

I felt in them something akin to myself. I envied them, I disdained them, I loved them tenderly; yes, their silly fat heads, where, of course, there were backs and stomachs lurking; and their dapper, much too tender tails.

And they grew not by the day but by the hour.

The yellow-brown monster disappeared behind the fat, black host.

But it was strange: my tadpoles fattened and grew, but they grew inexplicably fewer.

And then I saw *it* a third time and at first didn't understand. Already one-third the size of my pinky, it seemed enormous. The flat, rough body arched its linked back sharply upward, dropped its powerful tail like a stake, and as it paddled along with that rough tail, a different tail went down, its delicate muslin torn to shreds.

Then I saw both head and claws. The fat, silly, awkward head of a tadpole in the rough, powerful, piercing claws of the monster. And I understood.

I stared at the two bog brothers, held in such dreadful embrace. 'There's the trouble it will make,' I recalled the teacher's words.

And suddenly my heart stilled completely, as though it had stopped and gone into hiding, heavy as a lead weight, frightened and greedy, strangely greedy.

I stood still that way for a long time, and for a long time the silent bog doings carried on, in the murk of the boggy jar.

The black body-head turned grey, its colour grew closer and closer to that of the gentle grey tail, its form grew tapered and the ragged little tail shook more weakly . . . stopped shaking altogether. The film of grey fell slowly to the bottom of the jar.

In the pond there is an island, quite small, all covered in resinous old poplars that hang right down to the water, quiet and dark.

I sit beneath a poplar on the narrow shore, by the water, dark and quiet. My small boat doesn't move; it's an old one, with worn-off paint that was once a festive colour. The oar is tossed aside. I poled here with one oar, along the shallow pond's bottom, from the nearby shore.

So here I am, sitting in the shade above the water, and crying. There in the water move drowsy, lazing fish. For it's noon, and farther off, where the poplars' shadows don't hang along the water, the water is all overlaid with the thick viscous light of midday.

There are silver fish and thin ones – they're more lively – and then there are black ones with thick heads and bellies that sag downwards. Those are quite like my tadpoles, only they're five times bigger and just as awkward, just sleepier, and their tails aren't like muslin.

So I cry and cry. Not bitterly or abundantly, just crying, also with a noonday laziness.

And inside me I feel quite sour.

'Vera! Vera! Not again!'

It's the angry, somewhat raspy voice of my older brother.

'Bring me the boat, quickly. Since when are you allowed on the island alone?'

'Mama let me yesterday.'

'Well, yesterday isn't today.'

'She let me for today and tomorrow and for ever!'

But even as I'm shouting at the top of my voice, I'm in the boat and steering straight for my brother; I give a powerful shove and turn to the left from the stern like a wing, with my bow heading right. Quite a little minnow, I've grasped the long oar and turn with it. A shove to the right, a shove to the left.

To the right, to the left.

Uneven, impatient, shuddering passionately – just like my passionate, impatient, independent will – my boat flies up to the shore. The bow has almost touched. My brother is already rasping out, 'Where are you going? Where? And they let you go out alone!'

'You've got the dogs!'

The two sleek setters, Piron and Boyar, and the long, wavy-haired Gordon setter, Bertha, yelp by the water from excitement and nerves.

'What, you've only just noticed?'

'Are you going to let them swim?'

'Yes.'

'Can I come?'

I look pleadingly into the boat, because I've long since shifted to the planks of the pier, and my brother is in the boat, in my place.

'You can't; somebody was looking for you at home. You still haven't learned some scales or other.'

'Vasenka, Vasenka, please let me!"

'You can't, I tell you. I just remembered: it was Emiliya Lvovna looking for you. She's in the drawing room, and she's very angry. I'd get a move on.'

And then, quite gently, uncharacteristically, my brother adds, 'What's the matter, Vera? Were you crying? You're all puffy from tears. Were you punished?'

I flared up.

'Just the opposite.'

'And what's the opposite of punishment? A reward? Think we'll live that long? Let's ask Emiliya Lvovna at dinner, let's ask!'

Oh, how I hate this Emiliya Lvovna, the lazybones. She's only come to the country to give music lessons and she's ill-humoured from boredom, thrusting sheets of music in my face!

But I don't want to tell my brother about them and about it. And I'm afraid to keep silent: won't he really start to believe it? I mean, won't he believe I'm being punished? Shame! Shame! And he's kind today, even though his teasing is unpleasant, like always, and his voice is tender, and he's become just like Mama himself.

'Vasenka, it's the tadpoles.'

And once again I'm crying and telling him about them, and about *it* – the monster.

Vasya listens to me attentively, one foot planted on the bottom of the boat, the other thrust up on the high edge of the pier. Then for a fairly long time he's quiet.

And then, quite resolutely, he says, 'That's nature, Vera.'

I don't know what to make of it.

'A normal person gets used to nature. It becomes like second nature.'

I don't know what to make of it.

He notices my stupidity. He smiles at it condescendingly, but also a bit sadly.

'You see, don't you understand, all of that around us,' he drew a big arc with his hand, 'in the water, on the earth and in the earth, understand? It all lives according to nature, understand, and that means it can't do any differently. And, as a result, that's how it has to be. That's all very well, but then people sometimes want to live in ways they can't. That means making things complicated, understand, and not even obeying God, understand, God!? So don't cry . . . Piron! Piroshka! . . . You'll get used to it . . . Boyarka! Bertha! Here! . . .

There's no help for it . . . Into the water you cowards, you scoundrels!
. . . So don't cry, silly girl!'

He rowed standing up, to see the dogs better; he quietly worked
both oars, heading down along the pond towards the dam where the
water was deep, and the two dogs' heads, their ears laid back, swam
close behind the stern.

Only Bertha was still yelping and barking on the shore; she would
run into the water up to her belly and jump back out, shaking off the
diamond-like spray from her long, wavy hair. She looked up at me
with her big brown eyes; they were guilty and frightened, greedily,
restlessly beseeching. There was an exhausting, frightened longing in
her bark and in the unpleasant twists and turns of her body, wet
through and suddenly grotesquely thin.

My brother yelled wildly.

'Bertha! Come here, you bitch!'

With one leap Bertha is in the water. The long white back with a
patch of yellow in the middle still trembles unevenly above the water.
It's clear that her paws can still reach the bottom, they're stepping.
But now the back has sunk under, only the patch just sticks out. Bertha
swims evenly, effortlessly, and her luxurious tail lies on the water like
a trusty rudder. Soon in the distance I can see only her white head,
and with my too-seeing eyes I make out russet ears trembling with
fright, glistening with sun on their long, wavy silk.

'Or you know what? Throw out your jar!' my brother yells, his
overly loud voice travelling over the quiet water. 'Faster, Bertha, faster!
. . . Throw it in the wash pail . . . Hello, friends, after me! . . . What
are you keeping slime in your room for?'

'Why don't you throw that disgusting grub out of the jar?' asked my
teacher, quite unexpectedly interrupting the explication of Schiller's
ballad 'The Goblet'.

I stared straight into her eyes, but didn't see them and didn't answer.
She repeated the question.

'Because . . . that's how it has to be.'

'What has to be?'

'That – so it will eat.'

'And why is that?'

'That's how God made it.'

'And who explained that to you?'

'Vasya himself.'

And my eyes, still not heeding the tall, sinewy woman sitting opposite, grew hard and impudent.

Then I added with a laugh, drawling out my words: 'Because –
that's nature.'

'In no way is what you have in that disgusting stupid jar nature. It's
plain old capriciousness.'

She's very indignant. She's right and she's not right, because in the
swamp there is more room for them to hide, but then there are more
things to attack them.

So I say angrily, 'Well, so much the better.'

Now I saw the eyes I'd been staring at so long, so impudently,
without seeing. But the pale, unattractively flared-out eyes were unusually agitated, even frightened. My strict, righteous, extremely short-
sighted teacher is frightened by sure signs of resurgent rebellion.
Something pushed me to rebel. Words of some kind – incomprehensible even to me – squeezed upwards and out of my mouth. She kept
on asking, 'What is better? Why is it better?'

'It'll end quicker.'

'Dear Fathers! What will end?'

I didn't know what would 'end', didn't know what and why it was
'so much the better'; but I knew I would no longer read and explicate
Schiller's 'Goblet', with its repulsive sea monster. I stood up impertin-
ently from my chair opposite her and, with an air of importance,
walked out of the schoolroom unhurriedly.

I decided to head for the pond . . .

Of course, after the pond I was punished: three days without
playtime.

Now there were only thirteen tadpoles left, and nothing was left
alive in the boggy murk except for them and the monster.

Perhaps not less than two weeks had passed since the day we read
Schiller's ballad, and the tadpoles shown mercy were in essence no
longer tadpoles. Four flared paws with tiny webbed fingers had grown
out of each fat head. And the head itself proved not only a head, but
had a soft little belly and a round-shouldered frog's back.

And I laughed aloud now at the frogs with tails. Why did frogs in
the open, in the grass, not have tails, but in my jar they did?

My darlings, my darlings!

While the monster, who'd gobbled up everything that swarmed in
my bog catch – like Pharaoh's seven skinny cows, who gobbled up
seven fat ones and didn't get fat – stayed just as fat, rough and plated,
with a strong, menacing tail and greedy claws. It just got a bit longer.

I came to love the monster.

To me it seemed clothed in armour. And in the soundless bog-
water murk, where soft-bodied, witless, quite defenceless tadpoles

joggled and jostled, it alone ruled absolute over lives – precise, strong, swift.

And it devoured, triumphant. And I disdained the tadpoles.

I would run, though, to the river and to the pond. I would crouch down and stare for a long time in to the water. I was thinking of splashing it in there. In order to stop seeing it, and in order to save at least those thirteen tadpoles with tails.

Once more in the pond I saw black tadpoles, sleepy little fish. Maybe he'll start sucking them up? He'd grown to half the length of my little finger, the horrible thing.

And I returned to the jar empty-handed. There I saw the well-fed, lazy monster, nestled on the bottom among grey skins he'd sucked dry.

The monster was mysterious.

The teacher and I talked a great deal about him. We looked through three books where all sorts of things were described. We compared, we measured, but still weren't certain about his past, or his future.

'You know, I still think this grub of yours will turn into a water beetle!' the teacher announced decisively.

Then we both stood by the window and looked into the jar.

'Well, a water bug is black and round.'

'So, what do you make of that?'

'It's not at all alike.'

'Good Lord, how unreasonable you are! Do you think mosquitoes, that those silly stalks floating in your jar will turn into, look like their grubs? And butterflies?'

I'm not convinced.

'Water beetles are good.'

'How do you know?'

'Down below in the barrels, you know, the ones under the gutters, lots of them swim around.'

'Well, what of it? Have you gone swimming with them, like a little beetle maybe, or a fish?'

'Well, so what?'

'Why are you so sure they wouldn't eat you up?'

'Anyway, I don't believe that *it* is a water beetle.'

'Well, I'm not certain either. Strange, mysterious grub!'

The monster had to turn into something. But into what? What? What could things so evil, so brownish-yellow turn into, clawed and plated as they were, with tough tails that steer like a rudder toward the victim?

How terrible that the monster had to turn into something!

But maybe, after all, it would turn into a black water beetle, round, shiny and . . . maybe, probably even, of course, it would be good.

Where, then, would the evil go?

Could it disappear completely? Simply go nowhere, simply disappear? Like steam . . .

No, steam thickens from cold into clouds in the sky, and the rain comes down . . . Isn't that so?

Only one small frog was left. And at some point his tail had fallen off. He'd become such a fresh young thing! So, so dear! All green! With a strong back, feet spread wide and warty, with staring eyes.

He made it out of his home-made little bog by climbing up the glass; he breathed quickly, the way pocket watches whir, and his fat, soft little stomach fell in and rose at his short neck. He was so, so green and always fresh from a bath.

He watches wide-eyed with soft, crumpled lids. He doesn't climb down in the water.

Tame!

The monster?

So what am I to do with the monster?

Not in the river. Not in the pond. In the bog? There are baby frogs there, too.

I brought a rock for the jar, found a thick one and set it on end, so he could climb out on top. He has lungs now, he breathes with lungs now and not with gills. Both with lungs and gills: with whatever he needs. My teacher said so.

But he climbs down from the rock. He loves the water. And then . . .

To kill.

To kill the monster and save the soft, tame little frog, the last one. But how to kill something so tough and plated? You can't crush it. It will crunch. It's impossible. Disgusting.

Simply catch it and shake it out in the sun. It's sunny on the balcony. There's a door right here from the room on to the balcony; strictly speaking onto the roof, which is railed off with a balustrade and covered with iron sheeting. The iron heats up almost as much as my toy irons, which I use to press my doll's clothes. (I even tried to heat them that way in the sunshine.) That's the south. But even so, of course, for this one it's not enough . . .

Still, if you splash it out, it will bake to death there. It'll croak, the filthy thing.

Yes, Vasya was right. Better if I'd poured everything out together. Oh God! Why is it so hard?

Little green one sat on the stone till evening. Mouth like a rainbow, little warts everywhere. Looking. And then he lowers the soft folds over his eyes, and they become two stretched-out grey balloons.

I went about impatient, ill-tempered. My heart was in torment. I loved and hated the monster.

No, I hated the green one.

I went to bed that way, without deciding. Anyway, towards evening the sun had left my balcony . . .

I'm lying down and trying to sleep, not sleeping. It's very unpleasant.

I should light a candle. To see what's in the jar. What if it doesn't sleep at night? Does it have eyes? I didn't notice behind the claws. And anyway, it doesn't matter. Since at night your eyes can't see.

It will suck the frog to death. Oh, *it* will suck it to death before morning!

But the other one's on the rock . . . He'll climb down; oh, he'll climb down from the rock into his favourite murky water, boggy and homelike.

On purpose, I've been bringing water from a deep ditch, where slippery grass grows. Only I've tried hard not to scoop in a new creature together with the water . . .

My mind races and I've already lifted my foot towards the floor. Suddenly I remember angrily, 'Nature! Nature! Man wants to live in ways he can't. That means not even obeying God.'

And then I'm lazy! And it's dark! And it's awfully unpleasant to see him at night.

But what if suddenly it changed? Suddenly, right today? Right now has decided to change? And if it decided to change, maybe it's a sin to kill it. Maybe before it sucks the other one to death it will change, and then it will never suck anyone. But if I kill it? Kill it right at the moment when I shouldn't?

And then how to kill it? There's no sun at night. You have to crush it. It will crunch. It's hard.

I buried my head beneath the pillow, so everything would be muffled and soft.

So let it! . . . That's how it has to be. I fell asleep.

In the morning, the goggle-eyed, web-footed little frog was no more. It, it. It alone.

I don't feel sorry. I don't cry. Some sort of calm had descended.

I go down to the pantry for a spoon, in silence, biting my lip in businesslike fashion. I fish out the sleepy, well-fed monster with the spoon. And out on to the iron balcony.

The sun hasn't heated the iron sheets yet. It's still around the corner. Shall I wait? Impossible!

I splash out the water, shake him out on to the floor. I watch.

He coils about, beating disgustingly with his hard tail against the iron, lifting his clawed head with its vile yellow eyes. I see, now I see everything. I lean over close. He'd be half the length of my little finger, but I imagine that I'm looking into his eyes, right into them, vile, yellow, greedy, merciless.

I brought the stone that had been in the jar, where the green one would sit. I pressed the stone on the vile head with its claws and eyes. I crush it. It crunches. But the plated body still shakes, curving all over, and the tail lifts upright.

It's unbearably disgusting.

I throw the stone. The head is all crushed.

Nothing. Nothing. Now everything will be finished. Still business-like, I go to my room. I grasp the jar tight with two hands – and through the window.

The jar flies, splattering fetid, dead water, the dirty jar flies far beyond the window, towards the clean sand on the flower-bedded lawn. It's a heart that's grown spiteful, with a sharp feline claw.

Nothing. So everything in my jar 'finished quickly'. Let it.

But there, in the bog, it continues – as God ordained?

First published in 1907
Translated by Jane Costlow

IVAN ALEKSEYEVICH BUNIN

(1870–1953)

Bunin was born in Voronezh into a family of impoverished gentry.
After briefly attending Moscow University, he worked as a journalist,
then in rural administration. His first published works were in verse,
but he soon became better known for his prose; his models were
Pushkin, Tolstoy and Chekhov. He saw Tolstoy as the greatest ex-
emplar of a tradition of noblemen-writers of which he was himself the
last representative. Bunin left Russia in 1920 and settled in France,
remaining fiercely hostile to the Soviet regime. In 1933 he was awarded
the Nobel Prize for Literature.

In his autobiographical novel Life of Arseniev (written 1930–39),
Bunin wrote of himself as a young man: 'my sight was so good that
I could see all seven stars of the Pleiades; I could hear the whistle of
a marmot over half a mile away in the evening fields, and the smell
of a lily of the valley or an old book could make me drunk.' His
mature prose is sensual, musical and perfectly controlled. He claimed
that prose, like verse, 'must be in a definite key'; he also spoke about
the need to establish 'the general resonance' of a work.

Bunin was first translated into English as early as 1916 and was
admired by such writers as Katherine Mansfield, Virginia and Leonard
Woolf and D. H. Lawrence. During the second half of the twentieth
century, however, he was somewhat forgotten in the West – probably
because of a general lack of interest in émigré literature at a time when
it seemed more important to try to understand the Soviet Union.
Bunin's last volume of stories, Dark Avenues (1943), has been especially neglected – even though he rightly considered it his best book.
Two other important works by Bunin are his novel The Village (1910),
a dark and perceptive portrayal praised by Maksim Gorky of the
deepening crisis of peasant Russia, and his memoir Cursed Days, an
account of the anarchy and brutality Bunin witnessed between 1918
and his final departure from Russia in 1920.

The Koteliansky/Lawrence/Woolf translation of 'The Gentleman from San Francisco' is outstanding. Koteliansky provided a literal version; this was edited first by Lawrence, then by Leonard Woolf. Lawrence and Woolf both had a light touch as editors, clearly understanding that an intelligent literal translation can sometimes need only the most delicate of adjustments to become poetry. 'In Paris' (from Dark Avenues) is one of Bunin's few works set in his émigré present, rather than his Russian past.

THE GENTLEMAN FROM SAN FRANCISCO

Woe to thee, Babylon, that mighty city!
Apocalypse

The gentleman from San Francisco – nobody either in Capri or Naples ever remembered his name – was setting out with his wife and daughter for the Old World, to spend there two years of pleasure.

He was fully convinced of his right to rest, to enjoy long and comfortable travels, and so forth. Because, in the first place he was rich, and in the second place, notwithstanding his fifty-eight years, he was just starting to live. Up to the present he had not lived, but only existed; quite well, it is true, yet with all his hopes on the future. He had worked incessantly – and the Chinamen whom he employed by the thousand in his factories knew what that meant. Now at last he realized that a great deal had been accomplished, and that he had almost reached the level of those whom he had taken as his ideals, so he made up his mind to pause for a breathing space. Men of his class usually began their enjoyments with a trip to Europe, India, Egypt. He decided to do the same. He wished naturally to reward himself in the first place for all his years of toil, but he was quite glad that his wife and daughter should also share in his pleasures. True, his wife was not distinguished by any marked susceptibilities, but then elderly American women are all passionate travellers. As for his daughter, a girl no longer young and somewhat delicate, travel was really necessary for her: apart from the question of health, do not happy meetings often take place in the course of travel? One may find oneself sitting next to a multimillionaire at table, or examining frescoes side by side with him.

The itinerary planned by the Gentleman from San Francisco was extensive. In December and January he hoped to enjoy the sun of southern Italy, the monuments of antiquity, the tarantella, the serenades of vagrant minstrels and, finally, that which men of his age are most susceptible to, the love of quite young Neapolitan girls, even when the love is not altogether disinterestedly given. Carnival he thought of spending in Nice, in Monte Carlo, where at that season gathers the most select society, the precise society on which depend all the blessings of civilization – the fashion in evening dress, the stability of thrones, the declaration of wars, the prosperity of hotels; where some devote themselves passionately to automobile and boat races, others to roulette, others to what is called flirtation, and others to the shooting of pigeons which beautifully soar from their traps over emerald lawns, against a background of forget-me-not sea, instantly to fall, hitting the ground in little white heaps. The beginning of March he wished to devote to Florence, Passion Week in Rome, to hear the music of the Miserere; his plans also included Venice, Paris, bullfights in Seville, bathing in the British Isles; then Athens, Constantinople, Egypt, even Japan . . . certainly on his way home . . . And everything at the outset went splendidly.

It was the end of November. Practically all the way to Gibraltar the voyage passed in icy darkness, varied by storms of wet snow. Yet the ship travelled well, even without much rolling. The passengers on board were many, and all people of some importance. The boat, the famous *Atlantis*, resembled a most expensive European hotel with all modern equipments: a night refreshment bar, Turkish baths, a newspaper printed on board; so that the days aboard the liner passed in the most select manner. The passengers rose early, to the sound of bugles sounding shrilly through the corridors in that grey twilit hour, when day was breaking slowly and sullenly over the grey-green, watery desert, which rolled heavily in the fog. Clad in their flannel pyjamas, the gentlemen took coffee, chocolate or cocoa, then seated themselves in marble baths, did exercises, thereby whetting their appetite and their sense of well-being, made their toilet for the day, and proceeded to breakfast. Till eleven o'clock they were supposed to stroll cheerfully on deck, breathing the cold freshness of the ocean; or they played table-tennis or other games, that they might have an appetite for their eleven o'clock refreshment of sandwiches and bouillon; after which they read their newspaper with pleasure and calmly awaited luncheon – which was a still more varied and nourishing meal than breakfast. The two hours which followed luncheon were devoted to rest. All the decks were crowded with lounge chairs on which lay passengers wrapped in plaids, looking at the mist-heavy sky or the foamy hillocks which flashed behind the bows, and dozing sweetly. Till five o'clock, when, refreshed and lively, they were treated to strong, fragrant tea and sweet cakes. At seven, bugle-calls announced a dinner of nine courses. And now the Gentleman from San Francisco, rubbing his hands in a rising flush of vital forces, hastened to his state cabin to dress.

In the evening, the tiers of the *Atlantis* yawned in the darkness as with innumerable fiery eyes, and a multitude of servants in the kitchens, sculleries, wine cellars, worked with a special frenzy. The ocean heaving beyond was terrible, but no one thought of it, firmly believing in the captain's power over it. The captain was a ginger-haired man of monstrous size and weight, apparently always torpid, who looked in his uniform with broad gold stripes very like a huge idol, and who rarely emerged from his mysterious chambers to show himself to the passengers. Every minute the siren howled from the bows with hellish moroseness, and screamed with fury, but few diners heard it – it was drowned by the sounds of an excellent string band, exquisitely and untiringly playing in the huge two-tiered hall that was decorated with marble and covered with velvet carpets, flooded with feasts of light from crystal chandeliers and gilded girandoles, and crowded with ladies in bare shoulders and jewels, with men in dinner jackets, elegant waiters and respectful maîtres d'hôtel, one of whom, he who took the wine orders only, wore a chain round his neck like a lord mayor. Dinner jacket and perfect linen made the Gentleman from San Francisco look much younger. Dry, of small stature, badly built but strongly made, polished to a glow and in due measure animated, he sat in the golden-pearly radiance of this palace, with a bottle of amber Johannisberger at his hand, and glasses, large and small, of delicate crystal, and a curly bunch of fresh hyacinths. There was something Mongolian in his yellowish face, large teeth blazing with gold, and strong bald head blazing like old ivory. Richly dressed, but in keeping with her age, sat his wife, a big, broad, quiet woman. Intricately, but lightly and transparently dressed, with an innocent immodesty, sat his daughter, tall, slim, her magnificent hair splendidly done, her breath fragrant with violet cachous, and the tenderest little rosy moles showing near her lip and between her bare, slightly pow-dered shoulder-blades. The dinner lasted two whole hours, to be followed by dancing in the ballroom, whence the men, including, of course, the Gentleman from San Francisco, proceeded to the bar; there, with their feet cocked up on the tables, they settled the destinies of nations in the course of their political and stock-exchange conver-sations, smoking meanwhile Havana cigars and drinking liqueurs till they were crimson in the face, waited on all the while by negroes in red jackets with eyes like peeled hard-boiled eggs.

Outside, the ocean heaved in black mountains; the snowstorm hissed

furiously in the clogged cordage; the steamer trembled in every fibre
as she surmounted these watery hills and struggled with the storm,
ploughing through the moving masses which every now and then
reared in front of her, foam-crested. The siren, choked by the fog,
groaned in mortal anguish. The watchmen in the lookout towers froze
with cold, and went mad with their superhuman straining of attention.
As the gloomy and sultry depths of the inferno, as the ninth circle,
was the submerged womb of the steamer, where gigantic furnaces
roared and dully giggled, devouring with their red-hot maws mountains of coal cast hoarsely in by men naked to the waist, bathed in their
own corrosive dirty sweat, and lurid with the purple-red reflection of
flame. But in the refreshment bar, men jauntily put their feet up on
the tables, showing their patent-leather pumps, and sipped cognac or
other liqueurs, and swam in waves of fragrant smoke as they chatted
in well-bred manner. In the dancing hall, light and warmth and joy
were poured over everything; couples turned in the waltz or writhed
in the tango, while the music insistently, shamelessly, delightfully, with
sadness entreated for one, only one thing, one and the same thing all
the time. Among this resplendent crowd was an ambassador, a little
dry modest old man; a great millionaire, clean-shaven, tall, of an
indefinite age, looking like a prelate in his old-fashioned dress coat;
also a famous Spanish author, and an international beauty already the
least bit faded, of unenviable reputation; finally an exquisite loving
couple, whom everybody watched curiously because of their uncon-
cealed happiness: *he* danced only with *her*, and sang, with great skill,
only to *her* accompaniment, and everything about them seemed so
charming! – and only the Captain knew that this couple had been
engaged by the steamship company to play at love for a good salary,
and that they had been sailing for a long time, now on one liner, now
on another.

At Gibraltar the sun gladdened them all: it was like early spring. A
new passenger appeared on board, arousing general interest. He was
a hereditary prince of a certain Asiatic state, travelling incognito: a
small man, as if all made of wood, though his movements were alert;
broad-faced, in gold-rimmed glasses, a little unpleasant because of his
large black moustache, which was sparse and transparent like that
of a corpse; but on the whole inoffensive, simple, modest. In the
Mediterranean they met once more the breath of winter. Waves, large
and florid as the tail of a peacock, waves with snow-white crests
heaved under the impulse of the tramontane wind, and came merrily,
madly rushing towards the ship, in the bright lustre of a perfectly clear
sky. The next day the sky began to pale, the horizon grew dim, land

was approaching: Ischia, Capri could be seen through the glasses, then Naples herself, looking like pieces of sugar strewn at the foot of some dove-coloured mass; while beyond, vague and deadly white with snow, a range of distant mountains. The decks were crowded. Many ladies and gentlemen were putting on light fur-trimmed coats. Noiseless Chinese servant boys, bandy-legged, with pitch-black plaits hanging down to their heels, and with girlish thick eyebrows, unobtrusively came and went, carrying up the stairways plaids, canes, valises, handbags of crocodile leather, and never speaking above a whisper. The daughter of the Gentleman from San Francisco stood side by side with the Prince, who, by a happy circumstance, had been introduced to her the previous evening. She had the air of one looking fixedly into the distance towards something which he was pointing out to her, and which he was explaining hurriedly, in a low voice. Owing to his size he looked among the rest like a boy. Altogether he was not handsome, rather queer, with his spectacles, bowler hat, and English coat, and then the hair of his sparse moustache just like horsehair, and the swarthy, thin skin of his face seeming stretched over his features and slightly varnished. But the girl listened to him, and was so excited that she did not know what he was saying. Her heart beat with incomprehensible rapture because of him, because he was standing next to her and talking to her, to her alone. Everything, everything about him was so unusual – his dry hands, his clean skin under which flowed ancient, royal blood, even his plain, but somehow particularly tidy European dress; everything was invested with an indefinable glamour, with all that was calculated to enthral a young woman. The Gentleman from San Francisco, wearing for his part a silk hat and grey spats over patent-leather shoes, kept eyeing the famous beauty who stood near him, a tall, wonderful figure, blonde, with her eyes painted according to the latest Parisian fashion, holding on a silver chain a tiny, cringing, hairless little dog, to which she was addressing herself all the time. And the daughter, feeling some vague embarrassment, tried not to notice her father.

Like all Americans, he was very liberal with his money when travelling. And like all of them, he believed in the full sincerity and goodwill of those who brought his food and drinks, served him from morn till night, anticipated his smallest desire, watched over his cleanliness and rest, carried his things, called the porters, conveyed his trunks to the hotels. So it was everywhere, so it was during the voyage, so it ought to be in Naples. Naples grew and drew nearer. The brass band, shining with the brass of their instruments, had already assembled on deck. Suddenly they deafened everybody with the strains of their triumphant ragtime. The giant captain appeared in full uniform on the bridge, and like a benign pagan idol waved his hands to the passengers in a gesture of welcome. And to the Gentleman from San Francisco, as well as to every other passenger, it seemed as if for him alone was thundered forth that ragtime march, so greatly beloved by proud America; for him alone the Captain's hand waved, welcoming him on his safe arrival. Then, when at last the *Atlantis* entered port and veered her many-tiered mass against the quay that was crowded with expectant people, when the gangways began their rattling – ah, then what a lot of porters and their assistants in caps with golden galloon, what a lot of all sorts of commissionaires, whistling boys, and sturdy ragamuffins with packs of postcards in their hands rushed to meet the Gentleman from San Francisco with offers of their services! With what amiable contempt he grinned at those ragamuffins as he walked to the auto-mobile of the very same hotel at which the Prince would probably put up, and calmly muttered between his teeth, now in English, now in Italian – 'Go away! Via!'

Life at Naples started immediately in the set routine. Early in the morning, breakfast in a gloomy dining room with a draughty damp wind blowing in from the windows that opened on to a little stony garden: a cloudy, unpromising day, and a crowd of guides at the doors of the vestibule. Then the first smiles of a warm, pinky-coloured sun, and from the high, overhanging balcony a view of Vesuvius, bathed to the feet in the radiant vapours of the morning sky, while beyond, over the silvery-pearly ripple of the bay, the subtle outline of Capri upon the horizon! Then nearer, tiny donkeys running in two-wheeled buggies away below on the sticky embankment, and detachments of tiny soldiers marching off with cheerful and defiant music.

After this a walk to the taxi stand, and a slow drive along crowded, narrow, damp corridors of streets, between high, many-windowed houses. Visits to deadly-clean museums, smoothly and pleasantly lighted, but monotonously, as if from the reflection of snow. Or visits to churches, cold, smelling of wax, and always the same thing: a majestic portal, curtained with a heavy leather curtain: inside, a huge emptiness, silence, lonely little flames of clustered candles ruddying the depths of the interior on some altar decorated with ribbon: a forlorn old woman amid dark benches, slippery gravestones under one's feet, and somebody's infallibly famous *Descent from the Cross*. Luncheon at one o'clock on San Martino, where quite a number of the very selectest people gather about midday, and where once the daughter of the Gentleman from San Francisco almost became ill with joy, fancying she saw the Prince sitting in the hall, although she knew from the newspapers that he had gone to Rome for a time. At five o'clock, tea in the hotel, in the smart salon where it was so warm, with the deep carpets and blazing fires. After which the thought of dinner – and again the powerful commanding voice of the gong heard over all the floors, and again strings of bare-shouldered ladies rustling with their silks on the staircases and reflecting themselves in the mirrors, again the wide-flung, hospitable, palatial dining room, the red jackets of musicians on the platform, the black flock of waiters around the maître d'hôtel, who with extraordinary skill was pouring out a thick, roseate soup into soup plates. The dinners, as usual, were the crowning event of the day. Everyone dressed as if for a wedding, and so abundant were the dishes, the wines, the table waters, sweet-meats, and fruit, that at about eleven o'clock in the evening the chambermaids would take to every room rubber hot-water bottles, to warm the stomachs of those who had dined.

None the less, December of that year was not a success for Naples. The porters and secretaries were abashed if spoken to about the weather, only guiltily lifting their shoulders and murmuring that they could not possibly remember such a season; although this was not the first year they had had to make such murmurs or to hint that 'every-where something terrible is happening'. Unprecedented rains and storms on the Riviera, snow in Athens, Etna also piled with snow and glowing red at night; tourists fleeing from the cold of Palermo . . . The morning sun daily deceived the Neapolitans. The sky invariably grew grey towards midday, and fine rain began to fall, falling thicker and colder. The palms of the hotel approach glistened like wet tin; the city seemed peculiarly dirty and narrow, the museums excessively dull; the cigar-ends of the fat cabmen, whose rubber rain-capes flapped like wings in the wind, seemed insufferably stinking, the energetic cracking of whips over the ears of thin-necked horses sounded altogether false, and the clack of the shoes of the signorine who cleaned the tramlines quite horrible, while the women, walking through the mud, with their black heads uncovered in the rain, seemed disgustingly short-legged: not to mention the stench and dampness of foul fish which drifted from the quay where the sea was foaming. The Gentleman and Lady from San Francisco began to bicker in the mornings; their daughter went about pale and headachy, and then roused up again, went into raptures over everything, and was lovely, charming. Charming were those tender, complicated feelings which had been aroused in her by the meeting with the plain little man in whose veins ran such special blood. But after all, does it matter what awakens a maiden soul –whether it is money, fame or noble birth? . . . Everybody declared that in Sorrento, or in Capri, it was quite different. There it was warmer, sunnier, the lemon trees were in bloom, the morals were purer, the wine unadulterated. So behold, the family from San Francisco decided to go with all their trunks to Capri, after which they would return and settle down in Sorrento: when they had seen Capri, trodden the stones where stood Tiberius' palaces, visited the famous caves of the Blue Grotto, and listened to the pipers from Abruzzi, who wander about the isle during the month of the Nativity, singing the praises of the Virgin.

On the day of departure – a very memorable day for the family from San Francisco – the sun did not come out even in the morning. A heavy fog hid Vesuvius to the base and came greying low over the leaden heave of the sea, whose waters were concealed from the eye at a distance of half a mile. Capri was completely invisible, as if it had never existed on earth. The little steamer that was making for the island tossed so violently from side to side that the family from San Francisco lay like stones on the sofas in the miserable saloon of the tiny boat, their feet wrapped in plaids, and their eyes closed. The Lady, as she thought, suffered worst of all, and several times was overcome with sickness. It seemed to her that she was dying. But the stewardess who came to and fro with the basin, the stewardess who had been for years, day in, day out, through heat and cold, tossing on these waves, and who was still indefatigable, even kind to everyone – she only smiled. The younger lady from San Francisco was deathly pale, and held in her teeth a slice of lemon. Now not even the thought of meeting the Prince at Sorrento, where he was due to arrive by Christmas, could gladden her. The Gentleman lay flat on his back, in a broad overcoat and a flat cap, and did not loosen his jaws throughout the voyage. His face grew dark, his moustache white, his head ached furiously. For the last few days, owing to the bad weather, he had been drinking heavily, and had more than once admired the *tableaux vivants*. The rain whipped on the rattling windowpanes, under which water dripped on to the sofas, the wind beat the masts with a howl, and at moments, aided by an onrushing wave, laid the little steamer right on its side, whereupon something would roll noisily away below. At the stopping places, Castellamare, Sorrento, things were a little better. But even there the ship heaved frightfully; and the coast with all its precipices, gardens, pines, pink and white hotels, and hazy, curly green mountains swooped past the window, up and down, as it were on swings. The boats bumped against the side of the ship, the sailors and passengers shouted lustily, and somewhere a child, as if crushed to death, choked itself with screaming. The damp wind blew through the doors, and outside on the sea, from a reeling boat which showed the flag of the Hotel Royal, a fellow with guttural French exaggeration yelled unceasingly: 'Rrroy-al! Hotel Rrroy-al!' intending to lure passengers aboard his craft. Then the Gentleman from San Francisco, feeling, as he ought to have felt, quite an old man, thought with anguish and spite of all these 'Royals', 'Splendids', 'Excelsiors', and of these greedy, good-for-nothing, garlic-stinking fellows called Italians. Once, during a halt, on opening his eyes and rising from the sofa he saw under the rocky cliff-curtain of the coast a heap of such miserable stone hovels, all musty and mouldy, stuck on top of one another by the very water, among the boats, and the rags of all sorts, tin cans and brown fishing nets, and, remembering that this was the very Italy he had come to enjoy, he was seized with despair . . . At last, in the twilight, the black mass of the island began to loom nearer, looking as if it were bored through at the base with little red lights. The wind grew softer, warmer, more sweet smelling. Over the tamed waves, undulating like black oil, there came flowing golden boa constrictors of light from the lanterns of the harbour . . . Then suddenly the anchor rumbled and fell with a splash into the water. Furious cries of the boatmen shouting against one another came from all directions. And relief was felt at once. The electric light of the cabin shone brighter, and a desire to eat, drink, smoke, move once more made itself felt . . . Ten minutes later the family from San Francisco disembarked into a large boat; in a quarter of an hour they had stepped on to the stones of the quay, and were soon seated in the bright little car of the funicular railway. With a buzz they were ascending the slope, past the stakes of the vineyards and wet, sturdy orange trees, here and there protected by straw screens, past the thick glossy foliage and the brilliancy of orange fruits . . . Sweetly smells the earth in Italy after rain, and each of her islands has its own peculiar aroma.

The island of Capri was damp and dark that evening. For the moment, however, it had revived, and was lighted up here and there as usual at the hour of the steamer's arrival. At the top of the ascent, on the little piazza by the funicular station, stood the crowd of those whose duty it was to receive with propriety the luggage of the Gentleman from San Francisco. There were other arrivals too, but none worthy of notice: a few Russians who had settled in Capri, untidy and absent-minded owing to their bookish thoughts, spectacled, bearded, half-buried in the upturned collars of their thick woollen overcoats. Then a group of long-legged, long-necked, round-headed German youths in Tyrolese costumes, with knapsacks over their shoulders, needing no assistance, feeling everywhere at home and always economical in tips. The Gentleman from San Francisco, who kept quietly apart from both groups, was marked out at once. He and his ladies were hastily assisted from the car, men ran in front to show them the way, and they set off on foot, surrounded by urchins and by the sturdy Capri women who carry on their heads the luggage of decent travellers. Across the piazza, that looked like an opera scene in the light of the electric globe that swung aloft in the damp wind, clacked the wooden pattens of the women porters. The gang of urchins began to whistle to the Gentleman from San Francisco, and to turn somersaults around him, while he, as if on the stage, marched among them towards a medieval archway and under huddled houses, behind which led a little echoing lane, past tufts of palm trees showing above the flat roofs to the left, and under the stars in the dark blue sky, upwards towards the shining entrance of the hotel ... And again it seemed as if purely in honour of the guests from San Francisco the damp little town on the rocky little island of the Mediterranean had revived from its evening stupor, that their arrival alone had made the hotel proprietor so happy and hearty, and that for them had been waiting the Chinese gong which sent its howlings through all the house the moment they crossed the doorstep.

The sight of the proprietor, a superbly elegant young man with a polite and exquisite bow, startled for a moment the Gentleman from San Francisco. In the first flash, he remembered that amid the chaos of images which had possessed him the previous night in his sleep, he had seen that very man, to a T the same man, in the same full-skirted frock coat and with the same glossy, perfectly smoothed hair. Startled, he hesitated for a second. But long, long ago he had lost the last mustard-seed of any mystical feeling he might ever have had, and his surprise at once faded. He told the curious coincidence of dream and reality jestingly to his wife and daughter, as they passed along the hotel corridor. And only his daughter glanced at him with a little alarm. Her heart suddenly contracted with homesickness, with such a violent feeling of loneliness in this dark, foreign island, that she nearly wept. As usual, however, she did not mention her feelings to her father.

Reuss XVII, a high personage who had spent three whole weeks on Capri, had just left, and the visitors were installed in the suite of rooms that he had occupied. To them was assigned the most beautiful and expert chambermaid, a Belgian with a thin, firmly corseted figure, and a starched cap in the shape of a tiny indented crown. The most experienced and distinguished-looking footman was placed at their service, a coal-black, fiery-eyed Sicilian, and also the smartest waiter, the small, stout Luigi, a tremendous buffoon, who had seen a good

deal of life. In a minute or two a gentle tap was heard at the door of
the Gentleman from San Francisco, and there stood the maître d'hôtel,
a Frenchman, who had come to ask if the guests would take dinner,
and to report, in case of answer in the affirmative – of which, however,
he had small doubt – that this evening there were Mediterranean
lobsters, roast beef, asparagus, pheasants, etc., etc. The floor was still
rocking under the feet of the Gentleman from San Francisco, so rolled
about had he been on that wretched, grubby Italian steamer. Yet with
his own hands, calmly, though clumsily from lack of experience, he
closed the window which had banged at the entrance of the maître
d'hôtel, shutting out the drifting smell of distant kitchens and of wet
flowers in the garden. Then he turned and replied with unhurried
distinctness, that they would take dinner, that their table must be far
from the door, in the very centre of the dining room, that they would
have local wine and champagne, moderately dry and slightly cooled.
To all of which the maître d'hôtel gave assent in the most varied
intonations, which conveyed that there was not and could not be the
faintest question of the justness of the desires of the Gentleman from
San Francisco, and that everything should be exactly as he wished. At
the end he inclined his head and politely inquired: 'Is that all, sir?'

On receiving a lingering 'Yes,' he added that Carmela and Giuseppe,
famous all over Italy and 'to all the world of tourists', were going to
dance the tarantella that evening in the hall.

'I have seen picture postcards of her,' said the Gentleman from San
Francisco, in a voice expressive of nothing. 'And is Giuseppe her
husband?'

'Her cousin, sir,' replied the maître d'hôtel.

The Gentleman from San Francisco was silent for a while, thinking
of something, but saying nothing; then he dismissed the man with a
nod of the head. After which he began to make preparations as if for
his wedding. He turned on all the electric lights, and filled the mirrors
with brilliance and reflection of furniture and open trunks. He began
to shave and wash, ringing the bell every minute, and down the corridor raced and crossed the impatient ringings from the rooms of his
wife and daughter. Luigi, with the nimbleness peculiar to certain stout
people, making grimaces of horror which brought tears of laughter to
the eyes of chambermaids dashing past with marble-white pails, turned
a cartwheel to the gentleman's door, and tapping with his knuckles,
in a voice of sham timidity and respectfulness reduced to idiocy, asked:
'Ha suonato, Signore?'

From behind the door, a slow, grating, offensively polite voice: 'Yes,
come in.'

What were the feelings, what were the thoughts of the Gentleman from San Francisco on that evening so significant to him? He felt nothing exceptional, since unfortunately everything on this earth is too simple in appearance. Even had he felt something imminent in his soul, all the same he would have reasoned that, whatever it might be, it could not take place immediately. Besides, as with all who have just experienced seasickness, he was very hungry, and looked forward with delight to the first spoonful of soup, the first mouthful of wine. So he performed the customary business of dressing in a state of excitement which left no room for reflection.

Having shaved, washed, and dextrously arranged several artificial teeth, standing in front of the mirror, he moistened his silver-mounted brushes and plastered the remains of his thick pearly hair on his swarthy yellow skull. He drew on to his strong old body, with its abdomen protuberant from excessive good living, his cream-coloured silk underwear, put black silk socks and patent-leather slippers on his flat-footed feet. He put sleeve-links in the shining cuffs of his snow-white shirt, and bending forward so that his shirt front bulged out, he arranged his trousers that were pulled up high by his silk braces, and began to torture himself, putting his collar-stud through the stiff collar. The floor was still rocking beneath him, the tips of his fingers hurt, the stud at moments pinched the flabby skin in the recess under his Adam's apple, but he persisted, and at last, with eyes all strained and face dove-blue from the over-tight collar that enclosed his throat, he finished the business and sat down exhausted in front of the pier glass, which reflected the whole of him, and repeated him in all the other mirrors.

'It is awful!' he muttered, dropping his strong, bald head, but without trying to understand or to know what was awful. Then, with habitual careful attention examining his gouty-jointed short fingers and large, convex, almond-shaped fingernails, he repeated: 'It is awful . . .'

As if from a pagan temple shrilly resounded the second gong through the hotel. The Gentleman from San Francisco got up hastily, pulled his shirt-collar still tighter with his tie, and his abdomen tighter with his open waistcoat, settled his cuffs and again examined himself in the mirror . . . 'That Carmela, swarthy, with her enticing eyes, looking like a mulatto in her dazzling-coloured dress, chiefly orange, she must be an extraordinary dancer –' he was thinking. So, cheerfully leaving his room and walking on the carpet to his wife's room, he called to ask if they were nearly ready.

'In five minutes, Dad,' came the gay voice of the girl from behind the door. 'I'm arranging my hair.'

'Right-o!' said the Gentleman from San Francisco.

Imagining to himself her long hair hanging to the floor, he slowly walked along the corridors and staircases covered with red carpet, downstairs, looking for the reading room. The servants he encountered on the way pressed close to the wall, and he walked past as if not noticing them. An old lady, late for dinner, already stooping with age, with milk-white hair and yet décolleté in her pale grey silk dress, hurried at top speed, funnily, hen-like, and he easily overtook her. By the glass door of the dining room wherein the guests had already started the meal, he stopped before a little table heaped with boxes of cigars and cigarettes, and taking a large Manilla, threw three liras on the table. After which he passed along the winter terrace, and glanced through an open window. From the darkness came a waft of soft air, and there loomed the top of an old palm tree that spreads its boughs over the stars, looking like a giant, bringing down the far-off smooth quivering of the sea ... In the reading room, cosy with the shaded reading-lamps, a grey, untidy German, looking rather like Ibsen in his round silver-rimmed spectacles and with mad astonished eyes, stood rustling the newspapers. After coldly eyeing him, the Gentleman from San Francisco seated himself in a deep leather armchair in a corner, by a lamp with a green shade, put on his pince-nez, and, with a stretch of his neck because of the tightness of his shirt-collar, obliterated himself behind a newspaper. He glanced over the headlines, read a few sentences about the never-ending Balkan war, then with a habitual movement turned over the page of the newspaper – when suddenly the lines blazed up before him in a glassy sheen, his neck swelled, his eyes bulged, and the pince-nez came flying off his nose ... He lunged forward, wanted to breathe – and rattled wildly. His lower jaw dropped, and his mouth shone with gold fillings. His head fell swaying on his shoulder, his shirt-front bulged out basket-like, and all his body, writhing, with heels scraping up the carpet, slid down to the floor, struggling desperately with some invisible foe.

If the German had not been in the reading room, the frightful affair could have been hushed up. Instantly, through obscure passages the Gentleman from San Francisco could have been hurried away to some dark corner, and not a single guest would have discovered what he had been up to. But the German dashed out of the room with a yell, alarming the house and all the diners. Many sprang up from the table, upsetting their chairs, many, pallid, ran towards the reading room, and in every language it was asked: 'What – what's the matter?' None answered intelligibly, nobody understood, for even today people are more surprised at death than at anything else, and never want to believe it is true. The proprietor rushed from one guest to another, trying to keep back those who were hastening up, to soothe them with assurances that it was a mere trifle, a fainting-fit that had overcome a certain Gentleman from San Francisco ... But no one heeded him. Many saw how the porters and waiters were tearing off the tie, waist-coat, and crumpled dress-coat from that same gentleman, even, for some reason or other, pulling off his patent evening-shoes from his black-silk, flat-footed feet. And he was still writhing. He continued to struggle with death, by no means wanting to yield to that which had so unexpectedly and rudely overtaken him. He rolled his head, rattled like one throttled, and turned up the whites of his eyes as if he were drunk. When he had been hastily carried into room No. 43, the smallest, wretchedest, dampest and coldest room at the end of the bottom corridor, his daughter came running with her hair all loose, her dressing gown flying open, showing her bosom raised by her corsets: then his wife, large and heavy and completely dressed for dinner, her mouth opened round with terror. But by that time he had already ceased rolling his head.

In a quarter of an hour the hotel settled down somehow or other. But the evening was ruined. The guests, returning to the dining room, finished their dinner in silence, with a look of injury on their faces, while the proprietor went from one to another, shrugging his shoulders in hopeless and natural irritation, feeling himself guilty through no fault of his own, assuring everybody that he perfectly realized 'how disagreeable this is', and giving his word that he would take 'every possible measure within his power' to remove the trouble. The taran-tella had to be cancelled, the superfluous lights were switched off, most of the guests went to the bar, and soon the house became so quiet that the ticking of the clock was heard distinctly in the hall, where the lonely parrot woodenly muttered something as he bustled about in his cage preparatory to going to sleep, and managed to fall asleep at length with his paw absurdly suspended from the little upper perch ... The Gentleman from San Francisco lay on a cheap iron bed under coarse blankets on to which fell a dim light from the obscure electric lamp in the ceiling. An ice-bag slid down on his wet cold forehead; his blue, already lifeless face grew gradually cold; the hoarse bubbling which came from his open mouth, where the gleam of gold still showed, grew weak. The Gentleman from San Francisco rattled no longer; he was no more – something else lay in his place. His wife, his daughter, the doctor, and the servants stood and watched him dully. Suddenly that which they feared and expected happened. The rattling ceased. And slowly, slowly under their eyes a pallor spread over the face of the deceased, his features began to grow thinner, more transparent ... with a beauty which might have suited him long ago ...

Entered the proprietor. '*Già, è morto*!' whispered the doctor to him. The proprietor raised his shoulders, as if it were not his affair. The wife, on whose cheeks tears were slowly trickling, approached and timidly asked that the deceased should be taken to his own room.

'Oh no, Madame,' hastily replied the proprietor, politely, but coldly and not in English, but in French. He was no longer interested in the trifling sum the guests from San Francisco would leave at his cash desk. 'That is absolutely impossible.' Adding by way of explanation, that he valued that suite of rooms highly, and that should he accede to Madame's request, the news would be known all over Capri and no one would take the suite afterwards.

The young lady, who had glanced at him strangely all the time, now sat down in a chair and sobbed, with her handkerchief to her mouth. The elder lady's tears dried at once, her face flared up. Raising her voice and using her own language she began to insist, unable to believe that the respect for them had gone already. The manager cut her short with polite dignity. 'If Madame does not like the ways of the hotel, he dare not detain her.' And he announced decisively that the corpse must be removed at dawn: the police had already been notified and an official would arrive presently to attend to the necessary formalities. 'Is it possible to get a plain coffin?' Madame asked. Unfortunately not! Impossible! And there was no time to make one. It would have to be arranged somehow. Yes, the English soda water came in large strong boxes if the divisions were removed.

The whole hotel was asleep. The window of No. 43 was open, on to a corner of the garden where, under a high stone wall ridged with broken glass, grew a battered banana tree. The light was turned off, the door locked, the room deserted. The deceased remained in the darkness, blue stars glanced at him from the black sky, a cricket started to chirp with sad carelessness in the wall ... Out in the dimly lit corridor two chambermaids were seated in a windowsill, mending something. Entered Luigi, in slippers, with a heap of clothes in his hand.

'*Pronto?*' he asked, in a singing whisper, indicating with his eyes the dreadful door at the end of the corridor. Then giving a slight wave thither with his free hand: '*Partenza!*' he shouted in a whisper, as though sending off a train. The chambermaids, choking with noiseless laughter, dropped their heads on each other's shoulders.

Tiptoeing, Luigi went to the very door, tapped, and cocking his head on one side asked respectfully, in a subdued tone: '*Ha suonato, Signore?*'

Then contracting his throat and shoving out his jaw, he answered himself in a grating, drawling, mournful voice, which seemed to come from behind the door: '*Yes, come in . . .*'

When the dawn grew white at the window of No. 43, and a damp wind began rustling the tattered fronds of the banana tree; as the blue sky of morning lifted and unfolded over Capri, and Monte Solaro, pure and distinct, grew golden, catching the sun which was rising beyond the far-off blue mountains of Italy; just as the labourers who were mending the paths of the islands for the tourists came out for work, a long box was carried into room No. 43. Soon this box weighed heavily, and it painfully pressed the knees of the porter who was carrying it in a one-horse cab down the winding white highroad, between stone walls and vineyards, down, down the face of Capri to the sea. The driver, a weakly little fellow with reddened eyes, in a little old jacket with sleeves too short and bursting boots, kept flogging his wiry small horse that was decorated in Sicilian fashion, its harness tinkling with busy little bells and fringed with fringes of scarlet wool, the high saddle-peak gleaming with copper and tufted with colour, and a yard-long plume nodding from the pony's cropped head from between the ears. The cabby had spent the whole night playing dice in the inn, and was still under the effects of drink. Silent, he was depressed by his own debauchery and vice: by the fact that he gambled away to the last farthing all those copper coins with which his pockets had yesterday been full, in all four lire, forty centesimi. But the morning was fresh. In such air, with the sea all round, under the morning sky headaches evaporate, and man soon regains his cheerfulness. Moreover, the cabby was cheered by this unexpected fare which he was making out of some Gentleman from San Francisco, who was nodding with his dead head in a box at the back. The little steamer, which lay like a water beetle on the tender bright blueness which brims the bay of Naples, was already giving the final hoots, and this tooting resounded again cheerily all over the island. Each contour, each ridge, each rock was so clearly visible in every direction, it was as if there were no atmosphere at all. Near the beach the porter in the cab was overtaken by the head porter dashing down in an automobile with the lady and her daughter, both pale, their eyes swollen with the tears of a sleepless night . . . And in ten minutes the little steamer again churned up the water and made her way back to Sorrento, to Castellamare, bearing away from Capri for ever the family from San Francisco . . . And peace and tranquillity reigned once more on the island.

On that island two thousand years ago lived a man entangled in his own infamous and strange acts, one whose rule for some reason extended over millions of people, and who, having lost his head through the absurdity of such power, committed deeds which have established him for ever in the memory of mankind; mankind which in the mass now rules the world just as hideously and incomprehensibly as he ruled it then. And men come here from all quarters of the globe to look at the ruins of the stone house where that one man lived, on the brink of one of the steepest cliffs in the island. On this exquisite morning all who had come to Capri for that purpose were still asleep in the hotels, although through the streets already trotted little mouse-coloured donkeys with red saddles, towards the hotel entrances where they would wait patiently until, after a good sleep and a square meal, young and old American men and women, German men and women would emerge and be hoisted up into the saddles, to be followed up the stony paths, yea to the very summit of Monte Tiberio, by old persistent beggar women of Capri, with sticks in their sinewy hands. Quieted by the fact that the dead old Gentleman from San Francisco, who had intended to be one of the pleasure party but who had only succeeded in frightening the rest with the reminder of death, was now being shipped to Naples, the happy tourists still slept soundly, the island was still quiet, the shops in the little town not yet open. Only fish and greens were being sold in the tiny piazza, only simple folk were present, and among them, as usual without occupation, the tall old boatman Lorenzo, thorough debauchee and handsome figure, famous all over Italy, model for many a picture.

He had already sold for a trifle two lobsters which he had caught in the night, and which were rustling in the apron of the cook of that very same hotel where the family from San Francisco had spent the night. And now Lorenzo could stand calmly till evening, with a majestic air showing off his rags and gazing round, holding his clay pipe with its long reed mouthpiece in his hand, and letting his scarlet bonnet slip over one ear. For as a matter of fact he received a salary from the little town, from the commune which found it profitable to pay him to stand about and make a picturesque figure – as everybody knows . . . Down the precipices of Monte Solaro, down the stony little stairs cut in the rock of the old Phoenician road came two Abruzzi mountaineers, descending from Anacapri. One carried a bagpipe under his leather cloak, a large goatskin with two little pipes; the other had a sort of wooden flute. They descended, and the whole land, joyous, was sunny beneath them. They saw the rocky, heaving shoulder of the island, which lay almost entirely at their feet, swimming in the fairy blueness of the water. Shining morning vapours rose over the sea to the east, under a dazzling sun which already burned hot as it rose higher and higher; and there, far off, the dimly cerulean masses of Italy, of her near and far mountains, still wavered blue as if in the world's morning, in a beauty no words can express . . . Halfway down the descent the pipers slackened their pace. Above the road, in a grotto of the rocky face of Monte Solaro stood the Mother of God, the sun full upon her, giving her a splendour of snow-white and blue raiment, and royal crown rusty from all weathers. Meek and merciful, she raised her eyes to heaven, to the eternal and blessed mansions of her thrice-holy Son. The pipers bared their heads, put their pipes to their lips: and there streamed forth naïve and meekly joyous praises to the sun, to the morning, to Her, immaculate, who would intercede for all who suffer in this malicious and lovely world, and to Him, born of Her womb among the caves of Bethlehem, in a lowly shepherd's hut, in the far Judean land . . .

And the body of the dead old man from San Francisco was returning home, to its grave, to the shores of the New World. Having been subjected to many humiliations, much human neglect, after a week's wandering from one warehouse to another, it was carried at last on to the same renowned vessel which so short a time ago, and with such honour had borne him living to the Old World. But now he was to be hidden far from the knowledge of the voyagers. Closed in a tar-coated coffin, he was lowered deep into the vessel's dark hold. And again, again the ship set out on the long voyage. She passed at night near Capri, and to those who were looking out from the island, sad seemed the lights of the ship slowly hiding themselves in the sea's darkness. But there aboard the liner, in the bright halls shining with lights and marble, gay dancing filled the evening, as usual . . .

The second evening, and the third evening, still they danced, amid a storm that swept over the ocean, booming like a funeral service, rolling up mountains of mourning darkness silvered with foam. Through the snow the numerous fiery eyes of the ship were hardly visible to the Devil who watched from the rocks of Gibraltar, from the stony gateway of two worlds, peering after the vessel as she disappeared into the night and storm. The Devil was huge as a cliff. But huger still was the liner, many storeyed, many funnelled, created by the presumption of the New Man with the old heart. The blizzard smote the rigging and the funnels, and whitened the ship with snow, but she was enduring, firm, majestic – and horrible. On the topmost deck rose lonely among the snowy whirlwind the cosy and dim quarters where lay the heavy master of the ship, he who was like a pagan idol, sunk now in a light, uneasy slumber. Through his sleep he heard the sombre howl and furious screechings of the siren, muffled by the blizzard. But again he reassured himself by the nearness of that which stood behind his wall, and was in the last resort incomprehensible to him; by the large, apparently armoured cabin which was now and then filled with a mysterious rumbling, throbbing, and crackling of blue fires that flared up explosive around the pale face of the telegraphist who, with a metal hoop fixed on his head, was eagerly straining to catch the dim voices of vessels which spoke to him from hundreds of miles away. In the depths, in the underwater womb of the *Atlantis*, steel glimmered and steam wheezed, and huge masses of machinery and thousand-ton boilers dripped with water and oil, as the motion of the ship was steadily cooked in this vast kitchen heated by hellish furnaces from beneath. Here bubbled in their awful concentration the powers which were being transmitted to the keel, down an infinitely long round tunnel lit up and brilliant like a gigantic gun-barrel, along which slowly, with a regularity crushing to the human soul, revolved a gigantic shaft, precisely like a living monster coiling and uncoiling its endless length down the tunnel, sliding on its bed of oil. The middle of the *Atlantis*, the warm, luxurious cabins, dining rooms, halls, shed light and joy, buzzed with the chatter of an elegant crowd, was fragrant with fresh flowers, and quivered with the sounds of a string orchestra. And again amid that crowd, amid the brilliance of lights, silks, diamonds, and bare feminine shoulders, a slim and supple pair of hired lovers painfully writhed and at moments convulsively clashed. A sinfully discreet, pretty girl with lowered lashes and hair innocently dressed, and a tallish young man with black hair looking as if it were glued on, pale with powder, and wearing the most elegant patent-leather shoes and a narrow, long-tailed dress coat, a beau resembling an enormous leech. And no one knew that this couple had long since grown weary of shamly tormenting themselves with their beatific love-tortures, to the sound of bawdy-sad music; nor did anyone know of that thing which lay deep, deep below at the very bottom of the dark hold, near the gloomy and sultry bowels of the ship that was so gravely overcoming the darkness, the ocean, the blizzard . . .

First published in 1916
Translated by S. S. Koteliansky, D. H. Lawrence and Leonard Woolf

IN PARIS

When he had his hat on – walking down the street or standing in the metro – and you couldn't see the silver in his short, reddish hair, it was possible to imagine, given the freshness of his thin shaven face and the upright bearing of this tall thin figure in a long waterproof coat, that he was no more than forty. But his bright eyes had a look of dry sorrow, and he spoke and acted like a man who has been through a great deal. At one time he had rented a farm in Provence; he had heard any number of caustic Provençal jokes and he liked to drop them now and again, with a little smile, into his always clipped speech. Many people knew that his wife had left him long ago, back in Constantinople, and that ever since then he had lived with a wound in his soul. The secret of this wound was never revealed to anyone, but sometimes he couldn't help hinting at it, joking sourly if someone brought up the subject of women: '*Rien n'est plus difficile que de reconnaître un bon melon et une femme de bien*.'[1]

One damp, late autumn Paris evening he went into a small Russian restaurant on one of the dark sidestreets near Passy. Attached to the restaurant was some kind of a delicatessen, and he had inadvertently paused outside its wide window. On the shelf inside were cone-shaped pink bottles of rowanberry vodka and squat yellow bottles of zubrovka,[2] a plate of stale fried meat pasties, a plate of greying meat rissoles, a box of halva and a tin of sprats; further back was a counter of hors d'oeuvres, and behind that – the unfriendly Russian face of the woman who owned the establishment. There was light in the shop and, standing on the dark sidestreet with its cold, greasy-looking cobblestones, he felt drawn to this light. He entered, nodded to the owner and made his way through to a more dimly lit room adjoining the shop; this was still empty and the paper tablecloths looked clean and white. There he unhurriedly hung his grey hat and long coat on the horns of a coat-stand, sat down at a little table in the far corner and, absentmindedly rubbing together hands covered in reddish hair, began to read an endless list of hors d'oeuvres and main dishes, partly typed and partly written in violet ink which had smudged on the greasy paper. Suddenly a light went on in his corner, and he saw a woman of about thirty, with a look of distant politeness, coming towards him; she had black eyes and black hair parted in the centre, and she was wearing a white, lace-bordered apron over a black dress.

'*Bonsoir, monsieur*,' she said pleasantly.

She looked so pretty that he felt flustered. '*Bonsoir* – but you're Russian, aren't you?' he answered awkwardly.

'Yes, I am. I'm sorry – I've got used to speaking French to our customers.'

'Oh – do you get a lot of French people here?'

'Quite a lot, and you can be sure they'll order zubrovka, bliny and even borsch. Have you decided what you want?'

'No, there's so much to choose from. Tell me what you recommend!'

In a mechanical tone she began listing the dishes, 'Today we have sailor's cabbage soup, Cossack meatballs . . . Then there are veal chops or, if you like, you could have a shashlyk à la Kars[3] . . .'

'Splendid. I'll have cabbage soup, please, and then the meatballs.'

She took the little pad that hung from her belt and wrote on it with a pencil stub. Her hands were very white, aristocratic looking. Her dress was a little worn, but clearly from a good shop.

'Would you like some vodka?'

'I'd love some. It's horribly raw out there.'

'What would you like with the vodka? There's some wonderful Danube herring, our red caviar's only just come in, we've got lightly pickled gherkins . . .'

He looked at her again: the white lacy apron looked good against her black dress, and beneath the dress he could make out the fine breasts of a strong young woman. She had no lipstick on her full, fresh lips, her black hair was coiled into a simple knot, but her white hands looked well cared for, the fingernails shining and slightly pink, obviously manicured.

'What would I like to start with?' he said with a smile. 'I'll just have the herring, if that's all right, with some boiled potato.'

'What wine would you like?'

'Red. Just your ordinary house wine.'

She noted this down on her pad and brought over a carafe of water from another table. He shook his head: 'No, *merci*, I never drink water nor do I add water to wine. *L'eau gâte le vin comme la charrette le chemin et la femme – l'âme.*'[4]

'A fine opinion you have of us,' she observed calmly and went off for the vodka and herring. He followed her with his eyes, noticing how gracefully she held herself and the way her black dress swayed as she walked. Yes, she was polite and professional, and all her movements and gestures were those of a dignified, unassuming waitress. But what about her shoes? How could she afford those good-quality, expensive shoes? There must be some well-to-do, middle-aged *ami*. It was a long time since he had felt as animated as he did this evening –

thanks to her – and the thought of this *ami* was rather annoying. Yes, from year to year, from day to day, in our heart of hearts there's only one thing we wait for – a meeting that will bring happiness and love. Really, this hope is all we live for – and how vain it is.

He came back again the following day and sat down at his little table. She was busy at first, taking an order from two Frenchmen, repeating out loud what she was noting on her pad: '*Caviar rouge, salade russe . . . Deux shashlyks.*'

She went out to the kitchen, came back in and went up to him with a slight smile of recognition.

'Good evening. I'm glad you liked it here.'

He stood up and said cheerfully: 'Good evening to you! I like it here very much. And may I ask your name?'

'Olga Aleksandrovna. And may I know yours?'

'Nikolay Platonych.'

They shook hands; then she raised her notepad.

'We've got a wonderful soup today – rassolnik.[5] Our chef's quite remarkable, he used to work on the Grand Duke Aleksandr Mikhailovich's yacht.'

'Splendid, I'll have the rassolnik . . . And have you been working here long?'

'It's my third month here.'

'Where were you before?'

'I was a saleswoman at Printemps.'

'Staff cuts, I suppose?'

'Yes, I'd have stayed if I could.'

He realized with pleasure that he was probably wrong about the *ami*.

'Are you married?' he asked.

'Yes.'

'What does your husband do?'

'He's working in Yugoslavia. He was in the White Army. I imagine you were too?'

'Yes, I fought in the Great War and in the Civil War.'

'I knew straight away. And I imagine you're a general,' she said with a smile.

'I was once. Now foreign publishing houses commission me to write histories of those wars . . . But how come you're on your own?'

'I just am.'

The following evening he asked, 'Do you like the cinema?'

'It can be fun,' she replied as she placed his borsch on the table.

'They say there's a very good film showing at the Etoile. Would you like to come and see it with me? You do have days off, I assume?'

'*Merci*. I'm free on Mondays.'

'Well then, let's go on Monday. What's today? Saturday? The day after tomorrow, then. Is that all right?'

'Yes. So you won't be coming in tomorrow?'

'No, I'm going to see some people I know, out of town. But why do you ask?'

'I'm not sure . . . Somehow it'll feel strange not to be seeing you.'

He looked gratefully at her and blushed. 'Strange for me too. There are so few meetings in life that bring happiness.' And he quickly changed the subject. 'So, the day after tomorrow. Where shall we meet? Where do you live?'

'Near the Motte-Piquet metro.'

'Couldn't be better – the same line as the Etoile. I'll be waiting for you by the metro exit at 8.30 precisely.'

'*Merci*.'

He bowed with mock exaggeration and said, '*C'est moi qui vous remercie.*[6] Put the children to bed,' he said with a smile, wanting to know whether or not she had any children, 'and jump on the metro.'

'I haven't been blessed with children, thank God,' she said, and glided away with the plates.

He felt moved as he walked home, but there was a frown on his face. 'It'll feel strange not to be seeing you . . .' Perhaps this really was the providential meeting he had so long been waiting for. Only it was so late, so late. *Le bon Dieu envoie toujours des culottes à ceux qui n'ont pas de derrière.*[7]

It was raining on Monday evening; the sky over Paris was a dark, murky red. Hoping she would go on to dine with him in Montparnasse, he skipped lunch, went into a café on the Chaussée de la Muette, had a ham sandwich and a glass of beer, lit a cigarette and got into a cab. When they reached the Etoile metro, he told the driver to stop and stepped out into the rain; the fat red-cheeked driver waited trustingly. The wind blowing from the station could have been from a Russian bathhouse; dense, dark crowds of people were opening umbrellas as they climbed the stairs; a vendor beside him was calling out the names of evening newspapers in a low staccato quack. Suddenly she was there, among the people coming up. He walked joyfully towards her.

'Olga Aleksandrovna!'

She was elegantly and fashionably dressed and her eyes, outlined in black, looked at him freely, not like in the restaurant, and she graciously extended one hand, a small umbrella dangling from the wrist, as she held up the hem of a long evening dress with the other hand. 'An evening dress,' he thought, feeling happier still, 'so she's expecting to go somewhere after the cinema too.' Turning back the cuff of her glove, he kissed her white wrist.

'You poor man, have you been waiting long?'

'No, I've only just arrived. Let's get into the taxi.'

And with an excitement he had not felt for a long time he followed her into the cab, which was half-dark and smelt of damp cloth. The cab swayed as they turned a corner, a street lamp momentarily lit up the inside – and he instinctively put his arm round her waist, sensed the smell of powder from her cheek, saw her large knees under the black evening dress, the gleam of a black eye and her full lips with their red lipstick: this was a different woman.

In the dark hall, watching a white, shining screen where droning aeroplanes with wide wings were flying at oblique angles and dropping into the clouds, they quietly began to talk.

'Do you live on your own, or do you share with a girlfriend?' he asked.

'I'm on my own. It's awful, really. The hotel's clean and warm but, you know, it's the kind of place men bring girls to for the night, or even for an hour or two . . . I'm on the fifth floor, there's no lift, of course, and the red stair-carpet ends on the third floor . . . If it rains in the night, I feel such *toskà*. I open the window and there's not a soul to be seen. The whole city's quite dead. Just one solitary street lamp, somewhere or other down below in the rain . . . And you're a bachelor, I suppose, and you live in a hotel too?'

'I've got a small apartment in Passy. I live on my own too. I've been in Paris a long time. For a while I lived in Provence, I rented a farm there. I wanted to get away from everyone and everything, and to live by the work of my own hands – but that proved too much for me. I hired a Cossack to help out, but he turned out to be a drunkard – and a gloomy and frightening one at that. I tried breeding chickens and rabbits, but they all kept dying. Once I was nearly killed by a bite from my mule – an extremely vicious and clever beast . . . Worst of all was the utter loneliness. My wife left me when we were still in Constantinople.'

'Are you joking?'

'Not in the least. It's a common enough story. *Qui se marie par amour a bonnes nuits et mauvais jours.*[8] Though I didn't have much of either myself. She left me during the second year of our marriage.'

'Where is she now?'

'I don't know.'

She was silent for a long time. Some imitator of Charlie Chaplin kept running stupidly about the screen, his bowler hat cocked to one side and his feet splayed out in shoes that were down-at-heel and far too large for him.

'Yes, you must feel very lonely,' she said.

'Yes, and what can I do but be patient? *Patience – médecine des pauvres*.'[9]

'A very sad medicine.'

'It is indeed. So very sad,' he went on with a slight smile, 'that I've sometimes even glanced at *Illustrated Russia* – there's a section, you know, where they print little personal notices like: "Young Russian woman from Latvia feels lonely and would like to correspond with sensitive Russian Parisian. Please include photograph." Or "Serious lady, auburn hair, unsophisticated but *sympathique*, widowed with 9-year-old son, wishes to correspond, serious intentions, with sober gentleman at least 40, financially secure, employed as chauffeur or similar, enjoys home comforts. Intellectual interests not essential." I quite understand her – they really aren't essential.'

'But don't you have friends and acquaintances?'

'I have no close friends. And acquaintances are poor comfort.'

'Who keeps house for you?'

'There's not a lot of housekeeping to do. I make my morning coffee myself, and I make lunch myself. A *femme de ménage*[10] comes in the evening.'

'You poor thing,' she said, squeezing his hand.

And they sat like this for a long time, hand in hand, united by the gloom and the closeness of their seats, pretending to be watching a screen towards which, up above their heads, a beam of smoky, chalky-blue light was being shone from a little cabin on the back wall. The Chaplin imitator, whose battered bowler had risen off his head in horror, was hurtling, in the remains of an antediluvian automobile with a smoking samovar chimney for an exhaust pipe, straight at a telegraph pole. The loudspeaker let out a variety of musical roars while the smoke-filled pit down below – they themselves were in the balcony – resounded with thunderous applause and desperately joyous laughter. He leant over towards her:

'You know what? Why don't we go somewhere like Montparnasse? It's terribly boring here and there's no air.'

She nodded her head and began pulling on her gloves.

After sitting down again in a half-dark cab and looking at the windows – which were sparkling from the rain, flaring up from time to time like diamonds of different colours in the glow of street lamps or the reflections, now blood, now quicksilver, of advertisements up in the black height – he again turned down the cuff of her glove and gave her a long kiss on the hand. Her eyes too were strangely sparkling, their lashes thick and black as coal, as she sadly and tenderly leaned over towards him, till he could taste the sweetness of lipstick on her full lips.

At La Coupole they started with oysters and Anjou, then ordered partridge and claret. By the time they came to coffee and yellow chartreuse, they both felt a little tipsy. They smoked a lot; the ashtray was full of her blood-red cigarette-ends. As they talked, he looked at her flushed face and thought that she was quite a beauty.

'But tell me the truth,' she said, picking tiny crumbs of tobacco off the tip of her tongue. 'You must have met some women during these years.'

'Yes. But you can guess what kind . . . Nights in hotels . . . And you?'

She was silent for a moment. 'There was one very painful story . . . No, I don't want to talk about it. A boy, a pimp really . . . But how did you and your wife separate?'

'I'm ashamed to say. She met a boy too – a handsome young Greek, extremely rich. And after a month or two there was nothing left of that pure, touching young girl who had worshipped the White Army and all of us in it. She began dining with him in the most expensive bar in Pera and he would send her enormous baskets of flowers. "I don't understand. Surely you're not jealous, are you? You're busy all day long – and I have such fun with him. As far as I'm concerned, he's just a sweet boy – and nothing more." A sweet boy! And she was only twenty herself. It wasn't easy to forget her, to forget the girl I'd known back in Yekaterinodar.'

When the bill came, she checked carefully through it and told him not to leave more than ten per cent as a tip. After that, the thought of saying goodbye in half an hour seemed stranger still – to both of them.

'Let's go to my apartment,' he said sadly. 'We can sit and talk a bit longer . . .'

'Yes, yes,' she said, taking his arm and pressing it to her side.

A night taxi with a Russian driver took them to a lonely little sidestreet, stopping in front of a tall building beside which, in the metallic light of a gas lamp, light rain was falling onto a rubbish bin. They entered a suddenly bright hall, squeezed into the small lift, and went slowly up, embracing and quietly kissing one another. He managed to get the key into the lock of his front door before the corridor light cut out and led her first into a lobby, then into a small dining room where only one bulb lit up in the chandelier, shining bleakly. Their faces were already tired. He offered her more wine.

'No, my dear,' she said. 'I can't drink any more.'

He asked her again. 'Just a glass of white wine each. I've got some excellent Pouilly Fumé on the window ledge.'

'You drink, my dear, but I'm going to wash and undress. And to bed, to bed. We're not children and I'm sure you knew very well, when I agreed to come back with you . . . And anyway, why shouldn't we stay together?'

Too overcome to answer, he quietly led her into the bedroom; from there an open door led into the bathroom and he turned on the lights in both rooms. These lights were bright, it was warm from the radiators and the rain was drumming quickly and evenly against the roof. She immediately began to pull her long dress over her head.

He went out, drank two glasses of sharp, icy wine one after the other and, unable to wait any longer, went back into the bedroom. Opposite him, reflected in a large mirror on the wall, he could see the brightly lit bathroom. She was standing with her back to him, naked, white and strong, leaning over the basin and washing her neck and her breasts.

'No – keep out!' she said, and, throwing on a dressing gown yet not covering her full breasts, her strong white stomach or her taut white hips, she went up to him and embraced him as if she were his wife. And, as if she were his wife, he embraced her, all her cool body, kissing her still damp breasts that smelled of soap, her eyes, her lips from which she had wiped off the lipstick.

Two days later she left her job and moved in with him.

One day in winter he persuaded her to put all the money he had earned into a safe-deposit box in her own name at the Crédit Lyonnais. 'Just to be on the safe side,' he explained. '*L'amour fait danser les ânes*,[11] and I feel as if I'm twenty. But anything can happen . . .'

On the Tuesday before Easter he died in a carriage on the metro. As he was reading a newspaper, his eyes rolled back in his head and he slumped back against the seat . . .

As she returned in her mourning dress from the cemetery, it was a lovely spring day, spring clouds were floating here and there in a soft Paris sky and everything spoke of young, eternal life – and of how her own life was now finished.

Back at home, she began to tidy up the apartment. In the corridor, in a wall-cupboard, she found his old summer greatcoat, grey with a red lining. She took it off the peg, pressed it against her face and, still hugging it, sat down on the ground, her whole body convulsed by sobs, crying out, pleading with someone for mercy.

First published in 1942
Translated by Robert Chandler

TEFFI (Nadezhda Aleksandrovna Lokhvitskaya, 1872–1952)

Teffi was born in St Petersburg into a distinguished family that treasured literature; she and her three sisters all became writers. Her elder sister was considered a leading poet of the age, and both her younger sisters published articles in periodicals and had plays performed in theatres. Soon after the beginning of her career, in the early 1900s, she began to write under the name 'Teffi'; although this is sometimes thought to come from the English 'Taffy', she herself, in her story 'Pseudonym', says it derives from 'Steffi', a familiar form of 'Stepan' – the name of a friend. After the Russian Revolution, Teffi settled in Paris. There she played a prominent role in literary life, organizing a salon and, with impressive regularity, contributing weekly columns and stories to leading periodicals for the next twenty years.

During the course of her life she wrote in a variety of styles and genres: political feuilletons published in the Bolshevik newspaper New Life *(Novaya Zhizn) during her brief period of radical fervour after the 1905 Revolution; Symbolist poems that she declaimed or sang in the most important Petersburg literary salons; popular one-act plays, mainly satirical treatments of topical subjects – one was entitled* The Woman Question; *and a novel entitled simply* Adventure Novel *(1930). Her finest works, however, are her short stories and her* Memoirs *(1928–9), a witty, thoughtful yet tragic account of her last months in Russia before emigrating in 1919.*

As well as being admired by writers of the stature of Bunin, Bulgakov and Zoshchenko, Teffi was hugely popular throughout her life. In pre-Revolutionary Russia, candies and perfumes were named after her; after the Revolution, her stories were published and her plays performed throughout the Russian diaspora. Between her death and the first Soviet publication of her work in 1989, however, she was almost forgotten. This was probably for several reasons: because she was a woman; because she was considered 'lightweight' (critics noticed her humour more than her perceptiveness); and because some of her more than five hundred stories were obviously written in a hurry. Also, as I have said with regard to Bunin, there was a long period during which both Western and Soviet scholars paid little attention to émigré literature in general. Since the early 1990s Teffi has been ever more widely published.

'Love' is perhaps the finest of her stories about children; 'A Family Journey' is characteristic of her later work, as witty as it is sombre.

LOVE

It was during the wonderful days of my ninth spring – days that were long and saturated with life, full to the brim.

Everything during these days was interesting, important and full of meaning. Things were new and people were wise; they knew an astonishing amount, and they were keeping their great dark secrets until some future date, I didn't know when.

The morning of each long day began joyfully: thousands of small rainbows in the soapy foam of the washing stand; a new brightly-coloured light dress; prayers before the icon, behind which the fresh willow branches were still green; tea on a terrace shaded by lemon trees that had been carried out from the orangery in their tubs; my elder sisters, black-browed and with long plaits of hair, still unsettled, only just back from boarding school for the holidays; the slap of washing-bats from the pond beyond the flower garden, where peasant women shouted to one another as they did their laundry; the languid clucking of hens behind a clump of young, still small-leaved lilac: everything was not only new and joyful in itself but was a promise of something still more new and joyful.

And it was during this ninth spring that first love came into my life, that my first love came, passed by and went away – in all its fullness, with rapture and pain and disappointment, with all that is to be expected of any true love.

Four peasant girls, Khodoska, Paraska, Pidorka and Khovra – all wearing coin necklaces, Ukrainian wraparound skirts and linen shirts with embroidered shoulders – were weeding the garden paths. They scraped and hacked at the fresh black earth with their spades, turning over thick oily sods and tearing away tenacious crackling little roots that were as thin as nerves.

For hours on end, until I was called, I would stand and watch, and breathe in the heavy damp smell of the earth.

Necklaces dangled and clinked, arms red from the first of the sun slid lightly and gaily up and down the spades' wooden handles.

And then, instead of Khovra, who was fair and stocky, with a thin red band round her head, I saw a new girl – tall and lissom, with narrow hips.

'Hey, new girl, what's your name?' I asked.

A dark head encircled by thick four-stranded plaits and with a narrow white parting down the centre, turned towards me, and dark mischievous eyes looked at me from beneath round eyebrows that met in the middle, and a merry red mouth smiled at me.

'Ganka!'

And her teeth gleamed – even, white and large.

She said her name and laughed, and the other girls laughed, and I felt happy too.

Ganka was astonishing! Why was she laughing? And why did she make me feel so good and happy? She was not as well dressed as smart Paraska, but her thick striped skirt was wound so deftly round her shapely hips, her red woollen sash gripped her waist so firmly and vibrantly and her bright green ribbon trembled so arrestingly by the collar of her shirt that it was hard to imagine anything prettier.

I looked at her, and every turn of her pliant dark neck sang like a song in my soul. And her eyes flashed again, mischievous and teasing; they laughed, then looked away.

I was astonished by Paraska, Khodoska and Pidorka – how could they keep their eyes off her and how did they dare to behave as if they were her equals? Were they blind? But then even she herself seemed to think she was no different from the others.

I looked at her fixedly, mindlessly, as if I were dreaming.

A far-away voice called my name. I knew I was being called to my music lesson, but I didn't answer.

I saw Mother going down a nearby avenue with two smart ladies I didn't know. Mother called to me. I had to go and curtsy. One of the ladies lifted my face by the chin with her small hand, which was encased in a perfumed white glove. The lady was tender, white, all in lace; compared with her, Ganka seemed coarse and rough.

'No, Ganka's not nice.'

I wandered quietly back to the house.

The next morning I went out calmly, unconcernedly and cheerfully to see where they were weeding now.

Those sweet dark eyes met me as affectionately and merrily as if nothing had happened, as if I had never betrayed them for a perfumed lady in lace. And again the singing music of the movements of her shapely body took over, began to enchant.

The conversation at breakfast was about yesterday's guest, Countess

Mionchinskaya. My eldest brother was sincerely enraptured by her. He was straightforward and kind but, since he was being educated at the lycée, he felt it necessary to lisp and drawl and slightly drag his right foot as he walked.[1] And, doubtless afraid that a summer deep in the country might erase these distinguishing marks of the dandy, he greatly surprised us younger brothers and sisters with his strange mannerisms.

'The Countess is divi-i-inely beau-utiful!' he said. 'She was the reigning beau-ty of the se-ea-son.'

The second brother, who was studying at the military academy, did not agree. 'I don't see anything special about her. She may put on airs, but she's got the mitts of a peasant – the mitts of a *baba* who's been soaking neckweed.'[2]

The elder brother poured scorn over this: '*Qu'est-ce que c'est* mitt? *Qu'est-ce que c'est* baba? *Qu'est-ce que c'est* neckweed?'

'But I'll tell you who truly is a beauty,' continued the second brother, 'and that's Ganka who works in the garden.'

'Hah!'

'She's badly dressed, of course, but give her a lace gown and gloves and she'll beat your countess hands down.'

My heart started beating so fast I had to close my eyes.

'How can you talk such rubbish?' said my sister Vera, taking offence on the Countess's behalf. 'Ganka's coarse, and she has bad manners. She probably eats fish with a knife.'

I was in torment. It seemed as if something was about to be revealed, some secret of mine – but what this secret was I did not even know myself.

'That, I think we can say, has nothing to do with it,' said the elder brother. 'Helen of Troy didn't have French governesses, and she ate fish with her fingers – not even with a knife – yet her renown as a great beauty is unchallenged. What's the matter, Kishmish? Why have you gone so red?'

'Kishmish'[3] was my nickname. I answered in a trembling voice, 'Leave me in peace. I'm not doing you any harm. But you . . . you're always picking on me.'

In the evening, lying on the sofa in the dark drawing room, I heard my mother in the hall; she was playing a piece I love, the cavatina from the opera *Martha*.[4] There was something in the soft, tender melody that evoked in me the same singing languor I had seen in Ganka's movements. And this sweet torment, and the music, and my sadness and happiness made me cry, burying my face in the cushion.

*

It was a grey morning, and I was afraid it would rain and I wouldn't be allowed out into the garden.

I wasn't allowed out.

I sat down sadly at the piano and began playing exercises, stumbling each time in the same place.

But late in the morning the sun came out and I raced into the garden.

The girls had just thrown down their spades and sat down for their midday meal. They got out pots and jugs wrapped in cloths and began eating buckwheat kasha or milk curds. Ganka untied her little bundle, took out a thick slice of bread and a clove of garlic, rubbed the bread with the garlic and began to eat, shining her mischievous eyes at me.

I took fright and went away. It was terrible that Ganka ate such filth. It was as if the garlic had pushed her away from me. She had become incomprehensible and alien. Better if she'd eaten fish with a knife.

I remembered what my brother had said about Yelena the Beautiful,[5] but this brought me no consolation and I plodded back to the house.

Nanny[6] was sitting by the back door, knitting a stocking and listening to the housekeeper.

I heard the name 'Ganka' and froze. I knew from experience that if I went up to them they'd either send me away or stop talking.

'She worked for the steward's wife all winter. She's a hardworking girl. But every evening – the steward's wife began to notice – there was a soldier with her. The wife sent him on his way one evening and she sent him on his way a second evening – but she couldn't send him packing every evening.'

'Of course not,' said Nanny, 'not night after night.'

'So she scolded her now and again, of course, but Ganka just laughed – it was water off a duck's back. Then, on the Eve of Epiphany, she hears noises in the kitchen – it seemed Ganka was moving things around or something. In the morning she hears little squeals. She goes into the kitchen: Ganka's nowhere to be seen, there's just a baby covered in rags, squealing on the bed. The manager's wife takes fright. She starts to look for Ganka: what had become of her? Had something dreadful happened? She looks out through the window – and there's Ganka by the hole in the ice, barefoot, rinsing out her laundry and singing. The manager's wife wanted to dismiss her, but what would she do without her? She was such a sturdy, hardworking lass.'

I slipped quietly off.

So Ganka was friends with a simple uneducated soldier. This was horrible, horrible. And she had been tormenting some baby. There was something dark and terrible about all this. She had stolen it from

somewhere and hidden it in rags; and when it had cried, she'd run off
to the hole in the ice and sung songs there.

I felt miserable all evening, and in the night I had a dream from
which I awoke in tears. But my dream was neither sad nor frightening, and I was crying not from grief but from rapture. When I woke,
I could only half remember it and I was unable to recount it.

'I dreamed of a boat. It was quite transparent, light blue. It floated
straight through the wall into silver reeds. Everything was poetry and
music.'

'But then why are you howling?' asked Nanny in surprise. 'Why
does a boat make you howl? Maybe a boat means something good.'

I could see she didn't understand, but there was nothing more
I could say or explain. And my soul was ringing, singing, weeping in
ecstasy. A light blue boat, silver reeds, poetry and music . . .

I didn't go out into the garden. I was afraid I'd see Ganka and begin
thinking about terrible things I couldn't understand – about the soldier
and the little baby in rags.

The day dragged on. It was blustery outside and the wind was
bending the trees. They shook their branches and the leaves churned,
sounding like boiling waves.

In the corridor, outside the store room, was a surprise: on the table
stood an open crate of oranges. It must have been brought from town
that morning: they'd be given to us after lunch.

I adore oranges. They are round and golden, like the sun, and under
their peel are thousands of tiny pockets filled with sweet fragrant juice.
Oranges are beautiful, oranges are a joy.

And suddenly I thought of Ganka. She didn't know oranges. Warm
tenderness and pity filled my heart.

Poor thing! She didn't know. I should give her just one. But how?
To take one without asking was unthinkable. But if I did ask, I'd be
told to wait until after lunch. And then I wouldn't be able to take it
away with me. They wouldn't let me, and they'd ask questions – they
might even guess. They might start to laugh. Better just to take one
without asking. I'd be punished, I wouldn't be given any more – and
that would be that. What was I afraid of?

Round, cool and pleasant, it lay in my hand.

How could I? Thief! Thief! But all that could wait until later –
I must hurry to Ganka.

The girls were weeding right by the house, by the back door.

'Ganka! This is for you, for you! Try it – it's for you.'

Her red mouth laughed.

'What is it?'

'An orange. It's for you.'

She was turning it in her hand. I mustn't embarrass her.

I ran back into the house and, sticking my head out of the corridor window, waited to see what would happen. I wanted to share her pleasure with her.

She bit off a piece together with the peel (why hadn't I peeled it for her?), then opened her mouth wide, made a horrible face, spat out what she'd bitten off and hurled the orange far into the bushes. The other girls stood round her, laughing. And she was still screwing up her face, shaking her head, spitting, and wiping her mouth with the cuff of her embroidered shirt.

I climbed down from the windowsill and went quickly to the dark end of the corridor; hiding behind a large chest covered with a dusty carpet, I sat on the floor and began to weep.

Everything was over. I had become a thief in order to give her the best thing I knew in all the world. And she hadn't understood, and she had spat it out.

How would I ever get over this grief and this hurt?

I wept till I had no more tears. Then, a new thought came into my head: 'What if there are mice here behind the chest?'

This fear entered my soul, grew stronger there, scared away my previous feelings and returned me to life.

In the corridor I bumped into Nanny. She threw up her hands in horror.

'Your dress, your dress – it's all covered in muck! You're not crying again, are you?'

I said nothing. This morning humanity had failed to understand my silver reeds, which I had so longed to explain. And 'this' – this couldn't be spoken of at all. 'This' was something I had to be alone with.

But humanity wanted an answer and was shaking me by the shoulder. And I fended it off as best I could.

'I'm not crying. I . . . my . . . I've just got toothache.'

First published in 1924
Translated by Robert Chandler

A FAMILY JOURNEY

They argued for a long time about when it was best to leave – on the morning train or the evening train.

Grandmother was in favour of the morning train: 'At least you can look out of the window.'

Klavdiya was for the evening train: 'You can get some sleep, and the journey doesn't drag on for so long.'

Strokotov had no opinion of his own. Or maybe he had an opinion but didn't come out with it, since his opinion was never asked for. So he confined himself to nodding quietly in agreement – one moment with grandmother, the next moment with Klavdiya.

Preparations for the journey had been going on for a long time. Grandmother had unravelled her knitted jacket and made a sweater for little Petya. Then she had unravelled her woollen stockings and knitted little Petya some shorts. After that she had unravelled her warm gloves and made him some socks.

'At least the boy will be smartly dressed now. He'll be a little doll.'

Little Petya, the freckled and snivelling scion of the Strokotov family, looked like his cowed, despairing father, but the similarity was only external. In character, he was quite different. Petya thrust himself forward as much as his modest father tried to efface himself. He was bad-tempered, capricious and always dissatisfied. All he had inherited from his father were freckles, red hair and an eternally runny nose – from hay fever in summer, and from an ordinary cold in winter.

Klavdiya, the mother, a plain, skinny woman with short thick legs, saw herself as a victim and martyr and nagged away at her husband from morning till night. To bring about peace, the old woman would intervene on behalf of her son-in-law with the conciliatory words: 'Well, what do you expect from the fool?'

Klavdiya, who had dreamed in her youth of becoming a ballerina, believed that marriage to Strokotov had been her undoing. So as to bring a little solace to her life of sacrifice, she told people to call her 'Kate'. This name was pronounced by the family with a soft vowel, Russian-style: 'Kyate'.

Nature had set herself a very particular goal, one might say, in engendering the members of this family. The husband was intended for the role of a sheep, Kyate for that of an old spinster and seamstress, while the old woman was meant to be a peaceful lover of coffee and gossip. But Fate, like a third-rate director, had allotted everyone the wrong role, raised the curtain, played some little jingle and set her machine in motion.

Strokotov wore himself out, unable to live up to the role of destroyer of lives; Kyate was all too obviously no snake-charmer; while the old woman seemed to be struggling with a role a bit like that of a King Lear with no Cordelia: 'Blow, winds, and crack your cheeks!'

And now *tout ce joli monde*[1] was on its way to a French dacha. It had taken cries of despair, an advance deposit, and payment in instalments to rent this dacha. Kyate had sobbed and cursed Strokotov, who had utterly and completely destroyed her life and was now gradually destroying it all over again. Strokotov had got into the wall cupboard and crumpled his mother-in-law's coat while trying to hang himself. The old woman had tried to get Kyate to see reason: 'Don't torment the fool. If something happens, you'll have to answer to the police.'

Then they had baked some pies and set off on their way.

It happened to be an unusually hot day. Strokotov got so exhausted dragging all the suitcases, as well as the basket for the journey, that he even (quite unprecedentedly) began to answer back. This was somehow as absurd and even horrifying as if a guinea pig under a vivisector's scalpel were to look up indignantly and say: 'Why are you cutting my belly open, you bastard?'

On very hot days railwaymen like to temper their rolling stock in the sun, so that a carriage feels like a red-hot iron by the time the train leaves the station.

Little Petya did not want to look out through the window; instead he got straight to work on the pies. The old woman began mournfully listing the things they had forgotten and that were therefore sure to be devoured by moths.

A cinder suddenly flew into one of the hapless Strokotov's eyes. Cinders were always flying into his eyes: this was a misfortune that accompanied every one of the family's infrequent departures from Paris. Strokotov blinked, pulled at his eyelid, rubbed at his eye, rubbed towards his nose with his fist, rubbed away from his nose with his handkerchief; nothing made any difference.

Kyate got angry and began to hiss: 'Why doesn't this happen to anyone else? Columbus discovered the whole of America and nothing ever flew into *his* eye. Vasco da Gama . . . Hundreds like him . . . And did any of them? No, never . . . Whereas this ass . . . His eyes catch every bit of rubbish that's going!'

'Leave off, Kyate,' said the old woman. 'What do you expect from him? You don't seem to understand what kind of man he is. Give your nerves a rest.'

Strokotov felt hotter than ever as a result of his eye trouble. 'I'm dying, I need a drink,' he groaned. 'Why didn't we bring any water with us?'

'Because you never think of anything,' replied his wife, and went on to develop this thought sullenly and angrily: 'Is there anything you're capable of thinking about? No. There isn't. There never is. Not once have you ever thought about anything.'

'Ask him if he's still got the money,' the old woman instructed her daughter, preferring, because of the extraordinary contempt that she felt, not to address her son-in-law directly.

'It's still there, Maman,' Strokotov reassured her. 'The hundred francs are in my wallet. But all the same, I'm dying, and there's no water.'

The coach was getting hotter and hotter. Seeing her husband's sufferings, Kyate was suddenly filled with pity; her pity, however, because of the peculiar workings of her psyche, was directed not at Strokotov but at her mother. 'Mama, darling, you're sweating all over – you mustn't sit in a draught. Viktor, be so good as to close the window. Mama will catch cold. It probably makes no difference to you if my mother, who has made so many sacrifices for you, catches pneumonia. But to me it's not a matter of indifference. Close the window!'

The old woman almost protested against the closing of the window since she too was finding it unbearably hot, but she saw how desperately Strokotov wanted to disobey and instantly decided upon an act of self-sacrifice – anything to make things worse for her son-in-law: 'Thank you, Kyate, for taking care of your mother.'

With trembling hands Strokotov slammed shut the window, collapsed back into his seat with a groan and closed his eyes. The veins on his neck were protruding visibly.

The old woman looked at him thoughtfully out of the corner of one eye: 'Would this be too much for him?'

She decided it wouldn't.

'Blow, winds, and crack your cheeks!'

The train slowed down.

The martyr opened his eyes. 'I'll slip out and buy a bottle of Vichy,' he said, not looking at anyone.

And there was something in his tone that silenced both mother and daughter, preventing either of them from finding an appropriate rejoinder. The train came to a halt and Strokotov, trying not to look at his ladies in case they stopped him, leaped out on to the platform. But since Strokotov was unlucky with everything, the trolley with the drinks and sandwiches turned out to be at the other end of the platform. Strokotov gestured despairingly, trying to summon the trolley, but the trolley was busy with other passengers and he himself had to run the length of the train.

He found his Vichy.

'Combien?'

'Trois francs.'

He rummaged through each of his pockets. But he never had any change on him and was rummaging just on the off chance, just in case. He had to open his wallet and take out the sacred hundred-franc note.

The young lad in charge of the trolley took the note, spent a long time smoothing it out, inquired more than once if Strokotov didn't happen to have three francs about him, opened some little box, fiddled about inside it with one finger, handed a sandwich to a new customer, gave this man his change – and began fumbling about again, still holding onto the accursed hundred-franc note. Trembling with impatience, Strokotov glanced with hatred at the intruder and saw him suddenly quicken his pace and begin to gallop towards the train. Strokotov looked round. The train was moving.

His heart lurched. Everything went black. Clutching the cold, pot-bellied bottle of water against his chest, Strokotov rushed towards the train, grabbed hold and leaped into the last coach.

'Did you get the change?' the ladies yelled out together, with one voice. They had been observing this whole scene through the window.

'How could I?' he replied sullenly. Naïvely trying to change the subject, he then asked in a businesslike voice: 'Did you remember the corkscrew?'

The ladies choked. They were so enraged they couldn't breathe. They couldn't speak.

'Where?' said Kyate, recovering herself. 'Where are the hundred francs? Good God! This is hell. It's worse than being with a runaway convict.'

She let out such wild cries that even little Petya, who was used to everything and had been observing this entertaining little scene with curiosity, suddenly took fright and began to howl.

The old lady wanted to add her bit. She waited a long time, then couldn't wait any longer. She took umbrage.

'Don't shout like that,' she reprimanded her daughter. 'French people are listening. It's not right.'

'To hell with your French people,' the daughter snapped back. 'This cretin leaves us without a centime and it's all the same to you. You only care about looking good in the eyes of the French. You're wasting your time. You'll never get anything out of them except *sale étranger*.'[2]

Hearing unpleasant and entirely understandable words, a Frenchman sitting beside the other window took this *sale étranger* personally, flared his nostrils, took a deep breath, snorted and began – so it seemed – to compose a retort.

'Stop it, Kyate!' said the old woman sternly. 'This is getting out of hand.'

But Kyate was neither listening nor hearing.

'He felt like a little Vichy water. And why not? What do we care about money? So what if he has to pay a hundred francs? What does his wife matter? She can walk about naked as long as he gets his Vichy.'

And suddenly Strokotov leaped to his feet, terrible and black, his hair standing on end.

'To hell with you!' he howled. 'To hell with a-a-all! of you-ou-ou! I just can't . . .'

And, swinging the pot-bellied bottle above his head, as if he were an Indian and it were a tomahawk, he hurled it out through the window.

'Hold me back!' wheezed Kyate. 'Hold me back! I'm probably going to kill him.'

'Be quiet!' the old woman shouted hysterically, and suddenly, to universal astonishment, lifted up her leg and began to pull off her shoe. She then slipped a hand down her stocking and removed a piece of folded newspaper from beneath her heel. Everyone froze, silently watching in fear and wonder, the way people watch a conjuror as he produces a live chicken from an empty hat.

The old woman unfolded the newspaper and took out a compressed hundred-franc note.

'There! Maybe this will shut you up,' she said calmly, holding the money out to her daughter.

The daughter took the money, closed her hand over it, and pursed her lips.

'And now you'd better explain where you got hold of this money,' she said.

The old woman said nothing.

'You squirrelled it away, is that it? From the housekeeping, I suppose? My own mother! The person who should be a model of selfless . . . What's up?'

The train came to a halt.

'We've arrived,' shouted Strokotov. 'Quick – get out! The train only stops for three minutes. Hurry up! Kyate – your cardboard box! Maman – don't forget your parcel.'

'What a quick journey!' said the old woman, cheering up.

'Amazing!' Kyate joined in. 'I hadn't even noticed. Petya, darling, give Mummy your hand. Viktor, you take the basket. He always forgets something or other. Well, it's been a wonderful journey!'

First published in 1938
Translated by Robert Chandler

YEVGENY IVANOVICH ZAMYATIN
(1884–1937)

Zamyatin was born in Lebedyan, a small town around 200 miles south of Moscow. His father was an Orthodox priest and a schoolmaster; his mother a musician. After going to secondary school in Voronezh, he studied naval engineering in St Petersburg. In 1905 he was briefly imprisoned after joining the Bolshevik Party. He won recognition in 1913 with his 'A Provincial Tale'; like most of his early work, it is set in a provincial Russia that Zamyatin portrays as stifling and brutal. In March 1916 he was sent to Newcastle, to supervise the construction of icebreakers for the Russian navy. His stay in England inspired the satirical 'The Islanders' (1918) and 'The Fisher of Men' (1921). Shortly before the October Revolution, Zamyatin returned to Russia; now, however, he wrote critically of the Bolsheviks, and he was imprisoned twice more – in 1919 and 1922. Because of his moustache, neat tweed suits and formal behaviour, Zamyatin became known as 'the Englishman'.

After his return to Petrograd, Zamyatin collaborated with Maksim Gorky on various state-funded cultural initiatives; he edited translations of English and French literature and ran a creative writing workshop in the Petrograd House of Arts. A gifted literary critic and theorist, he was a teacher to the 'Serapion Brothers', a literary movement that defended the independence of art. His play The Flea (1926), based on Leskov's 'The Steel Flea', was a success, but the production was closed by the authorities. His anti-utopian novel We, a model for both Aldous Huxley's Brave New World and George Orwell's Nineteen Eighty-four, was published abroad, in English translation, after being turned down by Soviet publishers. Subjected to fierce criticism, Zamyatin appealed to Stalin for permission to emigrate. This, surprisingly, was granted, and he left for France in 1931.

Zamyatin at one time described himself as a Neo-realist. The Realists, he wrote, saw man and the world in a mirror. The Symbolists, reacting against the realists, used X-rays and therefore saw only skeletons. Neo-realism, unlike Symbolism, was concerned with life.

*Its practitioners, however, not content with merely holding a mirror
to life, aimed to study it through a microscope. The resulting picture
might seem distorted, but it was more authentic. Zamyatin's favourite
writer was Gogol: 'It was not without his influence that I developed
a tendency towards caricature, towards the grotesque, towards a
synthesis of fantasy and reality.'[1]*

The fame of We *has unjustly eclipsed Zamyatin's other work. His
stories 'The Cave' and 'Mamai' are powerful evocations of the frost,
famine and despair of post-revolutionary Petrograd, an era that
Zamyatin describes elsewhere as 'the merry, eerie winter of 1917–18,
when everything broke from its moorings and floated off somewhere
into the unknown'.[2] 'The Flood' is Zamyatin's most Dostoyevskian
work, about a childless woman who murders an orphaned teenager
whom she and her husband have taken in and who has become her
husband's mistress. 'The Lion', included here, is one of Zamyatin's
gentlest stories; it appeared first in French translation in 1935 and was
published in Russian only in 1939, two years after the writer's death.*

THE LION

It all began with a most bizarre incident: the lion, great king of the
beasts, was found hopelessly drunk. He kept tripping over all four
paws and rolling onto his side. It was an utter catastrophe.

The lion was a student at Leningrad University and at the same time
worked as an extra in the theatre. In that day's performance, dressed
in a lionskin, he was to have stood on a rock, waiting to be struck
down by a spear hurled at him by the heroine of the ballet; thereupon
he was to fall on to a mattress in the wings. At rehearsals everything
had gone off splendidly, but now suddenly, only half an hour before
the curtain was due to go up for the première, the lion had taken it
into his head to behave like a pig. No spare extras were available, but
the performance couldn't be postponed since a minister from Moscow
was expected. An emergency conference was in session in the office of
the theatre's Red director.

There was a knock on the door and the theatre fireman Petya
Zherebyakin came in. The Red director (now he really was red – with
anger) rounded on him.

'Well, what is it? What do you want? I've no time. Get out !'

'I . . . I . . . I've come about the lion, Comrade Director,' said the
fireman.

'Well, what about the lion?'

'Seeing, I mean, as our lion is drunk, that is, I'd like to play the lion, Comrade Director.'

I don't know if bears ever have blue eyes and freckles but, if they do, then the enormous Zherebyakin in his iron-soled boots was much more like a bear than a lion. But suppose by some miracle they could make a lion out of him? He swore that they could: he'd watched all the rehearsals from backstage, and when he was in the army he'd taken part in *Tsar Maximillian*.[1] So, to spite the producer, who was grinning sarcastically, the director ordered Zherebyakin to put on the costume and have a go.

A few minutes later the orchestra was already playing, con sordini, the 'March of the Lion' and Petya Zherebyakin was performing in his lion costume as if he'd been born in the Libyan desert rather than in a village near Ryazan. But at the last moment, when he was supposed to fall off the rock, he glanced down and hesitated.

'Fall, damn you, fall!' whispered the producer fiercely.

The lion obediently plumped down, landed heavily on his back and lay there, unable to get up. Surely he was going to get up? Surely there was not to be another catastrophe at the last moment?

He was helped to his feet. He got out of the costume and stood there, pale, holding his back and giving an embarrassed smile. One of his upper front teeth was missing and this made the smile somewhat rueful and childlike (incidentally, there is always something rather childlike about bears, isn't there?).

Fortunately he appeared not to be seriously hurt. He asked for a glass of water, but the director insisted that a cup of tea be brought from his own office. Once Petya had drunk the tea the director began to chivvy him.

'Well, Comrade, you've appointed yourself lion, you'd better get into the costume. Come on, come on, lad, we'll soon be starting!'

Someone obligingly sprang forward with the costume, but the lion refused to put it on. He declared that he had to slip out of the theatre for a moment. What this unforeseen exigency was he wouldn't explain; he simply gave his embarrassed smile. The director flared up. He tried to order Zherebyakin to stay and reminded him that he was a candidate-member of the Party and a shockworker, but the shock-worker-lion obstinately stood his ground. They had to give in, and with a radiant, gap-toothed smile Zherebyakin hurried off out of the theatre.

'Where the devil's he off to?' asked the director, red with anger again. 'And what are all these secrets of his?' Nobody could answer the Red director. The secret was known only to Petya Zherebyakin –

and of course to the author of this story. And, as Zherebyakin runs through the autumnal St Petersburg rain, we can move for a while to that July night when his secret was born.

There was no night that night: it was the day lightly dozing off for a second, like a marching soldier who keeps in step but cannot distinguish dream from reality. In the rosy glass of the canals doze inverted trees, windows and columns – St Petersburg. Then suddenly, at the lightest of breezes, St Petersburg disappears and in its place is Leningrad. A red flag on the Winter Palace stirs in the wind, and by the railings of the Aleksandrovsky Park stands a policeman armed with a rifle.

The policeman is surrounded by a tight group of night tram workers. Over their shoulders Petya Zherebyakin can see only the policeman's face, round as a Ryazan honey-apple. Then a very strange thing happens: somebody seizes the policeman's hands and shoulders, and one of the workers, thrusting his lips forwards in the shape of a trumpet, plants an affectionate smacking kiss on his cheek. The policeman turns crimson and blows a loud blast on his whistle; the workers run away. Zherebyakin is left face to face with the policeman – and the policeman disappears, just as suddenly as the reflection of St Petersburg in the canal, puffed away by the breeze: in front of Zherebyakin stands a girl in a policeman's cap and tunic – the first policewoman to be stationed by the Revolution on Nevsky Prospekt. Her dark eyebrows met angrily over the bridge of her nose and her eyes flashed fire.

'You ought to be ashamed of yourself, Comrade,' was all she said – but it was the way she said it!

Zherebyakin became confused and muttered guiltily, 'But it wasn't me, honestly. I was just walking home.'

'Come off it, and you a worker too!' The policewoman looked at him – but what a look!

If there'd been a trapdoor in the roadway, as there is in the theatre, Zherebyakin would have fallen straight through it and been saved; but he had to walk away slowly, feeling her eyes burning into his back.

The next day brought another white night, and again Comrade Zherebyakin was walking home after his duty turn in the theatre, and again the policewoman was standing by the railings of the Aleksandrovsky Park. Zherebyakin wanted to slip past, but he noticed she was looking at him, so he gave a guilty, embarrassed nod. She nodded back. The twilight glinted on the glossy black steel of her rifle, turning it pink; and, confronted by this pink rifle, Zherebyakin felt more cowardly than in the face of all the rifles which for five years had been fired at him on various fronts.

Not until a week later did he risk starting up a conversation with
the policewoman. It turned out that she too was from Ryazan, just
like Zherebyakin, and moreover she too remembered their Ryazan
honey-apples – you know, the sweet ones with a slightly bitter taste;
you can't get them here . . .

Every day on his way home Zherebyakin would stop by the Aleksandrovsky Park. The white nights had gone quite mad: the green,
pink and copper-coloured sky didn't grow dark for a single second.
The courting couples in the park had to look for shady spots to hide
in just as if it were daytime.

One such night Zherebyakin, with bear-like awkwardness, suddenly
asked the policewoman:

'Er, are you, that is, are policewomen allowed to get married, like,
in the course of duty? I mean, not in the course of duty, but in general,
seeing as your work is sort of military . . . ?'

'Married?' said policewoman Katya, leaning on her rifle. 'We're like
men now: if we take a fancy to someone, we have him.'

Her rifle shone pink. The policewoman lifted her face towards the
feverishly blazing sky and then looked past Zherebyakin into the
distance and completed her thought: 'If there was a man who wrote
poetry like . . . or perhaps an actor who came out on to the stage and
the whole audience started clapping . . .'

It was like the honey-apple – sweet and yet bitter at the same time.
Petya Zherebyakin saw that he'd better be off and not come back
there again, his cause was done for . . .

But no! Wonders haven't ceased! When there occurred that bizarre
incident of the lion, thank the Lord, drinking himself silly, an idea
flashed into Petya Zherebyakin's head and he flew into the director's
room . . .

However, that was all in the past. Now he was hurrying through
the autumn rain to Glinka Street. Luckily it wasn't far from the theatre
and luckily he found policewoman Katya at home. She wasn't a
policewoman now, but simply Katya. With her sleeves rolled up, she
was washing a white blouse in a basin. Dewdrops hung on her nose
and forehead. She had never looked sweeter than like this, in her
domestic setting.

When Zherebyakin placed a free ticket in front of her and told her
he had a part in the ballet that evening she didn't believe him at first;
then she grew interested; then for some reason she became embarrassed
and rolled her sleeves down; finally she looked at him (but what a
look!) and said she would definitely come.

The bells were already ringing in the theatre smoking room, in the corridors and in the foyer. The bald cabinet minister was in his box, squinting through a pince-nez. On the stage behind the curtain, which was still down, the ballerinas were smoothing their skirts with the movement swans use to clean their wings under the water. Behind the rock the producer and the director were both fussing round Zherebyakin.

'Don't forget, you're a shockworker. Mind you don't ruin everything!' whispered the director into the lion's ear. The curtain rose, and behind the bright line of the footlights the lion suddenly saw the dark auditorium, packed to the roof with white faces. Long ago, when he was simply Zherebyakin, and had to climb out of trenches with grenades exploding in front of him, he used to shudder and automatically cross himself, but still run forward. Now, however, he felt unable to take a single step, but the producer gave him a shove and, somehow moving arms and legs which seemed not to belong to him, he slowly climbed up on to the rock.

On top of the rock, the lion raised his head and saw, right next to him, policewoman Katya, leaning over the front rail of one of the second-row boxes. She was looking straight at him. The leonine heart thumped once, twice, and then stopped. He was trembling all over. His fate was about to be decided. Already the spear was flying towards him . . . Ouch! – it struck him in the side. Now he had to fall. But suppose he again fell the wrong way and ruined everything? He had never felt so terrified in all his life – it was far worse than when he used to climb out of the trenches . . .

The audience had already noticed that something wasn't right: the mortally wounded lion was standing stock-still on top of the rock and gazing down. The front rows heard the producer's terrible whisper:

'Fall, damn you, fall!'

Then they all saw a most bizarre thing: the lion raised its right paw, quickly crossed itself, and plumped down off the rock like a stone . . .

There was a moment of numbed silence, then a roar of laughter exploded in the auditorium like a grenade. Policewoman Katya was laughing so hard that she was in tears. The slain lion buried its muzzle in its paws and sobbed.

First published, in French, in 1935
Translated by David Richards

SIGIZMUND DOMINIKOVICH
KRZHIZHANOVSKY (1887–1950)

Krzhizhanovsky was, in his own words, 'known for being unknown'. The author of five short novels, more than a hundred stories, a dozen plays, screenplays and librettos, as well as hundreds of pages of essays, he went to his now-forgotten grave 'a literary non-entity'.

Born in Kiev to a Polish Catholic family, he took two degrees at Kiev University – in law, and in philology. The Revolution put an end to his career as a lawyer, freeing him to devote himself to writing and philosophy. In 1919 he wrote what he would later call his first real story, a 'fantasy-dialogue' between Jacobi, the German philosopher, and 'Supposedly', the sum of all human meanings.

At the same time, Krzhizhanovsky was becoming popular in Kiev as a lecturer – on the psychology of creativity, on the history and theory of the theatre, on art. He was erudite, a brilliant speaker and a bold and original thinker. He thought in images and constructed syllogisms out of these images. In 1920 he began collaborating with Anna Bovshek, a former Moscow Arts Theatre actress who became his lifelong companion.

In the spring of 1922 Krzhizhanovsky and Bovshek made their separate ways to Moscow; there they found separate rooms thanks – indirectly – to the 'Re-Measuring Commission'. This Commission remeasured Moscow apartments for purposes of enforcing the new 'ten-per-cent norm': ten per cent of all house space had to be surrendered for redistribution. To avoid being saddled with strangers, many owners – or rather former owners – of large apartments gave up rooms to friends or friends of friends. That is how Krzhizhanovsky came to live at No. 44 on the old Arbat. Apartment 5 was the home of an elderly count. On the recommendation of a mutual friend, the Count invited the tall, gaunt and impecunious intellectual to inhabit a small, dark unfurnished room at the end of a corridor. Krzhizhanovsky brought in a wooden bed with a horsehair mattress, a plain table with two drawers, an armchair with a hard seat, and hanging bookshelves. The Count died, the Countess moved out, and less sympathetic neigh-

bours moved in to what was becoming that symbol of Soviet life, a communal apartment.

By then there was a new norm stipulating that no one person could occupy more than nine square metres (ninety-seven square feet). An apartment intended for a single family thus became home to half a dozen families or more, with everyone obliged to use the same kitchen, bath and WC. Krzhizhanovsky's room was only six square metres, but his neighbours hated him none the less; he simply did not fit in. Bovshek pleaded with Krzhizhanovsky to join her in her own somewhat larger room, but he insisted he needed a room of his own. He also felt, she later recalled, that life in one apartment would destroy the enchantment of their relationship.

It was in that room, probably once a maid's room or a larder, that Krzhizhanovsky wrote his philosophical, satirical, lyrical phantasmagorias. Editors rejected them on the grounds that they were not 'contemporary'. According to Bovshek, however, Krzhizhanovsky was not concerned with life's easily observable surface; he was a 'writer-thinker'. Many of his stories have the quality of a problem or puzzle: 'I am interested,' he once said, 'not in the arithmetic, but in the algebra of life.'

'Quadraturin' belongs to a cycle of stories called 'What Men Die By', a title that recalls 'What Men Live By', a parable by Tolstoy in which an angel is sent down to earth to discover what men live by. He finds that men live (and thrive) not by looking after themselves, but by loving each other: 'He who loves is in God and God is in him, for God is love.' In 'What Men Die By' God is dead: people are engaged only in looking after themselves and what they imagine to be their own good.

Despite the constant rejections, Krzhizhanovsky went on writing his fictions and submitting them to publishers. The German invasion in 1941 frustrated a near-success: his Stories about the West had been accepted by a publisher and were in the process of being typeset. After this he gave up. Alcohol became an indispensable crutch. Asked what had led him to drink, he joked: 'A sober attitude towards reality.' Dangerously ill, he moved in with Bovshek in 1949; neighbours ranted about this 'illegal' resident (he and Bovshek had never married). A stroke then deprived him of the ability to read. He tried unsuccessfully to relearn the alphabet. On 28 December 1950 the critic Georgy Shengeli drew a black frame around an entry in his notebook: 'Today Sigizmund Dominikovich Krzhizhanovsky died, a writer-visionary, an unsung genius.'

Krzhizhanovsky's first book was published posthumously in 1989.

Three volumes of a projected five-volume collected works have recently appeared in Moscow, and they are already being translated into French.

Joanne Turnbull

QUADRATURIN

I

From outside there came a soft knock at the door: once. Pause. And again – a bit louder and bonier: twice.

Sutulin, without rising from his bed, extended – as was his wont – a foot towards the knock, threaded a toe through the door handle, and pulled. The door swung open. On the threshold, head grazing the lintel, stood a tall, grey man the colour of the dusk seeping in at the window.

Before Sutulin could set his feet on the floor the visitor stepped inside, wedged the door quietly back into its frame and, jabbing first one wall, then another, with a briefcase dangling from an apishly long arm, said, 'Yes: a matchbox.'

'What?'

'Your room, I say: it's a matchbox. How many square feet?'

'Eighty-six and a bit.'

'Precisely. May I?'

And before Sutulin could open his mouth, the visitor sat down on the edge of the bed and hurriedly unbuckled his bulging briefcase. Lowering his voice almost to a whisper, he went on, 'I'm here on business. You see, I, that is, we, are conducting, how shall I put it . . . well, experiments, I suppose. Under wraps for now. I won't hide the fact: a well-known foreign firm has an interest in our concern. You want the electric-light switch? No, don't bother: I'll only be a minute. So then: we have discovered – this is a secret now – an agent for biggerizing rooms. Well, won't you try it?'

The stranger's hand popped out of the briefcase and proffered Sutulin a narrow dark tube, not unlike a tube of paint, with a tightly screwed cap and a leaden seal. Sutulin fidgeted bewilderedly with the slippery tube and, though it was nearly dark in the room, made out on the label the clearly printed word: Q u a d r a t u r i n. When he raised his eyes, they came up against the fixed, unblinking stare of his interlocutor.

'So then, you'll take it? The price? Goodness, it's gratis. Just for advertising. Now if you'll' – the guest began quickly leafing through a sort of ledger he had produced from the same briefcase – 'just sign this book (a short testimonial, so to say). A pencil? Have mine. Where? Here: column III. That's it.'

His ledger clapped shut, the guest straightened up, wheeled round, stepped to the door . . . and a minute later Sutulin, having snapped on the light, was considering with puzzledly raised eyebrows the clearly embossed letters: **Q u a d r a t u r i n**.

On closer inspection it turned out that this zinc packet was tightly fitted – as is often done by the makers of patented agents – with a thin transparent paper whose ends were expertly glued together. Sutulin removed the paper sheath from the Quadraturin, unfurled the rolled-up text, which showed through the paper's transparent gloss, and read:

DIRECTIONS

Dissolve 1 teaspoon of the Quadraturin essence in 1 cup of water. Wet a piece of cotton wool or simply a clean rag with the solution; apply this to those of the room's internal walls designated for proliferspansion. This mixture leaves no stains, will not damage wallpaper, and even contributes – incidentally – to the extermination of bedbugs.

Thus far Sutulin had been only puzzled. Now his puzzlement was gradually overtaken by another feeling, strong and disturbing. He stood up and tried to pace from corner to corner, but the corners of this living cage were too close together: a walk amounted to almost nothing but turns, from toe to heel and back again. Sutulin stopped short, sat down and, closing his eyes, gave himself up to thoughts, which began: Why not . . . ? What if . . . ? Suppose . . . ? To his left, not three feet away from his ear, someone was driving an iron spike into the wall. The hammer kept slipping, banging and aiming, it seemed, at Sutulin's head. Rubbing his temples, he opened his eyes: the black tube lay in the middle of the narrow table, which had managed somehow to insinuate itself between the bed, the windowsill and the wall. Sutulin tore away the leaden seal, and the cap span off in a spiral. From out of the round aperture came a bitterish gingery smell. The smell made his nostrils flare pleasantly.

'Hmm . . . Let's try it. Although . . .'

And, having removed his jacket, the possessor of Quadraturin proceeded to the experiment. Stool up against door, bed into middle of room, table on top of bed. Nudging across the floor a saucer of transparent liquid, its glassy surface gleaming with a slightly yellowish tinge, Sutulin crawled along after it, systematically dipping a handkerchief wound round a pencil into the Quadraturin and daubing the floorboards and patterned wallpaper. The room really was, as that man today had said, a matchbox. But Sutulin worked slowly and carefully, trying not to miss a single corner. This was rather difficult since the liquid really did evaporate in an instant or was absorbed (he couldn't tell which) without leaving even the slightest film; there was only its smell, increasingly pungent and spicy, making his head spin, confounding his fingers and causing his knees, pinned to the floor, to tremble slightly. When he had finished with the floorboards and the bottom of the walls, Sutulin rose to his strangely weak and heavy feet and continued to work standing up. Now and then he had to add a little more of the essence. The tube was gradually emptying. It was already night outside. In the kitchen, to the right, a bolt came crashing down. The apartment was readying for bed. Trying not to make any noise, the experimenter, clutching the last of the essence, climbed up onto the bed and from the bed up onto the tottering table: only the ceiling remained to be quadraturinized. But just then someone banged on the wall with his fist, 'What's going on? People are trying to sleep, but he's . . .'

Turning round at the sound, Sutulin fumbled: the slippery tube spurted out of his hand and landed on the floor. Balancing carefully, Sutulin got down with his already drying brush, but it was too late. The tube was empty, and the rapidly fading spot around it smelled stupefyingly sweet. Grasping at the wall in his exhaustion (to fresh sounds of discontent from the left), he summoned his last bit of strength, put the furniture back where it belonged and, without undressing, fell into bed. A black sleep instantly descended on him from above: both tube and man were empty.

2

Two voices began in a whisper. Then by degrees of sonority – from piano to mf, from mf to fff – they cut into Sutulin's sleep.

'Outrageous. I don't want any new tenants popping out from under that skirt of yours . . . Put up with all that racket?!'

'Can't just dump it in the garbage . . .'

'I don't want to hear about it. You were told: no dogs, no cats, no children . . .' at which point there ensued such fff that Sutulin was ripped once and for all from his sleep; unable to part eyelids stitched together with exhaustion, he reached – as was his wont – for the edge

of the table on which stood the clock. Then it began. His hand groped
for a long time, grappling air: there was no clock and no table. Sutulin
opened his eyes at once. In an instant he was sitting up, looking
dazedly round the room. The table that usually stood right here, at
the head of the bed, had moved off into the middle of a faintly familiar,
large but ungainly room.

Everything was the same: the skimpy, threadbare rug that had trailed
after the table somewhere up ahead of him, and the photographs, and
the stool, and the yellow patterns on the wallpaper. But they were all
strangely spread out inside the expanded room cube.

'Quadraturin,' thought Sutulin, 'is terrific!'

And he immediately set about rearranging the furniture to fit the
new space. But nothing worked: the abbreviated rug, when moved
back beside the bed, exposed worn, bare floorboards; the table and
the stool, pushed by habit against the head of the bed, had disencum-
bered an empty corner latticed with cobwebs and littered with shreds
and tatters, once artfully masked by the corner's own crowdedness
and the shadow of the table. With a triumphant, but slightly frightened
smile, Sutulin went all round his new, practically squared square,
scrutinizing every detail. He noted with displeasure that the room had
grown more in some places than in others: an external corner, the
angle of which was now obtuse, had made the wall askew; Quadraturin,
apparently, did not work as well on internal corners; carefully as Sutulin
had applied the essence, the experiment had produced somewhat
uneven results.

The apartment was beginning to stir. Out in the corridor, occupants
shuffled to and fro. The bathroom door kept banging. Sutulin walked
up to the threshold and turned the key to the right. Then, hands
clasped behind his back, he tried pacing from corner to corner: it
worked. Sutulin laughed with joy. How about that! At last! But then
he thought: they may hear my footsteps – through the walls – on the
right, on the left, at the back. For a minute he stood stock-still. Then
he quickly bent down – his temples had suddenly begun to ache with
yesterday's sharp thin pain – and, having removed his boots, gave
himself up to the pleasure of a stroll, moving soundlessly about in
only his socks.

'May I come in?'

The voice of the proprietress. He was on the point of going to the
door and unlocking it when he suddenly remembered: he mustn't. 'I'm
getting dressed. Wait a minute. I'll be right out.'

'It's all very well, but it complicates things. Say I lock the door and
take the key with me. What about the keyhole? And then there's the

window: I'll have to get curtains. Today.' The pain in his temples had become thinner and more nagging. Sutulin gathered up his papers in haste. It was time to go to the office. He dressed. Pushed the pain under his cap. And listened at the door: no one there. He quickly opened it. Quickly slipped out. Quickly turned the key. Now.

Waiting patiently in the entrance hall was the proprietress.

'I wanted to talk to you about that girl, what's her name. Can you believe it, she's submitted an application to the House Committee saying she's . . .'

'I've heard. Go on.'

'It's nothing to you. No one's going to take your eighty-six square feet away. But put yourself in my . . .'

'I'm in a hurry,' he nodded his cap, and flew down the stairs.

3

On his way home from the office, Sutulin paused in front of the window of a furniture dealer: the long curve of a couch, a round extendable table . . . it would be nice – but how could he carry them in past the eyes and the questions? They would guess, they couldn't help but guess . . .

He had to limit himself to the purchase of a yard of canary-yellow material (he did, after all, need a curtain). He didn't stop by the café: he had no appetite. He needed to get home – it would be easier there: he could reflect, look round and make adjustments at leisure. Having unlocked the door to his room, Sutulin gazed about to see if anyone was looking: they weren't. He walked in. Then he switched on the light and stood there for a long time, his arms spread flat against the wall, his heart beating wildly: *this he had not expected* – not at all.

The Quadraturin was *still* working. During the eight or nine hours Sutulin had been out, it had pushed the walls at least another seven feet apart; the floorboards, stretched by invisible rods, rang out at his first step – like organ pipes. The entire room, distended and monstrously misshapen, was beginning to frighten and torment him. Without taking off his coat, Sutulin sat down on the stool and surveyed his spacious and at the same time oppressive coffin-shaped living box, trying to understand what had caused this unexpected effect. Then he remembered: he hadn't done the ceiling – the essence had run out. His living box was spreading only sideways, without rising even an inch upwards.

'Stop. I have to stop this quadraturinizing thing. Or I'll . . .' He pressed his palms to his temples and listened: the corrosive pain, lodged under his skull since morning, was still drilling away. Though the windows in the house opposite were dark, Sutulin took cover behind the yellow length of curtain. His head would not stop aching. He quietly undressed, snapped out the light and got into bed. At first he slept, then he was awoken by a feeling of awkwardness. Wrapping the covers more tightly about him, Sutulin again dropped off, and once more an unpleasant sense of mooringlessness interfered with his sleep. He raised himself up on one palm and felt all around him with his free hand: the wall was gone. He struck a match. Um hmm: he blew out the flame and hugged his knees till his elbows cracked. 'It's growing, damn it, it's still growing.' Clenching his teeth, Sutulin crawled out of bed and, trying not to make any noise, gently edged first the front legs, then the back legs of the bed toward the receding wall. He felt a little shivery. Without turning the light on again, he went to look for his coat on that nail in the corner so as to wrap himself up more warmly. But there was no hook on the wall where it had been yesterday, and he had to feel around for several seconds before his hands chanced upon fur. Twice more during a night that was long and nagging as the pain in his temples, Sutulin pressed his head and knees to the wall as he was falling asleep and, when he awoke, fiddled about with the legs of the bed again. In doing this – mechanically, meekly, lifelessly – he tried, though it was still dark outside, not to open his eyes: it was better that way.

4

Towards dusk the next evening, having served out his day, Sutulin was approaching the door to his room: he did not quicken his step and, upon entering, felt neither consternation nor horror. When the dim, sixteen candlepower bulb lit up somewhere in the distance beneath the long low vault, its yellow rays struggling to reach the dark, ever-receding corners of the vast and dead, yet empty barrack, which only recently, before Quadraturin, had been a cramped but cozy, warm and lived-in cubbyhole, he walked resignedly towards the yellow square of the window, now diminished by perspective; he tried to count his steps. From there, from a bed squeezed pitifully and fearfully in the corner by the window, he stared dully and wearily through deep-boring pain at the swaying shadows nestled against the floorboards, and at the smooth low overhang of the ceiling. 'So, something forces its way out of a tube, and can't stop squaring: a square squared, a square of squares squared. I've got to think faster than it: if I don't outthink it, it will outgrow me and . . .' And suddenly someone was hammering on the door, 'Citizen Sutulin, are you in there?'

From the same faraway place came the muffled and barely audible voice of the proprietress, 'He's in there. Must be asleep.'

Sutulin broke into a sweat: 'What if I don't get there in time, and they go ahead and . . .' And, trying not to make a sound (let them think he was asleep), he slowly made his way through the darkness to the door. There.

'Who is it?'

'Oh, open up! Why's the door locked? Re-measuring Commission. We'll remeasure and leave.'

Sutulin stood with his ear pressed to the door. Through the thin panel he could hear the clump of heavy boots. Figures were being mentioned, and room numbers.

'This room next. Open up!'

With one hand Sutulin gripped the knob of the electric-light switch and tried to twist it, as one might twist the head of a bird: the switch spattered light, then crackled, spun feebly round and drooped down. Again someone hammered on the door, 'Well!'

Sutulin turned the key to the left. A broad black shape squeezed itself into the doorway.

'Turn on the light.'

'It's burned out.'

Clutching at the door handle with his left hand, and the bundle of wire with his right, he tried to hide the extended space from view. The black mass took a step back.

'Who's got a match? Give me that box. We'll have a look anyway. Do things right.'

Suddenly the proprietress began whining, 'Oh, what is there to look at? Eighty-six square feet for the eighty-sixth time. Measuring the room won't make it any bigger. He's a quiet man, home from a long day at the office – and you won't let him rest: have to measure and remeasure. Whereas other people, who have no right to the space, but . . .'

'Ain't that the truth,' the black mass muttered and, rocking from boot to boot, gently and even almost affectionately drew the door to the light. Sutulin was left alone on wobbling, cottony legs in the middle of the four-cornered, inexorably growing and proliferating darkness.

5

He waited until their steps had died away, then quickly dressed and went out. They'd be back, to remeasure or check they hadn't under-measured or whatever. He could finish thinking better here – from crossroad to crossroad. Towards night a wind came up: it rattled the

bare frozen branches on the trees, shook the shadows loose, droned
in the wires and beat against walls, as if trying to knock them down.
Hiding the needle-like pain in his temples from the wind's buffets,
Sutulin went on, now diving into the shadows, now plunging into the
lamplight. Suddenly, through the wind's rough thrusts, something
softly and tenderly brushed against his elbow. He turned round.
Beneath feathers batting against a black brim, a familiar face with
provocatively half-closed eyes. And barely audible through the moan-
ing air: 'You know you know me. And you look right past me. You
ought to bow. That's it.'

Her slight figure, tossed back by the wind, perched on tenacious
stiletto heels, was all insubordination and readiness for battle.

Sutulin tipped his cap. 'But you were supposed to be going away.
And you're still here? Then something must have prevented . . .'

'That's right – this.'

And he felt a chamois finger touch his chest then dart back into the
muff. He sought out the narrow pupils of her eyes beneath the dancing
black feathers, and it seemed that one more look, one more touch,
one more shock to his hot temples, and it would all come unthought,
undone and fall away. Meanwhile she, her face nearing his, said, 'Let's
go to your place. Like last time. Remember?'

With that, everything stopped.

'That's impossible.'

She sought out the arm that had been pulled back and clung to it
with tenacious chamois fingers.

'My place . . . isn't fit,' he looked away, having again withdrawn
both his arms and the pupils of his eyes.

'You mean to say it's cramped. My God, how silly you are. The
more cramped it is . . .' The wind tore away the end of her phrase.
Sutulin did not reply. 'Or, perhaps you don't . . .'

When he reached the turning, he looked back: the woman was still
standing there, pressing her muff to her bosom, like a shield; her
narrow shoulders were shivering with cold; the wind cynically flicked
her skirt and lifted up the lappets of her coat.

'Tomorrow. Everything tomorrow. But now . . .' And, quickening
his pace, Sutulin turned resolutely back.

'Right now: while everyone's asleep. Collect my things (only the
necessaries) and go. Run away. Leave the door wide open: let *them*.
Why should I be the only one? Why not let *them*?'

The apartment was indeed sleepy and dark. Sutulin walked down
the corridor, straight and to the right, opened the door with resolve
and, as always, wanted to turn the light switch, but it spun feebly in

his fingers, reminding him that the circuit had been broken. This was an annoying obstacle. But it couldn't be helped. Sutulin rummaged in his pockets and found a box of matches: it was almost empty. Good for three or four flares – that's all. He would have to husband both light and time. When he reached the coat pegs, he struck the first match: light crept in yellow radiuses through the black air. Sutulin purposely, overcoming temptation, concentrated on the illuminated scrap of wall and the coats and jackets hanging from hooks. He knew that there, behind his back, the dead, quadraturinized space with its black corners was still spreading. He knew and did not look round. The match smouldered in his left hand, his right pulled things off hooks and flung them on the floor. He needed another flare; looking at the floor, he started towards the corner – if it was still a corner and if it was still there – where, by his calculations, the bed should have fetched up, but he accidentally held the flame under his breath – and again the black wilderness closed in. One last match remained: he struck it over and over: it would not light. One more time – and its crackling head fell off and slipped through his fingers. Then, having turned around, afraid to go any further into the depths, the man started back towards the bundle he had abandoned under the hooks. But he had made the turn, apparently, inexactly. He walked – heel to toe, heel to toe – holding his fingers out in front of him, and found nothing: neither the bundle, nor the hooks, nor even the walls. 'I'll get there in the end. I must get there.' His body was sticky with cold and sweat. His legs wobbled oddly. The man squatted down, palms on the floorboards: 'I shouldn't have come back. Now here I am alone, nowhere to turn.' And suddenly it struck him: 'I'm waiting here, but it's growing, I'm waiting, but it's . . .'

In their sleep and in their fear, the occupants of the quadratrures adjacent to citizen Sutulin's eighty-six square feet couldn't make head or tail of the timbre and intonation of the cry that woke them in the middle of the night and compelled them to rush to the threshold of the Sutulin cell: for a man who is lost and dying in the wilderness to cry out is both futile and belated: but if even so – against all sense – he does cry out, then, most likely, *thus*.

Written in 1926; first published in 1989
Translated by Joanne Turnbull

VERA MIKHAILOVNA INBER
(1890–1972)

Inber was born in Odessa. Her father worked in publishing and her mother taught Russian. As a young woman Inber lived for several years in France and Switzerland, returning to Russia shortly before the First World War. Between 1914 and 1922 she published three volumes of poetry; her poem 'Five Nights and Days' (1924), written in memory of Lenin, brought her wider recognition. She travelled regularly, making three trips to Western Europe between 1924 and 1934, as well as visiting Georgia and Soviet Central Asia.

Like all of her contemporaries, she was subject to a variety of pressures to write what was acceptable to the authorities. The critic Catriona Kelly observes that Inber 'complied partly because she felt under constant threat, being a first cousin of Lev Trotsky, and partly because she knew that literary conformity would secure her the trips abroad which were her one source of unalloyed pleasure'.[1] Inber is best known for the poetry and diaries she wrote between 1941 and 1943, during the Siege of Leningrad. The fame of her patriotic writing has perhaps led critics and readers to overlook the witty and graceful stories she wrote in the 1920s; several of these, like 'Lalla's Interests', are about children.

LALLA'S INTERESTS

The lift was old and very lonely in its cage. Embittered by incessant tottering from floor to floor, it had begun snapping the gate shut with a vicious click and whimpering on the way down like a wounded wolf. Sometimes it went out of service altogether and sulked between floors, glowering at people trudging up the stairs.

For chaperon the lift had Yakov Mitrokhin, someone's eleven-year-old son. He had appeared from the yard; the night watchman had taken to him and he to the lift. In accordance with his instructions from the house-manager's office, Yakov Mitrokhin did not allow anyone into the lift unaccompanied. He took everyone up himself and exacted from each, again as per his instructions, a fee of five kopeks.

During the long evening hours, while a blizzard hissed, howled and ran riot outside, Yakov Mitrokhin, ever at his post by the lift and waiting for people who had gone to the theatre or to see friends, would reflect upon life. He would reflect upon life, upon the fact that his felt boots were full of holes, that his adoptive father the night watchman Mitrofan Avdeyich hit hard and, worse, for no reason, and that it would be nice to find a pencil and take up book learning. Again and again he would examine the lift's mechanism, its inner workings, its seats, its buttons. One button in particular, a little red one: press it hard and the lift would stop dead. Very interesting.

In the evenings, when the grown-ups were out at the theatre or sitting quietly at home, giving their guests tea, boys in fur hats and sheepskin coats from all over the yard would come by for some talk with Yakov Mitrokhin. He was even visited, on occasion, by a velvet-bonneted six year old by the name of Lalla. Lalla's mother, a stout woman resembling a round chest of drawers, was deeply distressed by this friendship and always said, 'Why he's nothing but a waif, Lalla, wipe your nose! He could kill you or kidnap you, don't suck your thumb! Isn't there anyone else you'd rather play with?'

When Yakov Mitrokhin heard remarks like that, he would snort reproachfully, but he never said anything.

Lalla's nanny, a venerable old lady, was even more distraught: 'Lallachka, stop this foolishness, don't you even look at him! To think what you've found: a little lift boy, when your papa's writing desk is covered in leather and you drink hot cocoa every day. A treasure, you say? Don't be silly! He's not your sort!'

But little Lalla, fair and round as a button, invariably walked past Yakov Mitrokhin as close as she could, and smiled up at him.

One day downstairs by the lift, on the wall where people usually put up announcements to do with the building, there appeared one more:

All children what live in this house are invited to a meeting tomorrow after 5 under the stairs where the old coat is laying. Very importint things will be said. Enter free. The ones not from this house will have to pay (two licoriss sticks).

The announcement was unsigned.

The first to notice it was Lalla's mother. She read it through her pince-nez, then with her naked eye, and immediately rang the bell of the house-manager's office on the second floor. The house-manager's deputy emerged.

'What can you be thinking of, comrade Pelageyaitis?' said Lalla's mother. 'How can you permit such a thing?' She jabbed the notice with her reticule. 'Our children are being corrupted while you stand idly by! Why don't you say anything? Of course, my Lalla won't go, but that's not the point, what about the principle?'

Comrade Pelageyaitis blinked, blew his nose and took exception: 'I don't see anything wrong, ma'am. Children have a right to co-organize themselves for the protection of their professional interests.'

Lalla's mother spluttered with indignation and clenched her teeth: 'What interests can they possibly have when their noses are always running? I'm quite sure this is the work of that boy Yury from apartment eighteen. His father's a senior secretary.'

Senior secretary Seleznyov, a gloomy man with bad kidneys, looked askance at the announcement and thought: 'I can see that's Yury's writing. Who he'll be when he grows up, I don't know! An adventurer like that Pilsudsky.'

The children seemed not to notice the announcement. Only the stairs became unusually grubby with the marks of small boots, while the demand for liquorice sticks at a nearby co-operative rose so sharply that a fresh supply had to be laid in.

The night passed uneventfully, but the morning turned anxious.

To begin with the milkmaid arrived with the news that out-of-doors there was such a snowstorm you couldn't see an inch in front of your face and she'd nearly harnessed her horse the wrong way round, in consequence of which milk had gone up a kopek. A sense of trouble brewing hung over the house. But Seleznyov still went to the office with a dietetic lunch in his briefcase, while Lalla's mother set off for private trader Lapin's to see about this complication with the milk.

The children sat in their rooms and kept suspiciously quiet.

A little after five, when most parents – weary from the office, the blizzard and lunch – were resting, *Pravda* or *Izvestiya* slipping from their limp hands, small shadows began flitting down the stairs, clearly bound for the place where the old sheepskin coat was lying.

Lalla's mother, having stood in line at Lapin's for an hour and ascertained that milk had indeed gone up and that there was no cottage cheese at all, was also resting on the ottoman amid a quantity of pillows, mostly round, some as large as automobile wheels, others as small as saucers. In the kitchen, Lalla's nanny was arguing with the washerwoman about God.

The central heating was quietly snuffling. Suddenly a door slammed.

Lalla's mother jumped, up only to discover that little Lalla – Yelena Yegorovna Antonova – had disappeared.

Lalla's mother threw something on, stormed across the hall and rang the bell. The door was opened by Senior Secretary Seleznyov himself, holding a hot-water bottle: 'My Lalla is gone, and Yury, too, I imagine,' said Lalla's mother. 'They're having a meeting under the stairs, professional interests, but all they'll wind up with is pneumonia.'

'My Yury's not here,' Senior Secretary Seleznyov replied peevishly. 'Must have gone, too. I wouldn't be surprised if this was his doing. Let me put my coat on.'

They walked out together and started down. Just then the decrepit lift began to groan, hobbling down from the seventh floor. Seeing the two of them on the stairs, Yakov Mitrokhin stopped the machine, clicked open the gate crisply and said: ''Fyou please.'

Downstairs, meanwhile, the little room – where the old sheepskin coat was lying and the street-watering hose hibernating – had become so jammed with children you couldn't take a deep breath. The air was thick with the smell of liquorice.

Yury Seleznyov was standing on an old chair and getting ready to preside. His assistant, Viktor, age twelve and not a party member, kept running up to him with questions.

'Yury, there's a girl from another yard here with a baby. Can the baby give her its vote or not?'

Just then the baby began to vote all by itself, so loudly they were all nearly deafened.

'Comrades,' Yury tried to scream over it, 'comrades, I hereby inform you that in order to vote you must be able to walk! Anyone else must abstain. Votes are not transferable. Please put your name down if you'd like to speak – we don't have much time – about the problem of re-electing parents.'

Lalla, pale, eyes sparkling, squeezed her way through to Viktor and said quietly, 'Put my name down, too. I want to speak. Write: "Lalla from the fifth floor".'

'What do you want to speak about, comrade?'

'About prickly woollies, so we won't have to wear them any more. And lots of other things besides.'

Yury waved a liquorice stick and began: 'Comrades, I'd like to say a few words. All sorts of people – metalworkers, shop assistants, even bootblacks – have a union to protect them from exploitation, but we children can't do anything like that. Every parent, whether father or mother, and especially if he has bad kidneys, does whatever he wants with us. This can't go on. I suggest we present a list of demands and devise slogans in keeping with the times. Who's in favour? Against? Abstentions?'

'Yakov Mitrokhin's name is down next,' Viktor announced, 'to speak about not letting them box our ears. But he's not here.'

Yury frowned knowingly and said, 'Must be busy. He wouldn't run off for no reason. It's obviously something important. Leave him on the list.'

The meeting was hectic. Many problems were raised, all of them so pressing that no one could keep quiet. They talked about the fact that parents think too much of themselves and even forbid children to play in the corridor in communal apartments,[1] which is absolutely intolerable. They talked about the fact that washing one's shoes in puddles was necessary, and about all sorts of other things.

For the first time ever, the protection of children's interests was put on a professional footing.

The lift hung between the third and fourth floors for an hour and a half. Lalla's mother banged and bustled about in vain and senior secretary Seleznyov clutched the small of his back, while Yakov Mitrokhin kept insisting that the lift's insides were in a bad way and he couldn't do anything about it: the lift would hang there a while, then start up again all by itself.

When Lalla's mother, half dead from worry and the tense wait, finally returned to her round pillows, she found Lalla sitting at her father's writing desk. With a large blue pencil on a large sheet of paper she was painstakingly tracing out a slogan evidently devised at the meeting: CHILDREN, BE CAREFUL WHEN ELECTING PARENTS!

Lalla's mother was so horrified she turned pale green.

The next day she received a letter via Lalla's nanny. To her surprise, the bedraggled envelope contained something round. She opened it. Inside was a large, sticky five-kopek coin. The note said:

*Ma'am, I'm giving you back your five kopeks for the lift. To be fair.
I held you there on purpose so as your daughter Lalla could speak about
all her interests.*
  For illiterate Yakov Mitrokhin,
                              Yury Seleznyov

First published in 1925
Translated by Joanne Turnbull

MIKHAIL AFANASYEVICH
BULGAKOV (1891–1940)

Born in Kiev, Bulgakov studied medicine at Kiev University and served as a doctor during the First World War, working in both military and civilian hospitals in the provinces. He abandoned medicine in 1920 and moved to Moscow in 1921; like Chekhov, Russia's other doctor-writer, he made his living from writing humorous sketches for news-papers. His early works, Notes on the Cuff, The Diaboliad *and* The Fatal Eggs, *were well received, but the more sharply satirical* The Heart of a Dog *was declared unpublishable. During the late 1920s several of his plays were performed in leading Moscow theatres, but they were removed from the repertoire after official criticism. He then applied for permission to emigrate; this led to a telephone call from Stalin himself. Bulgakov – unlike Zamyatin – was refused permission to emigrate, but* The Days of the Turbins *(Bulgakov's adaptation of his Civil War novel* The White Guard*) was restored to the repertoire of the Moscow Arts Theatre, and Bulgakov was allowed to work there as an assistant producer from 1930 to 1936.* The Days of the Turbins *was one of Stalin's favourite plays, in spite of its sympathetic portrayal of the White Guard.*

During the 1930s Bulgakov wrote two novels which he knew would not be published in his lifetime: A Theatrical Novel *(translated as* Black Snow*) and* The Master and Margarita. *The latter, a complex novel writ-ten in a variety of styles from the laconic to the baroque, is Bulgakov's masterpiece. It is made up of three main elements: first, the story of Yeshua (Jesus) and Pontius Pilate; second, the story of the Master – the writer of the Pontius Pilate story – and his love for Margarita (Bulgakov introduced this element in 1931, shortly before his marriage to his third wife, Elena Shilovskaya); third, a visit paid to Moscow by the Devil, along with a retinue that includes an irrepressible black cat. The novel is frequently self-referential. In 1930, for instance, in a moment of despair, Bulgakov burned his first draft; his Master, in a similar despairing moment, also burns his manuscript – which is restored to him by the Devil, who remarks that 'Manuscripts don't burn.'*

The Master and Margarita *made a huge impact when it was first published in Moscow (in censored form) in 1966–7. In the critic Lesley Milne's words, 'it brought a sense of liberation akin to revelation'.*[1] *Two phrases, at least, quickly achieved proverbial status among the intelligentsia: 'Cowardice is the most terrible vice' – which was obviously intended to refer not only to Pontius Pilate but to the behaviour of Soviet society as a whole; and 'Manuscripts don't burn' – a declaration of faith on the part of Bulgakov that is sometimes repeated too glibly by those who wish to deny reality.* The Master and Margarita *survived, but there are works by Akhmatova, Mandelstam, Platonov and many others that did not.*

'The Embroidered Towel' is an example of Bulgakov's realistic manner; it is one of a group of semi-autobiographical stories published in periodicals in the 1920s and collected posthumously to form A Country Doctor's Notebook *(1963). Doris Lessing says of this 'little book' that it 'has an epic quality because of the background of Russia's vastness, the great distances, the weight of the ignorance, the need'.*[2] *It has recently been established that Bulgakov originally set the story in the 'unforgettable year' of 1917; his editor changed the year to 1916*[3] *– a change I have reversed. Bulgakov clearly intended the young girl, 'bloodless but still alive and beautiful none the less', as an image of Russia after the October Revolution. The red cockerel on the towel, for all its beauty and vitality, is an image of danger. This was a time when, all over Russia, peasants were setting fire to their landlords' estates, and the Russian idiom 'to let loose the red cockerel' means 'to commit arson'. This multi-faceted story can also be read as an account of an initiation into manhood and sexuality.*

THE EMBROIDERED TOWEL

If you have never driven over country roads it is useless for me to tell you about it; you wouldn't understand anyway. But if you have, I would rather not remind you of it.

To cut a long story short, my driver and I spent exactly twenty-four hours covering the thirty-two miles which separate the district town of Grachyovka from Muryovo hospital. Indeed so nearly exactly twenty-four hours that it was uncanny: at 2 p.m. on 16 September 1917 we were at the last corn-chandler's store on the outskirts of the remarkable town of Grachyovka, and at five past two on 17 September of that same unforgettable year 1917, I was in the Muryovo hospital yard, standing on trampled, withered grass, flattened by the September rain. My legs were ossified with cold, so much so that, as I stood there bemused, I mentally leafed through the textbook pages in an inane attempt to remember whether there was such a complaint as ossification of the muscles or whether it was an illness I had dreamed up while asleep the night before in the village of Grabilovka. What the devil was it in Latin? Every single muscle ached unbearably, like toothache. There is nothing I can say about my toes – they lay immobile in my boots, as rigid as wooden stumps. I confess that in a burst of cowardice I pronounced a whispered curse on the medical profession and on the application form I had handed in five years earlier to the rector of the university. All the time a fine rain was drizzling down as through a sieve. My coat had swelled like a sponge. I vainly tried to grasp my suitcase with the fingers of my right hand, but in the end spat on the wet grass in disgust. My fingers were incapable of gripping anything. It was then, stuffed as I was with all sorts of knowledge from fascinating medical books, that I suddenly remembered the name of the illness – palsy. 'Paralysis,' I said to myself in despair, God knows why.

'Your roads take some getting used to,' I muttered through stony, blue lips, staring resentfully at the driver, although the state of the road was hardly his fault.

'Ah, comrade doctor,' he answered, with lips equally stiff under their fair moustache, 'I've been driving fifteen years and I still can't get used to them.'

I shuddered and glanced round miserably at the peeling, white, two-storey hospital building, at the bare log walls of my assistant's house, and at my own future residence, a neat, two-storey house with mysterious windows blank as gravestones. I gave a long sigh. Suddenly instead of Latin words a faraway memory flashed through my head, a sweet phrase which a lusty tenor in blue stockings sang in my numbed and shaken head: *Salut, demeure chaste et pure* . . . Farewell, farewell, it will be a long time before I see you again, oh golden-red Bolshoy Theatre, Moscow, shop windows . . . ah, farewell.

'Next time, I'll wear a sheepskin coat,' I said to myself in angry desperation, tugging at the suitcase by its straps with my inflexible hands. 'I'll . . . though next time it'll be mid-October, I'll have to wear two sheepskin coats. I certainly shan't be going to Grachyovka for a month yet. Just think . . . I actually had to put up for the night en route! When we had only driven fifteen miles and it was as black as the tomb . . . it was night . . . we had to stop in Grabilovka, a school teacher put us up. This morning we set off at seven, and here we are . . . God, it's been slower driving here than if we'd come on foot. One wheel got stuck in a ditch, the other swung up into the air, my case fell on to my feet with a crash, we slithered from side to side, lurching forward one moment, backward the next. And all the time a fine rain drizzling down and my bones turning to ice. Who'd believe you can freeze as easily in the middle of a grey, miserable September as in the depth of winter? Ah well, it seems you can. And as you die a slow death there's nothing to look at except the same endless monotony. On the right the bare, undulating fields and on the left a stunted copse, flanked by five or six grey, dilapidated shacks. Not a living soul in them, it seems, and not a sound to be heard.'

In the end the suitcase yielded. The driver lay on his stomach and shoved it down on top of me. I tried to catch it by the strap, but my hand refused to perform and the beastly thing, crammed with books and all sorts of rubbish, flopped down on to the grass, crashing against my legs.

'Oh Lor . . .' the driver began fearfully, but I did not complain. My legs were no more sensitive than two sticks of wood.

'Hey, anybody at home? Hey!' the driver cried out and flapped his arms like a rooster flapping its wings. 'Hey, I've brought the doctor!'

At once faces appeared, pressed against the dark windows of the assistant's house. A door banged and I saw a man hobbling towards me in a ragged coat and worn old boots. He hurriedly and respectfully doffed his cap, ran up and stopped two paces short of me, then smiling somewhat bashfully he welcomed me in a hoarse voice, 'Good day, comrade doctor.'

'And who might you be?' I asked.

'I'm Yegorich,' he introduced himself, 'the watchman here. We've been expecting you.'

Without wasting a moment he grabbed the suitcase, swung it over his shoulder and carried it in. I limped after him, trying unsuccessfully to thrust my hand into my trouser pocket to get out my purse.

Man's basic needs are few. The first of them is fire. Back in Moscow, when I found out that I was to go to remote Muryovo, I had promised myself that I would behave in a dignified manner. My youthful appearance made life intolerable for me in those early days. I always made a point of introducing myself as 'Doctor So-and-So', and inevitably people raised their eyebrows and said, 'Really? I thought you were still a student.'

'No. I'm qualified,' I would answer sullenly, thinking, 'I must start wearing spectacles, that's what I must do.' But there was no point in this, as I had perfectly good vision, my eyes as yet unclouded by experience. Unable to wear glasses as a defence against those invariable, affectionately indulgent smiles, I tried to develop a special manner designed to induce respect. I tried to talk evenly and gravely, to repress impulsive movements as far as possible, to walk and not run as twenty-four-year-olds do who have just left university. Looking back, I now realize that the attempt did not come off at all.

At the moment in question I disobeyed my unwritten code of behaviour. I sat hunched up in front of the fire with my shoes off, not in the study but in the kitchen, like a fire-worshipper, fervently and passionately drawn to the birch logs blazing in the stove. On my left stood an upturned tub with my boots lying on top of it, next to them a plucked cockerel with a bloodstained neck, and its many-coloured feathers lying in a heap beside it. While still stiff with the cold, I had somehow managed to perform a whole set of vital actions. I had confirmed Yegorich's wife, the sharp-nosed Aksinya, in her position as my cook. As a result of this she had slaughtered the cockerel and I was to eat it. I had been introduced to everyone in turn. My feldsher[1] was called Demyan Lukich, the midwives were Pelageya Ivanovna and Anna Nikolayevna. I had been shown round the hospital and was left in no doubt whatever that it was generously equipped. With equal certainty I was forced to admit (inwardly, of course) that I had no idea what very many of these shiny, unsullied instruments were for. Not only had I never held them in my hands, but to tell the truth I had never even seen them.

'Hm,' I mumbled significantly, 'must say you have an excellent set of instruments. Hm . . .'

'Oh sir,' Demyan Lukich remarked sweetly, 'this is all thanks to your predecessor Leopold Leopoldovich. You see, he used to operate from dawn till dusk.'

I was instantly covered with cold sweat and stared glumly at the gleaming cupboards.

We then went round the empty wards and I satisfied myself that they could easily hold forty patients.

'Leopold Leopoldovich sometimes had fifty in here,' Demyan Lukich said consolingly, and Anna Nikolayevna, a woman with a diadem of grey hair, chose to say, 'Doctor, you look so young, so very young . . . it's simply amazing. You look like a student.'

'Oh, hell,' I said to myself, 'really, you'd think they were doing it on purpose!'

Through clenched teeth I grunted, 'Hm . . . no, well, I . . . yes, rather young looking . . .'

After that we went down to the pharmacy and a glance was enough to tell me that it was supplied with every conceivable medicine. Its two sombre rooms smelled strongly of herbs and its shelves were filled with an endless variety of preparations. There were even foreign patent medicines, which, need I add, I had never heard of.

'Leopold Leopoldovich ordered these,' Pelageya Ivanovna reported proudly.

'This Leopold was nothing short of a genius,' I thought and was filled with respect for the mysterious Leopold who had left the quiet little village of Muryovo behind him.

Besides fire, man also needs to find his bearings. I had long since eaten the cockerel, Yegorich had stuffed my mattress with straw and covered it with a sheet, and a light was burning in my study. Spellbound, I sat and stared at the legendary Leopold's third great achievement: the bookcase was crammed with books. I counted roughly thirty volumes of surgery manuals in Russian and German. And the books on therapeutics! The beautiful leather-bound anatomical atlases!

Evening drew on and I started to find my bearings.

'It's not my fault,' I repeated to myself stubbornly and unhappily. 'I've got my degree and a first-class one at that. Didn't I warn them back in town that I wanted to start off as a junior partner in a practice? But no, they just smiled and said, "You'll get your bearings." So now I've got to find my bearings. Suppose they bring me a hernia? Just tell me how I'll find my bearings with that? And more to the point, what will a hernia patient feel like when I get my hands on him? Will he find his bearings in the next world?' The thought made my blood run cold.

'What about peritonitis? Oh no! Or croup, that country children get? When is tracheotomy indicated? Even if it doesn't need tracheotomy I shall be pretty much at sea ... What about ... what about ... deliveries! I forgot about deliveries! Incorrect positions. What on earth will I do? What a fool I was! I should have refused this job. I really should. They should have found themselves another Leopold.'

Miserable, I paced up and down the twilit study. When I came up to the lamp I caught sight of the reflection of my pale face and of the light of the lamp in the window set against the boundless darkness of the fields.

'I'm like Dmitry the Pretender[2] – nothing but a sham,' I thought stupidly and sat down at the table again.

I spent about two lonely hours of self-torment and only stopped when my nerves could no longer bear the horrors I had summoned up. Then I started to calm down and even to work out a plan of action.

'Let's see now ... they tell me admissions are almost nil at the moment. They're braking flax in the villages, the roads are impassable ...'

'That's just when they will bring you a hernia,' thundered a harsh voice in my mind, 'because a man with a cold won't make the effort over impassable roads, but rest assured they'll bring you a hernia, my dear doctor.'

There was something in what the voice said. I shuddered.

'Be quiet,' I said to it. 'It won't necessarily be a hernia. Stop being so neurotic. You can't back out once you've begun.'

'You said it!' the voice answered spitefully.

'All right then ... I won't take a step without my reference book ... If I have to prescribe something I can think it over while I wash my hands and the reference book will be lying open on top of the patients' register. I shall make out wholesome but simple prescriptions, say, sodium salicylate, 0.5 grammes in powder form three times a day.'

'You might as well prescribe baking soda! Why don't you just prescribe soda?' the voice was blatantly making fun of me. 'What's soda got to do with it? I'll also prescribe an infusion of ipecacuanha, 180 c.c. Or 200 c.c. if you don't mind.'

And although no one was asking for ipecacuanha as I sat there alone by the lamp, I sheepishly turned the pages in the pharmacopoeia and checked ipecacuanha: meanwhile I automatically read in passing that there was a certain substance called 'Insipin' which is none other than 'ethereal sulphate of quinine-diglycolic acid'. Apparently it doesn't taste of quinine! What is it for? And how is it prescribed? What is it, a powder? To hell with it!

'That's all very well, but what are you going to do about a hernia?' The voice of Fear continued to pester me.

'I'll put them into a bath,' I defended myself in exasperation, 'and try to reduce it.'

'What if it's a strangulated one, old boy? Baths won't be much use then, will they! A strangulated hernia!' Fear chanted in a demoniac voice. 'You'll have to cut it out ... !'

I gave in and all but burst into tears. I sent out a prayer to the darkness outside the window: please, anything but not a strangulated hernia.

Weariness then crooned, 'Go to bed, unhappy physician. Sleep on it. Calm down and stop being neurotic. Look how still the dark is outside the window, the fields are cold and sleeping, there is no hernia. You can think about it in the morning. You'll settle down ... Sleep ... drop that book of diagrams, you won't make head or tail of it anyway ... hernial orifice ...'

*

I don't remember him arriving. I only remember the bolt grating in the door, a shriek from Aksinya and a cart creaking out in the yard.

He was hatless, his sheepskin coat unbuttoned, his beard was dishevelled and there was a mad look in his eyes.

He crossed himself, fell on his knees and banged his forehead against the floor. This to me!

'I'm a lost man,' I thought wretchedly.

'Now, now – what's the matter?' I muttered and pulled at his grey sleeve.

His face twisted and he started mumbling a breathless and incoherent answer, 'Oh doctor, sir . . . sir . . . she's all I've got, she's all I've got, she's all I've got,' he burst out suddenly in a voice so young-sounding and powerful that the lampshade trembled. 'Oh, sir, oh . . .' He wrung his hands in misery and started knocking his forehead against the floorboards as if trying to smash them. 'Why? Why am I being punished? What have I done to deserve God's anger?'

'What is it? What's happened?' I cried out, feeling the blood draining from my face.

He jumped to his feet, rushed towards me and whispered, 'Anything you want, doctor, sir . . . I'll give you money, take as much money as you want. As much as you want. We'll pay you in food if you like. Only don't let her die. Don't let her die. Even if she's to be a cripple, I don't mind. I don't mind!' He shouted to the ceiling. 'I've got enough to feed her, I can manage.' I could see Aksinya's pale face in the black rectangle of the door. I was overcome with anguish.

'Well, what is it? Speak!' I cried irritably.

He stopped. His eyes went blank and he whispered, as if telling me a secret, 'She fell into the brake.'

'Brake . . . brake? What's that?'

'Flax, they were braking flax, doctor,' Aksinya whispered in explanation, 'you know, brake, flax braking . . .'

'Here's a fine beginning. This is it. Oh why did I ever come?' I said to myself in horror.

'Who?'

'My daughter,' he answered in a whisper, and then shouted, 'Help me!' Once again he threw himself to the floor and his hair, cut like a mop in peasant fashion, fell into his eyes.

The pressure-lamp with its lopsided tin shade burned with hot beams of light. She lay on the operating table, on white, fresh-smelling oil-cloth and when I saw her all thoughts of hernia vanished from my mind.

Her fair, almost reddish hair hung down from the table in a matted clump. She had a gigantic plait which reached to the floor.

Her calico skirt was torn and stained with blood in various shades from brown to oily scarlet. The light of the kerosene lamp was a lively yellow in comparison with her paper-white face, and her nose was beginning to sharpen. On her white face, motionless as a plaster cast, a truly rare beauty was fading away before my eyes. Seldom in life does one see such a face.

The operating theatre was completely silent for about ten seconds, but from behind the closed doors came the muffled sounds of someone shouting and banging his head over and over again.

'Gone out of his mind,' I thought. 'The nurses must be seeing to him. Why is she so beautiful? Though he does have good bone structure; the mother must have been a beautiful woman. He's a widower . . .'

'Is he a widower?' I whispered automatically. 'Yes, he is,' Pelageya Ivanovna answered quietly.

Then Demyan Lukich, almost as if in anger, ripped the skirt from hem to waist, baring her instantly. I looked, and what I saw was even worse than I had expected. Strictly speaking there was no left leg. From the smashed knee down there were just bloody shreds, battered red flesh and splinters of white bone protruding in all directions. The right leg was fractured at the shin so that the tips of both bones had punctured the skin and her foot lay lifelessly on its side, as though disconnected.

'Yes . . .' the feldsher pronounced softly and that was all he said.

Thereupon I regained my wits and started feeling her pulse. Her cold wrist registered nothing. Only after a few seconds did I detect a barely perceptible, irregular ripple. It passed and was followed by a pause during which I had time to glance at her white lips and nostrils, which were turning blue. I already felt like saying 'It's all over', but fortunately controlled myself . . . there was another hint of a beat.

'The end of a mangled human being,' I said to myself. 'There's really nothing more to be done.'

But suddenly I said sternly, in a voice that I did not recognize, 'Camphor.'

Anna Nikolayevna bent over to my ear and whispered, 'What for, doctor? Don't torture her. What's the point of smashing her up any more? She'll die any minute now . . . you won't save her.'

I gave her an angry look and said, 'I asked for camphor . . .' in such a way that she flushed, marched resentfully to the little table and broke an ampoule. The feldsher obviously did not approve of the camphor either. Nonetheless he deftly and swiftly took hold of a syringe and the yellow oil went under the skin of her shoulder.

'Die. Die quickly,' I said to myself. 'Die. Otherwise what am I to do with you?'

'She'll die now,' whispered the feldsher as if guessing my thoughts. He glanced meaningfully at the sheet, but apparently changed his mind. It seemed a pity to stain it with blood. But a few seconds later he had to cover her. She lay like a corpse, but did not die. Suddenly my head became quite clear, as if I were standing under the glass roof of the anatomy theatre in that faraway medical school.

'Camphor again,' I said hoarsely.

And once again the feldsher obediently injected the oil.

'Is she really not going to die?' I thought in despair. 'Will I really have to . . .'

Everything lit up in my mind and I suddenly became aware without any textbooks, without any advice or help (and with unshakeable conviction), that now, for the first time in my life I had to perform an amputation on a dying person. And that that person would die under the knife. She was bound to die under the knife; after all, there was no blood left in her body. It had all drained out through her shattered legs over six miles and there was not even a sign that she was conscious. She was silent. Oh, why didn't she die? What would her maddened father say to me?

'Prepare for an amputation,' I said to the assistant in a voice that was not my own.

The midwife gave me a fierce look, but the feldsher showed a spark of sympathy in his eyes and began busying himself with the instruments. A primus-stove started to roar.

A quarter of an hour passed. I raised her cold eyelid and looked with superstitious fear at the expiring eye. It told me nothing. How could a semi-corpse stay alive? Drops of sweat ran uncontrollably down my forehead from under my white cap and Pelageya wiped away the salt sweat with gauze. What remained of the blood in the girl's veins was now diluted with caffeine. Ought it to have been injected or not? Anna Nikolayevna was gently massaging the swellings caused by the saline solution. And the girl lived on.

I picked up the knife, trying to imitate the man I had once in my life seen perform an amputation, at university. I entreated fate not to let her die at least in the next half hour. 'Let her die in the ward, when I've finished the operation . . .'

I had only common sense to rely on, and it was stimulated into action by the extraordinary situation. Like an experienced butcher, I made a neat circular incision in her thigh with the razor-sharp knife and the skin parted without exuding the smallest drop of blood. 'What will I do if the vessels start bleeding?' I thought, and without turning my head glanced at the row of forceps. I cut through a huge piece of female flesh together with one of the vessels – it looked like a little whitish pipe – but not a drop of blood emerged from it. I stopped it up with a pair of forceps and proceeded, clamping on forceps wherever I suspected the existence of a vessel. 'Arteria . . . arteria . . . what the devil is it called?' The operating theatre had begun to take on a thoroughly professional look. The forceps were hanging in clusters. My assistants drew them back with gauze, retracting the flesh, and I started sawing the round bone with a gleaming, fine-toothed saw. 'Why isn't she dying? It's astonishing . . . God, how people cling to life!'

The bone fell away. Demyan Lukich was left with what had been a girl's leg in his hands. Shreds of flesh and bone. This was all discarded and there remained on the table a young girl shortened, as it were, by a third, with a stump splayed out to one side. 'Just a little bit more . . . Please don't die,' I wished ardently, 'keep going till they take you to the ward, let me come out of this frightful episode with some credit.'

They tied the ligatures and then, knees knocking, I started sewing up the skin with widely spaced stitches. Suddenly I stopped, brought to my senses by an inspired thought: I left a gap for drainage in which I inserted a gauze wick. My eyes were dimmed with sweat. I felt as if I were in a steam bath.

I heaved a sigh of relief. I looked wearily at the stump and at her waxen face and asked, 'Is she alive?'

'Yes, she's alive,' came the immediate and almost soundless echo as the feldsher and Anna Nikolayevna replied in unison.

'She'll last perhaps another minute or so,' the feldsher mouthed voicelessly into my ear. Then he hesitated and suggested tentatively, 'Perhaps you needn't touch the other leg, doctor. We could just bandage it, you know . . . otherwise she won't last till the ward . . . all right? Better if she doesn't die in the theatre.'

'Let's have the plaster,' I uttered hoarsely, urged on by some unknown force.

The floor was covered in white blobs of gypsum. We were all bathed in sweat. The body lay lifeless. Its right leg was encased in plaster and the shin showed through where in another inspired moment I had left a window to coincide with the fracture.

'She's alive,' the assistant breathed in surprise.

Then we started lifting her and an enormous cavity could be seen under the sheet – we had left a third of her body on the operating table.

Shadows flitted down the passage, nurses darted to and fro and I saw a dishevelled male figure shuffle past along the wall and let out a muffled howl. But he was led away. Silence fell.

In the operating room I washed off the blood which had stained my arms up to the elbow.

'I suppose you've done a lot of amputations, doctor?' Anna Nikolayevna asked suddenly. 'That was very good, no worse than Leopold.'

She invariably pronounced the name 'Leopold' as if she were talking about the dean of a medical school.

I glanced suspiciously at their faces and saw respect and astonishment in all of them, including Demyan Lukich and Pelageya Ivanovna.

'Hm, well, the fact is I've done only two . . .'

Why did I lie? I cannot understand it to this day. The hospital was utterly silent.

'When she dies, be sure to send for me,' I told the feldsher in an undertone, and for some reason instead of just answering 'All right,' he said deferentially, 'Very good, sir.'

A few minutes later I was standing beside the green-shaded lamp in the study of the doctor's quarters. There was not a sound to be heard.

A pale face was reflected in the pitch-dark window.

'No, I don't look like Dmitry the Pretender, and, do you know, I seem to have aged, there's a furrow between my eyebrows . . . right now there'll be a knock . . . and they'll say, "She's dead."'

'Yes, I'll go and have a last look, any minute now there'll be a knock . . .'

There was a knock at the door. It was two and a half months later. One of the first bright days of winter was shining through the window.

He came in; only then did I really look at him. Yes, he definitely had good features. Forty-five years old. Sparkling eyes. Then a rustling sound. A young girl of enchanting beauty came bounding in on crutches; she had only one leg and was dressed in a very wide skirt with a red border at the hem.

She looked at me and her cheeks flushed pink.

'In Moscow . . . in Moscow,' I said and started writing down an address, 'they'll fix you up with a prosthesis – an artificial leg.'

'Kiss his hand,' the father suddenly commanded her.

I was so confused that I kissed her on the nose instead of the lips.

Then, hanging on her crutches, she undid a bundle and out fell a snow-white towel artlessly embroidered with a red cockerel. So that was what she'd been hiding under her pillow when I did my rounds

in the ward! And indeed I remembered seeing some thread on her
bedside table.

'I can't accept it,' I said sternly, and even shook my head. But she
gave me such a look that I took it.

It hung in my bedroom in Muryovo and then went with me on my
travels. In the end it grew threadbare, faded, wore out and disappeared
just as memories fade and disappear.

First published in 1926
Translated by Michael Glenny

ISAAK EMMANUILOVICH BABEL
(1894–1940)

Babel was born in Odessa, the son of a Jewish tradesman. He fought in the First World War from 1917 and spent most of 1918 in Petrograd and most of the next few years in Odessa, working in journalism and publishing. From 1923 he lived mainly in Moscow. His wife emigrated to France, but he himself decided against emigration; in 1928, while visiting his wife in Paris, he wrote: 'As regards individual freedom, life here is excellent, but we from Russia are homesick for the wind of great thoughts and great passions.' During the 1930s he worked in film and published relatively little. In a speech at the First Congress of Soviet Writers in 1934, mixing irony and pathos, he hailed Stalin's oratorical style as a model for writers, noted that Soviet power had taken away a writer's right to make mistakes, and claimed that he himself had now mastered the genre of literary silence. In 1937 Babel had a second daughter by Antonina Pirozhkova, whom he had met five years before. On 27 January 1940 he was shot, falsely accused of being a Trotskyist terrorist and foreign spy.

Babel's stories fall into three main groups: semi-autobiographical stories; The Odessa Tales *– an expressionistic celebration of the lives of the Jewish gangsters and whores of a city often seen as a Russian Naples; and the story-cycle* Red Cavalry *– the fruit of his months as what would now be called an 'embedded' war correspondent with a Cossack regiment in Poland in 1920.*[1] *The first stories from* Red Cavalry *were published in 1923–4 and brought Babel swift recognition: with their demotic language and vivid depictions of violence, they seemed a perfect response to demands for a new, post-revolutionary prose.*

The translator Clarence Brown has said of Babel's decision to serve with a regiment of Cossacks, 'This is something like a lone cat's voluntarily cultivating the society of a pack of hounds; for the image of the Cossack horseman, sabre in hand, is the quintessential horror in the collective Jewish nightmare of the pogroms that swept through Central and Eastern Europe.'[2] *Whatever motivated this decision –*

Babel's understanding of human violence is clear and penetrating: in Red Cavalry *sadism and vengefulness come in many guises, and victims and executioners absorb one another's identities with dizzying speed. These insights are conveyed with delicacy. In 'The Death of Dolgushov', for example, the intensity of the narrator's unconscious identification with the wounded Dolgushov is brought out by the repetition of a single word: Dolgushov's 'intestines were slithering down onto his thighs' and (eight lines later) 'Sweat was slithering down my body'.*

Primo Levi included 'Salt' in his personal anthology The Search for Roots. *'To what degree is it legitimate to exploit violence in literature?' Levi asks. 'That there is a limit is certain; as soon as you cross it you fall into mortal sins, aestheticism, sadism, prostitution for the cannibalistic consumption of a certain public. Babel is close to that limit but he doesn't cross it. He is saved by his compassion, which is modest and swathed in irony.'*[3]

The narrator of 'The Death of Dolgushov' and 'My First Goose' is a Jewish political commissar, similar to Babel in many ways but not to be identified with him.

MY FIRST GOOSE

Savitsky, commander of the Sixth Division, stood up when he saw me, and I was astonished at the beauty of his huge body. He got to his feet and – with his purple breeches, his crimson cap cocked to one side, his medals pinned to his chest – immediately split the hut in two, the way a banner splits the sky. He smelt of perfume and the cloying coolness of soap. His long legs were like two young women thrust up to their shoulders into shining boots.

He smiled at me, struck the table with his whip and drew towards him an order that had just been dictated by his Chief of Staff. Ivan Chesnokov was being commanded to advance with the regiment entrusted to him towards Chugunov-Dobryvodka and, on making contact with the enemy, to destroy him.

'*For which destruction,*' – the commander himself began to write, soon filling the whole sheet – '*I will hold the said Chesnokov entirely responsible, and liable to pay with his life, and I myself shall be the one who blows out his brains, and you, comrade Chesnokov, having been with me on this front for several months now, can entertain no doubt about this . . .*'

The Commander of the Sixth Division signed the order with a

flourish, threw it to his orderlies and turned his grey eyes, dancing with merriment, towards me.

I handed him the document detailing my secondment to the divisional staff.

'See to his papers!' said the Commander. 'See to his papers. Put him down for all front-line provisions except virgins and whores. Can you read and write?'

'Yes, I can,' I answered, envying him the iron and flowers of his youth. 'I graduated in law from the University of St Petersburg.'

'One of them milksops, are you?' he shouted out with a laugh. 'And with glasses on your nose. Mangy little runt! Nobody ever asked us if we want your sort here. People get killed for wearing glasses round here. Think you'll fit in, do you?'

'I'll fit in,' I answered, and set off with the quartermaster to look for a billet in the village.

The quartermaster carried my case on his shoulders, the village street stretched out before us; a dying sun, round and yellow as a pumpkin, was releasing its last rosy breath into the sky.

We went up to a hut with painted carvings around the windows. The quartermaster stopped and blurted out with a guilty smile: 'The lads 'ave a thing about glasses – there's nowt we can do about it. If you're a man of the 'ighest excellence – you've not got an 'ope in 'ell. But ruin a young lady, aye, ruin the purest of ladies – and you'll be the fighters' darlin'.'

He hesitated a moment, my case still on his shoulders, came right up to me, then threw me a despairing look and darted off into the outer yard. A group of Cossacks was sitting there on some hay; they were shaving one another.

'Fighters!' said the quartermaster, putting my case down on the ground. 'Orders from comrade Savitsky are you take this man in and no monkey business because this fella, who has suffered on the fields of learning . . .'

The quartermaster turned crimson and walked off without looking back. I raised my hand to my cap and saluted the Cossacks. A young lad with long flaxen hair and a handsome Ryazan face went over to my case and hurled it over the gate. Then he turned his backside to me and, with remarkable skill, let out a series of unmentionable sounds.

'Bog artillery!' an older Cossack shouted out, and then laughed. 'Rapid fire!'

The young lad exhausted his guileless artistry and walked away. I began crawling around on my hands and knees, gathering the manuscripts and tattered old clothes that had tumbled out of my case.

When I'd gathered them all up, I took them away to the far end of the yard. Near the hut, standing on some bricks round a fire, was a large pot of pork, slowly simmering, and the steam was like smoke drifting up from my childhood home back in the village, and it filled me with a confusion of desperate hunger and loneliness. I covered my battered little case with hay, made it into a pillow and lay down on the ground to read, in *Pravda*, the speech Lenin had given at the Second Congress of the Comintern. Sunlight fell on me through gaps in jagged little mounds, the Cossacks stepped now and again on my legs, the young lad made tireless fun of me, and Lenin's beloved lines travelled a thorny path, unable to get through to me. Then I put down the paper and went over to the mistress of the house, who was spinning yarn on the porch.

'Mistress,' I said, 'I need some grub.'

As if to look at me, the old woman raised, then lowered the rheumy whites of her half-blind eyes.

'Comrade,' she said, 'all this makes me want to go and hang myself.'

'Fuck and goddam you, woman!' I muttered crossly, and gave the old woman a shove in the chest with my fist. 'I'm not in the mood for discussion.'

Turning round, I saw someone's sabre lying on the ground close by. A haughty goose was roaming around the yard, imperturbably preening its feathers. I trapped it and pinned it to the ground; the goose's head cracked beneath my boot, cracked and began to bleed. Its white neck lay stretched out in the dung while, above the slaughtered bird, its wings flapped up and down.

'Fuck and goddam you!' I said, jabbing my sabre into the goose's insides. 'Roast it for me, mistress.'

Her glasses and her blindness glistening, the old woman picked up the bird, wrapped it in her apron and carried it off to the kitchen.

'Comrade,' she said, 'I want to go and hang myself.' And she closed the door behind her.

By now the comrades were sitting around their pot. They had been sitting motionless, upright as heathen priests, not watching the goose.

'The lad will do all right with us,' said one of them, winking as he took a spoonful of soup.

The Cossacks began to eat with the restrained elegance of peasants who hold one another in respect. I cleaned the sabre with some sand, went out through the gate and came back again in anguish. The moon hung over the yard like a cheap earring.

'Brother,' Surovkov, the eldest of the Cossacks, called out to me, 'sit down with us and have a bite to eat while you're waiting for your goose.'

He took a spare spoon out of his boot and handed it to me. We ate the pork and spooned up the cabbage soup.

'What does the newspaper say?' asked the lad with the flaxen hair, moving aside to make room for me.

'In the newspaper,' I said, pulling out my copy of *Pravda*, 'Lenin writes that everything is in short supply.'

In a loud voice, like a deaf man triumphant, I read the speech out to the Cossacks.

The evening wrapped me in the life-giving moisture of her twilight sheets; the evening pressed a mother's hands to my burning forehead.

I read and rejoiced, keeping track, as I rejoiced, of the mysterious curve along which Lenin went straight to the point.

'Truth tickles every nostril,' said Surovkov when I got to the end, 'yet not everyone can pick it out of the heap. But he's always spot on, like a hen pecking corn.'

After these words about Lenin from Surovkov, a platoon commander in the staff squadron, we went up to the hay loft to sleep. There we slept, all six of us, warming one another, legs entangled, beneath a roof whose holes let in the stars.

I dreamed, and I dreamed of women, and only my heart, crimson with murder, screeched and bled.

First published in 1924
Translated by Robert Chandler

THE DEATH OF DOLGUSHOV

The veils of battle swept towards the town. At noon Korochayev flew past us in a black cloak – the disgraced commander of the Fourth Division was battling alone, searching for death. As he galloped by, he shouted out: 'They've cut our supply lines. Radzivillov and Brody are in flames!'

And away he went – black and billowing, eyes like black coals.

Our brigades were regrouping on the board-flat plain. The sun rolled through purple dust. Wounded men in ditches were having a bite to eat. Nurses lay on the grass, singing in soft voices. Afonka's scouts were scouring the fields, searching for dead bodies and uniforms. Afonka rode by within two paces of me and said, without turning his head: 'They've given us a bloody nose – sure as two and

two makes four. Seems the commander will be fired. Our soldiers
aren't happy . . .'

The Poles had reached the forest a couple of miles from us, and
their machine-guns were not far away. Bullets whined and squealed,
an unbearable crescendo of lament. Bullets were wounding the earth,
burrowing into it, trembling with impatience. Vytyagaichenko, the
regimental commander, who had been snoring in the hot sun, cried
out in his sleep and woke up. He mounted his horse and rode over to
the lead squadron. His face was crumpled, an uncomfortable sleep
had left it covered in red streaks, and his pockets were full of plums.

'Son of a bitch!' he said angrily, and spat out a plum stone. 'What
a mess! Get out the flag, Timoshka!'

'Moving off, are we?' asked Timoshka. Pulling the flagstaff out
through his horse's stirrups, he unfurled a banner bearing a star and
some words about the Third International.

'Wait and see,' said Vytyagaichenko, and suddenly yelled wildly:
'To horse, girls! Squadron leaders, call your men!'

The buglers sounded the alarm. The squadrons formed a column.
A wounded man crawled out of a ditch and, shading his eyes with
one hand, said to Vytyagaichenko: 'Taras Grigoryevich, I've been
delegated to speak. It looks like we're going to have to stay put . . .'

'You'll fight them off all right,' muttered Vytyagaichenko, and made
his horse rear.

'We sort of feel, Taras Grigoryevich, that we might not be up to it,'
the wounded man called out after him.

'Don't whine,' said Vytyagaichenko, turning to face him. 'Don't
worry – we won't leave you behind.' And he gave the order to move
off.

At once the womanish voice of my friend Afonka Bida wailed out:
'Don't take us straight into a trot, Taras Grigoryevich. The enemy are
all of three miles away. How are we going to slash them down if our
horses are winded? There'll be time enough – God damn it – to meet
our Maker!'

'Walk on!' commanded Vytyagaichenko, not raising his eyes.

The regiment rode off.

'If I'm right about the Commander,' whispered Afonka, hanging
back a little, 'if he's really been fired, we're done for. Yes, soap the
rope and kick away the stool . . .'

Tears streamed from his eyes. I gazed at Afonka in amazement. He
span round like a top, clutched at his cap, snorted, whooped, and
charged off.

Grishchuk with his silly old cart and I – the two of us were left on our own, knocking around until evening in between walls of fire. Divisional HQ had disappeared. Other units wanted nothing to do with us. Our regiments went into Brody and were beaten back by a counter-attack. Grishchuk and I entered the town cemetery. A detachment of Poles sprang up from behind the graves, shouldered their rifles and opened fire. Grishchuk turned his cart round. All four wheels squealed.

'Grishchuk!' I called out, through the squeals and the wind.

'What a laugh,' he answered sadly.

'We're done for!' I called out, seized by the exhilaration of disaster. 'We're done for, my old fella!'

'Why do women bother?' he answered still more sadly. 'What's the use of matchmakin' and marryin'? What's the use of godfathers and godmothers, and dancin' at weddin's?'

Up in the sky a trail of pink glowed and faded. The Milky Way appeared between the stars.

'Makes me laugh,' said Grishchuk mournfully, pointing his whip at a man sitting beside the road. 'Makes me laugh – women goin' to all that bother . . .'

The man beside the road was Dolgushov, the telephonist. He was sitting with his legs wide apart, staring hard at us.

'Know what?' he said, as we came up to him. 'I've had it. Understand?'

'I understand,' said Grishchuk, stopping the horses.

'You'll have to waste a bullet on me,' said Dolgushov.

He was sitting propped up against a tree. His boots were sticking out in opposite directions. Without taking his eyes off me, he carefully lifted his shirt. His stomach had been torn out, his intestines were slithering down onto his thighs, and his heartbeats were visible.

'The Polacks are going to have some fun with me when they come. Take my papers. Write to my mother and tell her what happened . . .'

'No,' I answered, and urged my horse forward.

Dolgushov spread his blue hands out on the ground and looked at them in disbelief.

'Sneaking away?' he muttered, sliding down towards the ground. 'You're sneaking away, you bastard . . .'

Sweat was slithering down my body. The machine-guns were banging away, faster and faster, with hysterical obstinacy. Ringed by the halo of the sunset, Afonka Bida was galloping towards us.

'We're giving them quite a peppering,' he shouted out gaily. 'You having fun here?'

I pointed to Dolgushov and rode a little way off.

They spoke briefly – I couldn't hear what they said. Dolgushov handed the troop commander his papers. Afonka tucked them into his boot and shot Dolgushov in the mouth.

'Afonka,' I said, smiling pathetically as I rode up to the Cossack. 'I just couldn't.'

'Get lost,' he said, turning pale, 'or I'll kill you. You four-eyed lot feel as much pity for us as a cat does for a mouse.'

He cocked his gun.

I rode off at a walk, not turning round; in my back I felt the cold of death.

'Hey!' Grishchuk shouted out behind me. 'Stop fooling about!' He grabbed Afonka by the arm.

'The bastard!' shouted Afonka. 'I'll get him in the end . . .'

Grishchuk caught up with me by a bend in the road. No sign of Afonka. He'd ridden off in the opposite direction.

'Well, Grishchuk,' I said, 'today I've lost Afonka, my first friend.'

Grishchuk took out a wrinkled apple from under his seat.

'Eat this,' he said. 'Eat it, please.'

First published in 1923
Translated by Robert Chandler

SALT

Dear Comrade Editor,

I want to describe to you the political unconsciousness of women who are doing us nothing but harm. The men hope that, when you travelled and noted about the Civil War Fronts, you did not miss the most inveteranate station of Fastov which lies neither here nor there, miles from anywhere, but where we drank beer and felt good cheer. With regard to the abovementioned station, there is lots of stuff to be written, but as we say in our simple way, you can't clean up all the Lord's shit. So I shall describe to you only what I have seen first hand with my own eyes.

It was a quiet and glorious little night one week ago when our celebrated Red Cavalry train stopped there, loaded with fighters. All of us burning to promote the common cause and we had Berdichev as our destination. Only thing was our train wouldn't get moving, our Gavrilka's wheels wouldn't get turning – what was holding us up? And sure enough the stop proved of massive consequence for our common cause on account of blackmarketeers, those wickedest enemies of ours, among whom was a countless force of the female sex, and they treated towards the railway authorities with great insolence. Fearlessly did these wicked enemies grasp the handrails, in a whirl of sedition they roamed over the iron roofs and in every hand were the sacks we knew so well, each holding up to fifteen stone of blackmarket salt. But the triumph of the traders and their blackmarket capitalism was not to last long. Us fighters took the initiative, clambered out of the goods wagons and gave the insulted authority of the railwaymen a chance to breathe freely again. Only the female sex still remained hanging about with their sacks. Out of compassion the fighters let some women into the goods wagons, but they kept others out. And in our wagon too, the Second Platoon's, there was two girls at hand and when the first bell ringed we were approached by a representable woman with an infant in arms, saying, 'Let me on, dear Cossacks, all through the War I've wandered in misery from station to station with a baby in my arms and now I want to meet up with my husband but on account of the railway's condition it's impossible to travel, but don't I deserve better, good Cossacks?'

'Whatever the platoon consents, woman,' I say to her, 'that, in fact, is how your fate will turn out.' And I turn to the platoon and testify to them that this representable woman wishes to meet with her husband and she does indeed have a child with her so what will your consensus be – to let this woman on board or not?'

'Let her on board,' the lads shout, 'but she won't be wanting her husband when we've done with her!'

'No,' I say to the lads quite politely, 'I feel nothing but astonishment at hearing you come out with such bollocks. If you think back, platoon, over your own lives and remember how you yourselves were once infants in arms, you'll see that kind of talk isn't right.'

And the Cossacks talked together, saying as my words were persuasive, and they let the woman on board and she climbed in with gratitude. On fire with the truth of my words, the fighters all tried to find her somewhere to sit and every one of them was speaking at once: 'Sit in the corner, woman, and cuddle your baby in a motherly way. No one will touch you in that corner of yours and you'll reach your husband untouched, the way you desire, and we count on your conscience to raise a new change of guard for us because the old they don't stop growing older and youth, as you see, is in short supply. We have seen griefs, woman, in our first term of service and in our second. We've been choked by hunger and burnt by cold. But you sit here, woman, and have no fear.'

The third bell ringed and the train pulled out. And the glorious little night pitched her tent. And in that tent were stars like lamps. And the fighters remembered the Kuban night and the green Kuban star. And thoughts flew by like birds. While the wheels went clackety-clack, clackety-clack.

But when night's time was up and the guard changed and the red drummers of dawn had beaten reveille on their red drums, the Cossacks came over to me, seeing I was sitting there wide awake and gloomy as hell.

'Balmashev,' they say, 'why are you so down in the mouth? Why aren't you sleeping?'

'My deepest respect to you, fighters, and I ask only one request of you. Allow me to have a couple of words with that there citizeness.'

And, my whole body trembling, I rise from my couch, from which sleep has fled like a wolf from a pack of vicious dogs, and I go over to her and I take the babe from her arms and I tear off the swaddling clothes and underneath them I find a good forty-pound bag of salt.

'Here's a fine baby, comrades – one as doesn't ask for the tit, never does peepee on Mummy's skirt and never wakes anyone in the night.'

'Forgive me, kind Cossacks,' the woman butted in, cool as a cucumber. 'It wasn't me – it was this hard life of mine that deceived you.'

'Balmashev forgives your hard life,' I reply to the woman. 'It doesn't cost him anything much. Whatever Balmashev buys, he sells it on at the same price. But what about the Cossacks, woman, the Cossacks who looked up to you as a mother labouring for the Republic? What about them two girls now weeping after what they have suffered from us during the night. What about our women in the wheat fields of the Kuban, wearing out their womanly strength without husbands, while their husbands, no less forsaken themselves, can't help but violate young girls they happen across? And nobody laid a finger on you, you obscene woman, though they damn well should have. And what about Russia, crushed by suffering?'

And she answers back:

'I've no more salt, so all I have is the truth. You don't care about Russia, you only care about saving those Yids – Lenin and Trotsky.'

'We're not here to talk about Yids now, you troublesome bitch. Yids have got nothing to do with this. I don't say nothing about Lenin,[1] but Trotsky is the fearless son of a Governor of Tambov and he stands up for the working classes though he comes from a different class himself. They work like convicts, do Lenin and Trotsky, to drag us out onto life's free path, while you, you abominable bitch, are a worse counter-revolutionary than that White general threatening us with his keen-edged sabre from the back of a thousand-rouble horse.

That general can be seen from everywhere, from every road, and every worker's dream is to do him in. But you lot – you countless bitches with your strange children that don't ask to be fed and don't pee and don't crap, you can't be seen no more than a flea can and you go on biting and biting.'

And let me tell you straight that I threw that bitch of a citizeness onto the embankment from our moving train. But the coarse brute just sat there a while, shook out her skirts and went on her vile way. And seeing the woman unscathed, and Russia all around her like something beyond all words, and the peasants' fields without an ear of wheat, and the violated girls, and the many comrades on their way to the front few of whom would ever come back, I wanted to jump out after her and kill either myself or her. But the Cossacks took pity on me and said, 'Give her one from your rifle.'

So I took my faithful rifle down from the wall and wiped that shame off the face of the workers' land and republic.

And we fighters of the Second Platoon swear before you, dear comrade editor, and before you, dear comrades in the editorial office, that we shall deal mercilessly with all the traitors who are dragging us into the dirt and trying to turn the stream back to its source and cover Russia with nothing but corpses and dead grass.

In the name of all the fighters of the Second Platoon,
Nikita Balmashev, soldier of the Revolution.

First published in 1923
Translated by Robert Chandler

MIKHAIL MIKHAILOVICH
ZOSHCHENKO (1895–1958)

*Born in St Petersburg, Zoshchenko attended school and university
there. He served as an officer in the First World War but volunteered
for the Red Army in 1918. He joined the literary grouping 'The
Serapion Brothers' in 1921 (see p. 200). His humorous sketches
quickly became popular; 700,000 copies of Zoshchenko's books were
sold in 1926–7 alone. He also won the admiration of other writers –
from Maksim Gorky to Osip Mandelstam. Zoshchenko wrote his
finest, and sharpest, work in the 1920s, but he went on writing through
the 1930s and early 1940s. In 1943, he published part of* Before
Sunrise, *which can best be described as his attempt to psychoanalyse
himself and discover the reason for his lifelong depression. In 1946 he
was denounced as an 'enemy of Soviet literature' and expelled from
the Writers' Union. After this he wrote little of value.*

*Behind his mask of semi-literacy, Zoshchenko is a sophisticated and
self-conscious artist. A previous translator, Sidney Monas, has written,
'Zoshchenko uses careless language carefully. [His narrators speak in]
a weird mixture of peasant idiom, misunderstood highfalutin phrases,
rhetorical flourishes, explanatory asides that are anything but explanatory, repetitions, omissions, propaganda jargon absurdly adapted to
homey usage, instructional pseudoscientific words, foreign phrases,
and proverbial clichés joined to the latest party slogans.'[1]*

*The central criticism directed at Zoshchenko by the authorities was
that at a time of epic achievements he wrote only of trivia. Voronsky,
the editor of the influential journal* Krasnaya Nov' *(Red Virgin Soil),
wrote in a 1922 review of Zoshchenko's first book: 'This is supposed
to be Revolution? Here we get backyards, little crumbs and tiny
anecdotes. But that which shook all of Russia from end to end, the
loud rumble that was heard around the world [. . .] where is the echo
of all this?'[2] In reality, however – and this may be the true reason for
Voronsky's indignation – Zoshchenko registered this echo precisely;
his stories perfectly capture the texture of everyday life in Soviet
Russia, what Sinyavsky has called its 'outrageous small-mindedness':[3]*

the inescapable bureaucracy; the constant shortages of everyday necessities, especially living space; and people's strange eagerness to denounce one another.

Many of Zoshchenko's stories allude to the classics of Russian literature, above all to Gogol. The theft, or loss, of items of clothing is a motif that recurs especially often; a dozen or more stories can be read as a commentary on 'The Greatcoat'. 'The Galosh' also alludes to Pisarev, a utilitarian philosopher who claimed to value a good pair of galoshes more than any work of art. And 'The Bathhouse' is a parodic re-creation of Dostoyevsky's infernal bathhouse in his House of the Dead.

'Electrification', perhaps Zoshchenko's masterpiece, works on many levels. It can be read as a study of what psychoanalysts call 'resistance', the tendency to resist healing. What proves unbearable is not darkness and filth but light and cleanliness; the narrator's wife cuts the wires after *rather than* before *the apartment is redecorated. Politically, the story is still more bold. 'Communism is Soviet Power plus the Electrification of the Whole Country' was one of Lenin's most famous slogans; Zoshchenko is casting doubt on the whole Communist project.*

Zoshchenko is not only one of the funniest of Russian writers but also one of the most sober; no one is more aware – as he shows in 'The Hat' – of the harm carried out in the name of grand visions of progress. The cramped harsh world he portrays is a paradoxically eloquent assertion of the importance of what is so strikingly absent from it: small acts of kindness.

ELECTRIFICATION

What, brothers, is today's most fashionable word?

Today's most fashionable word of all is, of course, 'electrification'.

Lighting up Soviet Russia with light, without doubt, is a matter of massive importance. No one can argue with that. But it does, for the time being, have its downside. I'm not saying, comrades, that it costs too much. It costs money – that's all. No, I'm saying something different.

What I'm saying is this:

I was living, comrades, in a huge building. The whole of this building ran on paraffin. Some of us had lamps, some – cans of oil with a wick. The poorest had to make do with church candles. Life wasn't easy.

And then they start to install light.

First it's the house manager. Lights up his room – and that's that. A quiet fellow, doesn't let on what he's thinking. Though he wanders about a bit strangely and keeps absent-mindedly blowing his nose.

But he doesn't let on what he's thinking.

Then in comes my dear wife, Yelizaveta Ignatyevna Prokhorova. Says we should illuminate the apartment.

'Everyone,' she says, 'is installing light. The director himself has installed light,' she says.

So – of course – we do the same.

Light is installed, the apartment illuminated – heavens above! What foulness and filth!

Till then, you went to work in the morning, you came back in the evening, you drank down your tea and you went to bed. You never saw a thing with just paraffin. But now, with illumination – you see wallpaper flapping off the wall, and somebody's beaten-up slipper lying about on the floor. You see a bedbug trotting along, trying to get away from the light. An old rag here, a gob of spit there, a fag end, a flea frisking about . . .

Heavens above! It's enough to make you call the night watchman. Such a sight is sad to see.

In our room, for instance, we had a sofa. I'd always thought it wasn't a bad sofa – even quite a good sofa! In the evenings I used to sit on it. But now with this electricity – heavens above! Some sofa! Bits sticking up, bits hanging down, bits falling out. How can I sit on such a sofa? My soul protests.

No, I think, I don't live in luxury. Everything's revolting to look at. And everything I do goes wrong.

Then I see dear Yelizaveta Ignatyevna. She looks sad. She's muttering away to herself, tidying things up in the kitchen.

'What,' I ask, 'are you so sad about, dear wife?'

She shrugs her shoulders.

'I had no idea, my dear man,' she says, 'what a shabby life I've been living.'

I look at our bits and pieces. Not so great, I think. Foulness and filth. Rags of one kind and rags of another kind. All flooded with light and staring you in the eye.

So I start to get a bit down in the mouth, you might say, when I come back home in the evenings.

I come in. I switch on the light. I briefly admire the lamp, then bury my nose in the pillow.

Then I think again. I get my pay. I buy whitewash, I mix it up – and I set to work. I tear off wallpaper, I stamp out bedbugs, I sweep away cobwebs. I sort out the sofa, I paint, I adorn – my soul sings and rejoices.

I did well. But not that well. It was in vain, dear brothers, that I blew all that money. My wife cut the wires.

'Light,' she says, 'makes life seem horribly shabby. Why,' she says, 'shine light on our poverty? The bedbugs will die of laughter.'

I beg her. I argue arguments with her. No use.

'You can move,' she says, 'to another apartment. I don't want,' she says, 'to live with light. I've no money,' she says, 'to renovate and renew.'

But how could I move, comrades, after spending a fortune on white-wash? I gave in.

Light's all very well, brothers, but it's not easy to live with.

First published in 1924
Translated by Robert Chandler

PELAGEYA

Pelageya was illiterate. She didn't even know how to sign her name.

But Pelageya's husband was a Soviet worker in a position of responsibility. And though he was a simple lad from a village, five years in the city had taught him a lot. Not only how to sign his name. Goodness knows if there was anything he hadn't learned.

And he felt very ashamed of having an illiterate wife.

'You could at least, Pelageya, learn how to sign your name,' he would say to his wife. 'My surname's so easy. Two syllables – *Kuch-kin*. But you can't even do that. It's embarrassing.'

But Pelageya just shrugged her shoulders and said, 'Why, Ivan Nikolayevich? The years are going by for me. My fingers don't bend so well any more. What good will it do me to study and copy out letters? Study's for Young Pioneers[1] – I can't change myself now. I'll stay this way till the end of my days.'

Pelageya's husband was a very busy man and he couldn't afford to spend a lot of time on his wife. He would just shake his head. 'Ah, Pelageya, Pelageya . . .' And say no more.

But then one day Ivan Nikolayevich came home with a special little book.

'Pelageya,' he says, 'here is the very newest self-teaching ABC, compiled according to the latest methods. I'll show it to you myself.'

Pelageya smiled quietly, took the ABC from him, turned it this way and that way and hid it in the chest of drawers. 'Maybe future generations will need it,' she thought. 'Maybe it'll come in useful.'

But then one day Pelageya sat down to do some work. Ivan Nikolayevich's jacket needed mending – the sleeve was worn through.

Pelageya sat down at the table. She took a needle. She put one hand under the jacket. Something rustled.

'Money?' she thought.

It was a letter. A clean, neat little envelope, with fine little writing on it. And the paper, she thought, smelled of perfume or eau de Cologne. Pelageya's heart missed a beat.

'No,' she thinks. 'Don't say Ivan Nikolayevich is deceiving me. Don't say he's having intimate correspondence with ladies of importance and laughing at his illiterate fool of a wife!'

Pelageya looked at the envelope, took out the letter and unfolded it – but she couldn't make out a thing; she was illiterate.

For the first time in her life Pelageya was sorry she couldn't read.

'It may not be addressed to me,' she thought, 'but I need to know what it says. My whole life may be about to change. Maybe I should go back to the country and work in the fields.'

Pelageya began to cry. She thought how Ivan Nikolayevich seemed to have changed recently. Yes, he was fussing about his moustache more often. Washing his hands more often.

Pelageya sits there. She looks at the letter and howls. She can't read the letter. And how can she show it to anyone else?

Then Pelageya hid the letter in the chest of drawers, darned the jacket and began to wait for Ivan Nikolayevich. And when he arrived, Pelageya didn't let anything show. On the contrary, she talked calmly and quietly and even hinted that she wouldn't mind doing a little study. Really she had had enough of being a dark and illiterate peasant.

Ivan Nikolayevich was delighted. 'Splendid,' he said. 'I'll teach you the letters myself.'

'All right then,' said Pelageya.

And she looked very intently at Ivan Nikolayevich's neatly trimmed little moustache.

Day after day, for two months on end, Pelageya taught herself letters. Patiently, syllable by syllable, she formed words. She copied letters of the alphabet and learned sentences off by heart. And every evening she took the forbidden letter out of the chest and tried to divine its mysterious meaning.

This, however, wasn't at all easy.

Only during the third month did Pelageya fully master learning.

One morning, when Ivan Nikolayevich went off to work, Pelageya took out the letter and began to read it.

The fine handwriting was hard to decipher. Only the faint hint of perfume kept Pelageya going.

The letter was addressed to Ivan Nikolayevich.

Pelageya began to read:

Dear Comrade Kuchkin,

I'm sending you the promised ABC. I think that within two or three months your wife will be able to master learning completely. Promise, my dear, to make sure she does this. Explain things to her. Impress on her how awful it is, really, to be an illiterate peasant.

At this moment, for the coming anniversary, we are using every means to eliminate illiteracy from the whole of our Republic but we forget, for some reason, about those who are near and dear to us.

Do this without fail, Ivan Nikolayevich.
With Communist greetings,
Mariya Blokhina

Pelageya read this letter twice and, sorrowfully pursing her lips and feeling some kind of secret hurt, began to cry.

First published in 1924
Translated by Robert Chandler

THE BATHHOUSE

Bathhouses in America, citizens, are said to be excellent.

A citizen, for instance, walks in, throws his clothes into a special box – and off he goes for a wash. Doesn't even worry, for instance, that his things might get lost or stolen; doesn't even bother with a ticket.

Well, perhaps some anxious type of American has a word with the attendant: 'So long. Keep your eye on my stuff, will you?'

Simple as that.

And when this American's done washing, back he comes and picks up his clothes – all laundered and ironed. Foot-cloths[1] whiter than snow, no doubt. Drawers all patched and darned. Some life!

We've got good bathhouses too. But less good. Still, a man can get washed in them.

There's just one problem – tickets. I went to the bathhouse last Saturday (I can hardly, after all, go to America) and they gave me two tickets. One for my clothes, another for my hat and coat.

But where can a naked man put tickets? Quite frankly – nowhere. Not a pocket in sight. Just belly and legs. It's no joke. You can't tie tickets to your beard.

I tie a ticket to each leg. So I don't lose both at once. And in I go.

Now the tickets flap against my legs. Walking's no fun. But walk I must. I need a tub. How can you wash without a tub? It's no joke.

I look for a tub. Then I see a citizen getting washed in three tubs. He's standing in one tub, soaping his head in another and hanging on to the third with his left hand so it doesn't get swiped.

I give the third tub a pull. I want it, you see, for myself. But the citizen doesn't let go.

'Wotcha think yer up to?' he says. 'Thieving tubs as belong to others! I'll smash ye with this 'ere tub,' he says, 'right between yer eyes. That'll take the smile off yer face!'

'It was in the days of the Tsars,' I say, 'that people were smashed with tubs. Egotism, I call it, plain egotism! Other people, says I, need to wash too. We're not at the theatre.'

He turns his backside to me and goes on washing.

No point, I think, in standing over the soul of a man like him. Do that, I think, and he'll carry on washing for the next three days.

I walk on.

An hour later some fellow takes his hand off his tub. Daydreaming, I guess, or bending down for his soap. Anyway, I nick the tub.

I've got a tub but there's nowhere to sit. And a standing wash isn't what I call a wash. It's a joke.

Very well. I stand on my two feet, I hold my tub in one hand, and I wash.

And all around me, merciful heavens, it's laundry day. One man's washing his trousers, another's scrubbing his drawers, a third's wringing out some other item he owns. Soon as you get clean, you might say, you get dirty all over again. The bastards know how to splash all right. And all this laundering makes such a racket you no longer feel like washing. Can't hear what you're doing with the soap. It's no joke.

To hell with them all, I think. I'll finish washing at home.

I go back to the changing room. I hand them a ticket, they hand me my clothes. Everything's mine, I see, except for the trousers.

'My own trousers,' I say, 'have a hole just here. But look, citizens, at the hole on these here trousers!'

'We're not here,' says the attendant, 'to look after your holes. We're not at the theatre,' he says.

All right. I put on the trousers and go to collect my coat. But they won't give it to me – they want a ticket. And I've forgotten my ticket, it's on my leg. I have to undress. I take off my trousers and look for the ticket – it's gone. The string's there, tied to my leg, but where's the paper? Gone. Washed away.

I hold out the string. The attendant won't take it. 'I can't give out clothes,' he says, 'on the strength of string. Every citizen can cut himself pieces of string. We won't be able to lay in enough coats. Wait till the public's gone home. I'll give you what's left.'

'But comrade,' I say, 'what if what's left is rubbish? We're not at the theatre,' I say. 'Give me my coat,' I say, 'on the strength of distinguishing features. One pocket's torn,' I say, 'and the other's gone missing. And as for buttons, well, there's a top button, but I doubt you'll find many others.'

So I get back my coat. And he didn't even take the string.

I got dressed, and out I went. Then I remembered: I'd forgotten my soap. I went back. I'm not allowed in with my coat on.

'Take your coat off,' they say.

'I can't, citizens, undress a third time. We're not at the theatre,' I say. 'At least give me back the price of my soap.'

Nothing doing.

Nothing doing – then nothing doing. Off I go with no soap.

The reader may, of course, wish to know which bathhouse I'm talking about. Where is it? What's the address?

Which bathhouse? Any old bathhouse. A ten-kopek bathhouse.

First published in 1925
Translated by Robert Chandler

THE CRISIS

The other day, citizens, I saw a load of bricks being carted down the street. I really did!

My heart, you know, trembled with joy. Because, citizens, we are building. Bricks, after all, don't get carted around for no reason. Somewhere or other a building is being built. Things are getting going – touch wood!

In twenty years' time, maybe even less, every citizen, probably, will have a whole room to himself. And if the population doesn't multiply too rapidly and if, say, everyone is allowed abortions – two whole rooms. Or three. And a bathroom.

What a life it will be, citizens! One room, say, for sleeping. Another for receiving guests. A third . . . Who knows? There'll be more than enough to keep us busy when we're living lives of such freedom!

In the meantime, though, things are a little tight as regards square footage of space. Living space is a bit short because of the crisis.

I lived for a while, brothers, in Moscow. I only just got back. I experienced this crisis first hand.

I arrived, you see, in Moscow. I walked up and down the streets with my things. Not a hope. Not just nowhere to stay – nowhere even to leave my things.

Two weeks I walked the streets with my things. I grew a beard, my things went missing. I wandered about without any things. Travelling light. On the lookout, you see, for somewhere to live.

And then, in one building, a guy comes down the stairs. 'For thirty roubles,' he says, 'I can fix you up in a bathroom. The apartment, he says, is fit for a lord . . . Three toilets . . . A bathroom . . . You can live quite a life,' he says, 'in that bathroom. There's no windows,' he says, 'but there's a door. And water right there at hand. If you like,' he says, 'you can run yourself a bathful of water and dive in and out all day.'

'Dear comrade,' I say, 'I'm not a fish. I don't need to dive. I'd rather live on dry land. Can't you,' I say, 'knock a bit off on account of the damp?'

He says, 'I can't, comrade. I'd like to, but I can't. It's not up to me alone. This is a communal apartment. The rent we've agreed on is non-negotiable.'

'Well,' I say, 'what can I do? Take my thirty roubles,' I say, 'and let me in straight away. I've been pounding the pavements,' I say, 'for three weeks. I might,' I say, 'get tired.'

So. They let me in. I start living.

The bathroom, you know, truly is fit for a lord. Wherever you step – taps, a boiler, a bath made of marble. Only there doesn't happen to be anywhere you can sit. You can just about sit on the edge of the bath, but then you fall in, straight into the marble.

I made myself a plank lid for thirty roubles – and went on living.

A month later I happened to get married.

There she was – such a young, good-natured little spouse. With nowhere to live.

I thought she'd turn me down because of the bath. I thought I'd never get to know family happiness and comfort. But she didn't mind. Didn't turn me down at all. Just gave a little frown.

'What of it?' she says. 'There are good people living in bathrooms. And if the worst comes to the worst,' she says, 'we can put up partitions. This, say, could be my boudoir, and this – our dining room.'

'Partitions,' I say, 'would be good. Only the other tenants, the bastards, won't let us. No alterations, they keep saying.'

So. Life went on.

Within a year my spouse and I had a little baby.

We called him Volodya and on we lived. We bathed him right there in the bath. And life went on.

And really, you know, things were pretty excellent. Yes, the baby had a daily bath and never got a single cold.

Just one thing wasn't so very convenient. In the evening communal tenants were always barging in. Wanting to wash.

And then our whole family would have to move into the corridor.

Not that I didn't keep asking the tenants:

'Wash on Saturdays, citizens. You can't,' I say, 'wash every day. When are we meant to live? Put yourselves,' I say, 'in our place!'

But there were thirty-two of the bastards. Every one of them swearing. And threatening, if there was any trouble, to smash me in the face.

So what could I do? Not a thing. Life went on.

After a while my spouse's mother turns up in our bathroom. Settles in behind the boiler. Straight from the country.

'I've been dreaming for a long time,' she says, 'of rocking my grandson. You can't,' she says, 'deny me that pleasure.'

I say:

'I'm not denying it to you. Go on, babushka,' I say, 'rock away. What the hell. You can fill up the bath,' I say, 'and dive in with your grandson.'

And I say to the wife:

'Maybe, dear citizen, you've got more relatives planning to drop in. Tell me straight away. Don't keep me in suspense.'

She says:

'Only my kid brother. He might just come for the Christmas holidays.'

I left Moscow without waiting for the kid brother. I send money to the family by post.

First published in 1925
Translated by Robert Chandler

THE GALOSH

It's easy enough, of course, to lose a galosh in a tram.

Especially if one side of you's being squashed and there's some lout behind you treading on your heel. Suddenly – all gone galosh!

Losing a galosh is only too simple.

Mine came off just like that. In the blink, you could say, of an eye.

I got on to the tram – both galoshes were present. I can still almost see them. I even touched them as I climbed in – just to be sure.

Yet when I get off – one galosh, I can see, is there on my foot, but the other galosh has gone. My boot is there. And I can see my sock. And my drawers are in place. But no galosh.

And you can hardly, of course, run after a tram.

I took off the remaining galosh, wrapped it in newspaper – and off I went. 'After work,' I think, 'I'll make some inquiries. I can't let it go just like that. Wherever it is, I must track it down.'

Straight after work, I began. First I had a word with a tram driver I happen to know.

He really got my hopes up.

'Count yourself lucky,' he says, 'that you lost it on a tram. Any other public place and I wouldn't be so sure. But on a tram – heavens, your galosh is already as good as found! We have this special office, you see, for lost things. Just go and collect it. It's as good as found.'

'Well,' I say, 'thank you. That's a weight off my mind. The galosh, you see, is almost new. I've only been wearing it a couple of years.'

The next day I go along to the office.

'Brothers,' I say, 'is there any chance I could have my galosh back? It was taken off me in a tram.'

'Certainly,' they say. 'What kind of galosh?'

'An ordinary,' I say, 'kind of galosh. Size twelve.'

'We've got, so they tell me, around twelve thousand size twelves. Tell me some distinguishing features.'

'Its distinguishing features,' I say, 'are ordinary enough. The heel, of course, is a bit shabby. And there's no lining on the inside. The lining wore out.'

'We've got, so they tell me, over a thousand galoshes like that. Are there any special distinguishing features?'

'There are,' I say, 'special distinguishing features. The toe's been almost completely ripped off – it's only just hanging on. And there's hardly,' I say, 'any heel left. It's been worn down. But the sides,' I say, 'aren't doing badly. They're still in one piece.'

'Sit yourself down,' they say. 'We'll have a look right away.'

In no time at all, they come back with my galosh. I feel terribly pleased. Quite overcome. 'Yes,' I think, 'the system's functioning splendidly. And what men of principle they are,' I think, 'to go to such trouble over a single galosh.'

'Eternal thanks,' I say, 'till I'm dead and gone. Please let me have it. I'll put it on straight away. I'm truly grateful.'

'No, dear comrade,' they say. 'We can't let you have it. We can't be sure,' they say, 'whether it was you who lost it.'

'It most certainly was,' I say, 'I give you my word of honour.'

'We believe you and you have all our sympathy. And most probably you did indeed lose this very galosh. But we can't just give it to you. We need certification that you really have lost a galosh. Get this fact verified by your House Management Office[1] and then, without unnecessary red tape, we'll give you back what you have legitimately lost.'

'But brothers,' I say, 'dear, blessed comrades, no one in the office knows of this fact. They might not give me certification.'

'Yes, they will,' they say. 'It's their job. What else are they there for?'

I took one more look at the galosh and left.

The next day I went to the Head of our Office.

'Give me,' I say, 'a document. Or my galosh is as good as gone.'

'Ah,' he says, 'but did you really lose it? Or are you pulling a fast one? Maybe you just want to get your hands on an item of footwear?'

'I swear to God,' I say, 'that I lost it.'

'I can't, it goes without saying, take your word for it. Now if,' he says, 'you could bring me certification from the tram depot that you have lost a galosh, then I could give you your document. As it is, I can't do a thing.'

'But they just sent me to you.'

'In that case,' he says, 'write me a statement.'

'What shall I write?'

'Write,' he says, 'that on such and such a date a galosh went missing. And so on . . . And I undertake to remain at the above address until the matter has been cleared up.'

I wrote the statement. The following day I received official certification.

I went off with this certification to the office. And there, just imagine, without fuss or red tape, they gave me my galosh.

But once I had the galosh on my foot I felt still more overcome. Yes, I say to myself, the system well and truly functions! Can you imagine people taking such time and trouble over my galosh in some backward country? No, they'd have just thrown it out of the tram – simple as that. Here, though, I've got it back in less than a week. Quite a system!

Only trouble is, with all the to-ing and fro-ing that week, I lost the first galosh. I'd been carrying it under my arm all the time wrapped in newspaper and I couldn't remember where I'd left it. Not on a tram – that was the problem. It was a real shame I didn't leave it on a tram – where was I to look for it?

But I've got the other galosh. I keep it on my chest of drawers.

Any time I feel low, I just look at this galosh and I feel light-hearted and carefree. Quite, I say to myself, a system!

First published in 1927
Translated by Robert Chandler

THE HAT

Only now can one totally understand and grasp the great strides with which, in the last ten years, we have advanced forward.

Take any aspect of our life – nothing to be seen but total development and happy success.

And I, my brothers, as a former transport worker, can see very evidently what, for instance, has been achieved on this really rather important front.

Trains run backwards and forwards. Rotten sleepers are removed. Signals are repaired. Whistles give the right whistles. Travelling has become truly pleasant and satisfactory.

Whereas in the past! Back in 1918! You travelled, you travelled, and then – total standstill. And the engine driver, up at the head of the train, is shouting: 'Brothers! Come here!'

So the passengers gather.

And the driver says to them:

'I'm afraid I can't, brothers, for reasons of fuel, keep going. Those of you with an interest in further travel,' he says, 'should jump down from your carriages. And run along into the forest to collect firewood.'

Well, the passengers aren't too happy. They fuss and grumble about this kind of new innovation, but soon enough they're deep in the forest. Chopping and sawing.

They saw up a yard of firewood and we move off. The wood, needless to say, is green. Hisses like hell and our progress is halting.

And I remember another incident. In 1919. We were moving mod-

estly along towards Leningrad . . . We stop in the middle of nowhere.
Then – reverse drive. And we come to a standstill.

The passengers ask:

'Why have we stopped? And why all that way in reverse? Do we,
dear God, need firewood? Is the driver looking for birch trees? Is it an
upsurge of banditry?'

The fireman explains:

'There's been an unfortunate incident. The driver's hat's blown off.
He's gone to look for it.'

Passengers got off the train. Settled down on the embankment.

Suddenly they see the driver, coming out of the forest. Downcast.
Pale. Shrugging his shoulders.

'No,' he says. 'I can't find it. The devil knows where it's blown.'

They move the train back another five hundred yards. The passengers are divided into search parties.

About twenty minutes later some man with a sack shouts out:

'Here it is, you devils! Look!'

And there it is. The engine driver's hat. Hanging up on a bush.

The driver put his hat on, tied it with string to one of his buttons
so it wouldn't blow off again, and began getting up steam.

And half an hour later we were safely on our way.

Yes. Transport was in a totally bad state.

But today, even if a passenger – let alone a mere hat – were blown
off, we wouldn't stop more than a minute.

Because time is precious. We must keep moving.

First published in 1927
Translated by Robert Chandler

LEONID IVANOVICH DOBYCHIN
(1894–1936)

Born in the small town of Ludza in what is now Latvia, Dobychin grew up in Daugavpils.[1] His father, a doctor, died young; his mother was a midwife. He studied economics at the St Petersburg Polytechnic (1911–14). From 1918 he worked as a statistician in another small town, Bryansk, living until 1927 in a single room which he shared with four relatives. In 1934 Dobychin succeeded in moving to Leningrad; this, however, did little to lessen a sense of isolation that was probably compounded by his homosexuality – the Soviet Union was a homophobic society.

Dobychin's stories and The Town of N., *a short novel written in the voice of a child, have been compared to James Joyce's* Dubliners, *which Dobychin had probably read.[2] Important political events are reflected in the work of both writers, but only in so far as they impinge on the everyday lives of ordinary people. Like Joyce, Dobychin writes with unusual precision and delicacy; his minimalism, however, is such as to make even* Dubliners *seem wordy.*

Much of Dobychin's work is satirical, and it is not surprising that his two volumes of stories were harshly criticized – as was The Town of N., *first published in 1935. In March 1936 Dobychin was attacked as a 'class enemy' during a meeting at the Leningrad House of Writers. Shortly afterwards, he appears to have committed suicide.*

Though far from well-known, Dobychin was admired during his lifetime by members of both of the most interesting Leningrad literary groupings: the 'Serapion Brothers' and the OBERIU (Association for Real Art) (see pp. 200 and 296). The poet Korney Chukovsky was the first editor to publish Dobychin's work. During the fifty years after his death, Dobychin was almost, but not entirely, forgotten. One writer who helped to keep his name alive was Venyamin Kaverin; in each of the volumes of memoirs he published during the 1970s and 1980s, Kaverin included a different example of Dobychin's work, thus managing to return several complete stories to the reader long before Dobychin was finally republished in 1989, in the series 'The Forgotten

Book'. According to the contemporary poet Dmitry Prigov, only three Soviet writers brought something new into Russian prose: Dobychin, Platonov and Zoshchenko.

I have chosen three of Dobychin's simpler and more lyrical stories.

MEDICAL AUXILIARY

A man got off the train, took out a small mirror and turned his head from side to side. The telegraphist, who had been waiting by the bell, ran up to him.

'The doctor's assistant?' she asked – and, like a child, stood looking at him. He raised his eyebrows, which met on the bridge of his nose, and glanced condescendingly.

'Med-aux,' – he bowed.

It was slippery going. He took her arm.

'Oh!' she exclaimed.

The tiny fountain by the station was full, and spray flew on the wind beyond the cement basin.

'This way.' There were dark sheds on three sides, the puddles were rippled. Grass showed through the ice. They ran up the stairs, took off their coats in the kitchen and hung them on the door.

It was warm in the little room. Mother was breathing behind a screen.

'Shall I wake her?' said the telegraphist, on tiptoe, after she had looked.

'No,' he said with a gracious wave of his hands. 'My train's not for a long time. Let her sleep.' Turning round, she slipped off to the kitchen and clattered the samovar.

Cyclamen were flowering in a pot. The med-aux sniffed. Beneath the window was a path, straw had been scattered about. Beyond the wattle fence lay snow, and sticking up through the snow were beet tops.

They drank tea and quietly talked about the town.

'An interesting life,' enthused the med-aux. 'Mary Pickford[1] acts splendidly.'

He looked into the stove and, half-smiling, fell into thought. His eyebrows were slightly raised. A hair, missed by the razor, gleamed beneath his lip.

They moved to the sofa and sat in shadow. It was warm from the stove. The samovar kept going quiet, then hissing again.

'Jenny Jugo's[2] a brunette,' declared the med-aux, enthralled by his own words. 'She's the image of *you*.'

Huddling up and tucking her legs beneath her, the telegraphist said nothing. Her half-closed eyes were darkened by pupils that had dilated, as if from atropine.

'You're shivering,' said the med-aux, looking closely. 'You've caught a cold. Spring's played a trick on you.'

'No, I'm fine,' she said, and her teeth chattered. 'Perhaps, the ventilation pane . . .'

He looked round and gave a little shake of his head. 'It's closed. Put your coat on. I'll give you a sudorific. You must look after yourself, dress properly. Before you go out – eat.' She stood and began washing the dishes, knocking them against the bowl. The med-aux got to his feet, walked about on tiptoe, took some music off a little table, looked at the title and began humming a romance. Mother woke up.

First published in 1930
Translated by Robert Chandler

THE FATHER

The cross on the airman's grave was a propeller. Here and there lay interesting paper wreaths. A pot-bellied church with smashed windows peeped out from behind the maples. There was a circular bench round a linden tree.

The father and his boys were walking through the cemetery to the river. Mother was buried behind the bushes, where the hops grew. 'We'll go to her afterwards,' said the father, 'or we'll be late for the waves.'

There was the sound of a hooter. 'Quick!' shouted the boys. 'Quick!' – the father walked faster. They all began to run. Over the gate stood an angel, cut from a sheet of tin. In their hurry, they forgot to stop and, looking upwards, admire it.

They ran down the little path; the hooter sounded again. 'We'll be late,' urged father. Hearts pounded, heads too.

Throwing off their jackets, they reached the bank and, pulling legs out of trousers, dropped to the ground: they'd made it. There was a rumbling to their right, the smoke drew nearer, and from behind the bushes appeared the ship's white prow. They jumped up, danced about, waved their hats. The majestic captain was giving orders. The paddle-wheel churned, foam hissed, the wake seethed. They squatted down; on the deck were women, watching. Looking sideways at the women, they put their hands between their knees and squeezed them together.

'Smack!' went the first wave. 'Quick!' – they all leaped in.

The river was like a sea. 'Ooh!' people cried, and leaped up and down. 'Ooh!' cried father, holding the boys in his arms and jumping. 'Ooh, ooh!' cried the boys, flinging their arms round his neck and squealing.

The waves stopped. Father, hooting like a steamer, crawled on all fours through the water. The boys rode on him. Then he washed, and the boys took turns scrubbing his back, like grown-ups. Standing up again, he looked himself over and checked his muscles: in the evening he was seeing Lyubov Ivanovna. 'But at least I'm not a bad father,' he thought.

They walked back slowly. 'Otherwise,' said father, 'why get in the water at all?' Climbing back up the path took a long time. They blew dandelions and tore petals off daisies. They turned and looked down again. Cows were walking along the bank, mirrored in the river. Sometimes they mooed. Lights were being lit at the river-station; they glimmered. The sun set. There were not yet any stars. The angel over the gate had gone dark.

'You wait here,' father said by the linden tree. 'I'll be back.' They sat down, taking off their caps, and held hands. A mosquito whined.

Bushes turned black, blurring together. Tops of crosses poked out above them. The hops glowed. Father stopped and stood with his hat off. He had come because of Lyubov Ivanovna and was at a loss for words: what could he say, and how? The little boys felt frightened. Under the ground lay the dead. Someone might look out from the broken window of the church, an arm might reach out. It was good when father came back.

Soft with dust, the streets were pleasant to walk on. Here and there were street lamps. The stalls were lit up. In yards women were talking to sedate cows that had returned with the herd. Firemen had struck up a waltz in the town garden. Father bought a cigar and two spice cakes. Silent, they enjoyed them.

First published in 1931
Translated by Robert Chandler

PLEASE DO

The vet charged two roubles. The medicine was seventy kopeks. It did no good. 'Go and see the babka,'[1] said the women. 'She'll help.' Seleznyova locked the gate and, in a woollen shawl, tucking her hands up her cuffs, hunched, squat, in a long skirt and felt boots, set off.

Thaw was on the way. The trees were black. Garden fences divided the slopes of the hillocks into crooked quadrangles.

Factory chimneys smoked. The new houses had rounded corners. Engineers with little pointed beards, with badges on their hats, sauntered proudly. Seleznyova stepped to one side and, standing still, looked at them: she was paid forty roubles a month, they – it was said – six hundred.

Burdocks poked through the snow. Grey fences sagged. 'Hey, Auntie!' little boys yelled and slid past her feet on sleds.

Down below were dwellings, with little paths and apple trees, and meadows and forest could be seen in the distance. By the gate lay cinders. Seleznyova rang. Wearing a soldier's greatcoat, the dark curls on her forehead as if sewn to her kerchief, the babka let her in.

'Look at that pine there,' said the babka, 'and don't think.' The pine looked blue, poking up above a strip of forest. The babka muttered. A band was playing on the skating rink. 'Here's some salt,' – she nudged Seleznyova. 'Just slip her a little.'

The goat bent down over the water, then turned away. Hanging her head, Seleznyova went back out. 'So there you are,' said a woman who'd called round. She was squat, and wearing a home-made hat. Seleznyova greeted her. 'He's coming to have a look,' the woman announced. 'I would say Yes. His late wife was very dressy. Everything's still intact. The house is full of things.' Picking a lantern up off the ground, they set off, arms round one another's waists, slowly.

The visitor arrived – in a sealskin hat and a brown overcoat with an astrakhan collar. 'Do excuse me,' he began – and smirked, eyes gleaming, into his greying moustache.

'Not in the least,' said Seleznyova. The woman watched, delighted.

'Time flies,' marvelled the visitor. 'Spring will be here any day. We're learning the May Day anthem already.

'*Sisters,*'

– he unexpectedly began to sing, looking at Seleznyova and waving a spoon. The woman nudged Seleznyova, beaming.

> *'put on your wedding garb,*
> *Strew garlands of roses over the floor.*
>
> *Brothers,'*

– the woman sang along, rocking forward and winking at Seleznyova so she would join in too –

> *'open your hearts and your arms,*
> *The years of heartache and pain are no more.*[2]

Splendid!' the woman enthused. 'Marvellous, truthful words. And you sing superbly.'

'Yes,' nodded Seleznyova. She didn't like the visitor. She thought the song was stupid.

'Goodbye!' they said at last.

Throwing on a short jacket, Seleznyova ran out. There was a smell of damp. Music was wafting from far away. The goat didn't bleat when the lock rattled. She was lying on the straw, not moving.

It grew light. The roofs were dripping. The goat didn't need water now. After she had washed, Seleznyova went out, so as to get everything done before going to the office. She hired a man from the bazaar for fifty kopeks and, sitting in his sleigh, drove back with him.

'But she's alive,' he said, as he entered the outhouse. Seleznyova shook her head. Little boys ran off after the sleigh. 'Dead goat!' they shouted, and skipped about. Everyone left. Bending down, Seleznyova pulled up a sled with a box and began raking up the litter.

'Greetings!' said yesterday's visitor, suddenly appearing behind her. He was smirking, wearing the sealskin hat made from his late wife's muff, and his eyes gleamed. His cheeks were glossy. 'The gate's wide open,' he said. 'Too early for school, I thought, so why not?' Putting her rake down, Seleznyova pointed to the empty stall. He sighed politely. 'Scarcely do I glimpse death,' he began to intone, 'ere I weep and shed tears.'[3] Looking down at the ground, Seleznyova brushed her fingers against the outhouse wall and looked at them. Drops fell on her sleeves. A rook cawed.

'Well then,' said the visitor, twirling his moustache, 'I won't keep you. But I'll send the woman round: for a talk.'

'Please do,' said Seleznyova.

First published in 1931
Translated by Robert Chandler

ANDREY PLATONOVICH
PLATONOV (1899–1951)

Born in Voronezh, the eldest son of a gifted craftsman and railway worker, Platonov began work aged thirteen – in an office, then in a factory, then as an assistant engine driver. He welcomed the Russian Revolution and began publishing poems and articles in the local press in 1918. He worked as a land reclamation expert during much of the 1920s and as an engineer in the 1930s. Between 1927 and 1933 he wrote his most politically controversial works; two of these, Chevengur *and* The Foundation Pit, *were first published in the Soviet Union only in the late 1980s. Other stories were published in Platonov's lifetime but subjected to fierce criticism. His fifteen-year-old son was sent to a labour camp in 1938. He was released three years later – after the intervention of Platonov's influential friend Mikhail Sholokhov – only to die of the tuberculosis he had contracted there. During the Second World War Platonov worked as a war correspondent and published several volumes of stories, but he came under attack again after the publication in 1946 of 'The Return'. He died in 1951, also of tuberculosis.*

Platonov has often been called a satirist; he once wrote that 'satire must possess teeth and claws, its plough must dig deep into the soil so that the bread of our life can then grow.' His own satire – especially that of The Foundation Pit, *a response to Stalin's programme of crash industrialization and collectivization – is certainly not without teeth and claws; nevertheless, it is so intermingled with tenderness that the word 'satire' seems hardly appropriate. Platonov has also been called a surrealist; yet the more one learns about Soviet history, the more realistic his surrealism comes to seem. And few writers convey the texture, the smell and feel of everyday life more vividly.*

His subject matter is varied, but a theme to which he often returns is the search for utopia. In Chevengur *and* The Foundation Pit *he shows us the dreams of the builders of socialism in all their inarticulate confusion, his sympathy not lessened by a clear awareness of the consequences of these dreams. In his unfinished* Happy Moscow

Platonov examines the brave new world of 1930s Moscow, a time when the slogan most frequently repeated on posters and banners was Stalin's pronouncement that 'Life has become better, life has become merrier.' The short novel Soul, set in the remote deserts of Central Asia, is about an attempt to save a dying tribe and lead them to Communism. And the story 'Among Animals and Plants' is about the dissatisfied family of a railway worker in Soviet Karelia: the radio reports, and the splendour of the passing trains, lead them to believe that utopia has already been established in the Soviet Union – everywhere except in their own dismal hamlet.

'The Third Son' is one of Platonov's subtlest stories. After the death of an old woman, her six sons try three times – through 'occasional slow tears', through a perfunctorily performed Orthodox ceremony, and through almost heroic exuberance – to find a way to mourn her. Only when the third son blacks out, suddenly overwhelmed, are they freed to mourn her in their individual ways. According to Joseph Brodsky, who considered Platonov the finest Russian prose-writer of the last century, Ernest Hemingway greatly admired 'The Third Son'. A translation was published in the 1940s, so it is not impossible that Hemingway read the story and spoke about it to a Soviet journalist.

The delicately symmetrical narrative of 'The Return' represents the acme of Platonov's skill with regard to narrative construction. Without the least show of artifice, the story of Ivanov's return frames a second story, which frames a third story, which in turn frames a fourth. These framed stories help to bring about Ivanov's eventual change of heart; it is after listening to the story told by his son Petya, about another soldier's difficult homecoming, that Ivanov first begins to admit to himself that he might be less than perfect. It was probably Platonov's hope that, just as Petya's story helped Ivanov to renounce the distant utopia represented by the young woman he met on his journey home, so 'The Return' would help his own readers to return more easily to their peacetime lives.

In a 1999 article in The Moscow Times Penelope Fitzgerald chose 'The Return' as one of her 'three great Russian works of the millennium'. In 1946, however, this wise and humane story was considered a slander on Soviet Russia. Except for one story for children, it was the last work of his own that Platonov was able to publish.

On the surface, Platonov is the least 'literary' of writers. His language can seem crude, elemental – a friend once described it to me as 'the language that might be spoken by the roots of trees' – but it is also remarkably subtle, packed with the most delicate puns and allusions.

THE THIRD SON

An old woman died in a provincial town. Her husband, a seventy-year-old retired worker, went to the telegraph office and handed in six telegrams for different regions and republics, with the unvarying words: MOTHER DEAD COME HOME FATHER.

The elderly clerk took a long time doing the sums, kept making mistakes, and wrote out the receipts and stamped them with trembling hands. The old man looked meekly at her through the wooden hatch; his eyes were red and he was absent-mindedly thinking something, trying to distract grief from his heart. It seemed to him that the woman also had a broken heart and a soul now confused for ever – perhaps she was a widow or a wife who had been cruelly abandoned.

And so here she was, muddling money, losing her memory and attentiveness; even for ordinary, straightforward labour, people need to have inner happiness.

After sending off the telegrams, the old father went back home; he sat on a stool by a long table, at the cold feet of his dead wife, smoked, whispered sad words, watched the solitary life of a grey bird hopping from perch to perch in its cage, sometimes cried quietly to himself and then calmed down, wound up his pocket watch, glanced now and again through the window, beyond which, out in nature, the weather kept changing – leaves were falling, along with flakes of wet tired snow, then there was rain, then a late sun shone, with no warmth, like a star – and the old man waited for his sons.

The eldest son arrived by plane the very next day. The other five sons all gathered within two more days.

One of them, the third son, came with his daughter, a six year old who had never seen her grandfather.

The mother had been waiting on the table for more than three days, but her body did not smell of death, so neat and clean had it been rendered by illness and dry exhaustion; after giving plentiful and healthy life to her sons, the old woman had kept a small, miserly body for herself and had tried for a long time to preserve it, if only in the most pitiful state, so that she could love her children and be proud of them – until she died.

The huge men, aged from twenty to forty, stood in silence round the coffin on the table. There were six of them – seven including the father, who was smaller than even his very youngest son, and weaker too. In his arms he held his granddaughter, who was screwing up her eyes from fear of a dead old woman she had never met and whose white unblinking eyes could just see her from beneath their half-closed lids.

The sons silently wept occasional slow tears, twisting their faces in order to bear grief without a sound. The father was no longer crying; he had cried himself out alone, before the others, and now, with secret excitement and an out-of-place joy, he was looking at his sturdy band of sons. Two of them were sailors – captains of ships; one was an actor from Moscow; the one with the daughter was a physicist and a Party member; the youngest was studying to be an agronomist; and the eldest was a head engineer in an aeroplane factory and wore on his chest a medal for honourable labour. All six of them – seven including the father – were silent around the dead mother and mourned her without a word, hiding from one another their despair, their memories of childhood and of love's departed happiness, which had sprung up continually, making no demands, in their mother's heart and which had always found them – even across thousands of miles – and they had sensed it constantly and instinctively and this had made them stronger and they had been successful in life more boldly. Now their mother had turned into a corpse; she could no longer love anyone and was lying there like an indifferent stranger, an old woman who had nothing to do with them.

Each of her sons felt lonely and frightened now, as if somewhere in the darkness a lamp had been burning on the windowsill of an old house far from anywhere, and the lamp had lit up the night, the flying beetles, the blue grass, the swarms of midges in the air – an entire childhood world abandoned by those who had been born there; the doors of that house had never been locked, so that those who went out could always go back, but no one had gone back. And now it was as if the light had been extinguished in that night window, and reality had turned into memory.

On her deathbed, the old woman had asked her husband to have a priest sing prayers over her while she lay at home; after that she could be carried out of the house and buried without the priest, so as not to offend her sons and so they could walk behind her coffin. It was not so much that the old woman believed in God as that she wanted her husband, whom she had loved all her life, to feel a deeper grief and longing for her while prayers for the dead were chanted and wax candles shone on her lifeless face; she did not want to part from life without solemnity and memory. Once the children had arrived, the old man spent a long time looking for a priest; in the end, towards evening, he brought someone back with him, another little old man, dressed in ordinary civilian clothes, pink-faced from his vegetarian diet, purposeful little thoughts shining in his lively eyes. The priest had an army officer's kitbag on his hip. In it he carried his spiritual belongings: incense, thin candles, a book, a stole and a small censer on a chain. He quickly placed the candles round the coffin and lit them, fanned the incense in the censer and straight away, without warning, began muttering words from his book. The sons, who were all in the room, got to their feet; they felt awkward and somehow ashamed. One behind the other, eyes cast down, they stood motionless before the coffin. In front of them an elderly man was hurriedly, almost ironically, chanting and muttering, glancing now and again through small knowing eyes at this guard of honour – the offspring of the dead old woman. Partly he was a little afraid of them, and partly he respected them, and it seemed he would have been quite happy to get into conversation with them and even voice his enthusiasm for the construction of socialism. But the sons were silent and no one, not even the old woman's husband, crossed himself; they were standing guard around a coffin, not taking part in a service.

After completing the brief rite, the priest quickly gathered his things, then extinguished the candles burning around the coffin and packed all his goods back into his officer's kitbag. The father of the sons put some money into his hand, and the priest, without lingering, made his way through the line of six men, not one of whom looked at him, and timidly disappeared through the door. Really, he would have liked to stay in the house for the wake, discuss the prospects of wars and revolutions, and draw lasting comfort from a meeting with representatives of the new world he secretly admired but was unable to enter; he dreamed in solitude about how one day he would all of a sudden accomplish a heroic feat and so burst into the brilliant future, into the circle of the new generations – to this end he had even submitted a request to the local aerodrome, asking to be taken up to the very highest altitude and to be dropped from there by parachute without an oxygen mask, but he had not received any reply.

In the evening the father made up six beds in the second room and laid his little granddaughter down to sleep beside him, where his late wife had slept for forty years. The bed was in the same large room as the coffin; the sons went off into the other room. The father stood in the doorway while his children undressed and got into bed; then he pulled the door to and went and stood beside his granddaughter, first putting out the light. The little girl was already asleep, alone in the wide bed, the blanket pulled up over her head.

The old man stood over her in night's dim light; fresh snow out on the street was gathering up the scarce, scattered light of the sky and lighting the room's darkness through the window. The old man went up to the open coffin, kissed his wife's hands, forehead and lips and said to her, 'Rest now.' He lay down carefully beside his granddaughter and closed his eyes, so that his heart would forget everything. He dozed off and suddenly woke again. Under the door of the room where his sons were sleeping he could see light – the electric light had been switched back on and he could hear laughter and noisy conversation.

The noise made the little girl begin to toss and turn; perhaps she was awake too, simply too frightened to poke her head out from under the blanket – because of the night and the dead old woman.

The eldest son was talking about hollow-bodied metal propellers with animation and the delight of conviction, and his voice sounded rich and powerful – the voice of a man whose teeth were strong and in good repair and whose larynx was deep and red. The sailor brothers were recounting adventures in foreign ports and chortling about how their father had given them the same old blankets they had had in childhood and adolescence. White strips of calico had been sewn onto the top and bottom of each blanket with the words 'head' and 'feet', so they would keep the blankets the right way round and not cover their faces with the dirty, sweaty end where their feet had been. Then one of the sailors seized hold of the actor and they began rolling about on the floor, just like when they were children and all living together. And the youngest son egged them on, promising to take them both on at once – using only his left hand. The brothers clearly all loved one another and were glad to be together. It was many years since they had all met, and no one knew when they would meet again. Perhaps not until the funeral of their father. Getting carried away, the two brothers knocked over a chair and then fell silent for a minute, but, evidently remembering that their mother was dead and could hear nothing, they soon started up again. After a while the eldest son asked the actor to sing something in a low voice; after all, he must know some good Moscow songs. But the actor said it was difficult for him to start cold, with no cue. 'All right then, but first cover me up,' he agreed in the end. They found something to cover his face and the actor from Moscow began singing from underneath it, so he wouldn't feel awkward getting started. While he was singing, the youngest brother managed to do something that made another brother fall out of bed onto a third who was lying on the floor. They all laughed and told the youngest to pick up the brother who had fallen and put him back on the bed at once, using only his left hand. The youngest quietly answered his brothers, and two of them burst out laughing – so loudly that the little girl poked her head out from beneath the blanket in the dark room and called out, 'Grandad! Hey, Grandad! Are you asleep?'

'No, I'm not asleep, I'm not anything,' said the old man, and he coughed timidly.

The little girl couldn't bear it any longer, and she burst out sobbing. The old man stroked her face: it was wet.

'Why are you crying?' whispered the old man.

'Poor Granny,' said the granddaughter. 'Everyone's alive, and she's dead on her own.'

The old man said nothing. From time to time he just sniffed a bit, and coughed. The little girl felt frightened and she raised herself up a little so she could see her grandfather better and be sure he wasn't asleep. She looked at his face and asked, 'Why are you crying too? I've stopped.'

The grandfather stroked her head and whispered, 'I'm . . . I'm not crying. It's sweat.'

The little girl was now sitting next to the old man's pillow.

'Are you missing Granny?' she asked. 'Please don't cry. You're old too, you'll die soon and then you'll stop crying anyway.'

'I'll stop,' the old man answered quietly.

The other, noisy room went suddenly quiet. One of the sons had said something. Everyone had then fallen silent. One son again softly said something. The old man recognized the voice of the third son, the physicist, the father of the little girl. It was the first time there had been any sound from him; he had neither spoken nor laughed. Somehow he calmed down all his brothers, and they even stopped talking.

Soon after this, the door opened and in came the third son, dressed as if it were daytime. He went up to his mother in the coffin and bent down over her sad face in which there was no longer any feeling for anyone.

Late night made everything silent. No one was walking or driving down the street. In the other room the five brothers were quite still. The old man and his granddaughter, so intent they were hardly breathing, watched their son and father.

The third son all of a sudden straightened up, reached out his hand in the dark and clutched at the edge of the coffin, but, failing to get a proper grip, he just pulled the coffin a little across the table and fell to the floor. As if it no longer belonged to him, his head struck the floorboards, but the son uttered no sound – it was his daughter who screamed.

Wearing only their underclothes, the five brothers rushed to their brother and carried him into the other room to bring him round and calm him. A little later, when the third son came back to himself, all the other sons were already dressed or in uniform, even though it was not yet two in the morning. One by one, they went off in secret, about the apartment, through the yard and the entire night around the building where they had lived as children, and there they wept, whispering words and laments, as if the mother were standing over each one of them, listening to him and grieving that she had died and made her children yearn for her; had she been able to, she would have stayed alive for ever, so that no one would pine for her or expend on her a heart and body to which she had given birth. But the mother had not endured living long.

In the morning the six sons lifted the coffin onto their shoulders and carried it out to be buried, while the old man took his granddaughter in his arms and followed them; by now he was used to missing the old woman, and he was pleased and proud that he too would be buried by these six powerful men – and buried no less properly.

First published in 1936
Translated by Robert and Elizabeth Chandler

THE RETURN

Aleksey Alekseyevich Ivanov, a Guards captain, had been demobilized and was leaving the army. His unit, in which he had served all through the war, gave him a send-off, as was fitting, with regret, love and respect, with music and with wine. His close friends and comrades accompanied him to the railway station and, after saying their final goodbyes, left him there on his own. But the train had been delayed for hours; and, after those long hours had passed, it went on being even more delayed. A cold autumn night was already beginning; the station building had been destroyed in the war and there was nowhere to spend the night, so Ivanov got a lift from a car going his way and returned to his unit. The following day Ivanov's fellow-servicemen gave him another send-off; once again they sang songs and embraced the departing man to show their eternal friendship, but this time they expended their feelings more briefly and the party was just a group of close friends.

Then Ivanov set out for the station a second time; at the station he learned that yesterday's train had still not arrived, so he could indeed have gone back to his unit for one more night. But it would have been awkward to be seen off a third time and cause his comrades more trouble, and Ivanov stayed, ready for a long wait on the deserted asphalt of the platform.

Near the points just beyond the station stood a pointsman's hut which had survived the war. A woman in a padded jacket and a warm headscarf was sitting on a bench beside the hut; she had been there with her luggage the day before, and she was still sitting there, waiting for the train. The day before, as he left to spend the night with his unit, Ivanov had wondered whether to invite this lone woman back with him: she could sleep in the warm with the nurses; why leave her to freeze all night? – there was no knowing if she would ever get warm in the pointsman's hut. But while he was wondering, the car had begun to move and Ivanov had forgotten about the woman.

Now the woman was still there, still motionless and in the same place as before. Such constancy and patience showed the loyalty and immutability of a woman's heart – at least in relation to her possessions and her home, to which the woman was most likely returning. Ivanov went up to her: maybe she too would find it less dull to have company than to be on her own.

The woman turned her face towards Ivanov and he recognized her. It was a young woman they had called 'Masha the bathhouse-attendant's daughter' because this was what she had once called herself – she really was the daughter of someone who had worked in a bathhouse. Ivanov had come across her now and then during the war, on his visits to an Airfield Service Battalion where this bathhouse Masha worked as a civilian assistant to the canteen cook.

The autumn countryside around them felt gloomy and forlorn at this hour. The train which was to take both Masha and Ivanov to their homes was somewhere far off in grey space. There was nothing to divert or comfort a human heart except another human heart.

Ivanov got into conversation with Masha and began to feel better. Masha was a straightforward and good-looking girl, and there was a kindness in her large worker's hands and her healthy young body. She too was returning home and wondering what it would be like to start living a new civilian life; she had got used to the airforce women, and to the pilots who loved her like an elder sister, gave her chocolate and called her 'Big Masha' because of her height and the way she had room in her heart for all her brothers at once, like a real sister, and not just for one of them in particular. It was unaccustomed and strange, and even frightening, to be going home to relatives she was no longer used to.

Ivanov and Masha felt orphaned now without the army, but Ivanov could never stay sad or despondent for long; if he did, he would feel as if someone were laughing at him from a distance and being happy instead of him, while all he did was scowl like a half-wit. So he would always turn back quickly to the business of living; he would find something to be interested in or consoled by, some simple makeshift pleasure, as he put it himself, and would thus escape his depression.

He moved up closer to Masha and asked her to let him give her a comradely kiss on the cheek. 'Just a tiny one,' he said, 'because the train's late and it's so boring waiting for it.'

'Only because the train's late?' asked Masha, looking intently at Ivanov's face.

The ex-captain looked about thirty-five; the skin of his face was brown, wind-beaten and sunburnt; his grey eyes looked at Masha modestly, even shyly, and his speech, though direct, was tactful and courteous. Masha liked the hoarse, husky voice of this older man, his rough dark face and the expression it had of strength and defencelessness. Ivanov put out his pipe with a thumb that was inured to the smouldering heat, and sighed as he waited for permission. Masha drew away from Ivanov. He smelt strongly of tobacco and dry toast, with a hint of wine – pure substances that come from fire or else can give birth to fire. It was as if Ivanov fed solely on tobacco, rusks, beer and wine.

He repeated his request. 'I'll be careful, Masha, just a surface kiss . . . Imagine I'm your uncle.'

'I already have. Only not my uncle – my father.'

'Splendid. So you'll let me?'

'Fathers don't ask for permission,' Masha laughed.

Ivanov was to say to himself later that Masha's hair smelt of autumn leaves fallen in the forest, and he was never able to forget it . . . He walked away from the railway line and lit a small fire to fry some eggs for his and Masha's supper.

In the night the train arrived and carried Ivanov and Masha away, towards their homes. They travelled together for two days, and on the third day they reached the town where Masha had been born twenty years before. She collected her things together in the carriage and asked Ivanov to settle the bag more comfortably on her back, but Ivanov took her bag on his own shoulders and followed Masha out of the carriage, even though he had more than a day's journey still ahead of him.

Masha was surprised and touched by Ivanov's considerateness. She was afraid of finding herself suddenly alone in the town she had been born in, and had lived in, but which was now almost a foreign country to her. Her mother and father had been deported by the Germans and had died in some unknown place; now Masha had only a cousin and two aunts in her home town, people to whom she felt no real attachment.

Ivanov arranged with the station commandant to break his journey, and stayed with Masha. Really he should have hurried on to his own home, where his wife and two children, whom he had not seen for four years, were waiting for him. But Ivanov was putting off the joyful and anxious moment of reunion with his family. He was not sure why he was doing this – perhaps he wanted to enjoy his freedom a little longer.

Masha did not know Ivanov's family circumstances, and girlish shyness prevented her from asking. She trusted herself to him in the goodness of her heart, with no thought beyond the moment.

Two days later Ivanov resumed his journey home. Masha saw him off at the station. He kissed her in a habitual way and promised courteously to remember her image for ever.

Masha smiled in reply and said, 'Why remember me for ever? There's no need – and anyway you won't . . . I'm not asking you for anything. Forget me.'

'My dear Masha! Where were you before? Why didn't I meet you long, long ago?'

'Before the war I was at school, and long long ago I didn't exist at all.'

The train arrived and they said goodbye. Ivanov departed and did not see how Masha, left on her own, began to cry because she could not forget any friend or comrade, or anyone at all whose path had even once crossed hers.

Ivanov looked out of the carriage window at the small houses of the little town they were passing and which he was unlikely ever to see again in his life, and reflected that in a house just like one of these, though in another town, his wife Lyuba lived with their children, Petya and Nastya, and that they were expecting him; he had sent his wife a telegram when he was still with his unit, saying he was coming home without delay and that he longed to embrace her and the children as soon as he possibly could.

For the last three days Lyubov Vasilyevna, Ivanov's wife, had been to meet all the trains coming from the west. She took time off work, failed to fulfil her norm, and was unable to sleep at night for joy, listening instead to the slow indifferent movement of the pendulum of the wall-clock. On the fourth day Lyubov Vasilyevna sent Petya and Nastya to the station – to meet their father if he came during the day – but once again went to meet the night train herself.

Ivanov arrived on the sixth day. He was met by his son Petya. Petya was now getting on for twelve, and the father did not immediately recognize his son in this serious lad who seemed older than his years. The father saw that Petya was a thin, undersized little boy, but with a large head, a broad forehead and a calm face that seemed already accustomed to life's cares, while his small brown eyes looked at the world around him morosely and disapprovingly, as if all they saw everywhere was disorder. Petya was neatly dressed and shod: his boots were worn but still had some use in them, his trousers and jacket were old, cut down from his father's civilian clothing, but there were no holes in them, they had been darned and patched where necessary; all in all Petya was like a little peasant who had no money to spare but who took care of his clothes. His father was surprised, and he sighed.

'So you're my father, are you?' asked Petya, when Ivanov lifted him up and hugged and kissed him. 'You must be!'

'Yes, I am. Hello, Pyotr Alekseyevich!'

'Hello. Why have you been so long? We've been waiting and waiting.'

'It was the train, Petya. It was very slow. How are your mother and Nastya? Alive and well?'

'They're fine,' said Petya. 'How many decorations have you got?'

'Two, Petya, and three medals.'

'And mother and I thought your chest would be covered with them. Mother has two medals as well. She got them for good service . . . Why haven't you got any more luggage – just a bag?'

'I don't need any more.'

'I suppose a travelling trunk gets in the way when you're fighting?' asked the son.

'Yes,' the father agreed. 'It's easier with just a bag. No one there uses a trunk.'

'And I thought you all did. I'd keep my things in a trunk – in a bag things get crumpled and broken.'

Petya took the bag and carried it home while his father walked along behind him.

The mother met them on the porch; she had asked for time off work again, as if she had sensed in her heart that her husband would arrive that day. She had gone straight home from the factory, meaning to go on from there to the station. She was afraid: had Semyon Yevseyevich turned up at the house? He liked to drop in sometimes during the day; turning up in the afternoon and sitting with Petya and five-year-old Nastya had become a habit of his. True, Semyon Yevseyevich never came empty-handed, he always brought something for the children –

sweets or sugar, a small loaf of white bread or a coupon for shoes and clothing. Lyubov Vasilyevna had never had anything to reproach Semyon Yevseyevich for; all these two years they had known each other he had been good to her, and he had been like a father to the children, kinder, in fact, than many a father. But Lyubov Vasilyevna did not want her husband to see Semyon Yevseyevich today; she tidied up the kitchen and the living room, wanting the house to be clean, with nothing that did not belong there. Later, tomorrow, or the next day, she herself would tell her husband everything, all that had happened. Fortunately, Semyon Yevseyevich had not come that day.

Ivanov went up to his wife, put his arms round her and stood there with her, not moving away, feeling the forgotten and familiar warmth of someone he loved.

Little Nastya came out of the house and, after looking at the father she did not remember, started pushing at his leg, trying to separate him from her mother; then she burst out crying. Petya stood silently beside his father and mother, with his father's bag on his back; after waiting a while, he said: 'That's enough, you two – Nastya's crying, she doesn't understand.'

The father moved away from the mother and picked Nastya up. She was crying from fear.

'Nastya!' Petya called to her. 'Calm down, I tell you! This is our father, he's one of the family.'

Once inside the house, the father had a wash and sat down at the table. He stretched out his legs, closed his eyes and felt a quiet joy in his heart, a peaceful satisfaction. The war was over. During it his feet had walked thousands of miles. Lines of tiredness lay on his face, and his eyes felt a stabbing pain beneath their closed lids – they wanted to rest now in twilight or darkness.

While he sat there, the whole family bustled about in the living room and in the kitchen, preparing a celebration meal. Ivanov examined, one after another, all the objects around the house – the clock, the crockery cupboard, the wall thermometer, the chairs, the flowers on the windowsills, the Russian kitchen-stove. They had lived here a long time without him, and they had missed him. Now he had come back and he was looking at them, getting to know each one of them again, as if they were relatives whose lives had been poor and lonely without him. He breathed in the familiar, unchanging smell of the house – smouldering wood, warmth from his children's bodies, a burning smell from the grate. This smell had been just the same four years ago, it had not dispersed or changed in his absence. Nowhere else had Ivanov ever smelt this smell, although in the course of the war he had been in several countries and hundreds of homes; the smells there had been different, always lacking the special quality of his own home. Ivanov also recalled the smell of Masha, the scent of her hair; but that had been a smell of leaves in a forest, of some overgrown path he did not know, a smell not of home but once again of unsettled life. What was she doing now and how was she coping with civilian life, Masha the bathhouse-attendant's daughter? God be with her . . .

Ivanov could see that the busiest person around the house was Petya. Not only did he work hard himself, but he also told his mother and Nastya what to do and what not to do, and how to do everything properly. Nastya was obeying Petya meekly and was no longer afraid of her stranger-father; she had the alert and attentive face of a child who did everything in life seriously and truthfully, and she surely had a kind heart too, since she did not mind Petya.

'Nastya, empty the potato peelings out of the mug, I need it.'

Nastya obediently emptied the mug and washed it. Meanwhile their mother was quickly making a spur-of-the-moment pie, without yeast, to put in the stove; Petya had already got the fire going.

'Come on, Mother, get a move on!' Petya commanded. 'You can see I've got the stove ready. You're not much of a Stakhanovite,[1] you're a dawdler!'

'Just a minute, Petya, I'm nearly there,' said his mother obediently. 'I'll just put some raisins in and it'll be done. It must be a long time since your father had raisins. I've been saving them for ages.'

'He's had raisins all right,' said Petya. 'Our troops get raisins. Just look at their fat faces – they get enough food all right. Nastya, why are you sitting down – think you're a guest here? Go on, peel some potatoes, we're going to fry some for supper. You can't feed a whole family on nothing but pie!'

While his mother was making the pie, Petya took the large oven-fork and put a cast-iron pot of cabbage soup in the oven, so the heat would not go to waste; as he did this, he even admonished the fire: 'Why are you burning so messily, jumping about all over the place? Just burn evenly, and stay under the food – what do you think the trees in the forest grew up to make firewood for? And you, Nastya, why have you shoved the kindling into the stove just any old how? You should have laid it the way I taught you. And you're peeling too much off the potatoes again, you should peel them thinly and not dig out the flesh – that's how our food gets wasted! How many times do I have to tell you? This is the last time – do it again and you'll get a clout round the head!'

'Petya, why keep getting at Nastya?' their mother said gently. 'Just think for a moment! How can she peel so many potatoes, and do them all just as you want them, like a barber never nicking the flesh? Father's come home, and all you can do is find fault!'

'I'm not finding fault, I'm talking sense. Father needs feeding, he's just back from the war, and you two are wasting good food. Think how much we've wasted in potato peelings in a whole year! If we'd had a sow, we could have fed her all year on potato peelings alone, then taken her to the show and been given a medal. Just imagine it! But you don't understand.'

Ivanov had not known that his son had turned out like this; he sat and marvelled at his cleverness. But he preferred gentle little Nastya, who was also working away at household tasks. Her little hands were quick and deft – they must have had a lot of practice.

'Lyuba,' Ivanov said to his wife, 'why aren't you saying anything to me? Tell me how you've got on without me. How's your health been? And what work do you do?'

Lyubov Vasilyevna felt shy of her husband now, like a young bride; she was not used to him any more. She even blushed when he spoke to her and, just as in her youth, her face took on the timid, scared expression which Ivanov found so attractive.

'We've been all right, Alyosha. The children haven't been ill too often. I've taken care of them. The bad thing is that I've only been here with them at night. I work at the brick factory, at the press. It's a long way on foot.'

'Where do you work?' said Ivanov, not understanding.

'At the brick factory, at the press. I had no qualifications, of course, so at first I just did odd jobs outside. Then they gave me some training and put me on the press. It's been good to be working – only the children have been alone all the time. You can see how they've turned out. They know how to do everything themselves, they're like grown-ups,' Lyubov Vasilyevna said quietly. 'Whether that's a good thing, Alyosha, I just don't know.'

'We shall see, Lyuba . . . We'll all be living together now. There'll be time enough to work out what's good and what's bad.'

'Everything will be better now you're here. When I'm on my own I don't know what's right and what's wrong, and I've been afraid. Now it's for you to think about how to bring up the children.'

Ivanov stood up and paced about the room.

'So, all in all, you've kept in good spirits, have you?'

'It's been all right, Alyosha, and it's over now, we've stuck it out. Only we missed you dreadfully and we were afraid you'd never come back to us. We were afraid you'd die there, like others have . . .'

She began to cry over the pie, which she had already placed in its iron mould, and her tears dropped onto the dough. She had smeared the top of the pie with beaten egg and was still smoothing it with her palm, now smearing the festive pie with her tears.

Nastya gripped her mother's leg in her arms, pressed her face into her skirt and stared up at her father sternly from beneath her brows.

Her father bent down to her. 'What's the matter, Nastya, what's wrong? Are you cross with me?'

He gathered her up in his arms and stroked her head. 'What's the matter, little daughter? You've completely forgotten me, haven't you? You were tiny when I went away to the war.'

Nastya laid her head on her father's shoulder and she too began to cry.

'What is it, little Nastyenka?'

'Mummy's crying, so I'm crying too.'

Petya, who was standing in front of the stove, was bewildered and annoyed.

'What's the matter with you all? While you're all being moody, the heat's going to waste. Do you want the stove heated up all over again? Who'll give us coupons for more wood? We've used up the last lot, there's just a tiny bit left in the shed – about ten logs, and it's only aspen. Give me the dough, mother, before the heat all gets lost.'

Petya took out the big iron pot of cabbage soup and raked the embers on the floor of the stove, and Lyubov Vasilyevna, as if trying to please Petya, hurriedly put the two pies in, forgetting to brush the second one with egg.

Ivanov was finding his own home strange and rather hard to understand. His wife was the same, with her sweet, shy, though now deeply exhausted face, and the children were the same ones that had been born to him, except that they had grown older during the war, as was to be expected. But something was stopping Ivanov from feeling wholehearted joy at being back home – no doubt he was simply not used to family life any more and so was unable to understand even those nearest and dearest to him. Looking at Petya, his firstborn, now so grown up, listening as Petya gave commands and instructions to his mother and little sister, watching his worried, serious face, Ivanov confessed to himself with a sense of shame that he did not feel fatherly enough towards this boy, that he did not feel drawn to his own son. Ivanov was all the more ashamed of this lack of fatherly feeling because he was aware that Petya needed love and care more than the others did, for it was painful to look at him. Ivanov did not know in any detail how his family had lived while he was away, and he could not yet grasp at all clearly why Petya had come to be like this.

Sitting at the table, among his family, Ivanov realized what he had to do. He must get to work as soon as he could – he had to find a job and earn money, and help his wife bring up the children properly; then everything would gradually get better, and Petya would start running about with other children or sitting with a book, not standing at the stove with an oven-fork in his hands and giving orders.

During the meal Petya ate less than anyone else, but he scooped up all the crumbs and tipped them into his mouth.

'What are you doing, Petya?' his father asked him. 'Why are you eating crumbs when you haven't finished your pie? Eat it up and your mother will cut you another piece.'

'I could eat it all up,' Petya said with a frown. 'But I've had enough.'

'He's afraid that if he starts eating a lot, then Nastya will copy him and eat a lot too,' Lyubov Vasilyevna explained straightforwardly. 'And that worries him.'

'You two don't worry about anything,' said Petya unemotionally. 'I just want there to be more for you.'

Father and mother glanced at each other and shivered at their son's words.

'Well, and why aren't you eating?' the father asked little Nastya. 'Are you copying Petya? Eat up, or you won't grow up to be a big girl.'

'I am a big girl,' said Nastya.

She ate a small piece of pie, but pushed away another, bigger piece and covered it with a napkin.

'What are you doing?' her mother asked. 'Shall I put some butter on it for you?'

'No, I'm full up.'

'Well eat it like that then. Why've you pushed it away?'

'Because Uncle Semyon might come. I'm leaving it for him. It's not your pie, it's my pie I'm not eating. I'm putting it under my pillow so it doesn't get cold.'

Nastya got down from her chair; she took the pie wrapped up in a napkin over to her bed, and put it under the pillow.

Her mother remembered how she herself had once laid pillows over a pie she had baked for May Day, to keep it warm for Semyon Yevseyevich.

'Who is this Uncle Semyon?' Ivanov asked his wife.

Lyubov Vasilyevna did not know what to say. 'I don't know who he is,' she said. 'He comes on his own to see the children. His wife and his own children were killed by the Germans, he's grown fond of our two and he comes to play with them.'

'To play with them?' said Ivanov in surprise. 'What games do they play when he comes? How old is he?'

Petya looked quickly at his mother, then at his father; his mother did not answer his father's question, she only looked at Nastya with sad eyes. The father smiled unpleasantly, got up from his chair, lit a cigarette and then asked Petya, 'Where are the toys you and this Uncle Semyon play with?'

Nastya got down from her chair, climbed up onto another chair by the chest of drawers, took out some books and brought them to her father. 'They're book-toys,' she said. 'Uncle Semyon reads them out loud to me. Look what a funny teddy bear, he's a toy and he's a book too . . .'

Ivanov took the book-toys his daughter handed him: about Misha the Bear, and a toy cannon, and the little house where Granny Domna lived, spinning flax with her granddaughter . . .

Petya remembered it was time to close the damper in the stovepipe, so the warmth would not escape from the house. After closing the damper, he said to his father, 'Semyon Yevseyevich is older than you . . . He helps us out, leave him in peace.'

Glancing out of the window just in case, Petya noticed that the clouds in the sky were not the right kind of clouds for September. 'Look at those clouds,' he said. 'They're the colour of lead – they must be full of snow. Don't say winter's going to set in tomorrow! What will we do? We haven't dug up the potatoes yet, we haven't stocked up on food. What a situation to be in!'

Ivanov looked at his son, listened to him talking and realized he felt shy of him. He would have liked to ask his wife more about this Semyon Yevseyevich who had been coming to visit for the last two years, and whether it was Nastya this man came to see or his good-looking wife, but Petya distracted Lyubov Vasilyevna by talking about household matters: 'Mother, give me tomorrow's bread-coupons and the registration cards, and give me the paraffin coupons as well – tomorrow's the last day and we must get our charcoal, oh but you've lost the sack, they won't give us any charcoal without one, you must have a good look for the sack right now, or else sew a new one out of rags, how can we manage without a sack? And tell Nastya not to let anyone into our yard tomorrow for water – they take too much from the well; with winter coming the water will drop and our rope's not long enough to let the bucket down lower, and we don't want to have to eat snow, anyway we'd need firewood to thaw it out.'

As he said all this, Petya swept up around the stove and sorted out the kitchen utensils. Then he took the pot of soup out of the oven.

'We've had some pie and now we're having some cabbage-and-meat soup, with bread,' Petya announced. 'And you, father, must go first thing tomorrow to the District Soviet and the Military Commissariat. Then you'll be put on the list straight away and we'll get ration cards for you more quickly.'

'All right,' said the father obediently.

'Yes, and mind you don't oversleep and forget.'

'I won't,' the father promised.

Their first shared meal after the war – soup with meat – was eaten by the family in silence, with even Petya sitting there calmly; it was as if father and mother and children were afraid of destroying, through some chance word, the quiet happiness of a family sitting together.

Then Ivanov asked his wife, 'How have you managed for clothes, Lyuba? Is everything worn out?'

'We've been wearing all old things, but now we can buy something new,' Lyubov Vasilyevna smiled. 'I had to mend the children's clothes while they stood up in them. Then I cut down your suit, your two pairs of trousers and all your underclothes. There was no money to spare, you see, and the children had to wear something.'

'You did right,' said Ivanov. 'Children shouldn't have to go without.'

'They haven't had to. I even sold the coat you bought me. Now I wear my padded jacket.'

'Her jacket's too short. She could catch cold in it,' commented Petya. 'I'll go and work as a stoker at the bathhouse. I'll earn some money and get her a coat. People bring clothes to sell at the market, I've had a look and checked the prices. Some of the coats are all right.'

'We can get by without you and your wages,' said the father.

After dinner Nastya put a large pair of glasses on her nose and sat by the window to darn the little knitted mittens her mother now wore at the factory inside her work-mittens. It was already autumn; the weather had turned cold.

Petya glanced across at his sister and began to scold her: 'What are you up to now? Why have you got Uncle Semyon's glasses on?'

'I'm not looking through them, I'm looking over them.'

'Oh really! . . . I can see what you're doing! You'll ruin your eyesight and go blind, then you'll be on a pension and be a burden for the rest of your life. Take the glasses off this minute, I tell you, and stop darning those mittens, mother will darn them, or I'll do them myself as soon as I have a moment. Get out your exercise book and practise your writing – goodness knows when you last did any!'

'Does Nastya go to school then?' asked the father.

Their mother replied that Nastya was not yet big enough for school, but that Petya made her do lessons every day; he had bought her an exercise book, and she practised drawing the strokes for letters. Petya was also teaching his sister to do sums, adding and subtracting pumpkin seeds in front of her, while Lyubov Vasilyevna was herself teaching Nastya to read.

Nastya put down the mitten and took an exercise book and a pen and nib out of the chest of drawers, while Petya, satisfied that everything was being done properly, put on his mother's padded jacket and went outside to chop wood for the next day; he usually brought the firewood into the house at night and laid it behind the stove to dry out, so it would give out more heat and be more efficient.

In the evening Lyubov Vasilyevna got supper ready early. She wanted the children to go to sleep in good time so that she and her husband could sit together and talk. But the children did not fall asleep until long after supper; Nastya, lying on the wooden couch, kept watching her father from under the blanket, while Petya, who had lain down on the Russian stove he always slept on, winter and summer alike, tossed and turned, grunting and whispering something, and it was quite some time before he quietened down. But the night wore on, and Nastya closed her eyes that were tired from looking, while Petya started to snore on the stove.

Petya always slept lightly and on his guard: he was afraid something might happen in the night and he would not hear – a fire, or robbers breaking in, or his mother might forget to latch the door and it would come open during the night and all the warmth would escape. This time it was the troubled voices of his parents that woke him; they were talking in the room next to the kitchen. What time it was – midnight or nearly morning – he did not know, but his father and mother were not asleep.

'Alyosha, don't make so much noise, the children will wake up,' his mother was saying quietly. 'You mustn't say bad things about him, he's a good man, and he's loved your children . . .'

'We don't need his love,' said the father. 'I love my children myself. Loving other people's children – I like that! I sent you certificates regularly and you had your job – what did you need this Semyon Yevseyevich for? Still hot-blooded, are you? Oh Lyuba, Lyuba! You're not the woman I thought you were . . . You've made a fool of me.'

The father fell silent, then struck a match to light his pipe.

'What are you saying, Alyosha? How can you?' the mother burst out. 'When I've brought up the children and they've hardly ever been ill and they've got plenty of flesh on them.'

'So what?' said the father. 'Some women were left with four children, but they managed all right, and their kids are no worse than

ours. And as for Petya and the way you've brought him up – he carries
on like an old man, but it wouldn't surprise me if he's forgotten how
to read.'

From his place on the stove Petya sighed and then pretended to
snore, so he could go on listening. 'All right,' he thought, 'maybe I am
an old man, but it was all very well for you – you didn't have to worry
where your next meal was coming from!'

'Yes, but he's learnt some of life's hardest lessons!' said the mother.
'And he doesn't fall behind in his schoolwork.'

'Who is this Semyon of yours?' said the father angrily. 'Stop leading
me up the garden path.'

'He's a good man.'

'You love him, do you?'

'Alyosha, I'm the mother of your children.'

'Go on, give me a straight answer.'

'I love you, Alyosha. I'm a mother. It's a long time since I was a
woman, and that was only ever with you. I can't even remember when
it was.'

The father said nothing, smoking his pipe in the darkness.

'I've missed you, Alyosha. Of course I had the children, but that's
not the same as having you. I was waiting for you all the time, all
those long terrible years. Often I was afraid to wake up in the morning.'

'What's his job, where does he work?'

'He works at our factory, in the supplies section.'

'I see, a swindler.'

'He isn't a swindler. I don't know . . . His whole family were killed
in Mogilyov.[2] There were three children, the daughter was already
grown up.'

'Doesn't matter. He found himself another family, ready-made, and
a woman who's still quite young, and good-looking – so he's got
things nice and cosy again.'

The mother did not reply. There was a silence, but soon Petya could
hear his mother crying.

'He talked to the children about you, Alyosha,' she began, and Petya
could tell that big tears were hovering in her eyes. 'He told the children
how you were fighting for us and how you were suffering. They'd ask
why, and he'd say because you're a good man.'

The father gave a laugh and knocked the ash out of his pipe.

'So that's the kind of man he is, your Semyon Yevseyevich! Never
even seen me, yet he sings my praises. Quite a character!'

'No, he's never seen you. He made things up, so the children would
go on loving you, so they wouldn't lose touch with their father.'

'But why? Why was he doing it? Because he wanted you and he was in a hurry? Go on, tell me, what was he after?'

'Maybe he just has a kind heart, Alyosha, maybe that's why. Why shouldn't it be?'

'I'm sorry, Lyuba, but you're a fool. No one does things for nothing!'

'But Semyon Yevseyevich often brought things for the children. He always brings something – sweets, white flour, sugar. Not long ago he brought Nastya some felt boots, only they were no good, they were too small. And he's never asked for anything from us. We didn't need anything either, Alyosha, we could have managed without his presents, we'd got used to the way we were living, but Semyon Yevseyevich says he feels better when he's doing something for other people, it stops him missing his dead family so badly. It really isn't what you think – you'll see when you meet him.'

'You're talking nonsense!' said the father. 'Stop trying to trick me . . . I'm fed up with you, Lyuba. And I still want to enjoy life.'

'Enjoy life with us, Alyosha.'

'While you're carrying on with Semyon Yevseyevich?'

'I won't, Alyosha. He'll never come here again. I'll tell him to stop coming.'

'So something has been happening, if it's going to stop? Oh Lyuba, how could you? You women are all the same.'

'And what about you men?' the mother said in a hurt voice. 'What do you mean – we're all the same? I'm not the same. I've been working day and night, we've been making linings for locomotive fireboxes. I've grown thin in the face and horrible-looking, no one recognizes me, beggars don't even ask me for money. I've had a hard time too, and the children were alone at home. I'd get back from work – and there was the stove to light, the supper to cook, it was dark, and the children were miserable. They couldn't help round the house like they do now, even Petya was still little. And it was then that Semyon Yevseyevich started calling on us. He'd come round – and just sit with the children. He lives all on his own, you see. "Can I come and visit you sometimes," he asked, "so I can warm up a bit?" I told him our house was cold too, and the firewood was damp, but he said, "It's my soul that's chilled to the marrow. Just let me sit near your children, you don't need to heat up the stove for me." "All right," I said, "come round then. With you here the children won't be so frightened." Then I got used to his visits too. We all began to feel better when he came. I'd look at him and think of you, I'd remember we had you . . . It was so sad without you, it was awful. Why not let someone come round? I thought. Time will pass quicker, we won't be so miserable. What use is time to us when you're not here?'

'Well go on, what happened after that?' said the father impatiently.

'Nothing happened after that. Now you're back, Alyosha.'

'Well, all right then, if that's the truth,' said the father. 'It's time to get some sleep.'

'Stay up a bit longer,' the mother begged. 'Let's talk, I'm so happy to be with you.'

'Will they never quieten down?' thought Petya, lying on the stove. 'They've made it up – what more do they want? Mother's got to get up early for work, but she's still wide awake. A fine time to cheer up and stop crying!'

'And did this Semyon love you?' asked the father.

'Wait a minute. I'll go and tuck Nastya in, she gets uncovered in her sleep and she'll be cold.'

The mother covered Nastya up with the blanket, went into the kitchen and paused by the stove to check whether Petya was asleep. Petya knew what she was up to and started to snore. Then she went back and he heard her voice again.

'I dare say he did love me. I saw him looking at me affectionately – and I'm not much to look at now, am I? Life's been hard on him, Alyosha, and he had to love somebody.'

'You might at least have given him a kiss then, if that's the way things were,' said the father in a nice voice.

'Don't be silly! He did kiss me, twice, but I didn't want him to.'

'Why did he do it then, if you didn't want him to?'

'I don't know. He said he just lost his head, and that he was thinking of his wife, and I look a bit like her.'

'And does he look like me?'

'No, he doesn't. No one's like you, Alyosha, you're the only one who's like you.'

'The only one? Counting starts with one: first one, then two.'

'He only kissed me on the cheek, not on the lips.'

'Makes no difference where.'

'Alyosha, it does make a difference. And what do you know about how things have been for us?'

'What do you mean? I've fought through the whole war, I've been closer to death than I am to you at this moment.'

'While you were fighting, I was dying of worry. My hands were shaking from grief, but I had to keep working cheerfully. I had to feed the children and help our State against the Fascist enemy.'

She was talking calmly, but her heart was heavy, and Petya was sorry for his mother; he knew that she had learnt to mend shoes for all three of them, not to have to pay a lot of money to the cobbler, and that she had repaired electric cooking rings for their neighbours in return for potatoes.

'I couldn't go on like that, longing for you,' said the mother. 'And if I had, it would have been the end of me, I know it would, and there were the children to think of. I needed to feel something else, Alyosha, some sort of happiness, just to get some rest. There was a man who said he loved me, and he was gentle to me, like you used to be long ago.'

'You mean this Semyon Yevsey of yours?'

'No, someone else. He works as an instructor for our trade union district committee, he's an evacuee.'

'To hell with who the man is! So what happened? Did he console you?'

Petya knew nothing about this instructor, and this surprised him. 'So our mother's been naughty too,' he whispered to himself. 'Fancy that!'

'I got nothing from him, no joy at all,' the mother replied. 'Afterwards I felt even worse. My soul had been drawn to him because it was dying, but when he was close to me, really close, I felt nothing. All I thought about was household things, and I wished I hadn't let him be close. I realized I could only be calm and happy with you and that I'd only rest when you were close to me again. I'm lost without you, I can't even keep myself going for the children. Stay with us, Alyosha, we'll have a good life.'

Petya heard his father get up from the bed without speaking, light his pipe and sit down on the stool.

'How many times did you meet him and be really close?' asked the father.

'Only once,' said the mother. 'It never happened again. How many times should I have?'

'As many times as you like, that's your business,' declared the father. 'So why say you're the mother of our children, and that you've only been a woman with me, a long time ago?'

'It's the truth, Alyosha.'

'How can it be? What kind of truth? You were a woman with him too, weren't you?'

'No, I wasn't a woman with him, I wanted to be, but I couldn't. I felt I couldn't go on without you. I just needed someone to be with me, I was so worn out, my heart had gone all dark, I couldn't love my children any more, and you know I'd go through anything for them, I'd give the very bones from my body!'

'Just a minute,' said the father. 'You say you made a mistake with this second Semyon of yours. You didn't get any happiness from him – and yet here you are, you're still in one piece.'

'Yes,' whispered the mother. 'I'm still alive.'

'So you're lying to me again! So much for your truth!'

'I don't know,' whispered the mother. 'I don't know very much at all.'

'All right, but I know a lot, I've been through more than you have,' said the father. 'You're a whore, that's what you are.'

The mother was silent. The father's breathing was fast and laboured.

'So here I am, home at last,' he said. 'The war's over, and now you've wounded me in the heart . . . All right, you go and live with your Semyons. You've made a fool of me, you've turned me into a laughingstock. But I'm not a plaything, I'm a human being.'

In the dark the father began putting on his clothes and his shoes. Then he lit the paraffin lamp, sat down at the table, and wound up his watch.

'Four o'clock,' he said to himself. 'Still dark. It's true what they say: women aplenty, but not a wife to be found.'

It grew quiet in the house. Nastya was breathing evenly, asleep on the wooden couch. Up on the warm stove, Petya pressed his face into the pillow and forgot he was meant to be snoring.

'Alyosha,' said the mother in a gentle voice. 'Alyosha, forgive me.'

Petya heard his father groan, and then heard the sound of breaking glass; through a gap in the curtain he could see it had got darker in the other room, though a light was still burning. 'He's crushed the glass,' Petya guessed. 'And there's no lamp-glass to be got anywhere.'

'You've cut your hand,' said the mother. 'You're bleeding. Take a towel from the chest of drawers.'

'Shut up!' the father shouted at her. 'I can't stand the sound of your voice. Wake the children! Wake them up this very minute! Wake them, do you hear? I'll tell them what sort of mother they've got! I want them to know.'

Nastya cried out in fear and woke up.

'Mummy!' she called out. 'Can I get into bed with you?'

Nastya liked getting into bed with her mother in the night, to lie under the blanket with her and get warm.

Petya sat up on the stove, swung his legs over the edge, and said to everyone: 'Go to sleep! Why have you woken me up? It's not day yet, it's still dark outside! Why are you making such a noise? Why is the lamp burning?'

'Go to sleep, Nastya, go back to sleep, it's still early, I'll come to you in a minute,' the mother answered. 'And you lie down, Petya, and don't talk any more.'

'Why are you talking then?' said Petya. 'And what does Father want?'

'What's that to do with you?' the father replied. 'A right sergeant-major you are!'

'And why have you smashed the lamp-glass? Why are you frightening Mother? She's thin enough as it is. She eats her potatoes without any butter, she gives all the butter to Nastya.'

'And do you know what your mother's been up to here, do you know what she's been playing at?' the father cried plaintively, like a little boy.

'Alyosha!' Lyubov Vasilyevna said softly to her husband.

'Yes, I do, I know everything!' said Petya. 'Mother's been crying for you, she's been waiting for you, and now you've come back home – and she's still crying! You're the one who doesn't know!'

'You don't understand anything yet!' said the father furiously. 'A fine son we've produced!'

'I understand everything perfectly,' Petya answered from the stove. 'It's you who don't understand. There's work to do, we have to go on living, and you two are quarrelling like stupid fools.'

Petya stopped. He lay down on his pillow; and silently, without meaning to, he began to cry.

'You've had things too much your own way in this house,' said the father. 'But it's all the same now. You can carry on being the boss.'

Petya wiped away his tears and answered: 'Some father you are, saying things like that, and you a grown-up who's been through the war! You should go to the war-invalids' co-op tomorrow – you'll find Uncle Khariton there, behind the counter, he cuts the bread and he never cheats anyone. He's been in the war too and come back. Go and ask him – he tells everyone, he laughs about it, I've heard him myself. He's got a wife, Anyuta, she learnt to drive and now she delivers the bread, and she's a good woman, she doesn't steal any of it. Anyuta had a friend too, and she used to visit him and they'd have a drink and something to eat. This friend of hers has a decoration, he's lost an arm and he's in charge of the shop where you take your coupons to get clothes.'

'Stop talking nonsense and go to sleep,' said his mother. 'It'll soon be light.'

'Well, you two are stopping me sleeping . . . And it won't soon be light . . . This man with no arm made friends with Anyuta, life got better for them, but Khariton still lived at the war . . . Then Khariton comes back and starts cursing Anyuta. He curses her all day long and at night he has some vodka and something to eat, but Anyuta just cries and doesn't eat at all. He curses and curses, till he's tired out, then he stops tormenting Anyuta and says, "You fool of a woman, having only one man – and a man with only one arm at that! When I was away on my own I had Glashka and I had Aproska, and then there was Maruska and Anyushka your namesake, and then I had Magdalinka into the bargain!" And he laughs. And Anyuta laughs too. And she starts boasting about her Khariton: what a fine man he is, no better man anywhere, he killed Fascists and he had so many women after him he couldn't ward them off . . . Uncle Khariton tells us all this in the shop, he's taking in the loaves of bread one by one . . . And now they're quite peaceful, they have a good life . . . And Uncle Khariton laughs again and says, "But I deceived my Anyuta – I hadn't had anyone. No Glashka, no Nyushka, no Aproska, and no Magdalinka into the bargain. A soldier's the son of the Fatherland, he's got no time to fool around, his heart is levelled against the enemy. I just made all that up to give Anyuta a scare." Go to bed, father, put the light out – without the glass it just smokes!'

Ivanov listened in amazement to this story told by his son. 'What a devil!' he said to himself. 'I kept thinking he'd start talking about my Masha.'

Petya was exhausted and he began snoring; this time he really was asleep.

When he woke up it was broad daylight, and he was frightened to find he had slept so long and not yet done anything in the house.

No one was at home except Nastya. She was sitting on the floor turning the pages of a picture book her mother had bought her a long time ago. She looked through this book every day, because she had no other books, and traced the words with her finger, as if she were reading.

'Why are you messing up your book already?' Petya said to his sister. 'Put it away. Where's mother? Has she gone to work?'

'Yes,' answered Nastya quietly, closing the book.

'And where's father got to?' Petya looked round the house, in the kitchen and in the living room. 'Has he taken his bag?'

'Yes, he has,' said Nastya.

'What did he say to you?'

'Nothing. He kissed my mouth and my eyes.'

'Did he?' said Petya, and began to think.

'Get up off the floor,' he ordered his sister. 'I'll give you a proper wash and get you dressed, we're going out.'

At that moment their father was sitting in the station. He had already drunk a large glass of vodka and had got himself a hot meal with his travel voucher. In the night he had made up his mind once and for all to take the train to the town where he had left Masha and to meet up with her there again, perhaps never to part from her. A pity he was so much older than this bathhouse-attendant's daughter whose hair smelt of the countryside. But you can never tell – there's no knowing the future. All the same Ivanov hoped Masha would be at least a little bit glad to see him again; that would be enough, it would mean he too had a new and close friend, one, moreover, who was beautiful and cheerful and kind. You never can tell!

Soon the train arrived, going in the direction Ivanov had come from only yesterday. He took his kitbag and went on to the platform. 'Masha isn't expecting me,' he thought. 'She told me I'd forget her, whatever I said, and that we'd never meet again; yet here I am, on my way to her for ever.'

He got into a carriage and stood at the end of it, so that when the train pulled out he could look for a last time at the little town where he had lived before the war and where his children had been born. He wanted to look one more time at the house he had left; it could be seen from the train – the street it stood on led to the level crossing, and the train had to go over the crossing.

The train started, and went slowly over the points and out into the empty autumn fields. Ivanov took hold of the handrail and looked out from the carriage at what had been his hometown – at the little houses, the bigger buildings, the sheds, the lookout tower of the fire-station . . . In the distance he recognized two tall chimneys: one was the soap factory, the other was the brick factory – Lyuba would be working there now at the press. Let her live her own life now, and he would live his. Maybe he could forgive her, but what difference would that make? His heart had hardened against her now and there was no forgiveness in it for a woman who had kissed another man and lived with him just so that the war, and separation from her husband, would not make her so lonely and miserable. And the fact that it was the hardness of her life, and the torment of need and yearning, that had driven Lyuba to her Semyon or her Yevsey was no excuse; it was simply proof of her feelings. All love comes from need and yearning; if human beings never felt need or yearning, they would never love.

Ivanov was about to enter a compartment, to lie down and sleep; he no longer wanted a last look at the house where he had lived and where his children still did live: why torment oneself to no purpose? He looked out to see how far it was to the crossing – and there it was in front of him. It was here the railway crossed the track that led into the town; on this track lay wisps of straw and hay that had fallen off carts, and willow twigs and horse dung. There was rarely anyone on the track, except on the two market days of the week; just occasionally there would be a peasant on his way to the town with a full cart of hay, or on the way back to his village. That was how it was now: the track was deserted. All he could see, in the distance, running down the street that led into the track, were two children. One of them was bigger and one smaller, and the big one had taken the smaller one by the hand and was hurrying it along, but the small one, no matter how fast it tried to move its little legs, could not keep up with the bigger one. Then the bigger one began to drag the smaller one. They stopped at the last house of the town and looked towards the station, evidently wondering whether or not to go that way. Then they looked at the passenger train going over the crossing and began to run down the cart track, straight towards the train, as if suddenly wanting to reach it before it passed by.

Ivanov's carriage had passed the crossing. Ivanov picked up his bag, meaning to go through into the carriage and lie down for a sleep on the upper bunk where other passengers would not disturb him. But what about those two children? Had they managed to reach the train before the last carriage went by? Ivanov leaned out and looked back.

The two children, hand in hand, were still running along the track towards the crossing. They both fell down together, got up and ran on. The bigger one raised his one free hand and, turning his face towards Ivanov as the train passed by, began to beckon to someone, as if calling them to come back to him. Then they both fell down again. Ivanov could see that the bigger child had a felt boot on one foot and a rubber galosh on the other, which was why he kept falling.

Ivanov closed his eyes, not wanting to see and feel the pain of the exhausted children now lying on the ground, and then felt a kind of heat in his chest, as if the heart imprisoned and pining within him had been beating long and in vain all his life and had only now beaten its way to freedom, filling his entire being with warmth and awe. He suddenly recognized everything he had ever known before, but much more precisely and more truthfully. Previously, he had sensed the life of others through a barrier of pride and self-interest, but now, all of a sudden, he had touched another life with his naked heart.

Once more, from the carriage steps, he looked down the train towards the distant children. He knew now that they were his own children, Petya and Nastya. They must have seen him when the train was going over the crossing, and Petya had beckoned him home to their mother, but he had paid no attention, he had been thinking of something else and had not recognized his own children.

Now Petya and Nastya were a long way behind, running along the sandy path beside the rails; Petya was still holding little Nastya by the hand and dragging her along behind him when she was unable to move her legs quickly enough.

Ivanov threw his kitbag out of the carriage onto the ground, and then climbed down to the bottom step and got off the train, onto the sandy path along which his children were running after him.

First published in 1946

Translated by Robert and Elizabeth Chandler and Angela Livingstone

DANIIL IVANOVICH KHARMS
(1905–42)

Kharms was born in St Petersburg; his real name was Yuvachov. His father, a member of the terrorist organization 'The People's Will', had been arrested as a young man; after four years in solitary confinement and eight years of penal servitude on Sakhalin Island, he returned to St Petersburg in 1895 and remained a devout member of the Orthodox Church for the rest of his life. His son seems to have inherited something of both his courage and his spiritual concerns.

In his early twenties Kharms enrolled at a technical college but failed to graduate; later he enrolled on a film course, which he also failed to complete. Around 1927–8 Kharms helped to found the modernist OBERIU (Association for Real Art), one of the last independent Soviet artistic groupings; the poet Nikolay Zabolotsky was also a member. The pseudonym 'Kharms' may be derived from the English 'harm', 'charm' or even 'Holmes' (Sherlock Holmes has always been popular in Russia). During the 1930s, after official criticism of the OBERIU, Kharms earned his living by writing for children, publishing twelve books of stories between 1928 and 1940.

'The Old Woman' is by far the longest of his stories for adults, many of which are no more than ten lines. His short pieces include thirty numbered texts that constitute the cycle known as 'Incidents' or 'Happenings'. He also wrote plays, the most important of which is Yelizaveta Bam, *and poetry. Most of his adult work was published only after his death, although in 1937 he published a children's poem that included the lines:*

> *With a knapsack and a cudgel a man set off from home;*
> *He walked along, he walked along, so keen was he to roam . . .*
> *And then one dawn, one bright clear dawn, he went into a wood;*
> *He never has been seen again – just why's not understood.*

After this poem, which it is now difficult not to read as an evocation of one of the countless arbitrary arrests of the time, Kharms was unable to publish anything for a year. Arrested in 1941, after the outbreak of war, he died in a Leningrad prison hospital. It was not until 1988 that his work was first published in book form in the Soviet Union.

With its emphasis on guilt, the absurd and the spectral, 'The Old Woman', like 'The Queen of Spades', 'The Greatcoat' and much of Dostoyevsky, is very much a St Petersburg story. Kharms invokes Pushkin's Countess in the opening lines: the time given by the old woman, 'a quarter to three', is the time the dead Countess appeared to Hermann. The story is in fact so dense with literary reminiscence that it begins to seem as if the narrator either does not have a story of his own or else is being prevented by some external force from telling it. This is part of what makes 'The Old Woman' so powerful an evocation of alienation.

THE OLD WOMAN

And between them takes place the following conversation.
Hamsun[1]

Out in the yard stands an old woman, holding a wall clock in her hands. I walk past the old woman, stop and ask her, 'What time is it?'

'Look for yourself,' the old woman says to me.

I look, and I see the clock has no hands.

'There are no hands,' I say.

The old woman looks at the clock face and says to me, 'It's a quarter to three.'

'Ah, I see. Thank you very much,' I say, and walk away.

The old woman shouts something after me, but I carry on without looking round. I go out onto the street and walk on the sunny side. The spring sun is very pleasant. I walk, screw up my eyes and smoke my pipe. At the corner of Sadovaya Strect, I run into Sakerdon Mikhailovich. We say hello, stop and talk to one another for a long time. I get fed up with standing on the street and I invite Sakerdon Mikhailovich to a cellar bar. We drink vodka, eat hard-boiled eggs and sprats; then we say goodbye, and I walk on alone.

Suddenly I remember I've forgotten to turn off the electric stove at home. I feel very annoyed. I turn round and start to walk home. The day had got off to such a good start, and now something's already gone wrong. I shouldn't have gone outside.

I get back home and take off my jacket; I take my watch out of my waistcoat pocket and hang it on a nail; then I lock the door and lie down on the sofa. I'll lie there and try to get some sleep.

Out on the street, boys are shouting, making a horrible din. I lie there and think up ways of putting them to death. The one I like best would be to infect them with tetanus so they suddenly stop moving. Then their parents drag them back home. They lie in their little beds and can't even eat, because their mouths won't open. They're fed artificially. After a week the tetanus wears off, but the children are so weak they have to lie another whole month in bed. Then they slowly begin to get better, but I give them tetanus a second time and they all croak.

I lie on the sofa with my eyes open and can't get to sleep. I remember the old woman with the clock, the one I saw in the yard today, and I feel pleased there were no hands on her clock. Only the other day I saw a revolting kitchen clock in a used-goods store; its hands had been made to look like a knife and fork.

My God! I still haven't turned off the electric stove. I jump up and switch it off, then I lie down again on the sofa and try to fall asleep. I close my eyes. I don't feel sleepy. Spring sun shines in through the window, straight onto me. I start to get hot. I get up and sit in the armchair by the window.

Now I do feel like sleeping, but I'm not going to let myself. I'll take pen and paper and I'll write. Inside me I feel a terrible strength. Yesterday I thought through everything. It'll be the story of a miracle worker who lives in our time and doesn't work miracles. He knows that he is a miracle worker and can work any miracle he likes, but he does nothing. He's thrown out of his apartment. He knows he need only lift a finger and he could keep his apartment, but he does nothing; he moves out submissively and lives outside the town in a shed. He could turn this shed into a fine brick house, but he doesn't; he goes on living in the shed and in the end he dies, not having worked a single miracle in his entire life.

I sit and rub my hands with glee. Sakerdon Mikhailovich will burst with envy. He doesn't think I can write a work of genius any more. Quick, quick, to work! Down with dreams and indolence! I shall write for eighteen hours on end!

I tremble all over with impatience. I can't work out what to do: I needed to take pen and paper, but I grabbed all kinds of other things, not the ones I needed at all. I ran about the room: from window to table, from table to stove, then to the sofa and back again to the window. I choked from the flame that burned in my breast. It's only five o'clock now. A whole day lies ahead, and the evening, and a whole night.

I stand in the middle of the room. What am I thinking about? After all, it's already twenty past five. I must write. I move the table towards the window and sit down at it. In front of me there's a sheet of squared paper, in my hand – a pen.

My heart is still beating too fast, and my hand trembles. I wait, so as to calm down a little. I put the pen down and fill my pipe. The sun shines straight at me; I screw up my eyes and light my pipe.

Now a crow flies past the window. I look out and see a man with an artificial leg walking along the pavement. He makes a loud knocking noise with his leg and his stick.

'So,' I say to myself, and keep on looking out of the window.

The sun hides behind the chimney of the building opposite. The chimney's shadow runs along the roof, flies across the street and falls on my face. I must make use of the shadow and write a few words about the miracle worker. I seize the pen and write:

'The miracle worker was tall.'

That's all I can write. I sit till I begin to feel hungry. Then I get up and go over to the cupboard where I keep food. I rummage about but find nothing. A lump of sugar and that's all.

Someone knocks at the door.

'Who's there?'

No one answers. I open the door and see before me the old woman who in the morning had been standing out in the yard with the clock. I'm very surprised and I can't say anything.

'Here I am,' says the old woman, and comes into my room.

I stand by the door and don't know what to do: should I throw the old woman out or, on the contrary, should I ask her to sit down? But the old woman goes to my armchair by the window and sits down in it anyway.

'Close the door and lock it,' the old woman says to me.

I close and lock the door.

'Kneel down,' says the old woman.

And I get down on my knees.

But then I begin to see the full absurdity of my position. Why am I kneeling in front of some old woman? What indeed is this woman doing in my room, sitting in my favourite armchair? Why haven't I thrown this old woman out?

'Now listen,' I say. 'What right have you got to make yourself at home in my room and boss me about? I really don't want to be kneeling.'

'Quite right!' says the old woman. 'You must lie on your stomach now and bury your face in the floor.'

I at once obey her command.

Before me I see precisely traced squares. Pain in my shoulder and right hip makes me change position. I have been lying face down; now, with great difficulty, I get up onto my knees. All my limbs have gone numb and will hardly bend. I look round and see myself in my own room, on my knees in the middle of the floor. Consciousness and memory slowly return to me. I look round the room once more and see that someone appears to be sitting in the armchair by the window. It's not all that light in the room: it must be night now, white night. I look hard. Good Lord! Is that old woman really still sitting in my armchair? I crane my neck and look. Yes, of course it's the old woman. Her head has drooped onto her chest; she must have fallen asleep.

I get up and hobble over to her. The old woman's head has drooped onto her chest; her arms hang down over the sides of the chair. I feel like grabbing this woman and shoving her out of the door.

'Listen,' I say. 'You're in my room. I need to work. Please leave.'

The old woman doesn't move. I bend down and look into the old woman's face. Her mouth is half open; her false teeth have come loose and they're sticking out of her mouth. And suddenly I understand: the old woman has died.

I'm seized by a terrible feeling of irritation. Why did she die in my room? I can't bear dead people. And now what? I'll have to sort out this carrion, I'll have to go and talk with the caretaker and the house manager, I'll have to explain what the old woman was doing in my room. I looked with hatred at the old woman. But maybe she isn't dead? I feel her forehead. Her forehead's cold. So is her hand. What should I do?

I light my pipe and sit on the sofa. A mindless rage wells up in me.

'What a bitch!' I say out loud.

Like a sack, the dead old woman sits there in my chair. Her teeth are sticking out of her mouth. She's like a dead horse.

'What a horrible sight,' I say, but I can't cover the old woman with a newspaper, because anything can happen under cover of a newspaper.

I can hear movement the other side of the wall: my neighbour's getting up, he's an engine driver. All I need now is for him to sniff out that I've got a dead old woman sitting in my room. I listen to my neighbour's footsteps. Why is he being so slow? It's half past five now! He should have left long ago. My God! He's making himself a cup of tea. Through the wall I can hear the noise of the primus. Oh, if only this damned engine driver would hurry up and go.

I get on the sofa and put my legs up. Eight minutes pass, but my neighbour's tea still isn't ready and I can still hear the primus. I close my eyes and doze off.

I dream that my neighbour goes out and that I go out onto the staircase with him and slam the door behind me. It's a spring lock, I don't have the key on me, and I can't get back into the apartment. I'll have to ring and wake the other tenants, and that's not good at all. I'm standing on the landing, wondering what to do, and suddenly I see I don't have any hands. I tilt my head so I can see more clearly if I have any hands: to one side I can see a knife sticking out where there should be a hand, to the other – a fork.

'Look,' I say to Sakerdon Mikhailovich, who for some reason is sitting there on a folding chair. 'Look,' I say to him, 'at what's happened to my hands.'

Sakerdon Mikhailovich sits there in silence, and I see it's not the real Sakerdon Mikhailovich but one made out of clay.

Then I wake up and I understand at once that I'm lying in my room on a sofa and that a dead old woman is sitting in an armchair by the window.

I quickly turn my head towards her. There isn't any old woman in the chair. I look at the empty armchair and I'm filled with a wild joy. It must have all been a dream. Only where did the dream start? Did the old woman come into my room yesterday? Maybe that was a dream too. I came back home yesterday because I'd forgotten to switch off the electric stove. But maybe even that was a dream. Anyway, it's a good thing I don't have a dead old woman in my room and that I don't have to go to the house manager and sort out the corpse.

Still, how long have I been asleep for? I looked at my watch: half past nine, in the morning, no doubt.

Lord! The things one dreams in a dream!

I put my feet on the ground, I was about to get up and suddenly I saw the dead old woman, lying on the floor behind the table, next to the armchair. She was lying face up. The old woman's false teeth had jumped right out of her mouth and one tooth had sunk into one of her nostrils. Her arms were bent back under her torso and couldn't be seen; bony legs in dirty white woollen stockings poked out from beneath her skirt, which had ridden up.

'Bitch!' I shouted. I ran over to the old woman and kicked her in the chin.

Her false teeth flew off into the corner. I wanted to kick the old woman again, but I was worried marks might be left on her body, and then, of course, they would end up deciding that it was me who had killed her.

I moved away from the old woman, sat down on the sofa and lit my pipe. Twenty minutes went by. I realized there was going to be a criminal investigation anyway, and that in all the confusion I was sure to be found guilty of murder. Things were getting serious – and, to make matters worse, I'd gone and kicked her.

I went over to the old woman again, bent down and examined her face. There was a small dark bruise on her chin. No, nothing much could be made of that. It could have been anything. Maybe the old woman had bumped into something while she was still alive? I calm down a little and begin walking up and down the room, smoking my pipe and considering my position.

I walk up and down the room and begin to feel more and more hungry. I even start shaking from hunger. Once more I rummage about in my food cupboard, but all I can find is a lump of sugar.

I take out my wallet and count my money. Eleven roubles. So I can buy myself some pork sausage and bread and still have something left for tobacco.

I straighten my tie, which has got twisted during the night, take my watch, put on my jacket, go out into the corridor, carefully lock the door of my room, put the key in my pocket and go out onto the street. First of all I must eat something, then my thoughts will be clearer and I'll know what to do with this carrion.

On the way to the shop I have a thought: maybe I should go and see Sakerdon Mikhailovich and tell him everything? With two of us it might be easier to decide what to do. But I put this thought out of my head at once, because there are some things you have to do on your own, without witnesses.

There was no pork sausage in the shop; I bought myself half a kilo of saveloys. They were out of tobacco too. From the shop I went to the bakery.

There were a lot of people in the bakery, and a long queue waiting at the till. This made me cross, but I joined the queue all the same. The queue moved very slowly and then came to a complete stop, because there was some kind of rumpus going on by the till.

I pretended not to notice anything and just looked at the back of the pretty young lady standing in the queue in front of me. This young lady was obviously very inquisitive: she craned her neck first to the right, then to the left, and she kept standing up on tiptoe so as to get a better view of what was going on by the till. In the end she turned to me and asked, 'You don't know what's going on, do you?'

'I'm afraid I don't,' I answered, as coolly as I could.

The young lady looked one way, looked the other way and finally addressed me again, 'You couldn't go and find out what's happening up there, could you?'

'I'm afraid I'm not in the least interested,' I said still more coolly.

'What do you mean, not interested?' the young lady exclaimed. 'You're being held up in the queue too.'

I said nothing and just gave a slight bow. The young lady looked at me intently.

'Queuing for bread, of course, isn't really a man's job,' she said. 'I'm sorry you have to stand here. You must be a bachelor.'

'Yes, I am,' I replied, somewhat taken aback but continuing, out of habit, to answer rather coolly, giving slight bows at the same time.

The young lady looked me up and down once more, from head to toe, and then suddenly, touching me lightly on the sleeve, said, 'Why not let me buy whatever you want – and you can wait for me outside?'

I was quite taken aback.

'Thank you,' I said. 'That's very kind of you, but really, I can do it myself.'

'No, no,' said the young lady. 'You go outside. What were you going to buy?'

'Well then,' I said, 'I was going to buy half a kilo of black bread, only make sure it's a tin loaf, the cheap kind. It's my favourite.'

'All right then,' said the young lady. 'Off you go then. I'll buy it, and then we can settle up.'

And she even gave me a slight nudge on the elbow.

I went outside and stood by the door. The spring sun is shining straight in my face. I light a pipe. What a sweet young lady! So very unusual nowadays. I stand there, screwing up my eyes because of the sun, smoking my pipe and thinking about the sweet young lady. She even has light brown eyes. She's so pretty it makes my day.

'You smoke a pipe, do you?' I hear a voice beside me. The sweet young lady hands me the bread.

'Oh, I shall be forever grateful to you,' I say, taking the bread.

'And you smoke a pipe! That's something I really love,' says the sweet young lady.

And between us takes place the following conversation:

HER: So, you buy your own bread?
ME: I buy everything myself – not bread alone.
HER: And where do you have lunch?
ME: Usually I cook my own lunch. Sometimes I eat in the beer hall.
HER: Do you like beer?

ME: No, I prefer vodka.

HER: I like vodka too.

ME: You like vodka? That's splendid. I'd like to have a drink with you
some time.

HER: And I should like to drink some vodka with you.

ME: Forgive me, but may I ask you one thing?

HER (*blushing furiously*): Of course. Ask away.

ME: Very well, I will. Do you believe in God?

HER (*surprised*): In God? Yes, of course I do.

ME: And what would you say to us buying some vodka now and going
back to my place? I live very close.

HER (*eagerly*): Why not? That's fine by me.

ME: Let's go then.

We go to a shop and I buy half a litre of vodka. After that I've got
no more money left, only a little change. We keep talking about one
thing and another and suddenly I remember that in my room, lying
on the floor, is a dead old woman.

I look round at my new acquaintance; she's standing by the counter
and looking at jars of jam. I cautiously make my way to the door and
leave the shop. A tram is stopping just opposite the shop. I jump on
the tram, not even looking to see what number it is. I get off at
Mikhailovskaya Street and walk to Sakerdon Mikhailovich's. I'm
carrying a bottle of vodka, the saveloys and the bread.

Sakerdon Mikhailovich opened the door to me himself. He was
wearing a dressing gown with nothing on underneath, a pair of Russian boots with the tops cut off, and a fur hat with earflaps, but the
earflaps were turned up and the strings tied together in a bow.

'Glad to see you,' said Sakerdon Mikhailovich.

'I'm not interrupting your work?' I asked.

'No, no,' said Sakerdon Mikhailovich. 'I wasn't doing anything,
I was just sitting on the floor.'

'Look,' I said to Sakerdon Mikhailovich. 'I've brought some vodka
and a bite to eat. Unless you've got anything against the idea, let's
have a drink.'

'Fine,' said Sakerdon Mikhailovich. 'Come on in.'

We went through to his room. I opened the bottle of vodka and
Sakerdon Mikhailovich put two glasses and a plate of boiled meat on
the table.

'I've got some saveloys here,' I said. 'How shall we eat them – raw
or boiled?'

'Let's put them on to boil,' said Sakerdon Mikhailovich. 'And while they're cooking, we can have some vodka with the boiled meat. It's the very best kind of boiled meat – from soup.'

Sakerdon Mikhailovich put a pan on the kerosene stove and we sat down to the vodka.

'Vodka's good for you,' said Sakerdon Mikhailovich, filling the glasses. 'Mechnikov wrote that vodka's better for you than bread, because bread's just straw that rots in our stomachs.'

'Your good health!' I said, clinking glasses with Sakerdon Mikhailovich.

We drank, and we each ate a little cold meat.

'Tastes good,' said Sakerdon Mikhailovich. But just then there was a sharp crack from somewhere in the room.

'What's that?' I asked.

We sat in silence and listened. Suddenly there was another crack. Sakerdon Mikhailovich jumped up from the table, ran up to the window and tore down the curtain.

'What are you doing?' I shouted.

But Sakerdon Mikhailovich, without a word, rushed over to the stove, used the curtain to pick up the pan, and put the pan down on the floor.

'Oh hell!' said Sakerdon Mikhailovich. 'I forgot to put any water in the pan, and it's an enamelled pan, and now all the enamel's come off.'

'I see,' I said, and nodded.

We sat down at the table again.

'Oh, to hell with it,' said Sakerdon Mikhailovich. 'We'll eat them raw.'

'I'm terribly hungry,' I said.

'Help yourself,' said Sakerdon Mikhailovich, pushing the saveloys towards me.

'The last time I ate was yesterday, when we were in the cellar bar together. Since then I haven't eaten a thing,' I said.

'Yes, yes, yes,' said Sakerdon Mikhailovich.

'I've been writing all the time,' I said.

'Bloody hell!' Sakerdon Mikhailovich shouted out in an exaggerated tone. 'To be in the presence of a genius is quite something.'

'I'm sure it is!' I said.

'Been churning it out, have you?' said Sakerdon Mikhailovich.

'Yes,' I said. 'I've got through piles of paper.'

'To the genius of our day,' said Sakerdon Mikhailovich, and we lifted our glasses.

We drank. Sakerdon Mikhailovich ate the boiled meat, I ate the saveloys. After eating four saveloys, I lit my pipe and said, 'You know, I came to you to escape persecution.'

'Who's been persecuting you?' asked Sakerdon Mikhailovich.

'A lady,' I said. But Sakerdon Mikhailovich didn't ask me anything; he just silently filled our glasses with vodka. So I went on, 'We met in the bakery and I fell in love with her at once.'

'Is she pretty?' asked Sakerdon Mikhailovich.

'Yes,' I said, 'just my type.'

We drank, and I went on, 'She agreed to come and have some vodka in my room. We went to a shop together, but then I had to sneak out of the shop on my own.'

'Not enough money?' asked Sakerdon Mikhailovich.

'No, I had just enough,' I said, 'but I suddenly remembered I couldn't let her into my room.'

'Why, was there another lady in your room?' asked Sakerdon Mikhailovich.

'Yes, it could be said there's another lady in my room,' I said with a smile. 'I can't let anyone into my room at present.'

'Get married. You can invite me to the meal,' said Sakerdon Mikhailovich.

'No,' I said, snorting with laughter. 'I shan't be marrying *that* lady.'

'All right then, marry the one from the bakery,' said Sakerdon Mikhailovich.

'Why are you so keen to see me married?' I asked.

'Why not?' said Sakerdon Mikhailovich, filling up our glasses. 'To your conquests!'

We drank. The vodka was clearly starting to have its effect. Sakerdon Mikhailovich took off his fur hat with earflaps and flung it on the bed. I got up and began to pace about the room, already experiencing a certain giddiness.

'What are your feelings about the dead?' I asked Sakerdon Mikhailovich.

'Entirely negative,' said Sakerdon Mikhailovich. 'I'm afraid of them.'

'Yes, I can't stand the dead either,' I said. 'If a dead person came my way, unless he were a relative of mine, I'd probably boot him one.'

'One shouldn't kick corpses,' said Sakerdon Mikhailovich.

'I'd boot him in the mug myself,' I said. 'I really can't stand children or the dead.'

'Yes, children are vile,' said Sakerdon Mikhailovich.

'But which do you think are worse, children or the dead?' I asked.

'Children are probably worse. They get in our way more often. At least the dead don't burst into our lives,' said Sakerdon Mikhailovich.

'But they do!' I shouted, and at once fell silent.

Sakerdon Mikhailovich looked at me intently.

'Do you want more vodka?' he asked.

'No,' I said. Getting a grip on myself, I added, 'No, thank you, I don't want any more.'

I went and sat down again at the table. For some time we say nothing.

'I want to ask you,' I say in the end. 'Do you believe in God?'

A horizontal wrinkle appears on Sakerdon Mikhailovich's forehead and he says, 'Some things just aren't done. It's not done to ask a man to lend you fifty roubles if you've just seen him put two hundred in his pocket. Whether to give you the money or not is up to him; and the most pleasant and convenient way for him to refuse is to lie, to say he doesn't have the money. But you have just seen that the man does have the money and you have therefore made it impossible for him to refuse simply and pleasantly. You have deprived him of the right of choice – and that's mean. It's a rude and tactless way to behave. And to ask someone "Do you believe in God?" is also a rude and tactless way to behave.'

'No,' I said, 'the two things are quite different.'

'And I'm not comparing them,' said Sakerdon Mikhailovich.

'Well then,' I said, 'let's leave it at that. Only forgive me for asking such a rude and tactless question.'

'By all means,' said Sakerdon Mikhailovich. 'After all, I refused to answer you.'

'I wouldn't have answered either,' I said. 'Only for a different reason.'

'And what would that be?' Sakerdon Mikhailovich asked languidly.

'The way I see it,' I said, 'I don't think there are people who believe or who don't believe. There are only those who want to believe and those who want not to believe.'

'So, those who want not to believe must already believe in something?' said Sakerdon Mikhailovich. 'While those who want to believe are people who don't believe in anything at all?'

'You may be right,' I said. 'I don't know.'

'And in what do they believe or not believe? In God?' asked Sakerdon Mikhailovich.

'No,' I said. 'In immortality.'

'Then why did you ask me if I believe in God?'

'Somehow it just seems a bit silly to ask "Do you believe in immortality?"' I said to Sakerdon Mikhailovich. I got to my feet.

'What, are you leaving?' Sakerdon Mikhailovich asked me.

'Yes,' I said, 'it's time I went.'

'What about the vodka?' said Sakerdon Mikhailovich. 'There's only a little left – a glass each.'

'Let's finish it, then,' I said.

We finished up the vodka and ate the remains of the boiled meat.

'It's time I left,' I said.

'Goodbye,' said Sakerdon Mikhailovich, escorting me through the kitchen and out onto the stairs. 'And thanks for bringing something with you.'

'Thank you,' I said. 'Goodbye.'

And I left.

On his own now, Sakerdon Mikhailovich cleared the table, tossed the empty vodka bottle on top of the cupboard, put his fur hat with earflaps back on his head and sat on the floor beneath the window. Sakerdon Mikhailovich's hands were behind his back and could not be seen. His bare legs, in Russian boots with the tops cut off, poked out from beneath his dressing gown, which had ridden up.

I was walking down Nevsky Prospekt, deep in my own thoughts. I must go and see the house manager now and tell him everything. And once I've dealt with the old woman, I'll stand outside the bakery for days on end, until I meet that sweet young lady. After all, I owe her forty-eight kopeks for the bread. I have the perfect excuse to search for her. The vodka I had drunk was still having an effect, and everything seemed to be going well and straightforwardly.

On the Fontanka I stopped at a stall and, with my remaining change, I bought a large mug of kvass.[2] The kvass was sour and I went on my way with a foul taste in my mouth.

On the corner of Liteinaya some drunk staggered into me. It's a good thing I don't have a revolver; I'd have killed him there and then.

I must have walked all the way home with my face twisted with rage. In any event, almost everyone I met turned round to look at me.

I went into the house manager's office. A short, dirty, snub-nosed, one-eyed and straw-haired girl was sitting on the table; looking into a pocket mirror, she was daubing on her lipstick.

'Where's the house manager?' I asked.

The girl said nothing, continuing to daub on her lipstick.

'Where's the house manager?' I repeated sharply.

'He's coming tomorrow, not today,' answered the dirty, snub-nosed, one-eyed and straw-haired girl.

I went back out onto the street. The cripple with the artificial leg was walking along the other side; his leg and stick were knocking loudly. Six boys were walking behind the cripple, making fun of his gait.

I went in through the street door and began climbing the stairs. I stopped on the first floor. A horrible thought had entered my head: the old woman must have begun to decompose. I hadn't shut the windows and people say that the dead decompose quicker if a window is left open. How utterly stupid of me! And that damned house manager won't be here till tomorrow! I stood there for a few minutes irresolutely and then went on up the stairs.

I stopped again by the door to my apartment. Perhaps I should go to the bakery and wait there for the sweet young lady? I could beg her to let me stay two or three nights with her. But then I remember she has already bought some bread today, which means she won't be going to the bakery. And going there would have been a waste of time anyway.

I unlocked the door and went into the corridor. There was a light on at the end of the corridor and Marya Vasilyevna, holding some kind of rag in her hand, was rubbing it with another rag. Seeing me, Marya Vasilyevna shouted out, 'Shome old man came ashking for you!'

'What old man?' I said.

'Dunno,' answered Marya Vasilyevna.

'When was it?' I asked.

'Dunno that neither,' said Marya Vasilyevna.

'Was it you who talked to the old man?' I asked Marya Vasilyevna.

'Yesh,' answered Marya Vasilyevna.

'Then how come you don't know when it was?' I said.

'It were two hourzh ago,' said Marya Vasilyevna.

'And what did this old man look like?' I asked.

'Dunno that neither,' said Marya Vasilyevna, and went off into the kitchen.

I went to my room.

'What if,' I thought, 'the old woman's vanished? What if I go into my room – and there's no old woman there. Oh my God, surely miracles must happen sometimes?'

I unlocked the door and slowly started to open it. Maybe it was only my imagination, but I felt overcome at once by the sickly smell of decomposition in progress. I peered round the half-open door and, for a moment, was rooted to the spot. The old woman was on all fours, slowly crawling towards me.

I let out a yell, slammed the door, turned the key and jumped across to the opposite wall.

Marya Vasilyevna appeared in the corridor.

'Were you calling me?' she asked.

I was so upset that I couldn't answer and could only reply with a shake of the head. Marya Vasilyevna came up closer.

'You were talking to shomebody,' she said.

I gave another shake of the head.

'Inshane,' said Marya Vasilyevna, and went back to the kitchen, glancing round at me several times on the way.

'Can't just stand here. Can't just stand here,' I kept repeating to myself. This sentence had taken shape of its own accord somewhere within me. I said it over and over again until it reached my consciousness.

'Can't just stand here,' I said to myself, but I went on standing there as if paralysed. What had happened was terrible, but what had to be done was perhaps still more terrible than what had taken place already. My thoughts were in a whirl, and all I could see was the malicious eyes of the dead old woman as she crawled towards me.

Burst into the room and smash this old woman's skull in. That's what needs to be done! I even looked around and was happy to see a croquet mallet which, for some unknown reason, had been standing in the corner of the corridor for many years. Grab the mallet,[3] burst into the room and – thwack!

I was still trembling. I was standing with my shoulders hunched from the cold deep inside me. My thoughts jumped around, got in a tangle, returned to their point of departure and jumped around again, taking over new areas, while I stood and listened to these thoughts and it was as if I were removed from them and somehow not in command of them.

'The departed,' my thoughts explained to me, 'are a troublesome lot. It's not true to say they've gone to their rest – the dear departed give us no rest at all. They need to be watched all the time. Ask any mortuary attendant. Why, do you imagine, has he been put there? For one reason only: to stop the departed crawling all over the place. There have, while we're on this subject, been some amusing incidents. I've heard of a departed who, while the attendant, on orders from his superiors, was washing himself in the bathhouse, crawled out of the mortuary and into the disinfection room and ate up a pile of bed linen. The disinfection team gave him a good thrashing, but they had to pay for the spoiled linen out of their own pockets. Another of the departed got into the maternity ward and gave the expectant mothers such a fright that one of them had a miscarriage there and then, and the departed pounced on the aborted foetus and gobbled it up. And when a brave nurse hit the departed on the back with a stool, he bit this nurse in the leg and she died soon afterwards of infection by corpse poison. Yes, the dead are a troublesome lot, and you need to be on your guard with them.'

'Stop!' I said to my thoughts. 'You're blathering. The dead are immobile.'

'All right,' my thoughts said to me. 'Go into your room. In it you'll find one of your immobile departed.'

An unexpected stubbornness spoke up inside me.

'Yes, I will go into my room,' I said decisively to my thoughts.

'Just you try!' my thoughts said to me mockingly.

This mockery utterly enraged me. I grabbed the croquet mallet and rushed towards the door.

'Wait!' my thoughts yelled at me. But I had already turned the key and flung open the door.

The old woman was lying by the threshold, her face buried in the floor.

Croquet mallet raised, I stood at the ready. The old woman wasn't moving.

My trembling had stopped and my thoughts were flowing clearly and logically. I was in command of my thoughts.

'First, close the door!' I commanded myself.

I removed the key from the outside of the door and put it into the inside. I did this with my left hand, still holding the croquet mallet with my right hand and not once taking my eyes off the old woman. I turned the key in the lock and, stepping carefully over the old woman, reached the middle of the room.

'Now I'll get even with you,' I said. I had come up with a plan, the one usually adopted by murderers in crime novels and newspaper reports: I wanted simply to hide the old woman in a suitcase, take her outside the city and dump her in a bog. I knew one such place.

My suitcase was under the sofa. I dragged it out and opened it. In it were a few odds and ends: some books, an old felt hat and some torn underwear. I laid everything out on the sofa.

Just then the outside door slammed loudly, and it seemed that the old woman shuddered.

I jumped up at once and grabbed the croquet mallet.

The old woman is lying there peacefully. I stand up and listen. It's the engine driver, he's just come back, I can hear him walking about his room. Now he's walking down the corridor towards the kitchen. If Marya Vasilyevna tells him about my insanity, there'll be trouble. What a devilish nuisance! I must go along to the kitchen too and reassure them by appearing normal.

I stepped over the old woman again, placed the mallet just by the door so that, when I came back, I could pick the mallet up before I'd even entered the room, and went out into the corridor. I could hear voices in the kitchen but I couldn't make out the words. I closed the door to my room behind me and cautiously made my way to the kitchen: I wanted to know what Marya Vasilyevna and the engine driver were talking about. I walked quickly down the corridor, slowing down as I approached the kitchen. The engine driver was talking – evidently about something that had happened to him at work.

I went in. The engine driver was standing there with a towel in his hands and talking, while Marya Vasilyevna sat on a stool and listened. Seeing me, the engine driver waved his hand.

'Greetings, Matvey Filippovich, greetings!' I said to him, and went through to the bathroom. So far, everything was calm. Marya Vasilyevna was used to my strange ways and might even have forgotten the incident in the corridor.

Suddenly it dawned on me that I had not locked the door. What if the old woman crawls out of the room?

I spun round but remembered myself in time and, so as not to alarm the others, walked through the kitchen with calm steps.

Marya Vasilyevna was tapping on the kitchen table with one finger and saying to the engine driver, 'Shplendid! Shplendid! I'd have whishled too!'

My heart sinking, I went out into the corridor, then almost ran to my room.

From outside, everything seemed quiet. I went up to the door, half-opened it and looked inside. Just as before, the old woman was lying there calmly, her face buried in the floor. The croquet mallet was still standing there by the door. I seized the mallet, went into the room and locked the door behind me. Yes, the room definitely smelt of corpse. I stepped over the old woman, went up to the window and sat in the armchair. So long as I don't get ill from this smell that may only be faint but is none the less already unbearable. I lit my pipe. I felt a little nauseous and my stomach was slightly aching.

But what am I doing just sitting here? I must act quickly, before this old woman's gone completely rotten. But, whatever I do, I must be careful how I stuff her into the suitcase because that's just the moment she might take a bite out of my finger. And I don't want to die of infection by corpse poison – no, thank you!

'Hey!' I exclaimed suddenly, 'I'd like to know what you're going to bite me with. Where are those teeth of yours?'

I leaned over in the armchair and looked into the corner on the far side of the window where I reckoned the old woman's false teeth ought to be. But her false teeth weren't there.

I fell into thought: maybe the dead old woman had been crawling about my room in search of her teeth? Maybe she had even found them and stuck them back in her mouth?

I took the croquet mallet and poked about in the corner with it. No, the false teeth had disappeared. Then I took a thick flannelette sheet out of my chest of drawers and went over to the old woman. I held the croquet mallet in my right hand, at the ready, and in my left hand I held the flannelette sheet.

This dead old woman made me feel both fear and disgust. I raised her head with the mallet: her mouth was open, her eyes had rolled upwards and the whole of her chin, where I had kicked her, was covered by a large dark bruise. I looked into the old woman's mouth. No, she had not found her false teeth. I let her head go. Her head fell and knocked against the floor.

I spread the flannelette sheet out on the floor and pulled it right up to the old woman. With my foot and the croquet mallet, I turned the old woman first onto her left side, then onto her back. Now she was lying on the sheet. The old woman's legs were bent at the knees, and her fists pressed to her shoulders. Lying on her back like a cat, the old woman seemed to be preparing to defend herself against an eagle swooping down on her. Quick, away with this carrion!

I wrapped the old woman in the thick sheet and picked her up in my arms. She was lighter than I had expected. I lowered her into the suitcase and tried to close the lid. Here I expected all kinds of difficulties, but the lid closed relatively easily. I locked the suitcase and stood up again.

The suitcase is standing in front of me, looking perfectly respectable, as if it contains clothes and books. I took it by the handle and tried to lift it. Yes, it was, of course, heavy, but not excessively so. I could certainly carry it to the tram.

I looked at my watch: twenty past five. I sat in the armchair, to rest a little and smoke a pipe.

Evidently the saveloys I'd eaten that day had been a bit off; my stomach was aching more and more. Or maybe it was because I had eaten them raw? Or maybe my stomach-ache was purely from nerves?

I sit and smoke. And minute after minute goes by.

The spring sun shines in through the window, and I screw up my eyes against its rays. Then it hides behind the chimney of the building opposite, and the chimney's shadow runs along the roof, flies across the street and falls on my face. I remember how this time yesterday I was sitting and writing a story. Yes, here it is: squared paper and, in tiny writing, the words, 'The miracle worker was tall.'

I looked out of the window. The cripple with the artificial leg was walking along the other side; his leg and stick were knocking loudly. Two workers and an old woman were holding their sides and roaring with laughter at the cripple's ridiculous gait.

I got up. It's time! Time to be on my way! Time to take the old woman off to the bog! But I need to borrow some money from the engine driver.

I went out into the corridor and up to his door.

'Matvey Filippovich, are you there?' I asked.

'Yes,' answered the engine driver.

'Excuse me then, Matvey Filippovich, you don't happen to have any spare cash, do you? I get paid the day after tomorrow. You couldn't lend me thirty roubles, could you?'

'I could,' said the engine driver. And I heard him jangling keys, opening some box or other. Then he opened the door and handed me a new red thirty-rouble note.

'Thank you very much, Matvey Filippovich,' I said.

'It's nothing, don't mention it,' said the engine driver.

I put the money in my pocket and went back to my room. The suitcase was calmly standing in the same place.

'Off you go now, without delay,' I said to myself.

I picked up the suitcase and left the room.

Marya Vasilyevna saw me with the suitcase and called out, 'Where are you going?'

'To my aunt's,' I said.

'Are you coming back shoon?' asked Marya Vasilyevna.

'Yes,' I said. 'I just have to take some clothes over to my aunt. I might even be back tonight.'

I went out onto the street. I got to the tram without mishap, carrying the suitcase first in my right hand, then in my left.

I got in at the front of the rear car and beckoned to the conductress, so she'd come and take the money for my ticket and luggage. I didn't want my single thirty-rouble note to be passed from hand to hand all the way down the car, and I couldn't bring myself to leave the suitcase and go up to the conductress myself. The conductress came over to me and told me she had no change. I had to get off at the next stop.

I stood there in a rage, waiting for the next tram. My stomach was aching and my legs slightly trembling.

And suddenly I caught sight of my sweet young lady; she was crossing the street, not looking in my direction.

I grabbed the suitcase and rushed after her. I didn't know her name and couldn't call out to her. The suitcase was terribly in the way; I was holding it in front of me with both hands, and my knees and stomach were knocking against it. The sweet young lady was walking quite fast and I felt I'd never catch up with her. I was soaking with sweat and running out of strength. The sweet young lady turned into a side street. When I got to the corner, she was nowhere to be seen.

'Damn that old woman!' I hissed, throwing my suitcase down on the ground.

The sleeves of my jacket were soaking with sweat and sticking to my arms. I sat down on the suitcase and, taking out my handkerchief, wiped my neck and face with it. Two boys stopped in front of me and began staring at me. I put on a calm face and looked intently at the nearest gateway, as if I were waiting for someone. The boys were whispering together and pointing at me. I was choking with wild rage. If only I could infect them with tetanus!

And so, because of these obnoxious boys, I stand up, pick up the suitcase, walk with it to a gateway and glance inside. I look surprised, get out my watch and shrug my shoulders. The boys watch me from a distance. I shrug my shoulders once more and look inside the gateway.

'Strange,' I say out loud. I take the suitcase and carry it to the tram stop.

I get to the railway station at five to seven. I buy a return ticket to Lisy Nos and get into the train.

There are two other people in the carriage. One is evidently a worker; he is tired and has gone to sleep, his cap pulled over his eyes. The other, still quite young, looks like a village dandy; he is wearing a pink Russian shirt under his jacket and he has a curl of hair on his forehead, sticking out from beneath his cap. He is smoking a cigarette, in a bright green plastic holder.

I place the suitcase between the seats and sit down. My stomach cramps are so bad that I have to clench my fists not to groan with pain.

Some citizen or other is being led down the platform by two policemen to the police station. He walks with his hands behind his back and his head drooping.

The train moves off. I look at my watch: ten past seven.

Oh, what a pleasure it will be to dump this old woman in the bog! Only it's a pity I didn't bring my stick with me – the old woman's sure to need a bit of a push.

The dandy in the pink shirt is studying me insolently. I turn my back on him and look out of the window.

My stomach is racked by terrible spasms; I grit my teeth, clench my fists and tense my legs.

We pass through Lanskaya and Novaya Derevnya. I glimpse the golden top of the Buddhist pagoda, then the sea.

Then I jump up, forgetting everything around me. Taking very short steps, I hurry to the toilet. An insane wave is rocking and spinning my consciousness.

The train slows down. We're coming in to Lakhta. I sit there, afraid to move a muscle, scared I'll be thrown out of the toilet at the station.

If only the train would get going! If only the train would get going! The train gets going, and I close my eyes in delight. Oh, these moments can be as sweet as any moments of love. All my strength is summoned up, but I know this will be followed by a terrible collapse.

The train stops again. Olgino. The same torture again.

But now it's a matter of phantom urges. There's cold sweat on my forehead and a slight chill fluttering around my heart. I get up and stand for a while, my head pressed to the wall. The train travels on, and the swaying of the carriage feels very pleasant.

I gather all my strength and stagger out of the toilet.

The carriage is empty. The worker and the dandy in the pink shirt must have got out at Lakhta or Olgino. I walk slowly towards my little window.

And suddenly I stop and stare stupidly in front of me. The suitcase isn't where I left it. I must be by the wrong window. I leap to the next window. No suitcase. I leap back, I leap forward, I run up and down, I search each side of the carriage, I look under the seats, but there is no suitcase anywhere.

But how can there be any doubt about it? Of course, while I was in the toilet, my suitcase was stolen. Hardly surprising!

I sit there bug-eyed and for some reason I remember the cracking sound of the enamel coming off Sakerdon Mikhailovich's burning hot saucepan.

'So where's all this got me?' I ask myself. 'Now who's going to believe I didn't kill the old woman? I'll be arrested today, either right here or else back in the city, at the main railway station, like that citizen I saw walking along with his head drooping.'

I walk to the end of the carriage. The train's coming in to Lisy Nos. The white posts bordering the track flash by. The train stops. The steps on my carriage don't reach the ground. I jump down and walk towards the station building. It'll be half an hour till the next train back.

I go into a little wood. I see some juniper bushes. No one will see me behind them. I walk towards them.

A large green caterpillar is crawling along the ground. I kneel down and touch it with my fingers. Powerful and sinewy, it wriggles several times from side to side.

I look round. No one can see me. A slight shiver runs down my back. I bow down my head and say in a quiet voice, 'In the name of the Father and of the Son and of the Holy Ghost, now and for ever. Amen.'

....
.... Here I temporarily conclude my manuscript, considering it quite long-drawn-out enough as it is.

Written May–June 1939; first published in 1974
Translated by Robert Chandler

VARLAM TIKHONOVICH
SHALAMOV (1907–1982)

Born in Vologda, the son of a priest and a schoolteacher, Shalamov claims to have seen himself as a writer from childhood. He was inspired as a young man by Mayakovsky, whom he heard at a public recital. In 1929, while studying law at Moscow University, Shalamov was arrested and sentenced to three years in a camp in the Urals; he had been trying to distribute the suppressed letter that Lenin had written before his death, recommending that Stalin be removed from his post as General Secretary of the Party. In 1932 Shalamov returned to Moscow, where he worked as a journalist and published a number of short stories. In 1937 he was rearrested and sentenced to five years in Kolyma, the vast labour-camp empire in the north-east of Siberia. His sentence was extended in 1942, and in 1943 he was given an additional ten years for 'anti-Soviet agitation'; his crime was to have described the émigré Ivan Bunin as 'a Russian classic'. In 1953 Shalamov was allowed to leave Kolyma, and he returned to Moscow in 1956.

Solzhenitsyn wrote of Shalamov: 'His experience of the camps was longer and more bitter than mine, and I say with respect that it fell to him, not to me, to touch that bottom of brutalization and despair to which the whole of camp life dragged us.' Shalamov, however, rejected Solzhenitsyn's invitation to collaborate with him on The Gulag Archi-pelago. *In the early 1960s Shalamov was part of a circle that met at the home of Nadezhda Mandelstam, but with time he grew isolated and paranoid.* Kolyma Tales *was smuggled out to the West in the late 1960s, but it at first attracted little attention. Perhaps as a final gesture of despair, Shalamov compounded his troubles by offending against the dissidents' strict moral code; in 1972, under only slight pressure from the authorities, he signed a (somewhat ambiguous) denial of the truth of his own stories. In return, he was allowed to publish a small selection of his poetry. Denied the recognition enjoyed by others who had written about the Gulag, he spent his last years in poverty and obscurity. In 1979 he moved to an old people's home. He died in*

January 1982, shortly after being transferred, in bitter cold, to a psychiatric hospital.

A reader who knows only a few of the stories may well imagine the Kolyma Tales to be simply a factual account of Shalamov's experiences. The events described in each individual story seem entirely real. Only when we read further, when we try to grasp the whole of this epic cycle, do we begin to realize that its truth can never be grasped; we begin, at last, to sense the terrible unreality of the survivor's world. Successive narrators suffer identical fates, their stories intertwine impossibly, and time stands still. This fusion of realism and the surreal endows Kolyma Tales with extraordinary power.

Shalamov plays in several ways with a reader's initial assumption that he is reading a historical memoir: one example of his use of literary artifice is his choice of names for his characters. Several bear the names of Russian writers – Andreyev, Fadeyev, Platonov, Zamyatin – who were never themselves arrested or sent to the camps. In some cases the reason for the choice of name seems relatively simple; Fadeyev, the brutal guard in 'Berries', is clearly an image of the Fadeyev who was General Secretary of the Soviet Writers' Union from 1946 to 1953. Shalamov's reasons for naming the storyteller in 'The Snake Charmer' after Andrey Platonov are less obvious. It is possible that Shalamov is criticizing Platonov for attempting, during the second half of his career, to accommodate himself to the demands made of him by the authorities; just as Shalamov's fictional 'Platonov' tried to lie to himself about his reasons for telling stories to the criminals who held power in the camps, so the real Platonov may – Shalamov suggests – have deluded himself about his reasons for telling, or trying to tell, the stories demanded by the criminals who held power in the Soviet Union as a whole. In spite of this, Shalamov clearly felt respect – and more than respect – for Platonov; in the context of the loveless world of Kolyma tales, the repeated words 'I loved Platonov' are startling.[1]

Complete translations of the Kolyma Tales have appeared in many languages, but only a selection has been published in English. Shalamov ordered the cycle carefully; 'Through the Snow' is the opening story.

Robert Chandler and Nathan Wilkinson

THROUGH THE SNOW

How are roads beaten through virgin snow? A man walks in front, sweating and swearing, barely able to place one foot in front of the other, constantly getting stuck in the deep, powdery snow. He walks a long way, leaving behind him a trail of uneven black pits. He gets tired, he lies down on the snow, he lights a cigarette, and a blue cloud of makhorka[1] smoke spreads over the white shining snow. The man has already gone on further but the cloud still hangs where he rested – the air is almost motionless. Roads are always beaten on still days, so that human toil is not erased by the winds. The man chooses markers for himself in the snowy infinity: a cliff, a tall tree. He pilots his body through the snow, just as a helmsman steers a boat down a river, from headland to headland. Shoulder to shoulder, in a row, five or six men follow the man's narrow and uncertain track. They walk beside this track, not along it. When they reach a predetermined spot, they turn round and walk back in the same manner, tramping down virgin snow, a place where man's foot has never trodden. The road is opened. Along it can move people, strings of sleighs, tractors. If the others were to follow directly behind the first man, in his footsteps, they would create a narrow path, a trail that is visible but barely walkable, a string of holes more impassable than virgin snow. It's the first man who has the hardest task; when he runs out of strength, someone else from that vanguard of five goes out in front. Every one of them, even the smallest, even the weakest, must tread on a little virgin snow – not in someone else's footsteps. The people on the tractors and horses, however, will be not writers but readers.

Written in 1956; first published in 1978
Translated by Robert Chandler and Nathan Wilkinson

BERRIES

Fadeyev said: 'Hold on, I'll have a word with him myself.' He came up to me, then put the butt of his rifle beside my head.

I was lying in the snow, clutching the log I had let fall from my shoulder, unable to pick it up and regain my place in the line of men going down the mountain, each carrying on his shoulder 'a stick of firewood' – sometimes a big log, sometimes a smaller one. All of them – both guards and prisoners – were in a hurry to get back home, they all wanted to eat and sleep, they'd had more than enough of the endless winter day. And there I was – lying in the snow.

'Listen, old man,' said Fadeyev. He went on, addressing me, as he addressed all prisoners, with the polite, respectful word for 'you'. 'It really isn't possible that a giant like yourself should be unable to carry a log, or rather stick, as small as that. You're clearly a malingerer. You're a Fascist. While our Motherland battles the enemy, you jam sticks in the wheels.'

'I'm no Fascist,' I said. 'I'm a sick and hungry man. You're the Fascist. It says in the papers how Fascists kill old men. Think about what you're going to say to your fiancée – how will you tell her what you did in Kolyma?'

It was all the same to me. I couldn't bear the rosy-cheeked, the healthy, the well-fed, the well-clothed, and I wasn't afraid. I hunched up, protecting my stomach, but even this was just a primitive, instinctive movement – I wasn't in the least afraid of kicks to the stomach. Fadeyev booted me in the back. I felt a sudden warmth – no pain at all. If I died – so much the better.

'Listen,' said Fadeyev, when he'd turned me over, my face to the sky, with the toes of his boots. 'I've come across your sort before, yes, I've worked with people like you.'

Up walked another guard – Seroshapka.

'Let's have a look – so I can remember you. Nasty piece of work you are, ugly too. Tomorrow I'll shoot you myself. Understood?'

'Understood,' I said, picking myself up and spitting out salty, bloody spit.

I began to drag the log along the ground, to the sound of the whoops, yells and curses of my comrades – while I was being beaten up, they had been freezing.

The following morning Seroshapka took us out to work in forest that had been felled a year earlier: we were to gather up everything that could be burnt in the iron stoves that winter. Forests were always cut in winter – the stumps were tall. We levered them out, sawed them up and stacked them in piles.

Seroshapka marked off the forbidden zone, hanging tags – plaits of yellow and grey dry grass – on the few trees that remained around where we were working.

Our brigade-leader lit a fire for Seroshapka on a small hillock – only guards had the right to a fire while they worked – and brought him a supply of wood.

The snow on the ground had long ago been scattered by the winds. The chilled, frost-coated grass slipped through your fingers, changing colour when touched by a human hand. Slowly freezing on the hummocks were low bushes of mountain dog rose; the scent of their iced, dark-purple berries was extraordinary. Still tastier than the rosehips was the foxberry, nipped by the frost, overripe, dove-grey ... On stubby, straight little branches hung whortleberries – bright blue, wrinkled like empty leather purses, but still preserving within them a dark, bluey-black juice whose taste was ineffable.

Berries at this time of year, nipped by the frost, are quite unlike berries in their prime, the berries of the juicy season. Their taste is much subtler.

Rybakov, my comrade, was collecting berries in a tin can during our smoking breaks and even at moments when Seroshapka was looking the other way. If he picked a whole canful, the guards' detachment cook would give him some bread. Rybakov's enterprise had at once become a matter of major importance.

I had no such clients and I ate the berries myself, carefully and greedily pressing each berry against the roof of my mouth with my tongue – for a moment the sweet fragrant juice of the crushed berry was stupefying.

I didn't think of helping Rybakov, nor would he have wanted my help – then he would have had to share the bread.

Rybakov's little can was filling up too slowly, the berries were getting scarcer and scarcer, and, without noticing it, we had reached the boundaries of the zone – the tags were hanging right over our heads.

'Look!' I said to Rybakov. 'We'd better go back.'

But on the hummocks in front of us were rosehips, and whortleberries, and foxberries ... We'd seen these hummocks long ago. The tree with the tag on it should have been standing two yards further out.

Rybakov pointed at his can, which was still not full, and at the sun, now dipping towards the horizon, and slowly began to approach the enchanted berries.

There was the dry crack of a shot, and Rybakov fell face down among the hummocks. Brandishing his rifle, Seroshapka shouted out: 'Leave him where he is. Don't go near him!'

Seroshapka worked the bolt and shot again. We knew what this second shot meant. Seroshapka knew too. There must always be two shots – the first is a warning.

Lying there between the hummocks, Rybakov looked unexpectedly small. The sky, the mountains and the river were huge – God knows how many people these mountains could hold, laid out on the little paths between the hummocks.

Rybakov's little can had rolled a long way, I managed to pick it up and hide it in a pocket. Maybe I'd get some bread for these berries – I knew, after all, who Rybakov had been collecting them for.

Seroshapka calmly drew up our small detachment, counted us and gave the order to set off back home.

He tapped me on the shoulder with the tip of his rifle, and I turned round.

'It was you I wanted,' said Seroshapka. 'But you didn't cross the line, you bastard.'

Written in 1959; first published in 1973
Translated by Robert Chandler and Nathan Wilkinson

THE SNAKE CHARMER

We were sitting on an enormous larch that had been felled by a storm. In permafrost, trees can barely grip the inhospitable earth and it's easy for a storm to uproot them and lay them flat on the ground. Platonov was telling me the story of his life here – our second life in this world. I frowned at the mention of the Jankhara mine. I had been in some bad and difficult places myself, but the terrible fame of Jankhara resounded far and near.

'Were you in Jankhara long?'

'A year,' said Platonov quietly. His eyes narrowed, his wrinkles became more pronounced – before me was a different Platonov, suddenly ten years older.

'But it was only the beginning that was tough, the first two or three months. They're all criminals there. I was the only . . . literate person. I used to tell them stories, I used to "pull novels" for them, as the criminals say in their thieves' cant. In the evenings I told them stories by Dumas, Conan Doyle and Edgar Wallace. In exchange they fed and clothed me and I worked less. In this place that's the only advantage you get from being able to read and write – I suppose you've probably made use of it too.'

'No,' I said. 'No. To me that always seemed the ultimate humiliation, the end. I've never told novels for soup. But I know what you're talking about. I've heard "novelists".'

'Is that a condemnation?' asked Platonov.

'Not in the least,' I replied. 'A lot can be forgiven a hungry man – a lot.'

'If I stay alive' – this was the sacred formula that prefaced all reflections concerning any time beyond the next day – 'I'll write a

story about it. I've already thought of a title: "The Snake Charmer".
Do you like it?'

'Yes, I do. You just have to stay alive. That's the important thing.'

Andrey Fyodorovich Platonov, a scriptwriter in his first life, died
about three weeks after this conversation. He died the way many die
– he swung his pick, lost his balance, and fell flat on his face against
the rock. Intravenous glucose and strong cardiac medicines could
probably have brought him back to life – he wheezed on for another
hour or hour-and-a-half – but he was already silent by the time a
stretcher was brought from the hospital. The orderlies carried the little
corpse to the morgue – a light burden of skin and bones.

I loved Platonov because he didn't lose interest in the life beyond
the blue seas and the high mountains, the life we were cut off from by
so many miles and years and in whose existence we hardly believed
any longer – or rather we believed in it only as children believe in the
existence of some distant America. Platonov, God knows how, even
had some books, and when it wasn't very cold, in July for example,
he would avoid the kind of conversation that usually kept us all going
– what kind of soup we had had or would be having for supper, would
bread be given out three times a day or just once in the morning,
would it be rainy or clear the next day . . .

I loved Platonov, and I shall try now to write down his story: 'The
Snake Charmer'.

The end of work is by no means the end of work. After the whistle
you must gather your tools, take them to the storeroom, hand them
over, form up in ranks, and go through two of the ten daily roll-calls
to the accompaniment of the guards' curses and the pitiless shouts and
insults of your own comrades, comrades who are not yet as weak as
you are, but who are tired like you are, who are in a hurry to get back
like you are and who are made furious by every delay. Then you have
to go through yet another roll-call, form up in ranks, and walk five
kilometres to the forest to collect firewood – the forest nearby has
long ago been felled and burnt. The lumber brigade prepare the wood,
but the mineworkers each have to carry a log home. Goodness knows
how the heavy logs are brought back, the logs that are too heavy even
for two men to carry together. Trucks are never sent out for wood,
and the horses are all too sick even to leave their stables. A horse
weakens much more quickly than a human being, although the difference between its previous life and its present life is, of course,
immeasurably less than it is for human beings. It often seems, and
probably it is true, that man rose up out of the animal kingdom, that
man became man, the creature able to think up such things as this

archipelago and our improbable life here, simply because he had greater physical endurance than any other animal. What made an ape into a human being was not its hand, not its embryonic brain, not its soul – there are dogs and bears who act more intelligently and ethically than human beings. Nor was it a matter of mastering the power of fire – that too was secondary. Man had no other advantage at this time except that he turned out to be considerably stronger, he turned out to possess greater endurance – greater physical endurance. It's inaccurate to say that a man has nine lives like a cat. It would be more true to say of a cat that it has nine lives like a man. A horse can't endure even a month of our life here in winter, in cold quarters and with long hours of heavy labour in the frost. Unless it's a Yakut horse. But then Yakut horses aren't used for work. Nor, I admit, are they fed. Like deer, they hoof up the snow and drag out last year's dry grass. Yet man does stay alive. Maybe he lives on hope? But no one here has any hopes. No one here, unless he is a fool, can live on hope. That is why there are so many suicides. No, what saves man is his sense of self-preservation, the tenacity – the physical tenacity – with which he clings on to life and to which even his consciousness is subordinate. What keeps him alive is the same as what keeps a stone, a tree, a bird or a dog alive. But his grip on life is stronger than theirs. And he has greater endurance than any animal.

Platonov was thinking about all this as he stood by the gate with a log on his shoulder, waiting for the next roll-call. The firewood was brought in and stacked, and the people, jostling and swearing, hurried back into the dark log barrack.

When his eyes had got used to the dark, Platonov saw that by no means every worker had gone out to work. In the far corner, on the upper bed-boards, where they had taken the only light – an oil-lamp with no glass – seven or eight men were sitting in a circle round two other men who had their legs crossed like Tatars and were playing cards across a dirty pillow they had placed between them. The smoky lamp trembled, its flame lengthening and rocking the shadows.

Platonov sat down on the edge of the bed-boards. His shoulders and knees ached; his muscles were trembling. Platonov had been brought to Jankhar only that morning, and this had been his first day's work. There were no free places on the boards.

'Any moment now the game will break up,' thought Platonov, 'and I'll be able to lie down.'

The game up above finished. A black-haired man with a moustache and a long nail on the little finger of his left hand rolled over towards the edge of the boards.

'Well then, let's have a look at that Ivan Ivanovich over there!'
Platonov was woken by a prod in the back.
'Hey you – you're being called.'
'Well, where is this Ivan Ivanovich?' came the voice from up above.
'I'm not Ivan Ivanovich,' said Platonov, screwing up his eyes.
'He won't come, Fedechka.'
'Won't he now?'
Platonov was pushed out into the light.
'Hope to live?' Fedya asked him quietly, rotating his little finger
with its long dirty nail in front of Platonov's eyes.
'Who doesn't?' answered Platonov.
A powerful punch in the face knocked him off his feet. Platonov
picked himself up and wiped off the blood with his sleeve.
'That's no way to answer,' Fedya explained affectionately. 'I'm
sure that's not the way you were taught to answer at college, Ivan
Ivanovich!'
Platonov remained silent.
'Bugger off now,' said Fedya. 'Go and lie down by the shit bucket.
That's your place now. One squeak from you – and we wring your
neck.'
This was no empty threat. Platonov had already seen two men being
strangled with towels – in settlement of some 'thieves'' score. Platonov
lay down on the damp, stinking planks.
'Brothers, I'm bored,' said Fedya, yawning. 'Someone might at least
give my heels a scratch.'
'Mashka, hey, Mashka, come and scratch Fedya's heels.'
Into the strip of light emerged Mashka, a pale, pretty 'thief' about
eighteen years old.
He pulled off Fedya's worn yellow shoes, carefully slipped off his
torn dirty socks and, smiling, began to scratch Fedya's heels. Fedya
was ticklish; he was giggling and shaking.
'Get lost,' he said suddenly. 'You can't scratch. You don't know
how to.'
'But Fedya, I . . .'
'Get lost, I said. Scraping and clawing at me like that. No finesse.'
The onlookers nodded their heads sympathetically.
'In Kosoy, now, I had a Yid. He knew how to scratch. Brothers, did
he know how to scratch! An engineer.'
And Fedya plunged into his memories of a Yid who had once
scratched his heels.
'But Fedya, Fedya, what about the new boy? Don't you want to try
him?'

'Huh,' said Fedya. 'His sort don't know how to scratch. Still, you can bring him along.'

Platonov was brought out into the light.

'Ey, Ivan Ivanovich, you look after the lamp!' Fedya ordered. 'And at night you can put wood on the fire. Yes, and in the morning you can empty the slop pail. The orderly will show you where.'

Platonov remained obediently silent.

'In exchange,' Fedya explained, 'you will receive a bowl of soup. I don't eat that swill anyway. Right, now go and sleep.'

Platonov lay down in his former spot. The workers were nearly all asleep, huddled up in twos or threes for warmth.

'I'm bored,' said Fedya, 'the nights are too long. If only someone here could pull novels. In Kosoy, now . . .'

'But Fedya, Fedya, what about the new boy? Don't you want to try him?'

'That's an idea,' said Fedya, coming back to life. 'Bring him along.'

Platonov was brought along.

'Listen,' said Fedya, almost ingratiatingly. 'I got a little carried away just now.'

'That's all right,' Platonov said through clenched teeth.

'Listen now. Can you pull novels?'

A light gleamed in Platonov's dull eyes. He could – and how! In the investigation prison, his whole cell had been spellbound while he told the story of Count Dracula. But *they* had been people. Whereas this lot? Should he become court jester to the Duke of Milan – a jester who was fed for a good jest and beaten for a bad one? But there was another way of looking at it all. He would teach them about real literature. He would enlighten them. He would awaken in them an interest in art, in the word; even here, in the lower depths, he would do his duty, fulfil his calling. As had long been his way, Platonov did not want to admit to himself that it was simply a matter of being fed, of receiving an extra bowl of soup not for carrying out a slop bucket, but for other, more dignified work. More dignified? No, he wouldn't really be an enlightener – he would be more like someone scratching a criminal's dirty heels. But the cold, the beatings, the hunger . . .

Smiling tensely, Fedya waited for an answer.

'Y-yes, I can,' said Platonov, and smiled for the first time on that difficult day. 'I can pull novels.'

'You darling!' said Fedya more cheerfully. 'Come on then, climb up here. And here's some bread for you. Tomorrow you'll get something better. Come on, sit on this blanket. And have a smoke!'

Platonov, who had not smoked for a week, drew with painful pleasure on a stub of makhorka.

'What's the name then?'

'Andrey,' said Platonov.

'Well then, Andrey, how about something nice and long that's got
a bit of spice in it? Something like *The Count of Monte Cristo*. None
of that stuff about tractors.'

'*Les Misérables*, perhaps?' Platonov suggested.

'Is that the one about Jean Valjean? I heard that in Kosoy.'

'*The Club of the Knaves of Hearts* then. Or *The Vampire*?'[1]

'Fine. Let's have those Knaves . . . Silence, you swine!'

Platonov cleared his throat.

'In the city of St Petersburg, in the year 1893, a mysterious crime
was committed . . .'

It was getting light when Platonov found he had no more strength
left: 'And with that the first part comes to a close.'

'Great stuff!' said Fedya. 'That's the spirit! Come and lie down with
us now. There isn't much time left for sleep – it's dawn. You'll have
to snatch a bit of shut-eye while you're out at work – you must get
your strength up for this evening!'

Platonov was already asleep.

They were being taken out to work. A tall country lad, who had
slept through yesterday's *Knaves of Hearts*, gave Platonov a vicious
shove as they went through the door: 'Watch where you're going, you
reptile!'

Someone immediately whispered something in the lad's ear.

As they were forming into ranks, the tall lad went up to Platonov.

'Don't tell Fedya I hit you. I didn't realize, brother, that you're a
novelist.'

'I won't,' answered Platonov.

Written in 1954; first published in 1967
Translated by Robert Chandler and Nathan Wilkinson

DUCK

The mountain stream was already gripped by ice, and in the shallows
there was no stream at all. The shallows had been the first part to freeze
and after a month nothing was left there of summer's thundering,
threatening water; even the ice had been crushed, ground down and
shattered by horses' hooves, tyres and felt boots. But the stream was
still alive, its water still breathing – white steam was rising up from
the bits of open water, the patches still free of ice.

An exhausted duck, a diver, flopped onto the water. The flock had flown south long ago, the duck had been left behind. Everything was still bright, snowy – especially bright because of the snow that covered the whole naked forest, that covered everything up to the horizon. The duck wanted to rest, just a little, and then rise up and fly – fly away after its flock.

The duck had no strength to fly. The huge weight of its wings dragged it to the ground, but the water was a support, a refuge – the open patches of water seemed to the duck to be a living river.

But before the duck had looked round, before it had caught its breath, its keen ear registered danger – the rumble of danger.

A man was running down the snowy hillside, stumbling on frozen tussocks of grass that now, towards evening, had begun to freeze still harder. He had seen the duck long ago and had been watching it with a secret hope. Now this hope had been realized – the duck had settled on the ice.

The man had been creeping up on the duck but had lost his footing. The duck noticed him and the man began to run, no longer trying to hide. The duck was too tired to fly. It only needed to take off and, apart from threats and curses, nothing would have threatened it. But to lift itself up into the sky it needed strength in its wings – and the duck was too tired. All it could do was dive. It vanished in the water and the man, armed with some kind of heavy stick, stayed by the patch of water where the duck had gone under, waiting for its return. Soon, after all, the duck would need to breathe.

Twenty yards away, however, lay more open water. The man swore as he saw that the duck had swum under the ice and surfaced in this other patch of water. But it was no more able to fly than before. And it was wasting whole seconds in resting.

The man tried to break up the ice, to smash it, but with only rags for footwear this was impossible.

He thumped the ice with his stick. The ice began to crumble a little, but it didn't break. The man ran out of strength and, breathing heavily, sat down on the ice.

The duck swam round its patch of water. The man began to run, cursing and throwing stones at the duck, and the duck dived down and reappeared on the first patch of water.

And so they went on, man and duck, until darkness fell.

It was time to return to the barrack, to give up on this chance hunt. The man regretted wasting his strength on this mad pursuit. Hunger had prevented him from thinking properly, from working out a sure way of tricking the duck; the impatience of hunger had led him astray, stopping him from constructing a reliable plan. The duck was still out there in the middle of the ice, on its patch of water. It was time to return to the barrack. The man had not been trying to catch the duck in order to cook and eat the meat of a bird. A duck is a bird, and that means meat, doesn't it? To cook the duck in an iron pot or, better still, bury it in the embers of a fire. To coat the duck with clay and bury it in glowing purple embers, or simply throw it into the fire. The fire would burn down and the duck's clay jacket would crack. The fat inside would be hot and slippery. This fat would flow onto his fingers, it would congeal on his lips. No, this was not why the man had been trying to catch the duck. Hazily, confusedly, other plans had been forming, taking vague shape in his brain. He'd take this duck to the foreman, he'd give it to him as a present – and then the foreman would strike the man off the ominous list being drawn up that night. The whole barrack knew about this list, and a man tried not to think about what was impossible, what was beyond his reach – how to escape the transport and stay here on this site, with these work-brigades. Here the hunger was bearable, and enough is as good as a feast.

But the duck was still on the water. It had been very difficult for the man to take a decision himself, to act independently, to do something his daily life had not prepared him for. He had not been taught to hunt ducks. That was why his movements had been helpless, clumsy. He hadn't been taught to think about the possibility of such a hunt – his brain couldn't come up with correct answers to the unexpected questions life posed. He had been taught to live differently, without needing to take decisions of his own, with another will – someone else's will – in charge of events. It is uncommonly difficult to meddle in one's own fate, to 'refract' fate. And maybe that's all for the best – a duck dies on a patch of water, a man in a barrack.

His frozen, ice-scratched fingers tried to warm themselves against his breast – trembling from the aching pain of incurable frostbite, the man had tucked his hands, both of them, under his shirt. There was little warmth in his hungry body, and the man returned to the barrack, pushed his way through to the stove and still couldn't get warm. His body was shaking, shuddering unstoppably.

The foreman looked in through the barrack door. He'd seen the duck too, he'd seen the dead man chasing the dying duck. The foreman didn't want to leave this settlement either – who knew what lay in store for him at the next site? The foreman had been counting on a generous present – a live duck and a pair of trousers from a free worker – with which to soften the heart of the work superintendent, who was still asleep. When he woke up, the superintendent would then cross the foreman off the list – not the old slogger who'd caught the duck, but himself, the foreman.

In his bed, the work superintendent was rolling a 'Rocket' cigarette between practised fingers. He too had seen the beginning of the hunt, through the window. If the duck were caught, the carpenter could knock up a cage and the superintendent could take the duck along to the commandant, or rather to his wife, Agnya Petrovna. And the superintendent's future would be assured.

But the duck was left to die on its patch of water. And everything went on just as if the duck had never come to those parts at all.

Written in 1963; first published in 1970
Translated by Robert Chandler and Nathan Wilkinson

ALEKSANDR ISAYEVICH
SOLZHENITSYN (*b.* 1918)

Solzhenitsyn was born in Kislovodsk. He studied mathematics, and he worked as a schoolteacher for several months before the outbreak of the Second World War. Like his father under the Tsarist regime, he then served as an artillery officer. In 1945 he was sentenced to eight years in the Gulag for criticizing Stalin in a letter to a friend. Shortly before his release, he was operated on for stomach cancer. A year later, in 1954, he was admitted to an oncological clinic in Tashkent; he responded unusually well to treatment. At the height of Khrushchev's 'Thaw' in 1962, Solzhenitsyn's One Day in the Life of Ivan Denisovich, *a realistic evocation of life in a labour camp, was published to huge acclaim. Other short works were published in the Soviet Union, but the novels* Cancer Ward *and* The First Circle *could be published only in the West. Solzhenitsyn was expelled from the Writers' Union in 1969 and deported to the West in 1974, after the publication of* The Gulag Archipelago. *After two years in Zurich, he settled in Vermont. He returned to Russia in 1994.*

Few books have had the political impact of The Gulag Archipelago, *a long history of the Soviet system of labour camps. It is possible that Solzhenitsyn played an important role in the Soviet Union's eventual collapse. Solzhenitsyn's heroism, however, no longer commands automatic respect. Liberals have long been repelled by his reactionary Slavophilism, and he is now seen in Russia as an anachronism. Few people have read more than a small part of his most recent work,* The Red Wheel, *a cycle of huge novels set between 1914 and 1917. The subtlety and tenderness of some of his earlier work has been forgotten.*

The most striking chapter in Solzhenitsyn's memoir Invisible Allies *is about an experience of his while he was living in a small town in Kazakhstan, released from the Gulag but not yet officially 'rehabilitated'. One of the other exiles is the child-like Zubov, a born conspirator. When Solzhenitsyn first recites to him the poetry and plays he has composed and memorized in the camps, Zubov's only response is to express amazement that Solzhenitsyn should so burden his memory.*

*He makes Solzhenitsyn a box with a hidden drawer. Until then Solz-
henitsyn has never dared write anything down, and he has had to
devote one week in every month to 'reviewing' the material he has
memorized. Freed from this burden, and from the fear of confusing
his memory, he can afford for the first time to rework his texts.
Solzhenitsyn describes Zubov's gift as 'no less of a liberation than
stepping out of the camp gates'. ((London: Harvill, 1997), p.]sb[9).*

Solzhenitsyn's devotion to his cause is beyond question. What Invisible Allies *makes sadly, if inadvertently, clear is the emotional price
he paid for his heroism. He writes warmly and vividly about his friends
from his first years after being released. The 'allies' described in the
later chapters, however, are cyphers; people have ceased to matter to
him except as assistants in his heroic endeavour.*

*'What a Pity', one of Solzhenitsyn's earliest stories, is surprisingly
little known. Based on a true incident later recounted in Part Six of*
The Gulag Archipelago, *it is set in 1952, the year before Stalin's death.*

WHAT A PITY

The institution Anna Modestovna had to go to for the document was
closed for lunch. This was annoying but it made sense to wait: it would
only be another fifteen minutes, and she could get everything finished
before her own lunch break was over.

Anna Modestovna didn't want to wait on the staircase, so she went
back outside.

It was a late October day, damp but not cold. There had been some
fine drizzle during the night and in the morning, but it had stopped.
Lorries rushed by along the tarmac, sometimes sparing the passers-by
but more often spraying them with thin mud. There was something
appealing about the grey, raised boulevard between the carriageways,
and Anna Modestovna crossed on to it.

There was hardly anyone at all on the boulevard, even in the distance. Here, if you avoided the puddles, you could walk over the
coarse sand without getting your shoes in the least wet. Under the
trees lay a dark layer of damp leaves and, if you went close, a faint
smell seemed to waft up from them – perhaps left over from when the
leaves were alive, or perhaps the beginning of decay; in any case,
between the two carriageways of exhaust fumes, this boulevard was a
rest for your lungs.

Anna stopped. There was no wind and the whole dense network of
damp brown and blackish branches, smaller branches, still smaller

branches, twigs and next year's little buds was strung with countless drops of water, all silvery-white in the gloom. It was the moisture left by the rain on the smooth skin of the branches; there being no wind, the moisture had collected and formed into hanging drops – round drops on the underside of the little twigs, and oval drops on the underside of the curving branches.

Taking her folded umbrella in the same hand as her handbag, and pulling off her glove, Anna began running her fingers underneath the drops and sliding them off. When she did this carefully enough, the drop would transfer intact onto her finger, not breaking up but just slightly flattening. The wavy patterns on her finger showed up more clearly through the drop than elsewhere – the drop was like a magnifying glass.

But one and the same drop, while showing her what lay behind it, also showed her what lay above it; the drop was a convex mirror. In this mirror, against a light background of cloudy sky, she could see – yes! – dark shoulders in a coat, and a head in a woollen hat, and even the interwoven branches above her head.

Thus Anna forgot herself and began hunting for bigger and bigger drops, sometimes slipping them onto a fingernail and sometimes onto the fleshy part of her finger. Then, right beside her, she heard firm footsteps and she let her hand drop, ashamed to be behaving in a way more appropriate to her youngest son.

The passer-by, however, had seen neither the game she was playing nor Anna Modestovna herself – he was the kind of person who notices nothing on a street except a free taxi or a tobacco kiosk. He was a young man with the unmistakable stamp of a higher education; he was carrying a bulging bright-yellow briefcase, and he wore a bright overcoat of soft worsted and a fur hat with a crease down the middle. Only in the capital do you encounter men with such expressions – always self-assured, always victorious. Anna Modestovna knew people like this and she was afraid of them.

On her guard now, she walked on and came across a newspaper display board standing on pale blue posts. Beneath the glass lay both the inside and the outside pages of *Labour*. The glass had been chipped in one corner, water had got inside, and one sheet of newspaper was soaked. But at the bottom of this sheet Anna Modestovna saw a headline above two columns of print: THE NEW LIFE OF THE CHU RIVER.

This was somewhere she knew: she had been born there, in the Seven Rivers region.[1] Wiping the pane with her glove, Anna Modestovna began to skim through the article.

Its writer was no miser with words. He began with the Moscow aerodrome: how he had taken his seat in the aeroplane and, as if in contrast with the dismal weather, everyone had been in a joyful mood. Then he described his fellow travellers: who was flying with him and why. He even said a word about the stewardess. After that: the aerodrome at Frunze and how, as if in harmony with the sunny weather, everyone had been in a joyful mood. Then he recounted his journey along the Chu valley. Using a rich variety of technical terms, he described the hydraulic works, the spillway, the hydroelectric power station and the irrigation canals; he enthused at the sight of desert lands now irrigated and fruitful, and he expressed astonishment at the harvest statistics of the collective farms.

At the end he wrote: *But few know that this grandiose and majestic transformation of an entire region of nature was first conceived a long time ago. Our engineers did not have to carry out detailed surveys of the valley, its geological strata and water systems. The whole of the central project was completed on the basis of laborious calculations carried out in 1912, forty years ago, by the talented Russian hydrographer and hydraulic engineer, Modest Aleksandrovich V.,[2] who then, in the same year, began the initial works, risking his own capital.*

Anna Modestovna was neither shocked nor overcome with joy; it was rather that she had begun to tremble both inside and outside, as if at the start of an illness. She bent down, to see the final paragraphs right in the corner, and she tried to wipe the glass clean. With difficulty she read: *But under the bigoted Tsarist regime, indifferent as it was to the interests of the people, his plans could not be realized. They ended up gathering dust in the Department of Land Amelioration, and the excavations he had already completed were abandoned.*

What a pity! – the journalist exclaimed in conclusion – *what a pity that the young enthusiast did not live to see the triumph of his brilliant ideas! That he is unable to gaze upon the now transformed valley!*

Anna felt a sudden fear, surging up like boiling water, because she knew what she was going to do now: she was going to steal this newspaper! Like a thief, she looked round, first to her right, then to her left: there was nobody on the boulevard, just someone's back in the distance. What she was doing was unseemly, quite disgraceful, but . . .

The newspaper was held in place by three drawing pins across the top. Anna put her hand through the break in the glass. Where the newspaper was wet in the corner, it crumpled at once into a little damp ball and came off the pin. Standing on tiptoe, she managed to reach across to the middle pin, loosen it and pull it out. But the third, furthest pin was beyond her reach – and she just pulled on the newspaper. It tore – and the whole sheet came away in her hand.

Straight away, behind her back, she heard the piercing staccato of a policeman's whistle.

As if scalded (there was little she didn't know about fear, and a policeman's whistle was frightening enough at any time), Anna withdrew her now empty hand and turned round.

It was too late to run away, and it would have made things worse. Coming towards her – not down the boulevard, but through a gap in the boulevard fence, which Anna had not noticed before – was a tall policeman, looking all the bigger because of his wet raincoat, which he was wearing with the hood thrown back.

He did not call out. He came up to her, in no hurry. He looked down at Anna Modestovna, then at the newspaper – which had dropped down, somewhat crumpled, behind the glass – then at Anna Modestovna again. He towered over her, strict and severe. It was clear from his hands and from his pink, broad-nosed face that he was someone fit and strong – the kind of man to drag people out of a blaze or carry out an arrest without using firearms.

Not raising his voice, the policeman asked: 'What's all this, citizen? Do we want to be fined twenty-five roubles?'

(Oh, please let it just be a fine! She was afraid of some harsher interpretation of her behaviour.)

'Or do you not like people reading newspapers?'

(It was coming.)

'What do you mean? No, no! Forgive me!' said Anna Modestovna, somehow almost wriggling. 'I'll put it back straight away . . . if you'll allow me . . .'

No, hardly. Even if he did allow her, a sheet of newspaper with one wet corner and one torn corner would not be so very easy to put back.

The policeman continued to look down at her, giving no indication of his decision.

He'd been on duty a long time and it had been raining. It would be nice to take the woman back to the station, along with her newspaper. While he filed his report, he'd dry out a little. But he wanted to understand. A respectably dressed woman, middle-aged, not drunk.

She looked at him, waiting for her punishment.

'What have you got against the newspaper?'

'There's something about my father!' All apology, she was clasping to her chest the handle of her umbrella, her handbag and the glove she had taken off. She had not noticed that she had cut her finger against the glass.

WHAT A PITY 337

Now the policeman understood her. Pitying her because of her
bleeding finger, he gave a nod of the head.

'Being criticized, is he? But what difference is one copy going to
make?'

'No-o! No, no! The opposite – he's been praised!'

(Really, he didn't look unkind at all!)

At this point she saw the blood on her finger and began to suck it.
And she kept on looking at the policeman's large, simple face.

His lips barely parted. 'But why? Couldn't you have bought it in a
kiosk?'

'But look at the date!' She quickly took her finger from her lips and
pointed to the undamaged sheet of newspaper beneath the other half
of the glass. 'It's been there three days. Where am I going to find a
copy now?'

The policeman looked at the date. Again at the woman. And again
at the crumpled sheet of newspaper. He sighed: 'I should file a report.
And fine you . . . All right then, but don't do it again. Take it quickly,
before anyone sees.'

'Oh thank you! Thank you! How kind you are! Thank you!' Anna
Modestovna said the words over and over again, at the same time
as repeating some kind of wriggle or bow. Instead of putting her
handkerchief to her finger, she quickly slipped the hand with the pink
finger under the glass, seized the edge of the newspaper and pulled it
out. 'Thank you!'

The newspaper opened out. Anna, as best she could with one edge
being soaked and having only one free hand, folded it. With one more
polite little wriggle, she said: 'I'm very grateful to you. You can't
imagine what a joy this will be to my mother and father! May I go?'

Standing sideways on to her, he nodded.

And she walked quickly away, quite forgetting why she had come
to this street, clutching the newspaper, which she had folded skew-
whiff, and sucking now and again at her finger.

She must hurry back to her mother. So the two of them could read
this together! Once her father's place of exile had been determined,
mother would go and visit him. She could take the newspaper with
her.

The journalist hadn't known! He hadn't known – or he would never
ever have written that! And the editorial board didn't know – or they'd
never have let it through. The young enthusiast *had* lived to see the
day. He had lived to see the triumph of his brilliant ideas, because his
death sentence had been commuted and he had instead spent twenty
years in prisons and camps. And then, while on his way, under guard,

to some remote place of perpetual exile, he had petitioned Beria himself, asking to be sent to the Chu valley. But he had been sent elsewhere, and the local internal affairs office had no idea what to do with the useless old man: there was no suitable job for him – and as for a pension,[3] he had not put in enough years of work.

Written in 1956; first published in 1978
Translated by Robert Chandler

VASILY MAKAROVICH SHUKSHIN
(1929–74)

Shukshin was born in the village of Srostki in the Altai region of Siberia. In 1933 his father was executed, accused either of sabotage or of inciting a riot. For the sake of her family, Shukshin's mother resumed her maiden name; this name – Popov – was also used by Vasily until he was sixteen. After finishing his seven years at the village school, Shukshin enrolled in a technical college. He also began writing stories, which appear to have been rejected by a Moscow journal. Since Shukshin was living in another town, the village postmaster – according to Shukshin's sister – delivered the returned manuscripts to another Vasily Shukshin, the writer's illiterate uncle, who used the paper to roll cigarettes. This could be a story written by Shukshin, rather than a story about him – yet it may well be true.

Shukshin left Srostki during the famine of 1946. He wandered around Central Russia for two or three years, sleeping in workers' barracks or on park benches and working at a variety of labouring jobs. In 1949 he joined the Soviet navy, but he was discharged after four years because of stomach ulcers. He moved to Moscow in 1954, where he was a contemporary – and rival – of Andrey Tarkovsky at the most prestigious Soviet film college. As well as acting and making films, he wrote short stories, short novels and two longer historical novels, nearly all set in rural Siberia. His most famous work is the short novel Snowball Berry Red, *about an ex-convict trying to escape his old lifestyle; Shukshin played the lead role in his film of the book. Another important story is 'Before the Cock Calls Thrice', a parody of a Russian folk tale in which Ivan the Fool is sent on a search not for wisdom, but for a certificate attesting to his wisdom. Shukshin's bleak tone and his unsparing portrayal of village life did not escape criticism. In the 1970s, however, Russian nationalism was beginning to replace Marxism-Leninism as the State's binding ideology; none of Shukshin's work could be seen as in any way pro-Western or anti-Russian, and he was able to publish most of it.*

Shukshin has sometimes been criticized for spreading his talents too thinly. It seems likely, however, that all three of his careers – acting, directing and writing – were essential to him. He can perhaps best be seen as a folk storyteller – a figure he himself described as 'both a playwright and an actor, or, more likely, a whole theatre in one person'.[1] In the words of the critic Donald Rayfield, 'Shukshin has a cameraman's eye and a dramatist's ear'.[2]

Most of Shukshin's heroes are dreamers, searching for some escape from the monotony of the everyday. The émigré critic Mikhail Geller wrote, 'people who have lost an arm or a leg continue to feel pain in the amputated limb; Shukshin's characters feel pain where man's soul used to be.'[3] Some of Shukshin's stories are, nevertheless, extravagantly funny; others, like 'In the Autumn', would be depressing were it not for Shukshin's evident compassion towards his characters.

IN THE AUTUMN

Ferry operator Filipp Tyurin finished listening to the latest news on the radio, hung around at the table some more, and was sternly silent . . .

'There's just no stoppin' 'em!' he said angrily.

'Who you railin' at this time?' asked Filipp's wife, a tall old woman with manly hands and a man's deep booming voice.

'They're bombin' again!' Filipp nodded at the radio.

'Who're they bombin"?

'The Vietnamese, who else?'

The old woman didn't approve of her husband's passion for politics, and what's more this foolish passion irritated her. From time to time they'd had some serious quarrels because of politics, but the old woman didn't feel like quarrelling now – she didn't have time for it. She was getting ready to go to the bazaar.

Filipp, in a stern, intense frame of mind, put on some warmer clothes and set off for the ferry.

He'd been a ferry operator for a long time, ever since the war. He'd been wounded in the head and had to give up carpentry because it hurt to bend over his work. So he became a ferry operator.

It was the end of September; the wind had picked up after the rains, bringing with it cold, nasty weather. The ground squelched underfoot. From the loudspeaker in the village store you could hear an exercise programme being broadcast. The wind mixed with snatches of music and the buoyant voice of the Moscow trainer. Even so, the village pigs and roosters managed to hold their own, their squealing and crowing piercing through the other sounds.

The villagers Filipp met on his way nodded their greetings to him and hurried on, either to the village store for bread or to the bus – they were also in a hurry to get to the bazaar.

Filipp was used to making the trip from his house to the ferry each morning; he'd complete it without thinking. That is, he'd think about something, but not at all about the ferry or who, for example, he might be ferrying across the river that day. Everything was clear as far as that was concerned. Right now he was thinking about how to keep those Americans in check. He was surprised, but he never asked anyone why it was we didn't force them back with our missiles. Everything could be resolved in a couple of days.

In his youth Filipp had been very active politically. He'd taken an active part in the new life after the Revolution; he'd been an activist in the organization of the kolkhozes.[1] He hadn't dispossessed any rich peasants, it's true, but he'd done a lot of arguing and shouting, trying to convert the unbelievers and getting himself all worked up in the process. But he hadn't been a Party member either. Somehow that had never come up in conversation with the comrades in charge of everything, but still those in charge could never manage without Filipp. He helped them with all of his heart. And he was secretly proud that there was no way they could manage without him. He liked, for instance, to sit around in the village council on the eve of elections and talk to the district comrades about how best to hold the elections: who should take the ballot-box home, who would come on their own to vote, and of all things not to forget to run and remind them in the morning. Of course, there'd also be those who'd start getting all pigheaded about things as soon as you tried to get them to vote: 'And did they lend me a horse when I asked for one so's I could go get firewood?' This would absolutely amaze Filipp. 'What're you talkin' about, Yegor?' he'd say to the muzhik.[2] 'There ain't no comparison! Any fool can see that! What we got here is a political matter, and you're goin' on about some horse! They're as alike as a pie and a pussy.' And he'd rush all over the village, arguing his point. And folks would also argue back, they liked sparring with him. They wouldn't take offence. Rather, they'd say, 'Now, you tell them over there . . .' Filipp would feel the importance of the moment, he'd get all worked up, and take everything personally. 'Well, that's the common folk for you!' he thought, completely wrapped up in his great cause. 'They're all a bunch of backwoods blockheads.' As the years passed, Filipp's political activism subsided, his head wound began to bother him again, so he no longer had the strength to be an activist and get all worked up. However, he continued to take all political and social issues to heart, as he'd done formerly, and he worried a lot.

By the river the wind blew in strong gusts. It whipped and blustered. The cables creaked. But at least the sun peeped out, and that was nice.

Filipp went back and forth across the river. He ferried over the people who were in the biggest hurry and then, later on, things went more easily, without a lot of jumpy nerves. And Filipp was just about to turn his thoughts back to the Americans when a wedding party drove up, the kind they have nowadays, with everybody in cars all decked out with ribbons and balloons. This city-style wedding party had also become the fashion in the village. Three cars drove up. The wedding party piled out on the bank. They were loud, slightly tipsy and very showy and swaggering. Although it was the fashion – to go in cars with ribbons – it was still a rare sight. Not everybody could get hold of such cars.

Filipp watched the wedding party with interest. He didn't know these people – they weren't locals, they were going to visit somebody. One guy in a hat was pulling out all the stops, trying to attract attention to himself. It looked as though he was the one who'd managed to get the cars. He wanted everything to come off in a big way, with some dash to it. He made the accordion player perform on the ferry and he was the first one to break into a dance – he shouted, tapped out a beat with his feet and looked at everybody with the proud gaze of an eagle. But it made them uncomfortable. It was embarrassing. And it was embarrassing for the bride and groom – they were more sober than the others, more self-conscious. No matter how much that fellow in the hat showed off, he didn't infect anybody with his fake gaiety, and he soon got tired. The ferry made it to the other side, the cars drove off, and the wedding party rolled away down the road.

And Filipp began thinking about his own life. Here's how his marriage had come about when he was in his youth. There had been a girl in the village, Marya Yermilova, a beauty, round-faced, rosy, friendly. She took your breath away. She was the kind of bride you could only dream about at home, while lying on your sleeping bench. Filipp loved her very much, and Marya also loved him – it looked like they'd end up marrying. But Filipp got involved with the Komsomol[3] workers. And it was the same story then as later: he wasn't a member of the Komsomol himself, but he shouted and worked to overturn things just as much as they did. Filipp liked the fact that the Komsomol workers had risen up against the old villagers, against their hold on power. There was one conflict in particular: all the young, politically aware people declared their opposition to church weddings. The unheard-of happened. The village elders couldn't do anything. They got angry, reached for their whips, meaning to set those upstarts back on the straight and narrow with their whips alone if need be, but instead only succeeded in making them all the more dogged in their resistance. It was an exhilarating time. Filipp, of course, was all on the side of the Komsomol: he was also against church weddings. But that wasn't the case with Marya – she wasn't against them at all. Marya's mother and father were tough as flint on that issue and she herself had bowed out of the ranks of the progressive-minded once and for all: she wanted to have a church wedding. Filipp found himself in a very difficult position.

He tried to persuade Marya in every possible way (he was a masterful talker, which was probably why Marya loved him – it was a rare talent in the village). He tried to convince her, to thwart her peasant ignorance. He read her various articles, instructional and satirical. He made fun of her, but with a pain in his heart. Marya wouldn't budge an inch: it was a church wedding or nothing. Now, looking back on his life, Filipp knew that he'd been hopelessly stupid. He and Marya ended up parting ways. Filipp didn't change later on. He had never been sorry and wasn't sorry now that he had been able to participate to the best of his abilities in the restructuring of life in the village. But he was sorry about Marya. All his life his heart bled and ached. Not a day went by without him remembering Marya. At first it was so hard on him that he wanted to do away with himself. And as the years passed, the pain didn't disappear. He already had a family – it had been a civil marriage – and kids. But his heart longed and longed for Marya. When his wife, Fyokla Kuzovnikova, detected in Filipp this constant sorrow of his, she came to hate him. And that deep-seated, quiet hatred also took up permanent residence in her. For his part, Filipp didn't hate Fyokla. No. But during the war, for instance, whenever they were told 'You are defending your mothers and your wives,' instead of Fyokla, Filipp would picture Marya. And if he had ended up getting killed in the war, he'd have died thinking about Marya.

The ache didn't go away as the years went by, but of course, it didn't burn any more the way it had burned those first years of his marriage. By the way, he'd also stopped talking so much around then. He was an activist, as he'd been before; he spoke out because people had to be convinced, but all along it seemed as if all of his talk had less to do with politics than with his bitter thoughts about Marya. He'd be ever so pensive, then he'd suddenly snap out of it and once again he'd be trying to make people understand, once again trying to open their eyes to the new and the unprecedented. As for Marya . . .

Marya was taken away from the village at that time. Some guy came
to see her (not just some guy, later on Filipp met him many times), a
rich fellow from Krayushkino. They came, made the match, and took
her away. Of course, they had a church wedding. After a year had
gone by, Filipp asked Pavel, Marya's husband, 'Weren't you ashamed?
Draggin' yourself into a church . . . ?' Pavel acted surprised, then said:
'And why should I be ashamed?' 'You gave in to the old folks.' 'I
didn't give in,' Pavel said, 'I wanted a church wedding myself.' 'That's
what I'm asking,' said Filipp, now at a loss. 'Weren't you ashamed?
The old folks can be pardoned, you know, but what about you? We'll
never crawl out of the dark that way.' At that, Pavel started cussing.
'Get the hell outta here!' And he wouldn't talk with Filipp any more.
But here's what Filipp noticed: when they'd meet, Pavel would look
at him with some sort of suppressed rage, with pain even, as if he
wanted to understand something and just couldn't. Rumour had it
that Pavel and Marya weren't getting along well, that Marya was
unhappy. This was the last straw for Filipp. He even went on a drinking
binge to quell the new pain welling up inside him, but afterwards he
quit drinking and learned to live with his pain. He looked at his pain
as if it were a snake that he constantly carried inside himself, and no
matter how much it bit him, he put up with it.

These were the melancholy thoughts that the wedding party on
wheels had resurrected. These were the thoughts Filipp ferried from
shore to shore, back and forth, and it occurred to him that he'd
probably need a glass of vodka with his lunch – the wind cut to the
bone and his soul had begun to whimper for some reason. It started
to ache outright; it became alarmed and anxious.

'I'll do two more turns, then I'll have lunch,' Filipp decided.

As he approached 'their' bank (for Filipp, there was 'our' bank,
where his native village was, and 'their' bank opposite), he saw a
covered truck and a small group of people by the truck. Filipp's
experienced eye immediately guessed what kind of vehicle it was and
who was being transported in it: a dead person. People transport their
dead in exactly the same fashion. Waiting to board the ferry they
always climb out of the truck, away from the coffin, and somehow
just stand there like that and stare at the river and keep quiet, so that
it's clear from the start what kind of group it is.

'Who could it be?' Filipp wondered, peering at the people. 'They're
from some village upriver, seeing as we haven't heard about anybody
dying round here. But why on earth are they bringin' the body here
from somewhere else? Maybe the person didn't die at home, and so
they're bringin' him home to bury?'

When the ferry came closer to shore, Filipp recognized one of the
men beside the truck – it was Pavel, Marya's husband. And suddenly
Filipp realized who they were bringing . . . They were bringing Marya.
He remembered that in the beginning of the summer Marya had gone
to visit her daughter in town. She and Filipp had talked while they
rode on the ferry. Marya said that her daughter in town had had a
baby and that she needed to help her out for the time being. They'd
had a nice chat back then. Marya told him that they were doing fine,
quite well, that the children (there were three of them) were all settled,
she herself was getting a pension, Pavel was also getting a pension,
but he still worked, he did a little cabinet-making at home. They didn't
keep a lot of livestock, but somehow they had everything they needed.
They'd gotten into breeding turkeys. Last year they'd taken their house
apart and replaced the bad logs; their sons had come and helped.
Filipp also said that they too were doing well for the time being, he
was also getting a pension and he had no complaints about his health,
though his head would ache a bit when the weather was about to
change. And Marya said there was something the matter with her
heart. She was suffering from some sort of heart problem. Sometimes
she'd be feeling just fine and then suddenly her heart would constrict
and feel so heavy. It would happen at night: it would squeeze so bad,
it was enough to make you cry. And now, Marya clearly had met her
end. As soon as Filipp saw Pavel, he moaned under his breath. He felt
a sudden rush of heat.

The ferry bumped up against the rickety dock. They threaded the
chains for the ferry through the rings on the dock and secured them
with metal bars. The front wheels of the covered truck were already
touching the logs of the dock; the logs shook, creaked, and moaned.

Filipp stood by his rudder as if bewitched, looking at the truck. Oh
God, it's Marya they're bringing, Marya . . . Filipp was supposed to
show the driver how to park his truck because two more were rolling
up from behind, but he'd become rooted to the spot, he kept looking
at the truck, at the back of the truck.

'Where do you want me to put it?' the driver shouted.

'Huh?'

'I said, where do you want me to put it?'

'Put it over there,' Filipp gestured vaguely. It just would not completely sink in that they were transporting Marya's body. His mind was
all in a whirl, his thoughts were disjointed and couldn't focus on this
one sorrowful turn of events. First he remembered how Marya told him
– right here, on the ferry – that they were doing well. Then he saw her
as a young woman, when . . . Oh, God . . . Marya . . . Is it really you?

At last Filipp tore himself away from the place where he'd been standing and went up to Pavel.

Life had bent Pavel over. His face was fresh, his eyes were intelligent and clear, but his bearing was very poor. And there was a great, peaceful sorrow in his intelligent eyes.

'What happened, Pavel?' Filipp asked.

Pavel glanced momentarily at him, as if he didn't understand the question, and again he began looking down at the planks of the ferry. Filipp felt awkward about asking again. He turned back to his rudder. And as he went, he walked around to the back of the covered truck, glanced in and saw the coffin. And his heart started aching openly, and his thoughts came together: yes, this was Marya.

They floated along. Filipp mechanically steered the rudder and kept thinking: 'Maryushka, Marya . . .' The dearest person in the world to him was making her last crossing with him . . . All those thirty years that he'd been a ferry operator, he knew exactly how many times Marya had ridden on the ferry. Basically, she'd keep going to town to see her children: either when they were studying there or when they were setting up house or when they had kids. And now – Marya was no more.

He steamed up to the shore. Once again the chains rattled, the engines roared. Once again Filipp stood by the rudder and looked at the covered truck. It was incomprehensible. Never in all his life had he thought what it would be like if Marya died. Not once had he ever thought about that. This was the one thing he hadn't been ready for, her death. When the covered truck began to drive off the ferry, Filipp felt an unbearable anguish in his chest. He was seized by anxiety: shouldn't he do something? After all, they were taking her away right now. For good. He couldn't just let it go at that; he couldn't just see her off with his eyes and that's all. What was he thinking? And anxiety took hold of him all the more, but he didn't budge, and because of that, he became altogether out of sorts.

'Why, I should have said goodbye!' he realized, when the covered truck was already climbing up the slope. 'If only I could say goodbye! If only I could take one last look. The coffin hasn't been nailed shut yet, I could still take a look!' And it seemed to Filipp that these people, who had driven Marya past him, well, that they shouldn't have done that – just driven by and that's all. After all, if it was anybody's grief, then more than anybody else's, it was his grief. Marya was in the coffin. Where were they taking her? Everything that life had not wiped out, that was unravaged by time, that was unforgotten and painfully dear came crashing down on Filipp. His whole long life passed before his eyes – the most important part, the most necessary part, what had kept him alive. He didn't notice that he was weeping. His eyes kept following that monstrous truck where the coffin was. The truck made it to the top of the slope and turned into the street and disappeared.

And now life would go on differently somehow. He had been used to the fact that Marya was here on the earth with him. When things were difficult, when times were hard, he'd remember Marya and wouldn't feel so alone in the world. How on earth would he get along now? Oh God, what emptiness, what pain!

Filipp quickly got off the ferry: the last truck off the boat was still lingering close to the dock for some reason. Filipp went up to the driver.

'Catch up with that covered truck . . . the one with the coffin,' he said, climbing into the cab.

'How come? What for?'

'Just do it.'

The driver looked at Filipp, didn't ask anything else and took off.

While they were driving through the village, the driver levelled several sidelong glances at Filipp.

'Those are Krayushkinites,[4] right?' he asked, nodding at the covered truck up ahead.

Filipp nodded in silence.

'A relative of yours?' the driver asked again.

Filipp said nothing at that. Once again his eyes were glued to the covered truck. From where he was, you could see the coffin in the middle of the truck bed. The people who were seated along the sides of the truck bed suddenly seemed alien to Filipp – both to him and to this coffin. What in the heck were they there for? After all, it was Marya who was in the coffin.

'Want me to go around, or what?' the driver asked.

'Pass it, and let me out.'

They passed the vehicle. Filipp climbed out of the cab and raised his hand. And his heart began pounding, as if right here and now something was going to happen that would make it clear to everybody, Filipp included, who Marya had been to him. He didn't know what would happen, he didn't know what words he'd say when the truck with the coffin stopped. He just wanted to see Marya so badly, it had become something necessary and important. It was impossible for her to go off like that – after all, his life had also passed by and now there wouldn't be anybody for him any more.

The truck stopped.

Filipp got in at the back. He grabbed on to the side and climbed up that little set of iron steps which was at the base of the truck bed.

'Pavel . . .' he said pleadingly, not recognizing his own voice. He hadn't planned on speaking so pleadingly. 'Let me say goodbye to her. Let me at least have a look.'

Pavel suddenly stood up abruptly and stepped towards him. Filipp managed to see his face up close. It was a changed face. The eyes, which had not long ago been filled with sorrow, had now suddenly turned malevolent.

'Get outta here!' Pavel said quietly and harshly. And he shoved Filipp in the chest. Filipp hadn't expected that. He almost fell. He grabbed on to the side of the truck and held on. 'Go!' shouted Pavel. And he shoved him again and again – he shoved him hard. Filipp hung on to the truck with all his might. He looked at Pavel. He didn't recognize him. And he didn't understand a thing.

'Hey, hey, what's the matter?' The others in the back were alarmed. A young man – the son, probably – took Pavel by the shoulders and dragged him away from the rear of the truck. 'What are you doing! What's the matter with you?'

'He'd better clear outta here!' Pavel said, dripping with venom. 'He'd better clear out now! I've got my eye on you! He comes slitherin' up . . . the snake! Get outta here! Outta here!' Pavel stomped his foot. It was as if he'd gone mad with grief.

Filipp climbed down from the truck bed. Now he understood what the matter was with Pavel. He looked malevolently back up at him. And he spoke, not aware himself what it was he was saying, and yet, as it turned out, saying the very words that he'd been carrying inside him, words that had been waiting to come out.

'What, feelin' a little bitter? You snatched up what didn't belong to you and now you're all bitter about it. Were you happy about it back then?'

'As if you were any happier!' said Pavel from the back of the truck. 'Or maybe I don't know how happy you were!'

'That's what happens when you try to build your whole life on somebody else's misfortune,' Filipp continued, not listening to what was being said to him from the back of the truck. It was important to get everything out, very important. 'Did you think you were going to live in clover? No-o, it doesn't happen that way. Now I see what it was you got for your pains.'

'So, did *you* live in clover? You? Yourself? Then how come you're so old and bent over yourself? If you did live well – how come you're so bent over? From livin' the good life?'

'Were you happy back then? Well, now you can see what that happiness has brought you. You're just a beggar! A lousy beggar!'

'What's the matter with you two?' The young man became angry. 'Have you lost your minds? A fine time you've picked!'

The truck started up. Pavel still managed to shout from the back, '*I'm* a beggar? You spent your whole life whining like a dog at the gate! I'm not the one who's a beggar, you are!'

Filipp slowly started back.

'Marya,' he thought, 'oh, Marya, Marya ... Here's how you bent all our lives out of shape. A coupla fools snarlin' at each other ... Both of us are beggars, Pavel, so don't get so shook up. If you aren't a beggar, then why are you so angry? What should you be angry at? You carved out a piece of happiness in your youth – so live and be happy. But you didn't know joy either. She didn't love you, that's why the grief came rushin' out of you like that. There was nothing for you to snatch up back then. You just showed up and took her away ... and everybody was overjoyed about it.'

Filipp was sick at heart. But now vexation at Marya got mixed in with his bitter gall.

'You were a fine one, too: just couldn't wait, so you rushed off to Krayushkino! All impatient-like. And there was no sense in it, either ... And now what?

'I'll tell you what there is now,' Filipp said to himself in conclusion. 'There's nothing now. Except to find some way to live out my days. And get ready, too – to follow in her footsteps. You can't undo the past.'

The wind had slackened noticeably, the sky had become clear, the sun shone, but it was cold. All around it was somehow barren and cold. Well, it was autumn, after all. Why would it be warm?

First published in 1972
Translated by John Givens and Laura Michael

ASAR ISAYEVICH EPPEL (*b.* 1935)

*Eppel was born in Ostankino, a suburb of Moscow, and he studied
architecture at the Institute of Civil Engineering. Unable to publish
his own work under the Soviet regime, he worked for many years
as a translator. As well as translating Bruno Schultz and Wislawa
Szymborska from Polish (the foreign language he knows best), he
translated poems by – among others – Petrarch, Boccaccio, Kipling
and Brecht. It is possible that the exactness of Eppel's ear owes something to his experience of this demanding discipline. He is a master of
rhythm and tone: some sentences are short and staccato, others ramble
down half a page, but the reader is always in the presence of a speaking
voice. This rhythmic vitality – a quality also apparent in his libretto
for a popular musical based on Isaak Babel's* Odessa Tales *– reflects
both vivid perception and complex feeling. In one story Eppel
describes his writing as 'my bold and rambling prayer'.*

The first collection of Eppel's stories, The Grassy Street, *constitutes
a semi-fictionalized portrait of the decaying Moscow suburb where he
grew up during and after the Second World War. In the words of
the writer Andrey Sergeyev: 'Eppel introduces us to the world of
Ostankino, transformed after the Revolution from an elegant country
spot into a dustheap of people of all nationalities . . . His stories are
modern classics, some of them comparable to the best of Chekhov.'*[1]
*'Red Caviar Sandwiches' is one of the most joyful stories from this
collection.*

RED CAVIAR SANDWICHES

As you approached Ostankino Park, coming from Mariyna Roshcha
along wide Novo-Moskovskaya Street, on your right you would soon
see the Pushkin student dorm, an accumulation of stuccoed barracks.
A barrack is done fast and slapdash. And always for drastic action. Like
a barricade, its direct predecessor. But a barricade may fall, and then be

taken down, whereas a barrack will never fall, and never be taken down, witness that heir to the barricade, the Pushkin student dorm.

Having at some point performed its panicky mission, become a shelter for faceless working-class students, and cast the ones who finished out into the world of socialist achievements and rah-rah Soviet songs, it did not fall and was not taken down, but occupied: by the ones who never finished, by all manner of riffraff, and by good souls. Occupied permanently and in perpetuity.

I had various acquaintances there. Of the first, second, and third ilk. Take, say, of the third, the amazing Samson Yeseyich. But about him later. Not here. Instead I'll tell you about Aunt Dusya who took care of him. And not just about her. First, however, let's celebrate the barrack. The Pushkin student dorm.

The barrack is an oblong two-storey structure crouched low to the ground with two entrances along the front and two outside wooden staircases going to the second floor. It is a barely whitewashed construction under a black tarpaper hat inside which people walk, sit, lie down, and out of which they peer. I couldn't tell you the length of the barrack today, but we can easily establish the width. Since the plaster walls were nothing but timber inside, the barrack's butt-end could not have been more than twenty-four or twenty-five feet wide; or rather, that's exactly what it was, since that is the length of a timber. Said feet contained the lengths of two rooms plus the width of the corridor. Allow five feet for the latter, and that leaves eight feet for each room. That's right! Along the length you may fit a working-class student's bed (six-and-a-half feet) and, at the head or foot of the bed, a night-stand in which the working-class student may keep his Marx or his tattered little tome with the disturbing but trivial title *Without the Bird Cherries*.[1]

On each floor you have a corridor five feet wide and, on either side of this corridor, opening on to it, you have rooms stretched the length of their beds and, crammed into these rooms, people, children and belongings.

The corridor, which is also the kitchen, is absolutely endless, for beneath its ceiling burn only two yellow ten-watt bulbs, as sooty as oil-stoves, and in the smoke and steam the nightmarish chiaroscuro from many different objects creates countless screens and culs-de-sac, and all of this corroded by the rich, fetid, murky air.

Smoke and stench pervade. Along the walls loom washtubs, rags on nails, twig baskets, two-handled saws wrapped in dusty, brittle yellowed newspapers wound round with twine; the floor is a sea of trunks piled one on top of another, little padlocked cupboards painted white, and damp soapy stools supporting basins under small hanging washstands. There is no rule or rest from the dimly glinting buckets of water, the trash buckets, and the buckets of slops for the pig which someone's godmother is fattening in a nearby village, from the old-fashioned camp beds (canvas on crosspieces), from the sleds, the vats, the barrels, the bowls, from the shovels caked with yellow clay, the pitchforks and the rakes, for the ground-floor tenants have veg-etable patches under their windows, and some keep rabbits or chickens. There are children's skis, faded and flat as boards, one ski shorter than the other for lack of means. And there are plain boards, also of different sizes, with crooked brown nails bowed down to their rough surfaces.

There are even some things – marvellous but unsuited to the needs of barracks troglodytes – that once belonged to the ruling class: a broken chair lined with cord on velvet upholstery, a stand for walking sticks, and a settee (facing the wall) whose rounded back in tandem with the wall makes a marvellous receptacle for storing potatoes.

A frightful corridor, a foul labyrinth, no end to it! But even its endlessness is not beyond reproach, for it is broken up by open doors, by the odd conversation, always more akin to an argument, or by the um-pa-ra um-pa-ra-ra of an accordion, and from one of the rooms comes the astonishing voice of a portable gramophone which goes on valiantly playing the same popular tune from the last war on the same dull needle (sad to say, the record cracked badly not long ago).

Aunt Dusya lives in the cornermost and most pitiful room. The eight linear feet abovementioned multiplied simply by five become forty square feet, and anyone who has occupied such a room knows that opposite the door is the window, that to the left you sleep and rummage in your trunk, while to the right you sit at the table and keep moths in the closet. A treadle sewing machine, if you have one, may stand by the window; if not, you may put, say, a stool there.

The bedding on Aunt Dusya's cot forms a hummock, since non-seasonal things and big bunches of torn brownish stockings, the raw material for darning heels, are stowed under the mattress. The stock-ings tend to contain flakes of the epidermis of the once-young Aunt Dusya; the stockings are all knitted, though an occasional exhibit is of lisle or even Persian thread.

The ceiling is low, six feet ten inches, but that doesn't bother anyone because people were short and stumpy then, like the Oryol peasants in Turgenev's novels. Turgenev's stately Kaluga peasants did not settle here and were found no closer than Grokholsky Lane, and that was miles and miles away.

So then, on the bed there was a hummock and this caused us – me, pressing against my girl, so as to die, and my girl, pressing against me, so as to restore me to life, my girl who, unlike me, knew wide beds and how best to use them – various (we won't go into it!) inconveniences frustrating the ancient and inarticulate rite of embrace.

The barrack, its corridor, Aunt Dusya ... My blindingly beautiful girl, who knew other – Oh God, I slid down again! – much wider beds, and I, who knew only trestle-beds – Oh God, you slid down again! – but who also knew that my blindingly beautiful girl, who knew other wider beds, had come to see me. Why all this together? Why did all this couple, combine, connect on the ground floor of a barrack, more specifically in its right-hand rear corner, if facing the barrack from the front? – oh God, we slid down again! – here's why.

Little, wheezing, old Aunt Dusya took care of my old friend, the never-married physics teacher Samson Yeseyich, who lived in the barrack across the road. But about him, as I said, later and not here. So now, Aunt Dusya, who considered friendship with me good for the brilliant Samson Yeseyich (about which also later and not here), and therefore respected me, had supplied me with the key to her tiny room through the kind offices of Samson Yeseyich. She was in the habit – for a little something or simply for a word of thanks – of loaning her key to friends of the physicist, probably because the carnal life of others excited pleasant thoughts in her.

People with good memories will never forget how hopeless it was in those days to find a corner in which to consummate the unbearable half-meetings begun in bushes, in building entrances, on park benches or in dormitories when the room-mates had fallen asleep – as if they ever did! So to land on Aunt Dusya's lumpy bunk, while Aunt Dusya herself went to her employer's to tidy up or just dashed out somewhere, was a rare and welcome piece of luck.

Now about *her* – the girl for whose sake I had got hold of Aunt Dusya's key:

We were trudging, by now deeply chagrined, uphill – this climb up a rough, rutted road studded with round flat sea stones and shingle on which one's feet kept twisting, had been a very bad idea of mine, and it seemed that she, my new friend, a Calypso-like beauty with fear in her eyes, was on the point of rebelling and wanting to turn back, since even the pretext for our ascent had been unclear and unconvincing: either to survey the sea from on high or to see what the new fruit on a tangerine tree looked like.

But my companion did not rebel, though she could have turned

right around, and I waited in dread for her indignation, for her acquiescence to cease: I was young then, but I knew that acquiescence could
easily turn to indignation. After all, she suspected, or rather understood our secret, or rather my intention – my clammy and intolerable
hope. Of course she, too, was party to our tacit compact. If not for
that torrid climb! At first she agreed to look at the new fruit, then she
changed her mind.

We sat down under a tangerine tree on the baked earth, on the dry
hot clods, and my hand began to insinuate itself between her softish,
slightly cool, but also slightly flushed thighs. My five-fingered touch
was discovering the longed-for world tucked between those stunning
buttresses; suddenly my wrist was creeping along the dry hot clods of
cultivated earth under the tangerine tree, and my fingers were squeezing in between her thighs, now relaxed, now clenched, and burying
themselves like pups in the damp, vast – after the closeness of her thighs
– tangle of the thickets attained. My girl was quivering, twitching and
protesting, 'Don't, or else I'll get a headache, a really bad one!' Yet
she went on, with her slender, ringed fingers, squeezing whatever she
liked. 'Let's wait,' she whispered, 'this isn't the place. People will see
us, and the sun . . . Let's wait!' She went on twitching, her knees now
irrevocably parted, but she was right, and the arid incline under the
wayside tangerine tree was wilting and dying under the sun.

Wait till Moscow? Which one of us was going away that day, I
don't remember. Let's wait till Moscow!

We walked to Aunt Dusya's at the end of a warm summer afternoon
past the barrack and the mangy little vegetable patches, fenced in, or
rather off from one another, with all sorts of junk. Standing in the
windows of the low ground floors were people and insipid indoor
plants, growing out of cans either rusty or once gold, now peeling.

Note: Russian cans have always been the colour of tin, and it was
only the war, on top of all its meagre miracles, that produced the gilt,
black-lettered cans of stewed pork that were our salvation. And though
the war was over, and though it was already so over that we had
somehow decided to return the Dresden art collection to the Germans,
once we had shown it to all comers, these cans still rotted in the
windows of the Pushkin student dorm, though some were wrapped in
pretty white paper cut-outs, now shrivelled from the sun, mildew and
water.

We walked to Aunt Dusya's, past low buildings in the windows
of which stood people who seemed not to know me, though my
acquaintances might just as easily have been standing there. Our

skilfully chosen route allowed us to avoid meeting anyone since, in the first place, I was with a woman and, in the second place, a woman utterly unheard of in these parts.

People's first and most correct thought would be that she was a spy, since she was dressed and adorned as no woman to this day has ever been dressed and adorned, save the heroine of that universal film favourite *The Girl of My Dreams*. Even I, whose fingers retained the memory of her bathing suit, wondrous for those days, heavy to the touch, like a portière, and phosphorescent beneath the stars of our night-tide swim, when everything was beginning and when she kissed me with a kiss unknown in my once and future life, well . . . even I, who knew her sartorial means, was stunned by what I saw.

As I said, the war had ended to such an extent that it was remembered as a time of hunger, but hunger with stewed pork, as opposed to the hunger after the war without stewed pork. The wartime styles (noted for battlefield chic) varied with American gifts (by those who had them) had ended, and the captured finery – fabulous for its elegance, its shimmering linings, its neat seams, its lacy underthings, and the many possible ways of wearing all this even inside out if you liked – had faded. The wartime styles had ended for everyone, and everyone was arrayed in their own homemade clothes. But not my girl. She came to me in a fantastic guise, which one I no longer recall, though she had her own, very good reasons for her appearance.

Women came to Blok[2] wafting perfume and mist. This I learned later. She came to me sparkling with rings, earrings and necklaces. All this would become known as costume jewellery and over the years people would get used to it, despite their shame and prejudices, they would get used to wearing this stuff that made broads look like ladies. But where could it have come from when it wasn't supposed to exist yet? Where did she get it all: the strange dress, the shoes with golden clasps glittering with glass beads? Where? Here's where: she was with the occupation forces in the Eastern bloc, had lived a long time in East Germany, and recently come from there, where she worked as a staff translator and lived with her husband, an officer in the secret service.

She was deathly afraid of her spook. With his secretive way of life and omniscience he compelled her soul and flesh to suffer, generally treating the latter with an unbearable brittleness. And this flesh was not assuaged, neither beside the warm sea, nor under the tangerine tree, for fear of being seen by some acquaintance, a junior officer, say, dispatched by the spook.

Nor could we arrange a meeting in Moscow. Not for a long time.

But now Aunt Dusya had given me her key, had gone out somewhere, and I was walking with my girl, a little to one side and a step ahead or, you could say, behind, along the little paths and backways around the Pushkin student dorm to Aunt Dusya's barrack. It certainly tests a man's mettle: trying to sneak a glittering woman in the door of a teeming barrack right on the main street.

As it is, people are lolling dumbstruck in every window, old women perched on banks of earth are combing out wisps of grey hair with fine-tooth combs, former classmates may appear, and then there's the man by the shed who has been fixing his bicycle for a year now.

The summer street is light and sunny, and behind another shed boys are mating rabbits. Girls huddle at a deliberate distance, but still see how the rabbit, raptly nibbling grass beside the doe one instant, rears up on her the next, one of the long-eared little beasts squeals, then both wiggle their noses, and resume eating. The boys insist that the rabbits are *fucking*. The girls, watching from afar, know what the rabbits are doing, but don't use the word *fucking*. The brazen boys, wanting the girls' attention, make circles with thumb and forefinger, then insert the other forefinger, and slide it back and forth. The girls walk off.

Thus I lead my girl through my childhood, but she neither sees nor cares; she walks beside me in silence, thinking only of how her spook may have had her shadowed.

She walks with amazing calm. She is simply numb and blind with fear. *Her* fear. *My* fear has made me monstrously sharp-eyed and, when we pass from the daylight into the barrack's pitch-dark corridor, I manage to make out someone's slummy laundry hanging at the far end and a man sorting maggots for bait in a tin can.

Some trouble with Aunt Dusya's key . . . and we're in the room. I've brought sandwiches. Red caviar. Five of them. Cheap eats in those days. And she produces wine! She produces . . . wine . . . Never in my wildest dreams would I have expected such a thing. She produces a wine I don't know, the only wines I know (and those by hearsay) are Cahors and 'three-sevens' port, highly regarded by local experts in anything you like – but not *this*.

'Wait a moment!' she says when I, having drunk a little wine and eaten half a sandwich, begin aquiver to embrace her, freely fondling the heavy warm folds of her soft dress, in itself a voluptuous sensation.

'Wait a moment!' she says. 'I have to run out first!'

'Run out?'

'I have to! Or else I can't . . .'

I am crushed. In the Pushkin student dorm they run out, here's where: for the entire barrack there are all of two barns, resembling, as it were, rural granaries. Each one is high and light on account of the chinks in the walls and a lone dormer window. The barns are bleached with lime which drools down the dingy boards to create a unique atmosphere of slovenliness and untouchability. Each granary is divided by a wall that would have reached the ceiling, had there been one, but above the wall is empty space, and higher still one can see the ridge of the gable roof.

On either side of the wall – in the male and female halves – there is a platform made out of thick boards in which a series of eight holes has been cut. The effect of another presence is total. First, because of the low partition; second, because if you stand slightly back from the platform, the product of the performer on the other side of the partition is visible in the pit.

As if this weren't enough, huge holes have been punched in the wall at different levels. Here and there the holes have been boarded up with whatever came to hand. But only here and there. Now I was not born in a palace, and I have visited my share of latrines, and that one is supposed to sit, not stand on a toilet seat, I figured out all by myself at the age of twenty-three, but I never ventured into those monstrous outhouses except in dire need, though on sultry days the stench in their simmering semi-darkness grew somehow languorous, and through the breaches in the partition one could observe the determined squatting and listen to intriguing bits of female conversation. But that was in summer.

As we know, our people are uncommonly careless and sloppy with regard to earth closets. It costs our people nothing, given their disdain for basic aiming skills, to foul the rim of the orifice, soak the floor and leave fingerprints on the wall. The boards absorb everything, everything sticks to them, deliberate sloppiness begets forced sloppiness, and it becomes harder and harder to position oneself over the hole. Puddles further frustrate one's approach to the sloping grey gutter, especially if one is in soft soles or slippers.

And now, the cold is upon us. Everything that has been absorbed begins to freeze and form layers. By late December, crossing the ice crust to a hole is out of the question. There is less and less room for manoeuvre. The visiting public retreats closer and closer to the door, fouling the floor higgledy-piggledy. The walls (inside only, so far) are caked with tall ice crusts the colour of whey, rising up out of the floor like stalagmites, interspersed with fossilized brown clumps. The hoarfrost on the boards, the yellow newspapers frozen in the ice, the yellow crystals forming under the roof: nothing deters our people –

where else can they go? By mid-February, only by standing in the doorway may one celebrate the call of nature in the murk of the fossil world.

This circumstance decidedly alters the daily rhythms of the Pushkin student dorm. People put off going until dusk or after dark. By now the walls are caked even on the outside with turbid ice crusts, by now the expanse around the walls, if not covered with snow, is you can well imagine what.

But now spring arrives. Someone, cursing wildly, is cleaning out all this muck. Who, I don't know. For half an hour after it has been hosed down the granary looks human, then it begins all over again, and towards evening masturbator Mitrokhin walks in and takes a swift chisel to the rough-hewn wall's most promising hole. In no time at all, he is convulsing in a corner in response to the rustling behind the partition.

For this granary, then, my girl is calmly about to set out. In haste and confusion, I explain the long way round, unable to imagine how she will get there, and if she does, how she, wafting perfume and mist, will react to the shame, how she will ford the swollen floor in her velvet slippers.

I cannot take her there, for I simply cannot imagine how anyone could take a woman to that place, and so become unwittingly initiated into this utterly secret necessity, into this apotheosis of awkwardness and discouraged dignity.

She goes. I wait. I get it! Walking through the settlement, humiliated by the road to Aunt Dusya's, appalled by her forty-square-foot burrow – I'm used to it, but she's seeing it for the first time – by the musty humpbacked bed on which we *will*, by the table with the caviar sandwiches, red-and-white and sparkling beside the cloudy tumbler in whose putrid water a dirty swollen onion, now limp and splayed, has disgorged the repulsive greenish bud of an onion leaf ... seeing all this made her change her mind. She's gone. She's just up and gone! She took her purse, didn't she! True, she left the wine ... she brought wine ... It never ever occurred to me that anyone would bring wine for my sake. She's gone! And if she's not gone, then she's lost, and if she's not lost then somebody's picked her up: as I said, the neighbours might easily think she was a spy. Only recently, loyal and concerned citizens not far from here caught a spy, apparently American. Or even two.

'Hey, Kalinych, you mother, why'd you block my woodpile with your bicycle? Ain't you ever gonna be done with that thing?' the cheerful start of a friendly exchange by the shed can be heard outside the window. I startle, freeze, steal up to the window, and peek through the slit between the gauze curtain and the peeling wood.

A rivulet of tiny ants streams by my eye, skirting a stony tumour of oil paint on Aunt Dusya's window frame. They stream out of one chink and disappear an inch or so later into another. That's nothing! At this point, my eyes could make out an amoeba. My ears could pick up ultrasound.

'Kalinych, you fuck . . .' the usual sounds from the vicinity of the shed and then my pounding heart stops as the door, just behind me, opens with a jolt. I jerk round and am amazed to see my girl slip quietly into the room.

'Here I am,' she says, and I fasten my sharp eyes on her velvet slippers, especially the delicate line of her pretty dyed-black sole.

'Where can I wash my hands?'

Oh God! It will never end! I don't know where Aunt Dusya's washstand is in the endless corridor or which shard of soap on which of the thirty-three shelves belongs to her or what sort of soap it is. Maybe it's the marble soap sold by weight and boiled by the Ruzhan-sky soap-boiler – though boiled out of what? About that in due course. What if the basin under the washstand is full and has to be emptied? And if it's full, then of what?

'*Unmöglich!*'[3] I say, because my girl speaks German beautifully and at the time I too could get along in this language fairly well which, incidentally, is largely what drew me to her there, where the tangerine trees bear fruit.

'*Unmöglich, weil ich weiss nicht wo ist der* Aunt Dusya's washstand *und Seife!*'[4] I play the fool, and she, smiling, takes a sparkling perfume bottle from her bag, then some cotton wool, and neatly wipes her fingers with the many magnificent rings, among them a thick band binding her to her spook – not the custom then and also a surprising thing.

She went to the window, glanced through the slit to one side of the curtain, then turned around, undid her dress, took it off, then took off some other mysterious underthings, then took off everything else, and for the first time I saw a woman who had undressed for me.

'Now you take everything off!' said this miracle when I went up to her, embraced her and dazedly pressed myself into this unbearably various nakedness so unlike my own uniformity.

'Wait a moment! Stop! Metal inhibits love!' And she began to remove the sparkling objects from her neck, from her wrists, from her fingers, from her ears, and put them on the oilcloth-covered table where there soon accrued a small heap of watches, earrings, bracelets, rings – one rolled away under the bed. By her exquisite legs I, like the young Actaeon, found the gossamer ring in the desolation under the bed, and as I pulled my head out, I saw, still on my hands and knees, that the exquisite legs had been tucked up out of my way – taken off the floor: she had sat down on the humpbacked bed, and then lain down. I quietly placed the ring on the oilcloth. The ring clung trustingly to the others, and I just as trustingly entered the land where they kiss strangers sweetly, caress them, enchant them and yet sob, clinging to these strangers – the land of ripening tangerines and dry hot earth, the land of two, along whose damp sandy shores the wanderer Odysseus bends his firm steps towards Calypso languishing in the tangled thickets of her hair.

This was free love. All my previous conquests – hurried, prehensile, greedy and pitiful – were under-love compared with what happened in the land of the tangerine sun. Outside it was getting dark, in the room it was twilight, and this dusk increasingly isolated the land I had entered over and again, always to the sound of muffled laughter, muffled sobs, muffled words, and where I suddenly sensed moist lips humbly kissing my regal hand.

This was a meeting of two people who, for different reasons, dearly needed each other. A woman who needed me, and I, who needed this woman most in the world. A meeting without shame, or rather *outside shame*, celebrating with muffled sobs our triumph over the foul surround and over the hero of these out-of-the-way places, the spook; a meeting joining experience of vast Pomeranian beds with the entertaining erotica of Russian suburbs, slaking Mitrokhin's unbearable reverie, and sanctifying the ancient gesture made by the brazen boys in front of the girls at the rabbits' wedding.

The weary tangerine sun was already sinking when we heard a polite little cough through the door.

'Your landlady! She's been sitting there a long time, I think!'

When we came out of the room, leaving as a token of thanks two whole sandwiches and one almost whole, as well as half a bottle of wine, we found Aunt Dusya slumped on a sack of bran in the now empty corridor. She was dozing and softly grunting. I touched her padded jacket, I had to return the key. She jumped up, grinned slyly and surprised us with this phrase worthy of Sumarokov:[5] 'Love is by nature inherent in people!'

On the benighted street, my girl and I quickly went our separate ways, because she might run into undesirable acquaintances at the Ostankino tram stop, she said, scraping a fleck of red caviar off her teeth.

*

I walked away from the Pushkin student dorm and, by the last barrack, ran into Nasibullin, a shy and very modest Tatar boy who enrolled voluntarily in a secret service college after school.

'Good evening!' he said politely because he always strove to associate his cultivation, diligently acquired thanks to the concern of society, with my own innate cultivation and, by way of continuing this association, he asked shyly: 'Been to the Dresden show yet?'

'Na-a-ah!'

'Go, don't miss it!' And to pique my interest he glanced down the dusky alleys, looked terribly embarrassed and said: 'Lots of naked people!'

> Written 1979–80; first published in 1989
> Translated by Joanne Turnbull

SERGEI DONATOVICH
DOVLATOV (1941–90)

*Dovlatov considered his largely autobiographical stories to be untrans-
latable. He delighted, however, in the Russian translations of Mark
Twain, another celebrated storyteller whose best work hinges on the
humour in colloquial speech. Tom Sawyer's mock-casual confession
– 'I stopped to talk with Huckleberry Finn' – was filled with an
ineffable charm for Dovlatov, many of whose own characters – funny,
silly, unexpectedly astute, devil-may-care, vulnerable – have the sympathetic, democratic appeal of a Tom or Huck.*

*Half-Armenian and half-Jewish, Dovlatov was born in Ufa but grew
up in Leningrad; in 1962 he was expelled from university, drafted
into the Army and sent to the northern Komi republic to serve as a
prison-camp guard. He returned from there 'like Tolstoy from the
Crimea,' Joseph Brodsky later recalled, 'with a scroll of stories and a
certain look of bemusement'.[1]*

*Dovlatov's efforts to publish his stories in Soviet journals all failed.
He worked as a journalist and trained to be a stonecutter ('the most
fitting profession for me after literature'). In 1975 the proofs of his
first book were destroyed by the KGB. A year later several of his
stories appeared in the West. Dovlatov was expelled from the Union
of Journalists and ended up guarding an ice-bound barge on the Neva.
In 1978 he emigrated, first to Vienna, then to New York where he
published prolifically in both English and Russian.*

*Dovlatov held that a prose writer (as opposed to a poet, who is
inevitably constrained by the demands of metre and rhyme) must wear
'creative fetters' to guard against verbiage. His own 'creative fetter'
was to require that no two words in any one sentence begin with the
same letter (an impediment impossible to honour in English, if only
because of the articles). His stories combine humour and bitterness,
mischief and sentimentality, the impressionism of an anecdote and the
factualness of a document. As Brodsky has said, 'they are written like
poems'.*

'The Officer's Belt' comes from The Suitcase, *a cycle of stories*

inspired by the contents of the old suitcase that Dovlatov supposedly took with him when he left the Soviet Union: a decent double-breasted suit, a poplin shirt and shoes, a corduroy jacket lined with fake fur, a winter hat of imitation seal, three pairs of Finnish crêpe socks, driving gloves and, finally, a leather officer's belt.

Joanne Turnbull

THE OFFICER'S BELT

The worst thing for a drunk is coming to in a hospital bed. Not yet fully awake, you mutter, 'That's it! I'm going on the wagon! Going on the wagon for good. Not another drop!'

And suddenly you discover a thick gauze bandage on your head. You want to touch the dressings, but it turns out your left arm is in a cast. And so on.

This all happened to me in the summer of 1963 in the south of Komi.

The year before, I'd been drafted into the army. Enlisted as a prison-camp guard. I completed a twenty-day course for jailers near Sindor . . .

Still earlier I had spent two years learning to box. I'd entered major competitions. But I don't remember my trainer ever once saying, 'That's it! I don't have to worry about you any more.'

I did hear it, though, from Instructor Toroptsev at the school for jailers. After only three weeks. And despite the fact that I would be dealing not with boxers, but with recidivists . . .

I tried to look round. Patches of sunlight shone yellow on the linoleum. The bedside table was crammed with medicines. A wall newspaper hung by the door: LENIN AND PUBLIC HEALTH.

There was a smell of smoke and, oddly enough, seaweed. I was in the medical unit.

My tightly bandaged head ached. I sensed a deep gash over one eyebrow. My left arm was out of commission.

My army tunic was draped over the end of the bed. In the pocket, I thought, there had to be a few cigarettes. For an ashtray I used a jar containing some sort of inky solution. I had to hold the matchbox in my teeth.

Now I could think back over the events of yesterday.

In the morning I'd been crossed off the escort list. I'd gone to the first sergeant.

'What's happened? Am I really getting the day off?'

'More or less,' said the sergeant, 'you're in luck ... A prisoner's gone off his head in barrack 14. Barking like a dog, crowing like a cock ... He bit the cook, Aunt Shura ... Anyway, take him to the psychiatric hospital at Iosser and you can have the rest of the day off. Sort of a half-holiday.'

'When do I go?'

'Soon as you're ready.'

'Alone?'

'You can't go alone, it's against regulations. Take Churilin with you, or Gayenko ...'

I found Churilin in the tool shop. He was busy with a soldering iron. On the workbench something was crackling and giving off a smell of rosin.

'I'm doing some welding,' said Churilin. 'Very fine work. Take a look.'

I saw a brass buckle with a raised star. The inside of the star had been filled with tin. A belt with a weld like that was a dangerous weapon.

That was the fashion then among our enforcers: leather officers' belts. They filled the buckles with tin and went to dances. If a fight broke out, the brass buckles flashed overhead ...

I said, 'Get your things together.'

'What for?'

'We're taking some nut to Iosser. A prisoner in barrack 14's gone bananas. And bitten Aunt Shura to boot.'

'Good for him,' said Churilin. 'Obviously wanted some grub. That Shura sneaks prison butter home. I've seen her.'

'Let's go,' I said.

Churilin cooled the buckle under the faucet, then put on the belt: 'Let's roll ...'

They issued us guns; we went to the guardhouse. Two minutes later an inspector came in with a fat, unshaven prisoner. The prisoner was resisting and screaming:

'I want a pretty girl, an athlete! A medalist! Give me a medalist! How long do I have to wait?'

'At least six years,' replied the inspector, without irritation. 'And that's if they let you out early. You're in for grand larceny, you know.'

The prisoner ignored him and went on screaming, 'C'mon, creeps, gimme a medalist!'

Churilin sized him up, then nudged me with his elbow, 'Hey, what do you mean he's nuts? Nothing wrong with him. First he wanted grub, now he wants a broad. A medalist, no less ... The guy's got taste ... I wouldn't say no either ...'

The inspector gave me the papers. We went out on to the stoop.

Churilin asked, 'What's your name?'

'Do-re-mi-fat-so,' said the prisoner.

Then I said to him, 'If you're truly crazy, that's fine by me. And if you're faking it, that's OK too. I'm not a doctor. My job is to get you to Iosser. That's all I care about. On one condition: that you don't overact. Start biting and I'll shoot. But you can crow and bark all you like ...'

We had a three-mile walk ahead of us. No lumber trucks were going our way. Captain Sokolovsky had taken the camp chief's car. They said he'd gone to Inta to take some exams.

In short, we'd have to go on foot. The road wound through a settlement to some peat bogs. From there it went past a grove and up to a railroad crossing. Beyond the crossing began the camp watchtowers of Iosser.

Near a store in the settlement Churilin slowed down. I handed him a couple of roubles. You didn't have to worry about patrols at this hour of the day.

The prisoner clearly approved of our idea. In his joy, he became suddenly expansive, 'The name's Tolik ...'

Churilin came out with a bottle of vodka. I stuffed it in the pocket of my jodhpurs. Now all we had to do was hold off till we got to the grove.

The prisoner kept remembering his insanity. From time to time he got down on all fours and growled.

I advised him not to waste his strength. Save it for the medical examination. We wouldn't give him away.

Churilin spread a newspaper on the grass and pulled a few crackers out of his pocket.

We drank in turn, straight from the bottle. The prisoner hesitated at first, 'The doctor might smell it on me and think it was unnatural ...'

Churilin cut him off: 'And barking and crowing's natural? Eat some sorrel afterward and no one'll know the difference.'

The prisoner said, 'You've talked me into it.'

The day was warm and sunny. Light changeable clouds drifted across the sky. Lumber trucks honked with impatience at the railroad crossing. A bumblebee vibrated over Churilin's head.

The vodka began to take effect, and I thought, 'God, it's good to be free! When I'm demobilized I'll spend hours just walking in the streets. Stop by the café on Marat. Have a cigarette on a bench by the old Duma . . .'

I realize freedom is a philosophical concept. That doesn't interest me. Slaves, after all, don't care about philosophy. Go where you want: that's freedom!

My drinking companions were chatting easily. The prisoner was explaining, 'My head's not in good shape. Plus I've got gas . . . Frankly, they ought to release people like me. Write us off because of illness. The way they write off old equipment.'

Churilin interrupted him again, 'Head's not in good shape? Didn't you have enough sense to steal? Your papers say you're in for grand larceny. So tell us, what did you swipe?'

The prisoner pretended to brush the question aside, 'Oh, nothing much . . . A tractor . . .'

'A whole tractor?'

'Yeah.'

'How'd you pull it off?'

'Very simple. At a plant that casts reinforced concrete. I used psychology.'

'What d'you mean?'

'I walked into the plant, climbed onto a tractor – I'd hooked an empty oil drum on behind – and headed for the guard post. The metal drum made a racket so a guard came out: "Where are you going with that drum?" "On personal business," I said. "Got the papers?" "No." "Then unhook it, goddamn it!" I unhooked the drum and drove on. All in all, the psychology worked. Later we disassembled the tractor for parts . . .'

Churilin clapped the prisoner on the back in admiration, 'You're an artist, pal!'

The prisoner humbly concurred, 'I did win the respect of the people.'

Churilin suddenly stood up: 'Long live the labour reserves!'

He pulled a second bottle out of his pocket.

By this time the sun had invaded our glade. We moved into the shade and sat down on a felled alder.

Churilin gave the command, 'Let's roll!'

It was hot. The prisoner unbuttoned his shirt. On his chest a gunpowder tattoo cried out *Faina! Remember those golden days?*

Next to it were a skull, a bowie knife and a jar marked POISON . . .

Churilin was drunk before I knew it. I didn't even see it coming. Suddenly he was silent and glum.

I knew that our barrack was full of neurotics. Guard duty inevitably leads to that. But Churilin had always struck me as comparatively sane.

He had done only one crazy thing that I could remember. We had taken some prisoners out to fell trees. We were sitting by the stove in a wooden shack, warming ourselves and talking. Naturally, we were drinking.

Without a word Churilin went outside. He got a bucket from somewhere and filled it with crude oil. Then he climbed up on to the roof and poured the fuel down the stovepipe.

The shack filled with fire. We barely got out. Three of us had burns.

But that was a long time ago. Now I said to him, 'Calm down.'

Churilin reached silently for his pistol. Then we heard, 'On your feet! This two-man brigade is now under the escort's command! If necessary, the escort will use arms. Prisoner Kholodenko, forward march! Private First Class Dovlatov, fall in behind!'

I went on trying to calm him down: 'Snap out of it. Pull yourself together. And put that pistol away.'

The prisoner expressed surprise: 'What's all the ruckus about?'

Churilin meanwhile released the safety catch. I walked towards him, repeating, 'You've just had too much to drink.'

Churilin started to back away. I kept walking towards him, trying not to make any sudden moves. Out of fear I babbled something incoherent. I remember I even smiled.

Our prisoner, though, did not lose his presence of mind. He whooped merrily, 'Time to make my getaway!'

I could see the felled alder behind Churilin. Another step back and he'd trip over it. I bent down. I knew that in falling he might shoot. And that's exactly what happened.

A shot rang out and branches cracked . . .

The pistol fell to the ground. I kicked it aside.

Churilin got up. Now I wasn't afraid of him. I could knock him flat from any position. And I had the prisoner by my side.

I saw Churilin undoing his belt. I didn't realize what it meant. I thought he wanted to tuck his shirt in.

Theoretically I could have killed or at least wounded him. We were on a mission, after all. In a combat situation, so to speak. I would have been acquitted.

Instead I again made a move in his direction. Good breeding had gotten in my way even back in my boxing days.

As a result Churilin brought the brass buckle down on my head.

Fortunately, I remember everything. I didn't lose consciousness. I didn't feel the blow itself, but saw blood dripping on my trousers. So much blood that I had to cup my hands. I stood there and watched it drip.

At least the prisoner knew what to do. He grabbed the belt away from Churilin. Then bandaged my forehead with his shirtsleeve.

Here Churilin, evidently, began to realize what he'd done. He clutched his head in despair and, sobbing, trudged off towards the road.

His pistol was lying in the grass. Next to the empty bottles. I said to the prisoner, 'Pick it up.'

Now imagine what a picture we made: a wailing enforcer at the head of the procession, followed by a deranged prisoner with a pistol and, bringing up the rear, a private first class with a blood-soaked bandage round his head. A military patrol was coming towards us. A jeep with three soldiers pointing sub-machine guns and a gargantuan wolfhound.

I still can't believe they didn't shoot my prisoner. They could easily have sunk a few rounds into him. Or loosed the dog.

As soon as I saw the jeep, I lost consciousness. My volitional centres gave out. And the heat finally took its toll. I only managed to tell them that the prisoner wasn't to blame. As for who was to blame, they could figure it out for themselves.

On top of that, I broke my arm in the fall. Rather, I didn't break it, I damaged it. They found a crack in my forearm. That was really unnecessary, I thought.

The last thing I remembered was the dog. Sitting next to me, it yawned nervously, opening wide its lilac jaws . . .

A wall radio sputtered to life above my head. I heard a buzzing, followed by soft clicks. I pulled out the plug, without waiting for the triumphant strains of the Soviet anthem.

I was suddenly reminded of a forgotten sensation from my childhood. I'm running a temperature and so have been allowed to stay home from school.

I'm waiting for the doctor. He'll sit on my bed. He'll look into my throat. And he'll say: 'Well now, young man.' Mama will find him a clean towel.

I'm happy: I'm sick, and everyone feels sorry for me. I mustn't wash with cold water . . .

I began waiting for the doctor to appear. Churilin appeared instead. He peeped in the open window and swung a leg over the sill. Then he came towards me. His look was mournful and beseeching.

I tried to kick him in the scrotum. He stepped out of the way and said, wringing his disingenuous hands:

'Serge! I'm sorry. I was wrong . . . I repent . . . Truly repent . . . I was under the affluence . . .'

'Influence,' I corrected.

'All the more . . .'

Churilin took a few cautious steps in my direction:

'I meant it as a joke . . . Just for the hell of it . . . I have no grievances against you . . .'

'I should hope not,' I said.

What could I say to him? What can you say to a guard whose only use for aftershave lotion is internal?

I asked, 'How's our prisoner?'

'Fine. He's gone bananas again. Been singing "My Land So Vast and Free" all morning. He goes in for his examination tomorrow. For now he's in solitary.'

'And you?'

'And I, naturally, am in the guardhouse. That is, in fact I'm here, but in theory I'm in the guardhouse. A buddy of mine's on duty right now . . . I've got to talk to you.'

Churilin came a step closer and burst out, 'Serge, I'm finished, I'm cooked! The Comrades' Court! Trial's on Thursday!'

'Whose trial?'

'My trial. They say I've crippled you.'

'OK, I'll tell them I have no grievances. That I forgive you.'

'I already told them that. They say it doesn't matter, their patience has run out.'

'Well then, what can I do?'

'You're educated – think of something. Turn the pecker inside out, as they say. Or else those bastards'll pass the paperwork on to the tribunal. And I'll get three years in a disciplinary battalion. A disbat's worse than camp. You gotta help me . . .'

He screwed up his face and tried to cry, 'I'm the only son . . . My brother's in prison, sisters are all married . . .'

I said, 'I don't know what to suggest. There is one possibility . . .'

Churilin brightened up: 'What?'

'At the trial I'll ask a question. I'll say: "Churilin, do you have a civilian occupation?" And you'll say: "No." Then I'll say: "What's he supposed to do after he's demobilized – steal? Where are the promised courses in driver's education and crane operation? Why are we worse than a regular army?" And so on. Other soldiers in the hall will jump in and raise hell. They may even bail you out.'

Churilin brightened up even more and sat down on my bed, repeating, 'What brains! Now that's what I call brains! With brains like that you could, in theory, get by without working at all.'

'Especially,' I said, 'if you bash them in with a brass buckle.'

'That's behind us now,' said Churilin, 'it's all forgotten . . . Write down what I'm supposed to say.'

'I just told you.'

'And now write it out. Otherwise I'll get all mixed up.'

Churilin handed me the stub of an indelible pencil. Then he tore off a piece of the wall newspaper: 'Write.'

I spelled it out: *No*.

'What does that mean, "No"?' he asked.

'You said: "Write down what I'm supposed to say." And I've written it down: *No*. In court I'll ask you: "Do you have a civilian occupation?" And you'll say: "No." Then I'll do my bit about the crane operation courses. And the uproar will begin.'

'You mean I only have to say one word – "No"?'

'I guess so, yes.'

'That's not very much,' said Churilin.

'You may have to answer some other questions as well.'

'Like what?'

'I don't know.'

'But what'll I say?'

'Depends on what they ask you.'

'What'll they ask me? Roughly?'

'Well, for instance: "Do you plead guilty, Churilin?"'

'And what'll I say?'

'You'll say: "Yes."'

'That's all?'

'Or you could say: "Yes, of course I plead guilty and I am deeply sorry."'

'That's more like it. Write that down. First the question, then my answer. Write the questions the usual way and the answers in block letters. So I don't confuse them . . .'

Churilin and I conferred until eleven. The doctor's assistant wanted to kick him out, but Churilin said, 'May I not talk to my comrade in arms?'

As a result we wrote an entire play. Complete with dozens of possible questions and answers. What's more, Churilin insisted I indicate in parentheses: *(Coldly)*, *(Pensively)*, *(Confusedly)*.

Then they brought me my lunch: a plate of soup, fried fish and watery jelly.

Churilin was surprised: 'Food's better here than in the guardhouse.'

I said, 'Would you rather it were the other way round?'

I had to give him the jelly and the fish.

After that, we parted. Churilin said, 'My buddy in the guardhouse goes off duty at noon. Then some Ukrainian comes on. So I've got to be there.'

Churilin walked over to the window. He turned round: 'I forgot. Let's trade belts. Otherwise I'll get a longer sentence for this buckle.'

He took my soldier's belt. And hung his own on the end of the bed.

'You're lucky,' he said, 'mine's made of natural leather. And the buckle has a weld. One blow and a guy's out cold!'

'Yes, I know . . .'

Churilin went back to the window. And again turned round.

'Thank you,' he said, 'I'll never forget this.'

Then he climbed out of the window. Though he could just as easily have used the door.

At least he didn't walk off with my cigarettes . . .

Three days went by. The doctor told me I'd gotten off lightly. All I had was a scratch on my head.

I wandered round the cantonment. Spent hours in the library. Sunbathed on the roof of the woodshed.

Twice I tried going into the guardhouse. Once there was a first-year Latvian on duty. He raised his sub-machine gun as soon as he saw me. I wanted to leave some cigarettes, but he shook his head.

That evening I went by again. This time an instructor I knew was on duty.

'Come on in,' he said, 'you can even spend the night.'

He rattled his keys. The door swung open.

Churilin was playing cards with three other prisoners. A fifth was watching the game while he ate a sandwich. The floor was littered with orange peel.

'Hi there,' said Churilin. 'Now be quiet, I'm just about to get 'em down on all fours.'

I handed him a pack of Belomors.

'What, no booze?' said Churilin.

You had to admire his nerve.

I stayed for a minute and left.

Next morning notices were posted everywhere: *Open Komsomol Meeting. Entire Division Invited. Comrades' Court. Personal Case of Churilin, Vadim Tikhonovich. Attendance Compulsory.*

An old-timer walked by.

'Finally,' he said. 'Been getting away with murder . . . What goes on in those barracks, it's frightening . . . The liquor flows till they're ankle-deep . . .'

Some sixty people had gathered at the clubhouse. The Komsomol bigwigs were up on-stage. Churilin had been seated off to one side, by the flag. Everyone was waiting for Major Afanasyev.

Churilin looked utterly blissful. Maybe this was his first time in the spotlight. He was gesticulating, waving to friends. He waved to me, too, by the way.

Major Afanasyev went up on-stage.

'Comrades!'

Gradually the hall settled down.

'Comrade soldiers! Today we will discuss the personal case of Private Churilin. Private Churilin was sent on a responsible mission with Private First Class Dovlatov. Along the way Private Churilin got blind drunk and proceeded to commit irresponsible acts. As a result, bodily harm was done to Private First Class Dovlatov who, by the way, is just as much of a fuck-up, forgive me, as Churilin . . . They might have controlled themselves with a prisoner present . . .'

While the Major was saying all this, Churilin beamed with pleasure. He combed his hair a couple of times, fidgeted in his chair, fooled with the flag. He clearly felt like a hero.

The Major went on: 'In this quarter alone, Churilin has spent twenty-six days in the guardhouse. I'm not talking about benders – they're like snow in winter for Churilin. I'm talking about more serious crimes, like fights. You get the sense that for him Communism has already been built. He doesn't like your look – he socks you in the jaw. Soon everyone will be swinging his fists. You think there isn't anyone I'd like to take a swing at myself? Anyway, my patience has run out. Here's the question: Does Churilin stay with us or do his papers go to the tribunal? This is a serious matter, comrades! Now let's begin! Tell us, Churilin, what happened.'

Everyone stared at Churilin. A crumpled scrap of paper appeared in his hands. He twisted it, studied it and whispered something soundlessly.

'Tell us what happened,' repeated Major Afanasyev.

Churilin looked at me in confusion. We'd obviously forgotten something. Left something out of our script.

The Major raised his voice, 'Don't keep us waiting!'

'I'm in no hurry,' said Churilin.

He looked gloomy. His face was becoming more and more angry and morose. The irritation in the Major's voice, too, was growing. I had to step in: 'Why don't I tell what happened?'

'As you were!' shouted the Major. 'You're a fine one yourself!'

'O-oh,' said Churilin, 'well . . . I'd like to . . . you know . . . take a course in crane operation . . .'

The Major turned to him: 'What do courses have to do with it, for crying out loud? He got drunk, see, maimed his friend, and now he's dreaming of courses! Perhaps you'd like to go to university? Or study music?'

Churilin glanced at his paper again and said sullenly, 'Why are we worse than a regular army?'

The Major was choking with rage: 'How long can this go on? You try to meet him halfway, but he won't budge! You say "Tell us what happened," but he doesn't want to!'

'There's nothing to tell,' Churilin jumped up. 'Whad'ya want, a fucking *Forsyte Saga*?[1] "Tell us! Tell us!" What's to tell? The hell I will, bastard. Wanna make me mad? I could run you through, too, y'know!'

The Major grabbed his holster. Red spots bloomed on his cheek-bones. His breathing became laboured. Then he pulled himself together:

'Everything is clear to the court. Session adjourned!'

Two old-timers took Churilin by the arm. I pulled out my cigarettes and headed for the exit . . .

Churilin got a year in a disciplinary battalion. A month before his release I was demobilized. I never saw the crazy prisoner again, either.

That whole world has disappeared somewhere.

Only the belt remains.

First published in 1986
Translated by Joanne Turnbull

YURY VASILYEVICH BUIDA (b. 1954)

Buida's surrealism seems to derive partly from his early reading of Gogol, and partly from historical circumstances. His story-cycle The Prussian Bride *is set in the Kaliningrad region, the area once known as East Prussia, which Stalin seized from Germany in 1945. By the end of 1947, every last German had been deported. To Russian settlers the region was, in Buida's words, 'an alien land scattered with miracles mutating into monsters'.*

Buida has described how his mother, who had been brought up in Central Russia, first arrived in this region in 1947. Her train ticket bore the name of her destination: the town of Wehlau. She arrived, however, to find workmen blanking out this name from signs in the station. That night she and two friends speculated as to how the town would be renamed. Her own suggestion, 'Somewhere', was dismissed as too definite, not Russian enough. Her friends suggested 'Sometime or Other' or 'Any Old How'. In the event, the town was called Znamensk, after the Russian for banner.[1]

All the stories in The Prussian Bride *are set in Znamensk, where Buida was born and brought up. They resemble a collection of small-town myths whose truth has been embellished over the decades. Many of the characters are remarkable not only for their ready acceptance of the surreal, but also for their feats of memory. In a land with no past, memory is of supreme importance.*

Like Dante, from whom he claims to have learned economy of means, Buida is a poet of love – and the memory of love. And like Dostoyevsky, another writer of importance to him, he is afraid neither of emotional intensity nor of the profoundest philosophical themes. All this is apparent even from a story as short as 'Sindbad the Sailor'.

SINDBAD THE SAILOR

Before dying, Katerina Ivanovna Momotova sent for Doctor Sheberstov, who'd treated her all her life and had been pensioned off a long time ago. She handed him the key to her little house and a scrap of paper folded in four, asking him to burn it along with all the others.

'They're at home,' she explained in embarrassment. 'But please don't tell anyone. I'd have done it myself, only you see how it's all turned out . . .'

Sheberstov raised his eyebrows, but the old woman just smiled guiltily in reply. She was in a very bad way: dying from a sarcoma. The doctor looking after her at the hospital said she was unlikely to make it through the night.

Lyosha Leontyev was having a smoke on the bench by the hospital entrance. Next to hulking Sheberstov, he looked like a teenager in police uniform. His cap with its faded band was lying in the sidecar of his motorbike.

'Fancy a walk?' asked the doctor, gazing over Lyosha's head at the midges circling a dim streetlamp atop a wooden post turned green by the damp. 'To Katya Ivanovna's.'

'To Sindbad the Sailor, you mean? She hasn't died, has she?'

'No.' Sheberstov showed the policeman the key. 'She asked me to look in. I'm an outsider, at least you're law and order.'

Lyosha dropped his fag-end in a wide stone vase filled with water and got up with a sigh. 'Wish it were winter already . . .'

They set off at a leisurely pace along the slabbed pavement towards the mill, next to which lived Katerina Ivanovna, famous throughout the town for her exemplarily unsuccessful life.

She'd arrived here in East Prussia with the first settlers. Her husband had worked at the paper mill, she as a washerwoman at the hospital. They'd had four kids: two of their own and two they took from the children's home. The withered little woman had a big household to look after: a vegetable patch, a cow, a piglet, two dozen sheep, chickens, ducks, her ailing husband Fyodor Fyodorovich (who'd been wounded three times at the front) and the kids. In '57 she lost half a leg – she was run over by a train as she was bringing the heifer back from pasture. She'd had to leave the wash-house. Got a job as a caretaker at the nursery school. That same year her eldest boy, Vasya, drowned in the Pregolya. Three years later Fyodor Fyodorovich died too: an operation on his heart, which had been grazed by shrapnel proved too much for him. The girls grew up and left town. The youngest, Vera, married a drunken, thieving down-and-out; dumping their son on his granny, they upped and left for Siberia, hoping to make some money – and vanished. For the sake of the kid, Katerina Ivanovna knitted to order (before her fingers became riddled with arthritis), sheared sheep and herded all summer long. It wasn't easy for her chasing after the animals on her peg leg, but the pay wasn't bad and sometimes she'd even get fed out in the fields – she didn't grumble. The boy grew up, did his stint in the army, got married and only rarely – for New Year or May Day – sent his grandma a card wishing her success in her work and happiness in her private life. Katerina Ivanovna's pension was piddling. By and by, she found herself collecting empty bottles in vacant plots and backstreets or outside shops. She'd get into squabbles with her rivals, boys who yelled 'How much for a pound of old hag!' when they saw her and swiped her booty. Katerina Ivanovna got angry and swore, but her rage only lasted so long. Eventually she found a solution. She'd head out of town bright and early with a sack over her shoulders and hunt for empties in the ditches and woods by the road. Despite the pain from her leg, she trudged for miles each day, returning home with her rich pickings late in the evening, her eyes sunken and hot sweat streaming off her. She crumbled bread into a deep bowl, poured vodka over it and slurped it up with a spoon. Once in a while she'd start singing something afterwards in a quiet, tinkling voice. 'Others in her shoes would've croaked ages ago,' Battle-Axe, the town Tsarina, would say. 'But she's not even properly bonkers yet.' It was thanks to her bottle hikes that Katerina Ivanovna received the nickname Sindbad the Sailor.

Glancing furtively to both sides, Doctor Sheberstov opened the front door and motioned Lyosha ahead. Lyosha turned on the lights in the hall and kitchen. 'What did she want anyway?' he shouted from the other room. 'What is it we're after?'

Sheberstov didn't reply. He unfolded the piece of paper that Katerina Ivanovna had given him along with the key, and his face became flushed and swollen. He flung the scrap on to the kitchen table, bent down to avoid hitting his head on a beam and, wheezing noisily, came up behind Lyosha. The policeman was pensively inspecting the old woman's second room. A dim, unshaded bulb shone on an enormous pile of paper that took up nearly all the available space.

'What's she been doing, writing novels?' muttered Lyosha. 'Look here . . .' He picked up a scrap of paper from the floor. 'I loved you.

Even now, perhaps, love's embers . . .' He threw the doctor a puzzled look. 'What's it all about, eh?'

Sheberstov put his stick in his other hand and shoved Lyosha firmly to one side. Puffing and panting, he squeezed through a narrow gap to a bent-backed chair and sat down. He grabbed a handful of scraps from one of the piles and started reading.

'So what *is* all this?' Lyosha repeated, gazing in bewilderment at one of the scraps covered with an old woman's scrawl. 'She can't have . . .'

Sheberstov angrily looked him up and down.

'So who do you think invented the soul, the Devil?'

All night long they sorted through the papers that Sindbad the Sailor had asked to be destroyed and which she'd hidden from sight for almost fifty years. Every day, starting on 11 November 1945, she'd written out one and the same poem by Pushkin: 'I loved you.'[1] Eighteen thousand, two hundred and fifty-two pieces of paper of various sizes had been preserved, and those eight immortal lines were on every one of them, their beauty undimmed despite the lack of punctuation: the old woman had never used so much as a comma. She must have written from memory and had made many spelling mistakes; as for the word 'God', she'd always capitalized it, despite the Soviet orthography of the time. She'd put the date at the bottom of every scrap and, very rarely, added a few words: 5 March 1953 *Stalin died*; 19 April 1960 *Fyodor Fyodorovich is dead*; 12 April 1961 *Gagarin flew away to the moon*; 29 August 1970, *Petinka* (her grandson) *had a girl Ksenya*. Several sheets were burnt at the corners, others were ripped, and you could only guess at the emotional state she must have been in that day, when she wrote yet again, *I loved you* . . . Eighteen thousand, two hundred and fifty-two times she'd reproduced those eight lines on paper. Why? And why those eight lines in particular? And what were her thoughts when she wrote out the end of the poem, *As God grant you may yet be loved again*, adding neatly *Stalin died* or *Fyodor Fyodorovich is dead*?

Just before dawn, Sheberstov and Lyosha lit the stove and started burning the paper. The stove took only half an hour to warm up, and the room got stifling hot. Both felt uneasy, but when Lyosha said, 'What's the difference, burning a person or burning this . . . ?' the doctor just snorted angrily. There was one scrap – the one Katerina Ivanovna had given him – which Sheberstov decided to keep, even if he didn't know why. Perhaps just because, for the very first time, the

old woman hadn't written the date, as though she'd understood that
time is powerless not only over the eternity of poetry, but even over
the eternity of our wretched life . . .

First published in 1998
Translated by Oliver Ready

Note on Names

A Russian has three names: a Christian name, a patronymic (derived from the Christian name of the father) and a family name. The first name and patronymic, used together, are the normal polite way of addressing or referring to someone. Thus, Pushkin's Countess Anna Fedotovna is the daughter of a man whose first name is Fedot; Solzhenitsyn's Anna Modestovna is the daughter of a man whose first name is Modest; and Gogol's Akaky Akakiyevich bears the same first name as his father. Married or older peasants often addressed one another by the patronymic alone. By addressing the schoolteacher simply as 'Vasilyevna', the peasant driver in Chekhov's 'In the Cart' indicates that he sees her as one of them, just another peasant. Close friends or relatives usually address each other by one of the many affectionate forms of their first names. Masha and Mashenka, for example, are both affectionate forms of Mariya; Katya, Katyenka and Katyusha are affectionate forms of Ekaterina; Liza and Lizochka are modern affectionate forms, and Lizanka an older affectionate form, of Elizaveta.

Note on Ranks

Tsarist Russia was, in some respects, a highly organized and surprisingly meritocratic society. In 1722 Peter the Great decreed that all members of the nobility must serve the State, joining either the Army, the Navy or the civil service. He instituted the Table of Ranks given below; the higher civilian ranks all have precise military equivalents (and equivalents also exist for the clergy and the Imperial court). Compulsory State Service was abandoned under Catherine the Great, but the Table of Ranks remained in force throughout the eighteenth and nineteenth centuries with only minor modifications.

Table of Ranks

1. Chancellor	Field-Marshal
2. Full Privy Councillor	General
3. Privy Councillor	Lieutenant General
4. Full State Councillor	Major General
5. State Councillor	Brigadier
6. Collegiate Councillor	Colonel
7. Court Councillor	Lieutenant Colonel
8. Collegiate Assessor	Major
9. Titular Councillor	Captain
10. Collegiate Secretary	Lieutenant
11. Ship's Secretary	Lieutenant
12. Governor's Secretary	Second Lieutenant
13. Provincial Secretary	
14. Collegiate Registrar	

Holders of any rank were considered members of the nobility, and ranks from the eighth upwards conferred the status of hereditary nobility. It was thus easier in Russia than in many countries for a talented individual to join the nobility. Superiors were addressed according to their rank. Ranks nine to fourteen: Your Honour (*Vashe blagorodiye*); ranks six to eight: Your Highest Honour (*Vashe vysoko-blagorodiye*); rank five: Your Worship (*Vashe vysokorodiye*); ranks three and four: Your Excellency (*Vashe prevoskhoditelstvo*); ranks one and two: Your Highest Excellency (*Vashe vysokoprevoskhoditelstvo*); princes and counts: Your Radiance (Vashe siyatelstvo).

There are references to these ranks throughout much of nineteenth-century Russian literature. Both Gogol in 'The Greatcoat' and Dostoyevsky in 'Bobok' make fun of the importance attached to them.

Notes

ALEXSANDR PUSHKIN THE QUEEN OF SPADES

1. *Count Saint-Germain*: Famous, among other things, as a mystic, alchemist, magician, painter, musician and secret agent, the Comte Saint-Germain (?1690–?1784) is supposed never to have looked older than the age of forty or fifty.

2. *Casanova*: Giacomo Casanova (1725–98) is best known for his sexual adventures, as described in his *Memoirs*, first published in German in 1822.

3. *au jeu de la Reine*: In the Queen's gaming room (French, as are translations below).

4. *'Il paraît . . . plus fraîches'*: 'Monsieur seems to prefer the lady's maids to the ladies.'
   'But of course, Madam, the maids are fresher.'

5. *Vous m'écrivez . . . les lire*: 'You write four-page letters, my angel, more quickly than I can read them.'

6. *Mme Lebrun*: The French artist Louise-Elisabeth Vigée-Lebrun (1755–1842) painted mainly aristocratic ladies. She was well known in Russia, where she lived for five years.

7. *the celebrated Leroys*: Julien and Pierre Leroy were eighteenth-century French clockmakers.

8. *the Montgolfier balloon and Mesmer's magnetism*: The Montgolfier brothers invented the hot-air balloon in the early 1780s. Franz Mesmer (1734–1815) claimed to have discovered a hidden energy which he called 'animal magnetism'. This energy, and Mesmer's theories, came to be known as 'mesmerism'.

9. *Voltaire armchair*: A type of armchair with a high back.

10. *galvinism*: The eighteenth-century Italian scientist Luigi Galvani had shown that the muscles of dead animals could be made to contract if an electric current is passed through them.

11. *Homme . . . sans religion*: A man without morals or faith! (an unacknowledged quotation from the French Enlightenment philosopher Voltaire).

12. *mazurka*: A ballroom mazurka could last a long time. After a general

promenade, there were sections during which each couple, one after another, would dance a solo. There was plenty of opportunity for partners to converse, both while sitting out and during the promenades.

13. *oubli ou regret*: A way of randomly selecting partners during the mazurka. Each of a group of ladies would choose a word, such as *oubli* or *regret* ('forget' or 'regret'), to represent them. The gentleman would then have to pick one of these words – and dance the rest of the figure with the corresponding lady.

14. *à l'oiseau royal*: An eighteenth-century hairstyle; literally, 'his hair arranged in a "royal bird" style'.

15. *That night . . . Swedenborg*: The misattribution of these words to Emanuel Swedenborg, a Swedish mystic widely read in the eighteenth and nineteenth centuries, seems to be a deliberate mystification on Pushkin's part.

16. *Attendez, sir*: There were moments in the game of faro when a player was allowed to change his bet. If he wished to do so, he would call out to the banker *Attendez*! ('Wait!'). A contemporary of Pushkin recorded an occasion when the banker, a distinguished figure, took offence at being addressed so peremptorily.

17. *corner was being bent back by an absent-minded hand*: The implication is that a player might 'absent-mindedly' be doubling his stake after, rather than before, he sees the banker's cards.

MIKHAIL LERMONTOV THE FATALIST

1. *the left flank*: A line of Russian fortresses extended the whole length of the Caucasus, from the Black Sea to the Caspian.

2. *playing a seven*: In this variant of faro it is the banker who decides upon the sum to be played for. A punter then either agrees to the banker's terms or declines to take part in that round. Here, by saying he is playing a card, the punter indicates his agreement to play for the high stake determined by Vulich.

3. *chikhir*: A Caucasian new red wine.

4. *Nastya*: The most common affectionate form of the name 'Anastasiya'.

NIKOLAY GOGOL

1. Cathy Popkin, *The Pragmatics of Insignificance* (Stanford: Stanford University Press, 1993), p. 199.

THE GREATCOAT

1. *Yeroshkin . . . Senate*: Yeroshkin is derived from a word meaning 'tousled' or 'dishevelled'. The St Petersburg Senate was both a civil court and a legislative body.

2. *Belobryushkova*: The literal meaning of this improbable-sounding sur-name is 'white-bellied'.

3. *Khozdazat*: A fourth-century bishop. Before his conversion to Christi-anity, Khozdazat was a lawyer with a great reputation for his rhetorical powers – unlike Gogol's hero.

4. *promoted to state councillor*: That is, from the ninth grade to the fifth grade, a considerable leap (see 'Note on Ranks').

5. *chibouks*: Long-stemmed Turkish pipes.

6. *Falconet's Peter the Great*: Étienne-Maurice Falconet's *The Bronze Horseman* is the most famous statue in St Petersburg. The horse is rearing up on its hind legs. If the tail, which provides a third point of support, were to be cut off, the statue would collapse.

7. *Petrovich*: Younger or unmarried peasants were generally known by their Christian name or a nickname. The tailor's wish to be called by his patronymic indicates his desire for status.

8. *cross in the calendar*: In the Orthodox calendar there were twelve great festivals, printed in red, and a large number of saints' days, marked with a cross.

9. *a bonnet rather than a headscarf*: That is, a lady's bonnet, rather than a peasant woman's headscarf.

10. *foot-cloths*: A length of cloth wound round the foot and ankle. Socks or stockings were not worn by most Russians until the twentieth century.

11. *Kolomna*: In Gogol's day this district was on the outskirts of St Petersburg.

IVAN TURGENEV THE KNOCKING

1. *Filofey . . . more appropriate at the christening*: The only well-known Filofey in Russian culture is a monk who lived in the early sixteenth century and helped to popularize the idea that Moscow was the 'Third Rome', i.e. the successor to Constantinople, which fell to the Turks in 1453.

2. *Zhukovsky*: Vasily Zhukovsky (1783–1852) was one of the greatest Russian Romantic poets. The poem is 'On the Death of Field Marshal Count Kamensky' (1809).

FYODOR DOSTOYEVSKY

1. Donald Rayfield, 'The Pram in the Hall was his Fulfilment', *Literary Review* (London, August 2002).

2. Ibid.

3. Fyodor Dostoyevsky, *The Brothers Karamazov* (London: Vintage, 1992), p. xvi.

BOBOK

1. *Attic salt*: That is, Athenian wit, refined wit.

2. *collegiate councillor*: A civil servant of the sixth grade (see Note on Ranks).

3. *Suvorin's Almanac*: Aleksey Suvorin (1834–1912), a well-known publisher and later a friend and mentor to Chekhov, published an annual almanac. It was used widely as a reference source.

4. *Pervoyedov*: Means 'First Eater'.

5. *court councillor*: A civil servant of the seventh grade.

6. *fortieth day*: Russian Orthodox custom is to hold the funeral on the third day after someone's death, and a memorial service on the ninth and fortieth days. On the fortieth day a place is laid for the deceased at table; this is popularly believed to be the last time he or she eats with the family.

7. *Full Privy Councillor*: A civil servant of the second grade, the equal of an admiral or a full general.

8. *Valley of Jehoshaphat*: Named in the Bible (Joel 3:2) as the Place of Judgement.

9. *state councillor*: Fifth grade.

10. *Lebezyatnikov*: This name is derived from the Russian for 'to fawn'.

11. *en haut lieu*: French for 'in high places' – presumably, in court.

12. *Yulka Charpentier de Lusignan*: An obviously incongruous name. *Yulka* is a diminutive form of the Russian equivalent of Julie; *Charpentier* is a common French surname, and *Lusignan* a very aristocratic one.

13. *Katiche*: A Frenchified form of the Russian Katya, the affectionate form of Ekaterina.

14. *Prussians ... make mincemeat of us*: Prussia was at this time the dominant military power in Europe.

COUNT LEO TOLSTOY

1. See Hugh McLean, 'Could the Master Err?', in *Tolstoy Studies Journal* (University of Toronto, 2005). The revised text was used in the Sytin edition of Tolstoy's *Collected Works*, ed. P. I. Biryukov (Moscow, 1913).

NIKOLAY LESKOV

1. Hugh McLean, *Nikolai Leskov: The Man and His Art* (Harvard: Harvard University Press, 1977), p. 115.

2. Hugh McLean, 'Nikolai Leskov', in *Encyclopedia of Literary Translation into English*, ed. Olive Classe (London/Chicago: Fitzroy Dearborn, 2000), p. 829.

3.   Nikolay Leskov, *Satirical Stories of Nikolay Leskov*, tr. William Edger-
       ton (New York: Pegasus, 1969), p. 24.

THE STEEL FLEA

1.   *Council of Vienna*: The Congress of Vienna (1814–15), held after the
       defeat of Napoleon, established a balance of power in Europe that was
       to last until 1848. Aleksandr I died in 1825 and was succeeded as Tsar
       by his brother Nicholas I.

2.   *Don Cossack Platov*: Matvey Ivanovich Platov (1751–1818), a general
       in the Russian army and a Cossack hetman, accompanied Tsar
       Aleksandr I to London. (William Edgerton's note.)

3.   *Apollo Velvet Ear*: The 'correct' name of this sculpture is the Apollo
       Belvedere. A Roman copy of a Greek original, it has itself been copied
       many times.

4.   *Tula Town*: The Central Russian city of Tula was famous for its
       gunsmiths.

5.   *'Molvo'*: At the beginning of the nineteenth century there was a sugar
       factory in St Petersburg owned by a certain Ya. N. Molvo. Apparently
       this name was a Russified form of the French name Mollevaut. If this
       supposition is true, then the irony of Platov's patriotic Russian defence
       of 'Mollevaut' sugar becomes all the sweeter. (W.E.)

6.   *Bobrinsky's factory*: Count A. A. Bobrinsky owned a sugar refinery in
       southern Russia during the 1830s. (W.E.)

7.   *Father Fedot in Taganrog*: 'Father Fedot' was not made up out of thin
       air. Before his death in Taganrog, Tsar Aleksandr I did go to confession
       to the priest Alexey *Fedotov*-Chekhovsky, who was known after that
       as 'Confessor to His Majesty' and loved to call everybody's attention
       to this completely chance occurrence. This *Fedotov*-Chekhovsky is
       apparently the legendary 'Father Fedot'. (Leskov's note.)

8.   *Zhukov tobacco*: A popular brand in Russia during the first half of
       the nineteenth century, was manufactured in St Petersburg in a factory
       owned by Vasily Zhukov. (W.E.)

9.   *chibouk*: A long-stemmed Turkish pipe.

10.   *Count Nestlebroad*: Count Karl Vasilyevich Nesselrode (1780–
       1862) was Russia's Minister of Foreign Affairs from 1816 to 1856.
       (W.E.)

11.   *Riga Dunamunde*: A port town at the mouth of the Western Dvina
       river. (W.E.)

12.   *Count Kleinmichel*: Count Peter Andreyevich Kleinmichel (1793–
       1869) served from 1842 to 1855 as Chief Administrator of Highways
       and Public Buildings. (W.E.)

13.   *Commandant Skobelev*: General Ivan Nikitich Skobelev (1778–1849)
       was commandant in 1839 of the Fortress of Peter and Paul in
       St Petersburg, which was used as a prison. (W.E.)

NOTES387

14. *Martyn-Solsky*: Martyn Dmitriyevich Solsky (1798–1881) was an army doctor and a member of the medical council of the Ministry of Internal Affairs. (W.E.)
15. *Count Chernyshov*: Aleksandr Ivanovich Chernyshov (1786–1857) served as Minister of War from 1827 to 1852. (W.E.)
16. *'affairs . . . yore'*: Echoes of Pushkin's poem 'Ruslan i Lyudmila' (1820). (W.E.)

ANTON CHEKHOV

1. Vasily Grossman, *Life and Fate*, tr. Robert Chandler (New York: Harper & Row, 1985), pp. 282–3.
2. Janet Malcolm, *Reading Chekhov* (London: Granta, 2003), p. 21.
3. Rosamund Bartlett, *Chekhov: Scenes from a Life* (London: Simon and Schuster, 2004), p. 349.

IN THE CART

1. *zemstvo*: An elected local administrative assembly in late-ninteenth- and early-twentieth-century Russia.

LIDIYA ZINOVYEVA-ANNIBAL

1. From the Voloshin archive in Pushkinsky dom, St Petersburg.
2. Jane Costlow, 'Lidiia Zinov'eva-Annibal', in *Reference Guide to Russian Literature*, ed. Neil Cornwell (London: Fitzroy Dearborn, 1998), pp. 927–8.

THE MONSTER

1. *Konstantin Aleksandrovich Siunnerberg*: (1871–1942), an art critic, a theoretician and a contributor to the Symbolist journal the *Golden Fleece*; his work elaborates a theory of intuitive creativity.

IVAN BUNIN IN PARIS

1. *'Rien n'est . . . de bien'*: 'There's nothing harder than picking out a good melon or a decent woman' (French, as are the sentences below).
2. *zubrovka*: A spicy vodka.
3. *shashlyk à la Kars*: A shashlyk is much the same as a kebab. Kars is a town in Eastern Turkey.
4. *L'eau gâte . . . l'âme*: 'Water spoils wine as a cart spoils a road and a woman – a man's soul.'
5. *rassolnik*: A meat or fish soup made with pickled cucumbers.
6. *C'est moi qui vous remercie*: 'It's I who should thank you.'
7. *Le bon Dieu . . . pas de derrière*: 'The good Lord always sends trousers to those who have no bottom.'

8. *Qui se marie . . . mauvais jours*: 'He who marries for love enjoys good nights and bad days.'
9. *Patience . . . pauvres*: 'Patience – the medicine of the poor.'
10. *femme de ménage*: A cleaning lady.
11. *L'amour . . . ânes*: 'Love makes even donkeys dance.'

TEFFI LOVE

1. *lisp . . . drag his right foot as he walked*: Probably in imitation of Lord Byron.
2. *baba . . . neckweed*: A *baba* is a peasant woman; *neckweed* is a word for hemp.
3. *'Kishmish'*: A Russian borrowing from the Turkic languages of Central Asia, it means 'raisins'.
4. *Martha*: *Martha, or Richmond Fair* (1847) by the German composer Friedrich von Flotow (1812–83).
5. *Yelena the Beautiful*: The heroine of a Russian folk tale, here confused with Helen of Troy.
6. *Nanny*: In a gentry household typically a peasant woman employed first as a wet-nurse to a baby and then kept on as a household servant. She was often more intimately involved with a child's life than its mother was.

A FAMILY JOURNEY

1. *tout ce joli monde*: 'All these fine people' (French).
2. *sale étranger*: 'Dirty foreigner' (French).

YEVGENY ZAMYATIN

1. From a 1931 questionnaire (IMLI archive, f. 47, op. 3, ed khr. 2).
2. Yevgeny Zamyatin, *A Soviet Heretic* (London: Quartet, 1991), p. 13.

THE LION

1. *Tsar Maximillian*: A Russian folk play.

VERA INBER

1. Catriona Kelly, *A History of Russian Women's Writing* (Oxford: Clarendon Press, 1998), p. 235.

LALLA'S INTERESTS

1. *communal apartments*: See introductory note to Sigizmund Krzhizhanovsky, pp. 206–7.

MIKHAIL BULGAKOV

1. *Reference Guide to Russian Literature*, ed. Neil Cornwell (London: Fitzroy Dearborn, 1998), p. 203.
2. Doris Lessing, preface to Mikhail Bulgakov, *The Fatal Eggs* (London: Hesperus, 2003), p. xii.
3. Bulgakovskaya Entsiklopediya, www.bulgakov.ru/p/polotentse (May 2004).

THE EMBROIDERED TOWEL

1. *feldsher*: A partly qualified medical assistant.
2. *Dmitry the Pretender*: A pretender to the Russian throne who, in 1604, invaded Russia with Polish support.

ISAAK BABEL

1. In *A Jew on Horseback: Isaac Babel in Life and Art* (Stanford: Stanford University Press, 2005), Gregory Freidin refers to Babel as 'the first "embedded" war correspondent'.
2. Clarence Brown, *The Portable Twentieth-Century Russian Reader* (London: Penguin, 1985), p. 204.
3. Primo Levi, *The Search for Roots* (London: Penguin, 2001), p. 140.

SALT

1. *Yids . . . Lenin*: Many Cossacks imagined Lenin to be Jewish.

MIKHAIL ZOSHCHENKO

1. Mikhail Zoshchenko, *Scenes from the Bathhouse* (Ann Arbor: University of Michigan Press, 1961), pp. viii–ix.
2. Quoted by Cathy Popkin, *The Pragmatics of Insignificance* (Stanford: Stanford University Press, 1993), p. 60.
3. Andrey Sinyavsky, *Soviet Civilization* (New York: Arcade, 1990), p. 199.

PELAGEYA

1. *Young Pioneers*: The Communists' children's organization.

THE BATHHOUSE

1. *Foot-cloths*: See note 10 to Gogol, 'The Greatcoat'.

THE GALOSH

1. *House Management Office*: Responsible for all matters relating to the administration and physical upkeep of a residential building. It had an internal passport office to register new residents, to de-register those who had left or died, and to make sure that no one was living there illegally. And it certified all manner of documents.

LEONID DOBYCHIN

1. Ludza was formerly known as Lyutsin, Daugavpils as Dvinsk. See L. Dobychin, *Polnoye Sobraniye sochinenii i pisem* (St Petersburg: Zvezda, 1999), p. 7.
2. Ibid., p. 41.

MEDICAL AUXILIARY

1. *Mary Pickford*: American film actress (1893–1979).
2. *Jenny Jugo's*: Austrian film actress (1905–2001). The translator Richard Borden has pointed out that, in this story, 'only the representatives of the world of far away . . . have names'.

PLEASE DO

1. *babka*: A *baba* is a peasant woman; the diminutive form *babka* means a traditional woman healer.
2. *'Sisters'*: The words are from 'A May Day Song' (1918) by the Proletkult poet Vladimir Kirillov.
3. *'Scarcely do . . . shed tears'*: These words are part of the Orthodox burial rite.

ANDREY PLATONOV THE RETURN

1. *Stakhanovite*: Aleksey Stakhanov was a coal-miner whose improbably vast output of coal – twelve tonnes a day – led to his being held up as a model for Soviet workers.
2. *killed in Mogilyov*: This suggests that he was Jewish. Mogilyov was a major centre of Jewish life, and most of its Jews were killed by the Nazis. See Philip Bullock's 'A Modern Ahasuerus' in *Essays in Poetics*, 27 (Autumn 2002) (Keele University).

DANIIL KHARMS THE OLD WOMAN

1. *Hamsun*: Kharms was an admirer of the Norwegian writer Knut Hamsun (1859–1952), who was influenced by Dostoyevsky; the epigraph is from Hamsun's novel *Mysteries* (1892).
2. *kvass*: A very slightly alcoholic drink made from bread.

3.   *Grab the mallet*: It is worth pointing out that croquet remained popular in Russia for a surprisingly long time (20,000 copies of Chesnokov's *Descriptions and Rules of the Game* were printed in 1930).

VARLAM SHALAMOV

1.   See R. Chandler, 'Varlam Shalamov and Andrei Fedorovich Platonov', in *Essays in Poetics*, 27 (Autumn 2002) (Keele University).

THROUGH THE SNOW

1.   *makhorka*: Coarse tobacco.

THE SNAKE CHARMER

1.   *The Club of the Knaves of Hearts ... The Vampire*: The first 'novel' is derived from Pierre-Alexis Ponson du Terrail's 1857–70 feuilleton saga, *Rocambole or The Dramas of Paris*, whose anti-hero was the mastermind of a criminal organization known as 'The Club of the Knaves of Hearts'; Platonov's transposition of the action to St Petersburg in 1893 can be seen as an indication of the liberties that camp 'novelists' took with their material. Shalamov is probably also alluding to Pushkin's 'The Queen of Spades'. The second 'novel' is derived from *The Vampyre* by John Polidori. A huge success when published in 1819, this novella was at first thought to have been written by Lord Byron.

ALEKSANDR SOLZHENITSYN WHAT A PITY

1.   *the Seven Rivers region*: In what are today the independent republics of Kazakhstan and Kyrgyzstan.
2.   *Modest Aleksandrovich V.*: *Modest* is an uncommon name and the heroine's patronymic is *Modestovna*. It is clear that this man is the heroine's father.
3.   *pension*: Work in a labour camp did not count towards a pension; it was considered as payment for the (alleged) crime.

VASILY SHUKSHIN

1.   Quoted by John Givens, Introduction, in Vasily Shukshin, *Stories from a Siberian Village* (DeKalb: Northern Illinois University Press, 1996), p. xxx. My information about Shukshin derives mostly from this source.
2.   Donald Rayfield, 'Cussedly Independent', *Times Literary Supplement*, 8 August 1997.
3.   Quoted by Geoffrey Hosking, *Beyond Socialist Realism* (London: Granada, 1980), p. 179.

IN THE AUTUMN

1. *kolkhozes*: Collective farms. Hundreds of thousands of peasants were deported in 1929–30 as a result of Stalin's policy of 'Total Collectivization'.
2. *muzhik*: Peasant. Often the word is used as a synonym for 'man'.
3. *Komsomol*: The Communist Youth organization.
4. *Krayushkinites*: Inhabitants of the village of Krayushkino, where Pavel and Marya have been living.

ASAR EPPEL

1. Andrey Sergeyev, on the back cover of Eppel's *The Grassy Street* (Moscow/Birmingham: Glas, 1994).

RED CAVIAR SANDWICHES

1. *Without the Bird Cherries*: A sentimental love story by Panteleimon Romanov (1884–1938).
2. *Blok*: Aleksandr Blok (1880–1921), the Symbolist poet. His works include *Verses on the Beautiful Lady* (1904) and *Nocturnal Hours* (1911).
3. *'Unmöglich!'*: 'Impossible!' (German).
4. *'Unmöglich . . . und Seife!'*: 'Impossible, because I don't know where *Aunt Dusya's washstand* and soap are!' (German).
5. *Sumarokov*: Aleksandr Petrovich Sumarokov (1717–77) was a Russian dramatist and poet.

SERGEI DOVLATOV

1. Joseph Brodsky, *Sergei Dovlatov Sobranie Prozy v Trekh Tomakh* (St Petersburg: Limbus Press, 1995), Vol. III, p. 358.

THE OFFICER'S BELT

1. *Forsyte Saga*: John Galsworthy's *The Forsyte Saga* (1922) was surprisingly well known in Soviet Russia.

YURY BUIDA

1. Yuri Buida, 'Zamok Lokhshtedt', *Znamya*, 2 (2000) pp. 179–80.

SINDBAD THE SAILOR

1. *'I loved you'*: This is probably the single most famous Russian lyric poem:

I loved you. Even now, perhaps, love's embers
Within my heart are not extinguished quite.
But let me not disturb you with remembrance
Or cause you any sadness, any fright.
I loved you hopelessly, could not speak clearly,
Shyness and jealousy were ceaseless pain,
Loved you as tenderly and as sincerely
As God grant you may yet be loved again.

   (Translated by Jim Reed)

Acknowledgements

Editing this anthology has impelled me not only to read fine writers I had never read before, but also to enter into conversations with friends and colleagues from many countries. Olive Classe, Musya Dmitrovskaya, Olga Kuznetsova, Olga Meerson, Mark Miller, Natasha Perova, Ian Pindar, Natalya Poltavtseva and Joanne Turnbull have made invaluable contributions. I also wish to thank Denis Akhapkin, Hafiza Andreeva, Andrey Aryev, Carol Avins, Rosamund Bartlett, Ksana Blank, Natalya Bragina, Yury Buida, Peter Carson, Jane Chamberlain, Lucy Chandler, Sylvana Chandler, Jenefer Coates, Neil Cornwell, Jane Costlow, Julie Curtis, Richard Davies, Martin Dewhirst, Tom Dolack, Carol Dougherty, Katya Dovlatova, Sibelan Forrester, Gregory Freidin, Kobi Freund, Anne-Marie Fyfe, Yury and Therese Galperin, Genevra Gerhart, Elizabeth Ginzburg (and all eighteen members of her 2004 'Chekhov to Zoshchenko Seminar' at DePaul University in Chicago), Igor Golomstock, Julian Graffy, Jane Grayson, Robert Hodel, Hamid Ismailov, Daniel Jeffreys, Masha Karp, Nina Karsova, Catriona Kelly, Elena Kolesnikova, Natalya Kornienko, Sally Laird, Angela Livingstone, Olga Makarova, Hugh McLean, Robin Milner-Gulland, Allegra Mostyn-Owen, Eric Naiman, Dora O'Brien, Cathy Popkin, Donald Rayfield, Oliver Ready, Robert Reid, Ruth Rischin, Omry Ronen, Caroline Sigrist, Christopher Tessone, Anat Vernitskaya, Faith Wigzell, Evgeny Yablokov, Elizabeth Sara Yellen, Zinovy Zinik, and my translation students at Queen Mary College, London. The SEELANGS e-mail discussion group has been a great help; my thanks to everyone who offered advice, and my apologies to those whose advice I did not follow. I cannot imagine having completed this book without the help of my wife Elizabeth, who has been deeply involved at every stage of my work on it. I also wish to thank my first two teachers of Russian, both of whom were unusually gifted, imaginative and generous: Gordon Pirie and Count Nicholas Sollohub.

*

The editor and publisher gratefully acknowledge permission to reprint the following copyright material. YURY BUIDA: 'Sindbad the Sailor' from *The Prussian Bride* (London: Dedalus, 2002) by permission of the publisher; MIKHAIL BULGAKOV: 'The Embroidered Towel' from *A Country Doctor's Notebook* (London: Harvill, 1975) by permission of the publisher; IVAN BUNIN: 'The Gentleman from San Francisco' from *Russian Short Stories* (London: Penguin, 1941) by permission of Random House; 'In Paris' from *'Zhizn' Arsen'eva'* (Moscow: Pressa, 1996) by permission of the Ivan Bunin Estate; ANTON CHEKHOV: 'In the Cart' from *About Love and Other Stories* (Oxford: Oxford University Press, 2004) by permission of the publisher; SERGEI DOVLATOV: 'The Officer's Belt' from *Chemodan* (St Petersburg: Azbuka, 2001) by permission of the Dovlatov Estate, translation by permission of Joanne Turnbull; ASAR EPPEL: 'Red Caviar Sandwiches' from *The Grassy Street* (Moscow/Birmingham: Glas, 1994) by permission of Asar Eppel, translation by permission of Joanne Turnbull; VERA INBER: 'Lalla's Interests', translation by permission of Joanne Turnbull; SIGIZMUND KRZHIZHANOVSKY: 'Quadraturin', translation by permission of Joanne Turnbull; NIKOLAY LESKOV: 'The Steel Flea' from *Satirical Stories of Nikolai Leskov* (New York: Pegasus, 1969) by permission of David Edgerton; ANDREY PLATONOV: 'The Return' from *The Return and Other Stories* (London: Harvill, 1998) by permission of the publisher; VARLAM SHALAMOV: 'Through the Snow', 'Berries', 'The Snake Charmer' and 'Duck' from *Sobranie Sochinenii* (Moscow: Vagrius, 1998) by permission of Irina Sirotinskaya; VASILY SHUKSHIN: 'In the Autumn' from *Stories from a Siberian Village* (DeKalb: Northern Illinois University Press, 1997) by permission of the publisher; ALEKSANDR SOLZHENITSYN: 'What a Pity' from *Na Krayakh* (Moscow: Vagrius, 2000) by permission of Editions Fayard; TEFFI: 'Love' from *Gorodok* (Moscow: Lakom, 1999) and 'A Family Journey' from *Vse o Lyubvi* (Moscow: Lakom, 2001) by permission of Madame Szydlowski; IVAN TURGENEV: 'The Knocking', translation by permission of Martin Dewhirst; YEVGENY ZAMYATIN: 'The Lion' from *The Penguin Book of Russian Short Stories* (London: Penguin, 1982), translation by permission of David Richards; LIDIYA ZINOVYEVA-ANNIBAL: 'The Monster' from *The Tragic Menagerie* (Evanston: Northwestern University Press, 1999) by permission of the publisher; MIKHAIL ZOSHCHENKO: 'The Galosh' from *Sobranie Sochinenii v trekh tomakh* (Leningrad: Khudozhestvennaya Literatura, 1986–7) and 'Electrification', 'Pelageya', 'The Bathhouse', 'The Crisis' and 'The Hat' from *Sochineniya 1920-e Gody* (St Petersburg: Kristall, 2000) by permission of the Limbus Press. My own translation of Solzhenitsyn's 'What a Pity' was first published in *Prospect* (London: January 2003), and my translation of Zoshchenko's 'Electrification' in *Moving Worlds* (Leeds: 2004, Vol. 4, No. 1).

Every effort has been made to obtain permission from all copyright holders whose material is included in this book, but in some cases this has not proved possible at the time of going to press. The editor and publisher therefore wish to thank those copyright holders who are included without acknowledgement, and would be pleased to rectify any errors or omissions in future editions.

Robert Chandler
2005